FRANCESCA

GILLIAN GODDEN

Boldwood

First published 2019. This edition first published in Great Britain in 2022 by Boldwood Books Ltd.

Cover Design by Colin Thomas

Cover Photography: Colin Thomas

A CIP catalogue record for this book is available from the British Library.

Paperback ISBN 978-1-80280-126-2

Large Print ISBN 978-1-80280-127-9

Hardback ISBN 978-1-80280-125-5

Ebook ISBN 978-1-80280-129-3

Kindle ISBN 978-1-80280-128-6

Audio CD ISBN 978-1-80280-120-0

MP3 CD ISBN 978-1-80280-121-7

Digital audio download ISBN 978-1-80280-122-4

Boldwood Books Ltd
23 Bowerdean Street
London SW6 3TN
www.boldwoodbooks.com

1

REMEMBERING THE PAST

Getting out of the black cab, I handed over the fare and put my coat over my arm. The skies had looked dull this morning, and it had surprised everyone when the sun had shone and the clouds had disappeared.

Walking towards the huge building in front of me and reaching my hand up to the door handle, I was just about to pull it open when, through the glass pane in the centre of the door, I saw the man I loved standing at the bar. On either side of him were two beautiful leggy young blonde women, each with her arm around his waist, laughing and joking without a care in the world.

I instantly pulled my hand away from the handle. Although the sun was blocking my view slightly, I surveyed the happy scene before me, thinking of how I had once dreaded walking in on such a cosy scene like this and how all my insecurities had risen at the thought of it.

Looking at my watch, I noticed it was another half an hour before I was due to meet him. The journey into the West End of London hadn't taken as long as I had thought. Deciding to leave them all to it, I looked around and spotted a coffee shop with people sitting outside under umbrellas enjoying the sunshine and watching the crowds passing by.

The West End was in all its glory on a sunny day. Tourists were walking along the footpaths, while would-be artists drew chalk drawings of famous celebrities on the pavements, people watching in awe at their talent. Buskers with their guitars sang away, hoping for tips from the crowds of people passing by.

Taking a seat at a table, I ordered a coffee from the smiling waitress who came out to meet me, notepad in hand, waiting for my order. I looked across at the huge building with its flags heralding the owner's name and remembered the happy scene I had left behind me. The waitress put my black coffee on the table before me and asked if I wanted anything else.

Shaking my head, I lifted the cup to my lips to take a sip. My mind wandered off again. I'd been thinking a lot about the past lately. I didn't know why, but sometimes in quiet moments, things that I hadn't thought about for years suddenly popped into my mind at the oddest moments.

Staring at the hustle and bustle of the crowds before me reminded me of how I'd felt the first time I'd come into the West End and seen all the fantastic sights before me – the famous theatres advertising famous plays had been so exciting. But I'd also been so nervous, too. At this moment, that all seemed like a life-time ago. I'd been young and foolish; and worst of all, I'd been in love. Or had thought I was. But what is love? It makes you blind and ignorant to the harsh truths it brings with it. I, Francesca, had been the biggest fool of all.

I'd been broken and penniless when my husband Luke had eventually left me for my work colleague and friend, Emma. She was everything I wasn't: beautiful, clever, and a homeowner with plenty of money in the bank.

Frowning to myself, I picked up my cup again and took another sip of the hot coffee. It warmed my throat. Remembering that time still made me feel sick inside. How stupid and naive I'd been. How gullible and desperately lonely.

I'd been flattered when Luke had sought me out at an office party. He was tall, handsome, and when he'd asked me to dance, I couldn't refuse.

All the other ladies had smiled, jealous at my achievement, or so I'd thought. He was the original London cockney gent, and I was surprised he'd even noticed me: eighteen, on work experience, and as naive as they came.

After that dance, we'd dated for a while. When Luke had asked me to move in with him, I'd instantly agreed. He had a typical bachelor flat, which needed a lot of attention, but he'd said we could decorate it together and make it ours. After all, we were in love.

Luke was always borrowing money from me, even though he was the one with the real job. He came home late, saying he'd had to work overtime, and I'd supposed because he was paying the rent and most of the bills that was why he had no money, but none of it made much sense.

Our wedding was cheap and cheerful at the local registry office. We had a few drinks at a pub around the corner afterwards – again, because we couldn't afford anything else – and I had felt like the luckiest woman in the world. He had married me.

One drunken night, when yet again I was moaning about the fact that we were both working and still never had any money, he blurted out the truth. He'd proposed simply to shut me up. But he'd followed it through anyway.

Wincing to myself now at my stupidity, I felt sorry for that young woman I'd once been – alone in the big city, miles away from home and family, with no one to talk to. I didn't even tell my mam about all the arguments Luke and I were having. I knew she would worry and I hadn't wanted that. She had enough to deal with looking after my three younger brothers on her own since Dad had died.

I knew for a fact that she would have insisted I go home, back where I belonged. But I couldn't do that. I wanted to make something of myself. I felt that in the big city I would be given the opportunity to do that. Maybe I'd even make some extra money to send home to Mam to help her out. I just knew I couldn't go back a failure. Mam had been so proud of me moving to London and that was why I hung on to my marriage, lived hand to mouth even though I was working every hour possible, and even put up with my newlywed husband lashing out and using me as a punching bag. Of course, he was always sorry, and even though I made excuses at work about my bruises, they all knew the truth.

Then the worst had happened and I'd discovered I was pregnant. Luke had hit the roof. I had never seen him so angry. His face was flushed, and the angry words just spewed out of his mouth. 'You have to get rid of it, you stupid cow. How on earth could you let something like this happen?'

I had actually found myself apologising, as though it was all my fault! You do, though, in those kinds of marriages. You're brain washed into believing you're always in the wrong and you actually believe it yourself.

I never mentioned my pregnancy again. I wouldn't 'get rid of it', and Luke never acknowledged the fact or spoke of it again. He was happy as long as I continued working for as long as I could. He'd seen it as my problem. The last thing I'd wanted was for him to lash out at me, so I had kept a low profile. I had no idea what I was going to do when I had to give up work for a while, but I knew I'd cross that bridge when I had to.

As time went on, I saw less and less of him, which I was glad of. There had been lots of gossip about Luke cheating on me. But there was a particular woman that everyone around the office talked about more than most. The silence, which was accompanied by knowing looks, when I walked into the office canteen was deafening.

So I had tried putting a little money aside, some days going without food or heating. I knew, though, that, come the end of the week, Luke would always return and take the lion's share out of the money pot and then disappear again. I hadn't dared hide it all. That would have been asking for trouble.

When I had gone into labour and the pains were coming thick and fast, I had tried contacting him at work, to no avail. So I rang my supervisor, Emma, who had always been so kind to me in the past. I had rung her at home, knowing it was her day off. But to my utter surprise, it had been Luke who had answered the telephone. The shock in his voice when he realised it was me was nearly as bad as the shock I had in hearing him.

So there it was – my friendly, understanding supervisor and my husband. I hung up the telephone. There was no point saying anything now. I had other things to do. I rang a taxi to take me to the hospital.

A few hours later, I had given birth to a precious son, who I called Bobby. And when I held him I knew that at least something good had come out of my terrible marriage. But when I had returned home a few days later, I found the house empty. Still holding Bobby in my arms, I walked the full length of the bare flat towards the bedroom. My heart was in my mouth and I could feel the panic rising inside of me.

There, the wardrobe was empty, all of Luke's belongings had gone and the money pot was empty. He had left me and my baby with nothing. Tears rolled down my face. That was it then, the end of my marriage – not even a goodbye.

There'd been a knock at my door. When I opened it, I saw the elderly lady who lived next door, who was called Christine.

'He's gone, love. Came with a van and took everything. He said you were moving, and he was making a start. But I knew he was lying.' She had given me one of those pitiful looks I had come to know so well.

She handed me a supermarket bag full of food she'd bought. Then she'd given me another plastic bag. I was slightly perplexed at this one, as it was full of unopened envelopes.

'He asked me to give you this when you got home. That's how I knew he was lying. Why wouldn't he give it to you himself?'

She looked at the small bundle fast asleep in my arms and moved the blanket aside to see. 'Boy or girl?' she asked.

'Bobby, a boy. Thank you for the groceries. I'll just find my purse.'

She smiled at me. We both knew I had no money. I was embarrassed, and she knew it. 'Never mind, love. You just sort yourself and little Bobby out. If you need anything, I'm next door.' With that, she turned and walked away.

Looking inside the shopping bag, I saw that she'd bought some bread, milk, and even a tin of formula for Bobby. It seemed she had been prepared for me coming home to face all of this, even if I hadn't.

I looked into the bag filled with envelopes next. I laid Bobby down on the sofa and took one out. They were all final demands for money.

The rent hadn't been paid in months. Loans had been taken out in my name. And the gas had been cut off. What a homecoming.

Bobby started to cry and I too was crying with utter despair. What was I going to do?

Without knowing why, only that I was feeling at such a loss, I went next door and knocked apprehensively on the door. Christine opened it as though she'd half been expecting me. She invited me and Bobby in and offered us a warm welcome and a hot cup of tea. I showed her the bag full of final demands. Slowly but surely, we drank our tea and opened them all. There was an eviction notice in there too.

Christine took charge of everything, spreading out all of the letters on her floor and sorting out the more serious ones first; the ones that involved keeping a roof over our heads. She picked up her telephone and contacted the landlord and explained the situation. Maybe, just maybe, he would have a heart and let me pay off the arrears bit by bit.

The landlord, after a long drawn out argument and given the fact that I had just had a baby, agreed to give me another chance – that was, if I applied for benefits. Then the local council would pay the rent, and I would be responsible for any outstanding arrears, which he agreed to let me pay off in instalments. Breathing space.

Next was the gas and electric. Both utilities also agreed to help. Budget payment metres would be installed, so that I paid for what I used and a little extra towards what was owed for arrears.

What a mess I had been in back then! I remembered how weak and tired I'd felt but Christine had been a godsend. This stranger who I had known for a few hours had basically helped me sort my life out. I would be eternally grateful for her help. All I had to do was keep my word and try and pay those companies the money I owed them.

* * *

Days passed into weeks. I had electricity, gas, and food in the cupboard. Strangely enough, thinking back now, I realised I had more when Luke left me than I'd ever had when I lived with him. I also had peace of mind for me and Bobby.

I never heard another word from Luke; he had no curiosity about his baby. He didn't even know if it was a boy or girl. When I bumped into people from my old work place, they informed me that Luke and Emma were living together, and that she was quite well off financially. I felt a pang, but I also felt pity for her, knowing he would lead her in the same merry dance he had me and drain all her savings. He had cheated and used me, and he would do the same to her.

I realised that I needed a job. So I set about scouring the local papers, pushing Bobby in his pram around the streets, handing in CV after CV to anyone and everyone.

Employers didn't seem interested, especially as my flexibility was limited. Chris, who had now become a very good friend and confidant, had offered to babysit if and when needed, but it still didn't get me a job.

Then one fateful day when I was totally exhausted and little Bobby was sleeping, I sat outside a café and asked for a coffee, much the same as now really. Only that time, it was the East End of London, known for its gangland history, including the Kray twins.

Across the road, I saw a public house. Groups of men came pouring out, laughing and joking. When they opened the doors, loud music blared out. Bar work? I hadn't even considered it, but it was an option. I knew nothing about it, and had no experience, but there was no harm in asking. What did I have to lose?

Summoning up the courage, I finished my coffee and crossed the road. I felt a bit silly pushing my pram into a pub, but I had no choice. It was dark inside and packed to the hilt with men. I looked across towards the well-lit bar and, leaving the pram in the door-way, walked towards it.

The bar staff looked at me strangely as I stood there with a baby in my arms, though the majority of customers never even noticed me. The manager came over, and I told him I was looking for a job. I explained I had no experience but I was prepared to learn.

Leaning over the bar, he looked at me. 'You do know what kind of pub this is, don't you?' he'd asked me. He had a smiley face and reached out and stroked Bobby's hand. I looked at him oddly, curious as to what he meant.

Again, he smiled and just pointed over to the far end of the pub. There on a stage at the back was a half-naked woman dancing to the music. I hadn't even noticed the stage behind the crowds of men. I turned and looked at the manager again. I was a little shocked. I had never seen anything like it or even heard of it before.

'It's a stripper pub, love – you, know exotic dancers, striptease. Are you sure you want to work here?'

Curiosity got the better of me, and I turned again to the stage and saw the now naked young woman taking a bow and accepting applause from the crowd. Then she disappeared behind a curtain. I turned back to the manager, and he was laughing to himself. 'Not quite what you expected was it?'

It wasn't, and I felt myself blushing. But at least this manager was listening to me, unlike all the other managers who'd just taken my name and said they would be in touch if anything turned up.

'I need a job,' I almost shouted at him over the music. 'Do you have any spare shifts?'

Again he looked at me oddly, as though thinking to himself, and stroked his chin. Then he looked down at Bobby and up at me again. He could see how desperate I was. 'Yes, I have some spare shifts going if you want them. Start tomorrow night at 7 p.m. I'll give you a trial, and we'll see how it goes.' He held out his hand to shake on the deal, and I nearly shook his arm off.

My huge smile alone would make him feel as though he had done his good deed for the day!

I had walked out of there on air. I'd done it. I had a job. I didn't remember walking home, but when I got there I went straight to see Chris and told her I had a job and where it was.

She didn't seem as pleased as I'd thought she would be, and had warned me of what people thought of those kinds of pubs. I explained something was better than nothing and argued my case until she eventually gave in. It wasn't my lifelong ambition, but it was paid work, wherever it was. And this man had given me a chance and I knew that was all I needed.

My first evening passed in a blur. The pub had been busy and the manager and the other bar staff showed me how to work the till and laughed at my first attempts at pulling a pint of lager. The strippers were at the other end of the pub on the stage, and you didn't really see them much. All you saw were the men's backs who were watching them.

It wasn't seedy like Chris had described it at all. There were no dirty old men in long mackintosh coats, as was the usual myth. The men were from all walks of life: businessmen in suits, coming in during their lunch breaks and before their train home was due; normal men having a laugh and a drink with their colleagues and friends; and, of course, the football supporters, who sang their songs and shouted out the usual innuendos at the dancers.

I had been nervous meeting the strippers, not knowing what to expect. But they were normal working women with normal lives. One was paying her way through university, and working the pubs gave her the flexibility to carry on with her studies. And there were lots of different shifts to choose from. Two dancers worked the lunchtime between 12.30 p.m. and 3 p.m., and another two dancers worked from 6 p.m. till 8 p.m. Then there was a late shift from 8.30 p.m. till 11 p.m.

I learnt they all worked above board for an agency. They were paid a basic wage, which covered their expenses, and the rest of their wages was made up in tips. They did two or three dances and each dance lasted approximately six minutes. Before they started, they went around the crowds of men with an empty pint glass and the men promptly took out a few pound coins and put the money in the glass.

At the end of each shift, the dancers would walk around the back of the bar and cash up their change into notes. I remember how shocked I'd been when I saw how much money they were earning!

All in all, the dancers were a nice bunch of women. Some of the more popular girls acquired their own fan club of men who followed them from pub to pub. Apparently, there were a lot of these pubs in London, and the girls worked maybe two or three shifts a day! It was another world, and it seemed a very lucrative one.

None of the strippers mentioned sex. Most of them were in relationships or married. Unlike how Chris had described this seedy world, it seemed no one was forced into having sex. They talked about normal day-to-day things, including their children and their husbands.

One of the strippers was called Candy, a beautiful Jamaican woman. She and her husband were buying their house, and he was a mechanic who paid the mortgage and the bills whilst her wages paid for those little extras for the children. As I said, it wasn't that seedy or exotic really – just normal women earning extra cash.

After a few months it all became normality for me. Chris looked after Bobby more and more as my shifts increased. I soon had the hang of it, and the manager seemed pleased. I even knew the regular customers by name and what they wanted to drink before they asked. All in all, it was good fun.

Knowing I had Bobby, who was now growing, some of the strippers actually brought in bags of baby clothes their own children had grown out of. I never divulged anything about myself, just that I was a single mum. No one pushed for more gossip, and I left it at that. All the strippers worked a long way from home, and they never told any of their families what they did for a living in case it caused embarrassment. It was a shame really, having to hide it this way. But I knew from Chris what people's opinions were about women who took their clothes off. They assumed they had to be prostitutes, but that just wasn't the case.

It wasn't long before Bobby was a year old. Time had passed so quickly. I was still paying off the debts Luke had left behind and even managed to send some money home to my mam to help her out. Chris was a great help babysitting for me, which I insisted on paying her for.

'You're wasted behind that bar, Francesca,' Candy said to me one day and her friend nodded in agreement. When I looked at them curiously, they went on. 'You get a lot of male attention and apart from your wages, you're not earning a penny for it. Why don't you come to this side of the bar and try striptease? There's money in it, as you know.' They laughed and nudged each other, giving me a knowing wink.

I felt my face flush red with embarrassment, I wasn't sure if they were laughing at me or with me. 'I couldn't do that. I'm not pretty enough, and I couldn't take my clothes off in front of everyone.' I stopped short. I knew I had offended them, and I hadn't meant to. It had come out wrong.

They were pretty women, glamorous and confident. I, on the other hand, was plain and lacked confidence. All of my self-worth had been crushed by Luke. Time after time, he had said I was dull.

'Francesca, we all say that in the beginning, but the money tempts you and even becomes addictive. Think about it. You're not bad looking. And you're young, with a decent figure. What are you, a size ten?'

'Size eight,' I replied.

'Bloody hell, Fran. Didn't you eat when you were pregnant? Do you have any stretch marks?' They were laughing now, although it wasn't funny to me. There were days in the past when I had gone without food, even when I had Bobby. I had done that so I could buy food for him.

'Not a stretch mark in sight.' I smiled. 'My mam told me to oil my stomach every day to try and prevent it, and she should know. She had four of us.'

We all laughed together this time. They looked at their watches and walked to the changing area by the side of the stage.

The manager, who had been listening to the friendly banter while polishing his glasses, came up behind me. 'They're not wrong you know. You could do okay. I shouldn't be saying this because I could lose myself a decent barmaid.'

I just smiled at him. Thankfully, the silence was broken by the first customers coming in. Still, the thought lingered in my mind. And this time, I watched the strippers and their teasing ways and how all their clothes were adapted to come off easily. I couldn't do that. Could I?

The conversation wasn't mentioned again, and life carried on as normal. I did pay more attention to the strippers, though. And every time I saw the money they were earning, my mind started working overtime. But each time I considered what Candy and her friend had said, I realised how ridiculous the idea was and decided they were just having a laugh at my expense.

A few weeks later, Candy and a few of the other girls came in for a drink and a gossip.

'I have a surprise for you tonight.' She smiled. The other girls turned and looked at each other as though they were all in on the joke.

A man and two women walked into the pub. Everyone, even the regulars, seemed to know them. The girls were sitting on the stools at the bar, and the strippers who were working that evening came across and said hello to the well-known trio.

'These are our agents,' said Candy. 'And we've all decided it's time for you to have a go. So tonight, Francesca, you're going to audition.'

The agents introduced themselves and informed me they didn't have long, but they had heard a lot about me. Candy had convinced them to come and see for themselves.

The manager started serving the customers and waved my way. 'Go on then. It's the graveyard shift. Look around you. There are only a dozen blokes in here. Don't waste everyone's time, Fran.' He laughed encouragingly.

Inside, I was panicking. I felt cornered, but I knew they meant well.

2

NEW BEGINNINGS

Candy and the others frogmarched me to the little changing room. They opened their 'work bags' full of costumes and one by one, out came glamorous exotic garments they thought would suit me. Just the thought of going through with this made me squirm, but I did as I was told.

I was wearing stockings and suspenders. All of the shoes were too high and too big, so they stuffed the fronts with toilet paper. Then Raquel, a petite blonde stripper, handed me a white PVC nurse's outfit. I felt ridiculous and looked like I was going to a fancy-dress party!

'Right. Next, some lipstick. Let's put a bit of make-up on that face of yours. Here, take this and go and collect some money.' They were fully in charge of the situation.

'I can't. I feel silly,' I said, 'and they won't give me any money.'

They could see my dwindling confidence and knew I was going to back out and run for it, back to the safe haven behind the bar.

Raquel took my arm and opened the changing room door to the pub. I still wasn't sure if they were using me as an object of ridicule. She walked me towards the customers and said, 'Come on, guys, fresh meat. And no auditions are for free.' She pushed the glass towards them.

Fresh meat! That was how she described me? I lowered my eyes to the floor and was expecting rejection, which would end this drama. But to my surprise, the guys started putting money in the glass. Raquel walked with me to each one and joked and bantered with them, encouraging them to put more money in.

'Right, Fran. The DJ has picked out some music for you. The agents are at the bar. All you have to do is the same as you have seen us do a million times. Dance slowly, and most of all, take that worried look off your face and smile.'

It was a weak smile as I stumbled in those high heels stuffed with toilet roll. But after all the effort everyone had put in, I didn't want to let them down.

The ambience was of nervous excitement. Most of the men had seen me behind the bar, but this was a different Francesca. They were curious. The lights were very bright on the stage area, which made the crowd look dark and I could hardly see anyone. So when the music started, I began to move around the stage as I had seen the others do, day in, day out.

I looked towards the girls, who were smiling and giving me the thumbs up and mouthing at me to start undoing my clothes.

And in that moment I'd thought, *Oh, to hell with it – in for a penny*. I followed their silent instructions and clumsily took off the nurse's outfit. It was all over before I knew it. The men clapped their hands and the girls were all smiles as I wobbled back into the changing room. My legs felt weak, but most of all I couldn't believe what I had just done!

The trio of agents walked into the cramped changing area and one held out an agency card towards me. 'I'm Amanda. This is Jill, and this is Pete. You're a little wooden, love, but polish up your act a bit, get some costumes and give us a call if you're interested.' She turned towards Candy, who she treated like an old friend, and said, 'You were right, Candy. You can always spot a good one. I'll call you and we'll meet for lunch and a catch up.'

With that, they turned and left.

I looked at the long black card in my hand. Then I looked at the glass with the money in it and wondered how much was in there. Raquel picked it up and handed it to me. 'Well, go on. Cash it out. Let's see how much you got.'

Back behind the bar, I counted out forty pounds. Oh, my God. That was much more than I'd expected. Forty pounds for six minutes of work. The manager let out a deep sigh and jokingly said he was going to have to get another barmaid.

'No. No way,' I said. 'I'm not going to let you down, not after everything you've done for me.'

He put his arm around my shoulder reassuringly. 'Oh yes you are, girl,' he said in that deep cockney accent of his. 'And you're going to pack this place out and make me a fortune. Now go for it.'

His blessing made me feel better, but I insisted on finishing the rest of my shifts while I thought it over.

But me dancing permanently? It seemed a little far-fetched. Candy and the other dancers kept doing their best to convince me. I explained that I couldn't afford any costumes. Nor did I have the confidence to do it on my own.

The girls all assured me that these were non issues, but it was Candy most of all who spoke up in that reassuring voice of hers. 'Costumes we can sort, no problem. Confidence will come. We'll make a point of working with you for the first few times until you're feeling bold enough. Come on. Give it a go. You have nothing to lose and a lot of money to gain.'

They were right, of course. And they were really trying to help me. A couple of weeks later, my mind was made up. I knew this was an opportunity that could change mine and Bobby's life.

* * *

I couldn't believe how quicky time passed. Two years flew by and the girls had been proved right. I had grown in confidence and even established my own little fan club. I had, in time, developed my own banter for the men and chatted and joked with them, encouraging them to put tips into my collection glass.

The money rolled in. I took driving lessons, and Candy's husband found me an old banger of a car he'd seen at an auction. He had fixed it up and made it road worthy and that gave me the opportunity to work further afield and not depend on tube trains and buses all the time.

Bobby was a toddler now and thoroughly enjoyed our days out in the car and I loved being able to spend time with him and provide him with those extra little treats which brought him joy.

I worked hard long hours. But life was good. I kept my schedule as close to my old barmaid work as possible and put my make-up on in the car. That way, as much as she had her suspicions, Chris never said anything. She also liked the increase in babysitting money I gave her. It was a win-win situation.

I was still paying off Luke's debts, but I could pay more now and there was light at the end of the tunnel.

For once in my life, I didn't feel like a failure. Things seemed to be working out, and life felt good. I enjoyed the work and the friendship with the other strippers. Everyone seemed to look out for each other.

I never really contemplated the future, just the here and now. All I wanted was to build up a home and some decent sort of life for Bobby. He was the innocent party in all of this, and it was my duty to sort that out.

And even now, when I looked in the mirror these days, and saw a very different woman looking back at me, inside I was still that same shy Francesca, who'd lived in fear for so long. It had seemed then like it would take forever for me to regain my confidence and move on.

3

THE BEGINNING OF THE END

The day started normally. I got Bobby ready for his morning at nursery as usual and rang the agency to confirm my bookings for the day. It was nearly December, and that was usually when the pubs were busier than ever. All the office parties came into the pub, which meant everyone was in the festive spirit and feeling more generous than usual.

I heard the post drop through the letter box and went into the hallway to see what bill was due. Most of it was junk mail. Then I spotted one with a solicitor's stamp on the front. I opened it nervously. Maybe this was another of those threatening letters demanding money.

To my utter shock, it was from a solicitor instructed by Luke to apply for a divorce. They were advising me to get my own solicitor so they could go ahead with proceedings. It had never occurred to me that Luke would apply for a divorce and I stared at the letter in my hand, reading it again, waiting for the words to register in my brain.

It was clear now he wanted nothing more to do with me and

Bobby and although I'd known it was all over, seeing it in black and white gave me a sick feeling in my stomach.

I made a coffee and rang Candy. I had told her by now that my husband and I had separated and she wasn't very shocked when I asked her if she knew any solicitors I could use. I didn't know where to start looking, but Candy seemed to know everyone and anyone.

I rang one of the contacts she gave me and made an appointment. The solicitor's secretary said they could squeeze me in that morning for a preliminary chat to see if they could help.

The solicitor advised me that I should have started proceedings earlier myself, but it wouldn't make much difference, as we hadn't lived together for a couple of years. I would have liked some form of justice, something that acknowledged that Bobby and I were victims in all of this. The solicitor said she would mention it in her letter, including the fact Luke had never paid any maintenance for Bobby.

I carried on, on autopilot.

Another couple of weeks passed when another solicitor's letter dropped through the letter box. Luke had denied any knowledge of Bobby and didn't intend paying for him. My solicitor informed me that we could get a DNA test to prove Bobby was Luke's son and then apply for maintenance.

It felt as if Luke was still manipulating me from afar. I felt sick inside that Luke didn't want to know little Bobby. He knew Bobby was his child, and yet he wasn't even curious about his son.

I learnt through my solicitors that Luke had a daughter and was still living with Emma who now wanted marriage. It seemed she could call the shots because she held the purse strings, and I knew first-hand how much Luke wanted an easy life without it costing him anything. She was also older and wiser than I had been and wouldn't fall for any of his lies the way I had. But anyway, I had my own life to live now.

* * *

The agency always held a Christmas party for all the strippers and publicans they worked with throughout the year. It gave everyone a chance to meet and get acquainted, showing good relationships between the agency and the other publicans.

That year's party was held in early December, as the run-up to Christmas was such a busy and hectic time. Apart from the usual shifts, you also had the bonus of doing 'Santa Kissograms'. These were lucrative and, wearing your sexy Santa dress and hat, you were paid by staff at offices to make a fuss of one of the poor unsuspecting workers. These gigs paid well, but they were a little embarrassing. You were walking into an office environment and dancing topless in front of men and women alike, but the money was a good bonus to your wages.

The strippers were all excited about the Christmas party, which each year was held at a different pub. I had bought a new dress, but walking into the crowded pub full of girls I worked with and their husbands or boyfriends, I really didn't feel in the party mood. It was a free bar and buffet, so people were drinking more than usual, given they weren't paying for it, and having a great time. But I just felt flat.

'Francesca! Francesca!'

Hearing my name, I turned and saw Candy and her husband. She was waving for me to go over and join them. She'd put her handbag on the seat beside her, saving it for me. I painted on my best smile, which by now was well rehearsed.

Christmas was a strange time. It could either be full of excitement and happiness, or it could be the loneliest time of the year.

Here I was, laughing and chatting as though I didn't have a care in the world. But I was lonely. My forthcoming divorce had dragged up old ghosts, and I felt bitter that Luke and his newfound girlfriend seemed happy and would be looking forward to a cosy Christmas with their child.

Stupid I know. But I still felt a pang of failure inside. Why couldn't we have brought our son up together and been a family? What had I done so wrong that he couldn't wait to escape me? There were no answers and I ended up having a couple of glasses of wine, wallowing in my own self-pity and trying to blot out what I was feeling inside.

In another week, I would be home, spending Christmas with my mam and my family and hopefully feeling in a better mood than I did now.

As the evening progressed, I decided to stay for another half an hour and then leave. At least I had gone and made the effort. And no one would really notice. They were all too busy taking advantage of the free bar and discussing their Christmas plans.

I walked to the bar and ordered another glass of wine. As I raised it to my lips, someone bumped into me, sending me backwards. I felt a pair of hands hold my shoulders, steadying me. As I turned, half spilling my drink, I looked up into the bluest eyes I had ever seen.

Standing before me was a tall and extremely handsome man, immaculately dressed in a well-tailored grey suit with a pink shirt. His hair was blond and wavy and looked even blonder against his tanned face. I noticed he had a cleft in his chin, giving his face that extra something. He was handsome, verging on pretty, but very masculine indeed.

My throat felt dry as I looked down at the damp wine stain on the arm of his suit. 'Sorry.' I instinctively moved to wipe his sleeve.

'I'll get a bar towel.' What a stupid thing to say, considering the state of the cloths on the bar.

He shook his head and smiled. 'Don't worry about it, no harm done.'

Heat rushed to my face. 'I'm so sorry, I couldn't help it, I was bumped. Are you sure I can't get you something to wipe your arm?'

He shook his head again, his blue eyes twinkling. 'Why don't you have a drink with me? That'll make up for it,' he said.

Someone behind the bar passed me a fresh glass of wine. They'd clearly seen what had happened with the previous one. I took a very large gulp, bigger than expected. Those eyes were hypnotising, and I couldn't stop gazing into them. I felt myself blushing and looked around the room. I was half expecting one of the girls to come up to the bar and introduce this Adonis as her partner. But no one did.

He then did something I hadn't expected. He put his hand to the bottom of my wine glass and tipped it gently towards my lips. I took a sip, my eyes locked firmly on his.

'Are you having a good time?' he asked me, removing his hand from the glass. His voice was deep, and his words were crisp and well spoken.

Who the hell was he? I didn't want to ask and seem rude, and I was waiting for him to mention who he was with. But he didn't. 'Yes, thank you. It's a nice party, isn't it?'

He said something and there was a natural pause in the conversation. I felt like I should leave him to get on with the party, so I left the bar and sat back down next to Candy and her husband. The whole experience had left me feeling flushed and hot so within minutes of smiling and nodding and pretending to listen, I told her I was going to the beer garden for some fresh air. This was usually where everyone went to have a cigarette.

I started to walk towards the back and realised he was following my lead.

It was hot and stuffy inside, and the fresh air hit me instantly and sobered me up a little. The beer garden had been decorated with fairy lights to give it a Christmas feeling, and they glowed in the December night air.

I turned and noticed the man was behind me. There was no one out there, just us. We looked at each other for what seemed like forever, yet not a word was spoken. I could feel my heart pounding in my chest, and then suddenly, we were kissing. Each kiss was more ardent and intense than the last. His strong arms were around me and holding me tight. The smell of his aftershave was intoxicating. I felt his hands roaming over my body, and I responded by holding him closer and kissing him more. I had never been kissed so passionately in my life. His kisses were arousing feelings inside me that I had never felt before. With my back against the wall, I felt his strong arms hoisting me upwards, our lips never parting. My legs wrapped around him. And then suddenly we were having sex.

It felt so good, and I clung onto him with every fibre in my being, and then suddenly my legs began to tremble and my body tensed. I couldn't breathe. Later I realised I'd had my first ever orgasm. I had been a married woman, even had a child, and yet I had never experienced anything like that before.

Afterwards, we were both panting heavily, and the cold realisation of what I had just done creeped in. I heard voices and laughter. Someone was coming. Without a second thought, I pulled down my dress and picked up my bag, noticing for the first time that this stranger's trousers were at his knees. I pushed past him and ran for the side gate and fled without a backward turn. Once outside on the pavement, I saw a black cab coming towards me and waved at it to stop.

'Wait!' I heard the man shout behind me as I fled. I quickly got into the cab and left, leaving my sordid encounter behind me.

I couldn't believe what I had just done. I didn't even know the man's name. What must he think of me? I'd had too much to drink, wallowed in my own self-pity, and this was the outcome.

Whoever he was, I hoped I would never have to see him again. I felt ashamed of myself. What an awful night. But something inside of me warmed when I thought of him. Stupid I know. Still, it had been an instant attraction, even a fatal one in the heat of the moment, and no one's fault. I was as eager for his kisses as he had been for mine. How we had ended up like that I'll never know, but we had and that was the end of it.

4

CHRISTMAS

Before I knew it, it was Christmas Eve and me and Bobby could go home at last. It felt great opening the door to my mam's after a long week. As soon as I went through the door, I was hit by the warmth of the oven and the smell of the mince pies she was baking.

It was dark and icy outside. It had been snowing, and the Christmas tree with its fairy lights and tinsel made the house feel warm and welcoming. The television had some Christmas movie on, and all of my younger brothers were lounging on the sofa watching it. The welcome was lovely. Hearing my voice, they all ran towards me and gave me a hug, each of them wanting to tell me their news. Mam walked into the lounge from the kitchen, her hands covered in baking flour. She walked towards me and gave me a hug. This was what I needed. This was what I had missed.

Christmas came and went in a mayhem of overindulgence, wrapping paper, and smiles all around. My mam saved all year round for Christmas, buying saving stamps at the supermarkets for the food and paying weekly towards presents she thought the boys, including Bobby, would like.

We hardly had a chance to have a proper chat until New Year's

Eve. The boys were all playing with a car racing game, and my mam came through to the lounge with two large cups of coffee.

'You're still my baby you know. I know when something is wrong and when you're lying to me. You're not getting all this money working behind a bar or temping as a secretary. What is it, love?' she asked.

My face burned, and before I knew it, I was spilling the beans on my work, the divorce, and even my encounter with the stranger in the beer garden. It felt good to let it all out and be able to tell the truth. The one person who wouldn't judge me was my mam. And once I started, I couldn't stop.

She didn't approve, but she accepted it and admired me for standing on my own two feet. As for Luke and the divorce, she said I was well out of it. I had never told her all about Luke and my married life, but at this moment, I knew she had already guessed it had been an abusive relationship. For the first time I felt like a grown-up, chatting and confiding in my mam, the two of us talking woman to woman. It made me realise how much I had grown as a person. I loved being there, it was my roots, but my life was so different now.

No sooner had Christmas come and gone I was back in London and on my way to work. Walking into the changing rooms, I found half a dozen of my workmates excited and bubbling over with enthusiasm.

'What's happening here?' I asked, putting my bag down.

Candy was the first to turn around. Beaming, she announced, 'You'll never guess what. Lambrianu's is having an open audition day next Sunday. My God, Fran, this is big time.'

'What is Lambrianu's?' I asked curiously. Whatever it was, it had created a great deal of excitement.

They all looked at me as though I was an idiot.

'Good God, Fran. Have you lived in a cave or something all

your life? It's only the most exclusive nightclub in the West End. The owner, Mr Lambrianu, is some sort of gangland boss, who owns one of the biggest clubs in town and only hires the very best.'

Shrugging my shoulders and feeling a fool, I said simply, 'I've never heard of it or him. Why is he having an audition day if he hires only the best? What is the best anyway?' I couldn't understand what all the excitement was about.

Candy explained that anyone who was anyone knew Mr Lambrianu, and those who didn't, wanted the prestige of knowing him by going to his clubs. He was, I also learnt, a total womaniser, famous for having a different woman on his arm every night – usually some model who wanted her photo taken with him so it would end up in some glossy magazine.

She explained that people paid a lot of money to get into his clubs. The entry fee was 100 pounds, which stopped the riff-raff from going. Apparently, working for this guy would be a whole different ball game. No pint glass collections; he paid the highest wages and wanted only the best.

'Why would a famous gangland boss with loads of money and influential friends own some strip club?' I asked.

Candy just laughed at me. 'Supply and demand, Fran. Men are men whatever class they are from. And if this guy thinks there's money to be made, he'll make it, only bigger, better, and classier than anyone else. He even has pole dancers.'

'You seem to know a lot about him. What's he like?' I asked. All this excitement intrigued me.

'No idea, Fran. All I know is what I've read in the newspapers and magazines. I know of him but, I don't know him, and I don't know anyone who does. We move in very different circles.'

* * *

Days passed. I didn't think much more about Lambrianu's and the audition until the call came.

Candy informed me that she had been put forward, which didn't surprise me. She was, after all, a close friend of the agents. Then she told me that I had also been put forward.

I was astounded. I wasn't beautiful like the others. I scraped by and was comfortable in these little backstreet pubs. Why would I want to humiliate myself by auditioning and getting rejected?

I didn't want to do it and gave my argument to Candy. She started getting angry. I could hear it in her voice. 'For God's sake, Fran. You are a beautiful young woman: long dark, wavy hair down your back; a size eight waist; and boobs to die for. When are you going to look into the mirror and see the real you?'

I was surprised at her description of me. No, I didn't see that. All I saw was plain old Francesca, someone who had repulsed her husband and made him want to cheat on her. If I looked so good, why had he done it? Eventually I agreed to go with her, just as moral support.

The day of the auditions arrived.

Pulling up outside of the huge building, I realised exactly what Candy and the others were excited about.

The club was four storeys high, and it was situated on the corner and took up both sides of the street. Black flags with neon pink writing at the top of the building advertised the club's name: Lambrianu's. It took my breath away. This was truly a totally different league.

I was surprised by how many girls were already there. There must have been nearly a hundred – all from other agencies around the city and even outside of London. The penny was beginning to drop. This really was a big deal. Inside, the club was enormous. Huge chandeliers hung from the ceiling. The stage area was a full professional stage with pink velvet curtains at the sides. It was like something out of a movie and I was in awe.

Eventually a woman walked towards us all. She was immaculately dressed in a black suit and white blouse. Her heels were high, and her blonde hair was in a fancy ponytail, trailing down her back. She introduced herself as Sharon. She seemed very professional with her clipboard in her hand. She made everyone line up in a regimental fashion. She had another woman with her, who every now and again, she would turn to and whisper something.

I definitely didn't like this. No way could I come up to this woman's expectations. She just wanted to see you naked to make sure there were no stretch marks or blemishes and to see whether you had any rhythm. This disappointed Candy, because she had spent a fortune on a new sequined costume especially for the occasion.

Already, I noticed people were leaving and I looked to Candy for an explanation.

'They are either over a size-twelve waist, or she doesn't like the look of them. Either way, she's getting that assistant of hers to thank them for coming and giving them twenty pounds for cab fare home,' she whispered.

The girls were leaving in droves. We waited for our twenty-pound farewell. But it never came.

We were led into the changing rooms, which were bigger than my front room. It was just like you see in the theatres with huge mirrors surrounded with lights. This was a far cry from the little East End pubs I was used to – it oozed sophistication!

We were down to about twenty of us. Sharon sat opposite with her clipboard, not showing any emotion on her face.

Candy did her dance, and then Sharon's assistant turned to me and told me I was next. I was trembling and on the verge of backing out. But Candy told me to get on with it. At least I hadn't been thrown out yet. We were still in with a chance.

Looking back, it was all a bit of a daze. I just remember going through the motions, and then the music finished. It was over.

Sharon stood up at the end and clapped her hands at all of us. 'Thank you, ladies. We'll be in touch in a few days when we have decided.' With that, she got up and walked away.

Sharon's assistant gave us our cab fare and showed us out. That was it. It was over, and as we left, we both felt a little deflated. All that hype and adrenalin for nothing.

Then the call came. Candy screamed down the telephone at me that she had been offered a job. I was pleased for her. I really was. She had set a lot of store by the auditions, and at last her dream had come true. She went on and on about what Sharon had said to her, and then she told me again, just in case she had forgotten anything.

Putting down the telephone after wishing her well, I walked into the kitchen to put the kettle on and noticed the message flashing on my answer phone. I had been offered a job as well and was to turn up the following Monday at 8 p.m.

As we arrived, bouncers were standing outside with their radios and headpieces with microphones on. They opened the door for us, and we walked up to the bar. Sharon greeted us and informed us that, in future, we were to use the staff entrance and not the front. She explained it kept up the mystery and expectation of the men. Also, we were in our street clothes, and that just wouldn't do. Lambrianu girls turning up in their jeans? No way.

In the changing rooms, there were some dancers who had obviously worked there a while. They were sitting with their heated rollers in, and the room smelt of hairspray and make-up. They seemed to look down their noses at us.

I was very nervous, especially when Sharon pulled us to one

side and went through the rules of the house – it was a very long list!

Firstly, there was no dating or drinking with the customers. We were there to work. Punctuality was a must. Costumes were changed weekly. She pointed to the back of the room, where there were rails of costumes on hangers. She informed us they were there for anyone to use. She would discuss with us later how many shifts we would like to work. In a week or two, she would decide whether to offer us more or fewer shifts, depending on the reviews she'd had from the men.

She also informed us that they had VIP booths where you could do one-to-one dances. With a wagging finger, she also explained that the booths had CCTV cameras in them. 'Any funny business, and you're sacked. This is a reputable club, not a knocking shop.'

I felt like crawling under a stone. All the other women were making themselves busy doing their hair but having a good listen to the toasting we were getting.

She handed us our timetables, smiled, and then, thankfully, walked out.

'So,' said Candy, trying to break the ice with the other girls, 'when do we get to meet the big boss then?'

'You don't. It's as simple as that. He's not interested in us. He likes models and actresses who put him on the red carpet at movie premieres. The best thing you can do is keep your head down, do your work, and don't cause any trouble. He's ruthless.'

The response seemed to take the smile off Candy's face. She had wanted so much to be associated with this famous gangland boss and the reputation of working for him. But, like all of us, she was just another employee.

'So, where is he then?' Candy persisted now she had their

attention. She looked around the dressing room, waiting for an answer.

'Mr Lambrianu is usually at his casino. Sharon takes care of us, and she's in charge,' said one of the strippers in a bored way while putting the finishing touches to her make-up.

That was the end of it. One of the girls moved aside to where there were some spare seats in front of a mirror, and we started getting ready. I was nervous. These women were gorgeous, absolute perfection.

I looked across at Candy and gave a weak smile. She looked crushed. This hadn't lived up to her expectations at all.

5

LAMBRIANU'S

The weeks flew by. Surprisingly enough, I quickly got the hang of dancing at Lambrianu's. You were like some famous showgirl in a West End show and I loved the atmosphere. As much as I missed the East End pubs I found myself enjoying the stardom of my new workplace, even though it was regimented.

I polished up my act a lot and put more effort into the way I looked under Sharon and the other girl's guidance. More than anything, the money was amazing – even though you didn't do a collection before you danced. That didn't stop the men waving you over towards them and putting a twenty-pound note at the side of the stage or in your garter.

Candy, on the other hand, didn't like the strict ways. You weren't allowed to work for anyone else; yet that didn't stop her sneaking off back to the East End pubs. She said she liked being able to do as she pleased.

I figured Sharon knew what she was up to, because Candy's shifts got fewer and fewer, until eventually she was down to two a week.

I was able to buy Bobby new clothes and toys, not just stuff from charity shops. And I was able to pay off my debts at long last. When I looked in the mirror, I saw someone else. I was tanned and slim. My hair was shiny because of all the oil serum the girls showed me to use so that my wavy hair hung into ringlets down my back. I didn't recognise myself!

Although the pubs had been very good to me and I still kept in touch with some of the publicans I had known, I kept my head down and abided by the rules. This was a bigger, more exclusive place and we were known as the 'Lambrianu girls' although none of us had ever met the man himself.

* * *

In no time at all, a year had come and gone, and Bobby was just about ready for primary school. My beautiful baby was now a young boy.

The Boss, as Mr Lambrianu was referred to, always held a great big party at the end of the year for all of his workers, and even a few of the VIP customers were invited. This apparently was a grand occasion, and even the hard-faced bouncer, who I knew quite well by now, looked forward to it.

The club was closed for the evening. Buffet tables had been brought in, full of food; silver buckets of champagne, packed in ice, lined the tables; and the huge pine Christmas tree in the corner of the room gave off a scent of its own.

It was nice having a night off and just mingling and chatting with the others, but we were still expected to keep up appearances, even though we weren't working, and so were all dressed in our best dresses.

Suddenly the club went quiet. Everyone, including me, turned to see why. Instantly, I recognised the man at whom they were all staring. I would have known those blue eyes anywhere. Seeing them again after all this time shocked me and wiped the smile from my face.

I had often wondered who that man had been and, on occasion, looked through the crowds of men before me wondering if he could be among them. Of course, he never had been.

We stared at each other for what seemed an eternity. The darkness of the club and its flashing lights hid my embarrassment.

Sharon's husband, who I knew was called Jake, and had seen a few times before, spoke first. 'Evening ladies, gents,' he added, looking towards some of the security men who were chatting to us. 'I hope you're all having a good time.' He went around introducing everyone to the man by his side, and then he pointed at me. 'This is Francesca.'

I stared. My feet were rooted to the floor. The man beside Jake smiled, displaying a perfect line of white teeth, and held out his hand to shake mine.

'Tony Lambrianu,' he said. 'It's nice to meet you.' He had taken my hand and had shaken it but still held on to it. I wasn't sure if he recognised me, but, as he turned to his friend and smiled, something inside me knew that he had.

Slowly the words 'Tony Lambrianu' seeped into my brain. I felt the bile rise in my throat, and I wanted the ground to swallow me up. This was my boss – the man who paid my wages! This was the very same man who I'd had casual sex with last year. Now here, standing before me, smiling, was my Achilles heel.

'Francesca? Have we met before?' he asked with a wry grin on his face. I felt he was playing with me now, and my heart was hammering in my chest.

'No,' I said, which was all I could muster up, as my mouth had gone dry.

He looked straight into my eyes and said, 'Are you sure? I never forget a face.'

Now I knew he was toying with me, finding amusement in my embarrassment, watching me squirm. I shook my head emphatically. 'No, sir. We have never met,' I lied.

'She must have one of those faces,' one of the other girls slurred, a little worse for wear.

Thank God someone had broken the moment. He nodded, raised my hand and kissed the back of it before letting go and walking away with Jake. Seeing them laugh and give each other a high five made me feel sick. I knew I was the brunt of their joke.

Feeling the vomit rising up in my throat, I ran to the bathroom. I couldn't breathe and it felt like I was having a heart attack! Locking myself in the toilet cubicle, I threw up. Beads of sweat were on my brow. My boss knew everything about me and how 'easy' I had been. I worked for him. I would probably lose my job. He wouldn't want anyone knowing he'd been slumming it with one of his employees!

'Fran! Fran, are you okay?' Candy had come into the toilets to find me.

I shouted that I was fine, but she knocked on the door for me to open it.

When I did, she looked worriedly at me. 'Fran you look awful, what's the matter?'

I made up an excuse about drinking on an empty stomach and tried calming my breathing, realising I had suffered a panic attack. I started rinsing my mouth and washing my hands in the basin, while Candy chatted on about the fantastic-looking boss we had.

'I was beginning to doubt he ever existed, Fran. But, God, women must throw themselves at his feet.'

I looked at myself in the mirror. I was as white as a sheet, and I also knew Candy was right. Women did throw themselves at his feet – me being one of them!

I made my excuses about feeling ill and assured Candy that she should stay at the party and enjoy the rest of the night. I just needed to get out of there and get some fresh air in my lungs.

6

BAD TIMES

I worried that I had overreacted the evening of the party, but when I turned up for work, nothing was said and life went back to normal. I had enjoyed Christmas with my family, but there had been a cloud over the festivities. My mam's new boyfriend, George, had taken it upon himself to be lord of the manor and boss the boys around and I felt angry when my mam allowed it, always giving the excuse that my brothers needed a male example in their life.

I'd made a point of informing my mam that he would not boss Bobby around, and I had intervened when he had got on his high horse and tried. I could tell that he didn't like me or the fact that I reminded him that he was a 'guest' in the house. If he didn't like what he saw, maybe he should leave. I hadn't wanted to upset the apple cart, but I also felt I should make my feelings known, for my brothers' sakes.

A couple of months passed when I got a call from the eldest of my brothers. 'Fran, you have to come home,' he said. 'Things are really bad here. Will you come?'

He didn't go into detail but I knew I had to go, because he

wouldn't have telephoned me if it wasn't important.

I packed a few things and put Bobby in the car. I decided it was quicker to drive to the club and tell Sharon personally I had to go home to my mam's. Unlike the other girls, this was the first time I had cancelled my shifts or thrown a sickie.

'Oh, Fran,' Sharon shouted when I was leaving with Bobby, 'as you're passing that way, will you drop this off at Tony's other club?' She held out a brown envelope to me, and although it was inconvenient and in the wrong direction, I took it.

It was a small favour to ask, considering how understanding she had been about my forthcoming absence.

When I arrived at the club, I couldn't get in. The doors were locked, and even though I knocked and banged, no one answered. I had to go if I was going to make it home at a reasonable time, so I decided I would take it to the club when I got back in a day or two.

When I arrived at my mam's, she was as shocked to see me as I was at the sight that greeted me. I asked her what was going on and she admitted that she had given George the money I had sent to her for him to rent a bigger house for them all.

Somewhere in the midst of this, they had argued, and he had left without returning the money. The electricity had been cut off, and she couldn't pay the bill and George had even taken the boys' bunk beds with him, leaving the boys with nothing to sleep on.

Everything seemed a mess, and my mam had tried saving face by not telling me. She didn't want to be a burden. Thank God my brother had taken the initiative and telephoned me.

First things first – I sent the boys to the local fish and chip shop so I could listen in private to the rest of the happenings. Poor Mam. I'd only brought 100 pounds with me and I hadn't been expecting anything like this.

I left the boys to eat their fish and chips and contacted the electric company and paid the bill in full. As I reached into my bag for my purse, I noticed the brown envelope Sharon had given me. Curiously, I opened the corner of it and saw that it was full of money! My heart pounded. I couldn't believe my eyes. Sharon had trusted me with all of this money but, listening to my mam's problems and feeling helpless, the overwhelming temptation to borrow some of the cash engulfed me. I decided that maybe I could borrow just a little bit to help Mam out.

So this was what I did and the next few days were a whirl. I bought new beds for the boys and paid the rent in advance. The happier it made my family, watching their smiles, the more I dipped into this pot of gold in my handbag – anything to ease my mam's pain. I had a telephone installed so I could be instantly reachable if needed.

I stayed for the week, spending and spending, until eventually, I had to leave. In my eagerness to sort everything out, I hadn't realised just how thin the envelope had become. I was a little afraid and nervous driving home, knowing I would have to face the consequences.

When I arrived home I noticed my answer phone flashing. It had thirty messages on it. Each message in turn that I listened to was Sharon's voice asking me to ring her.

Eventually on the last message, I heard Mr Lambrianu's voice.

'I believe you have something of mine, Francesca. When you get this message, I expect you to come to my office. Don't make me come to you.' The tone was threatening and made my blood run cold.

Now I had to face the music. I had never meant to spend that much money and I still didn't know how much I'd spent. But I guessed it went into the hundreds, maybe even a few thousand pounds!

I rang Sharon who was not at all pleased with me and kept

going on about how I had betrayed her trust. She told me I was to go to the casino and see Mr Lambrianu himself.

Dealing with Mr Lambrianu had been the last thing I'd expected, but Sharon said I had humiliated her and it was obvious that she had been on the receiving end of his wrath. Now I was frightened and nervous. I didn't know what to expect.

I had never been to a casino before and on arriving there, I was in awe. I thought the clubs looked amazing but this completely blew me away with its splendour.

Two bouncers were standing outside in their tuxedos and they looked down their noses at me, which obviously meant they had heard why I was there. One spoke into his radio, announcing that I had arrived. He nodded towards me and beckoned me to follow him past the huge casino tables and roulette wheels.

I was led down a huge corridor, and the man in front of me stopped and another guy came to meet me. I could feel the tension building. If Tony Lambrianu had wanted to intimidate me, he had achieved his goal.

I was then told to wait. After only a few moments the man came back and indicated that I was to follow him to two large double doors. He opened one of them and simply said, 'She's here, boss.' Then he stood aside for me to walk in.

Sat at a huge wooden desk in a leather chair was Mr Lambrianu, with Jake standing at his side.

I had expected to walk in and find an angry man, full of abusive language, but no. Jake held his hand out to me and asked for the envelope, which I handed to him.

'Sit down, Francesca.' Mr Lambrianu pointed to a chair at the opposite side of the table from him. 'Coffee?'

This all seemed very calm and civil, not at all what I had expected. Yet I knew my head was on the chopping block, and sat before me was my executioner.

Tony looked towards Jake, who by now had opened the envelope and was counting the contents. He looked up and informed us both that I had spent 3,000 pounds! My God, I didn't realise I had spent that much. I'd showed off, spending money and buying clothes, food, and furniture and I realised now that I had been ridiculous. I felt like crying and my heart sank. I was a thief; nothing more, nothing less.

'Are you going to call the police?' I asked. I found some courage to try and defend myself and announced that I intended to pay it all back. I couldn't go to prison. What about Bobby?

I apologised again and nervously rambled on, wringing my hands in the process.

Mr Lambrianu held up his hand to stop me. 'Some spending spree. And no, I won't be calling the police.' He and Jake looked at each other and smiled. They both seemed to find this amusing. 'Of course you will pay me back, Francesca. I already know that.'

I breathed a sigh of relief and managed an awkward smile of my own. Maybe this wasn't going to be as bad as I thought. At least the police weren't going to be involved.

He then asked me why I had stolen his money and what it had been for.

I felt sure that anyone who was called to his office to face his anger would make all kinds of excuses, and he had heard them all before. This was personal. I didn't want him to know that my family had been in a real mess because of my mam's boyfriend. It sounded pathetic to say it out loud, so I just let him think what he liked and was prepared to face the music.

Taking a deep sigh, he informed me that 3,000 pounds plus the interest he charged meant that I now owed him 9,000 pounds!

'What? You can't be serious,' I yelled at him, stunned. He couldn't mean it. Could he?

He then informed me in that slow deep crisp voice of his that he wanted it paid back in twenty-eight days, or more interest would be added.

Jake walked to the door and opened it for me. The meeting was over. I was about to walk out, still in a daze, when he said my name again, and calmly and quietly informed me that I was also sacked!

'How am I supposed to pay you back if I'm not earning any money?' I said. The panic inside me made me raise my voice and almost screech.

'Not my problem, Francesca.' He then went on to explain that he couldn't be seen to employ someone with her fingers in the till. If that was the case, then other people would think they could do it and get away with it.

'Twenty-eight days and counting Francesca. I want it in full, the same way you took it.'

Then I was dismissed.

I walked out of there, not even waiting for his suited escorts to show me the way. My mind was spinning, and tears were pouring down my face. His words were going around and around in my brain. I was back at the beginning: in debt, and with no job.

I didn't know why, but out of desperation, I telephoned Sharon and tried appealing to her better nature about my job. It was like talking to a brick wall. The decision had been made, and that was final. Mr Lambrianu's word was law.

I had some savings set aside but nothing that amounted to what that loan shark was demanding. I was angry and bitter. Yet I realised it had been my own fault. I wished I had never heard the name Lambrianu, let alone worked for him. Damn him! Damn them all. And damn me for being so stupid.

I telephoned Candy and poured out the whole miserable story. She had left Lambrianu's as I had presumed she would and gone back to the East End pubs. I asked her if I would be able to get my old job back, but she informed me that word had already spread, and publicans had been warned not to employ me.

I cried buckets of tears. The more I thought about my fate, the more I cried. I did the only thing a girl could do and telephoned my mam. Even though I told her I had been sacked, I didn't want her to know it was because I had helped her and so I said that I owed Mr Lambrianu some money. I mentioned that I had some savings but not enough. I didn't know what else to do. Even after selling my car, I would still be 3,000 short.

Mam knew best of course. She told me to take what I had to him; something was better than nothing, and it showed I was willing. Surely that stood for something?

But counting up everything I had and everything I could sell, it still wasn't enough. What a cold-hearted man he was. Poor Bobby – he didn't deserve this. Just as we were getting on our feet again, my stupidity had wrecked it.

* * *

Twenty-eight days later, I had to go and face the music. I was still two thousand pounds short.

Sharon had given me a set time and date I was to go back to the casino. I was nervous, and it showed. After the same pomp and ceremony I'd had the first time, I was shown into the office.

Mr Lambrianu sat in his large leather chair at his desk, with Jake stood by his side. I took the money out of my bag and put it on the table. I looked at them both, nervously waiting while Jake counted it. I explained that was all I could get together at such short notice.

But Mr Lambrianu didn't seem to be listening. He was looking at me, and then he sat back in his chair and gave a little sigh. He turned towards Jake and smiled.

'Francesca do you think you could use your acting skills and escort me for the evening at a very grand social event? People will be curious about you and some ladies possibly bitchy. But this is important to myself and Jake – nearly as important as that money and what you owe me is to you.' His voice was deep, and he spoke eloquently, but his eyes were smiling as he turned towards Jake and nudged him with his elbow. 'I've thought of something,' he said, with a large grin on his face.

I didn't know what they were talking about. I obviously wasn't in on the joke. But I felt, as usual, I was going to be the brunt of it.

'Why would you want me to come to a social event with you?' I said. My throat felt dry. 'I'm sure you are not short of escorts for the evening. Why me?' I shifted uneasily in my chair, waiting for an answer.

His explanation was short and sweet. He explained about the evening, the people I would meet, and the questions that would be fired at me. He told me that, to pull this off, they wanted a professional, someone who had acted and lied through many shifts at work, convincing men to part with their money. Worst of all, he explained to me that I was to pretend to be his girlfriend, long term.

My jaw almost dropped, and the look on my face must have been pure horror. This was crazy. Why did he need a pretend girlfriend? He had lots of girlfriends. Everyone knew that.

7

LADIES' NIGHT

I was offered no explanation, only that, if I accepted, my debt would be cleared once and for all. If not, the interest was already mounting up on what I still owed.

I cleared my throat and decided to ask a few of my own questions.

'If I was to do this, whatever it is, would you be prepared to take the ban off my working the local East End pubs? I need to work. And although I don't know what you expect of me – and I get the feeling that you expect a lot – I've never been to any grand social events before. I don't even own a dress for such an occasion.' There, I had said my piece while I had their attention.

I saw them glance at each other and then nod. Mr Lambrianu handed me over 1,000 pounds and told me to buy a dress and whatever I needed. And yes, they would lift their ban and let me get some work, although not at their club.

All of my scrimping and saving, and he had just pushed 1,000 pounds of the money I had given him towards me and told me to spend it on a dress.

The thought of clearing my debt and getting my job back was

tempting. But you know what they say: if it sounds too good to be true, then it probably is. On the other hand, he had hinted that, if I didn't accept, I would still owe him a lot of interest, and so it would be a never-ending circle of debt. I had no option but to agree. I half expected a smile, but I didn't receive one. Their poker faces showed nothing.

Jake explained that Sharon would be in touch with the details. And then I was dismissed.

With the money in my bag, I walked out of the casino, not wondering about this crazy deal to clear my debts but the fact that I could work again. Okay, it meant starting from scratch, but at least I had the opportunity to work. Thank God for that!

* * *

Before I knew it, the evening was upon me. Sharon had schooled me on the details and the lies. I'd had to memorise things like how long I had known Tony, where we had met, and so on. She had also been shopping with me and helped me pick out something suitable. She had always been decent to me, but I actually felt a bond with her now. I had a feeling she thought I was a bit naive. And, yes, I was. What did I know about evening gowns and hair salons that did your make-up and nails?

We had both decided it would be better to rent one rather than buy one, because I would never wear it again. Together we had picked out a beautiful, deep purple satin evening gown. It was sleeveless, save two thin satin straps holding up the bustier top half, and it hung straight down until it reached passed my knees and bowed out into a fish tail, swishing around my legs as I walked.

It was the most luxurious thing I had ever owned and stupidly, I couldn't wait to wear it.

My hair was straightened and put up into a French pleat that was puffed out on the top, with two kiss curls at either side of my face. My high court shoes matched the colour of my dress. And my fake tan, make-up and false eyelashes finished off the whole combination. What a transformation. I'd never worn anything like this and probably never would again.

The chauffeur-driven Rolls-Royce arrived, and I got in, feeling like a princess. But now, reality was also dawning. What did the evening have in store for me?

Arriving at the huge hotel, I could already see lots of other cars dropping off couples. The women in their real fur coats and best jewellery caused a rainbow of colour outside. My nerves were kicking in now and I felt like an imposter. When we stopped, the chauffeur got out and opened the door for me. He must have sensed my uncertainty and walked me to the main doors and gave me a thumbs up. I was to meet the others at the bar in the reception.

I spotted Sharon first, and she came to meet me. She was wearing a traditional black ball gown with a bustier top, which emphasised her blonde hair. She was stood next to Jake. Then I spotted Mr Lambrianu. He had a purple bow tie and cummerbund around his waist, the exact same colour as my dress. I also noticed that the colour highlighted his blondness, making him look very handsome indeed. Sharon really had done her homework.

I wasn't sure If I looked okay or not, because Tony and Jake just stared at me and then at each other and then at me again. Sharon handed me a small brandy. 'Drink this for your nerves,' she said.

I didn't particularly drink, but looking around and watching all of these people coming towards me terrified me. I took a huge gulp of it and felt it slide down my throat, warming my chest.

A man in a red tail coat, who Sharon whispered to me was the master of ceremonies, started announcing that people were to stand near some huge wooden double doors that were roped off from the bar. When we stood in the queue, the doors opened. One by one, this man announced us all by name until we walked through the wooden doors, full of dining tables and waiters going about their business. I was in awe. It was so grand.

I was so stunned by all this glamour all I could do was look around me in wonderment and I was having trouble putting one leg in front of the other.

'Tony! Jake!' a man shouted. 'Over here, boys.'

The man was standing by a long table, dressed in all his finery and wearing what looked to me like a Lord Mayor's chain around his neck. Sharon gave me the look, which I took to mean this was the man that all of this was for. This man and his wife were the people I was supposed to impress. Sharon had given me a summary of Ralph Gold and warned me about his wife, Julie, who would try and trip me up in any lie.

The men shook hands. Looking to the man's side, I noticed a woman with a blonde bob. She was wearing an elaborate gold taffeta ball gown, and every part of her seemed to have jewellery on it. I was slightly surprised because she seemed a lot younger than the man, who I believed to be her husband – definitely not what I had expected.

'You must be the lovely Francesca.' Ralph Gold held his hand out and shook mine and then introduced me to his wife Julie.

It almost makes me smile when I think back to my first meeting with Ralph and Julie. I had no idea who they were. Sharon had missed out the parts in her summary that Ralph and Julie owned most of England and were deeply involved with the mafia. Tony and Jake had desperately wanted to do business with him. The only problem had been Tony's lifestyle. Ralph liked a respectable front, married men, because at that time wives could not testify in court against their husbands. He didn't like girlfriends who might kiss and tell. I realised afterwards that was where I came in. The humble, single parent who had never been in the tabloids, ticked all of Ralph's boxes... which meant I was perfect for Tony's plan.

* * *

Julie Gold surprisingly gave me a hug, including a kiss on the cheek. 'You must tell me, darling Francesca, how you stole Tony's heart,' she drawled, 'although, I can see for myself why.'

I blushed and smiled back. Mr Lambrianu slipped his arm around my waist, and I felt my body tense. My God, what did I call him? Tony? Before I had to worry or answer Julie, we were led to our tables, and the dinner was served. I looked down at the cutlery and then at Sharon, who was talking to Jake. I didn't know why, but I felt as though I was being stared at, as though eyes were burning into me. When I looked up, I saw Julie Gold.

She smiled and then picked up her cutlery from the outside and lifted them higher for me to see. She had already seen past my posh dress and finery and knew it wasn't what I was used to.

Mr Lambrianu played the doting boyfriend well and once the speeches had finished, everyone was free to mingle. The band started up, and finally people could enjoy themselves.

Instantly, Julie Gold, followed by an entourage of women similarly dressed, came and sat at my side of the table. Ralph was talking to the men, while I was left to be interrogated by Julie and her friends. It was bad, if not worse, than predicted. She wanted to know everything about me: where I was from, how old I was, and so on. I spent most of the evening being questioned and I saw Mr Lambrianu look over now and again. Even he looked nervous to a point.

But I felt I held my own. As much as possible, I told the truth. I was from a small Yorkshire town, I was divorced with a young son, and I'd met Tony at a party.

Julie was permanently having her glass filled by the waiters and she was already a little loud and tipsy as she held court with all these women around her, who admired her jewellery and flattered her.

I was tired of being interrogated, and after two glasses of wine and a lot of soda water, I found my tongue at last. 'I really don't know why you are asking me all of this. I'm sure you know most of it already – just as I'm sure that you know I also worked for Tony. I have a young son and bills to pay.'

The deathly silence around the table was deafening. I knew I had gone too far.

I saw all the men and Sharon look up at me. The other women with Julie stared at me, almost open-mouthed. The awkward silence was broken by Julie Gold's loud laughter. 'You have to hand it to these straight-talking northern women. They give as good as they get.'

Everyone started to laugh, and then she announced the truth. 'Of course we knew you worked for Tony, but we wondered how you would lie your way out of that. Well done, Francesca. You might have embarrassed Tony, but you speak the truth.'

With that, she shouted over to Ralph that it was time for a dance and they headed onto the dance floor.

'What the hell did you say that for, big mouth?' said Jake after the Golds had left the table.

'No, Jake. Hang on a minute,' said Sharon, 'this could work in our favour. No lies. They didn't expect that confession, not tonight. If anything, the tables have been turned. That is why she has gone to dance and talk to Ralph. The questions are over.' Sharon smiled and seemed pleased.

Sharon had been right. When the Golds returned, they talked about other things.

A beautiful young woman came over and draped herself over

Tony's shoulders. 'Tony, darling, I thought you would have brought Roxy with you. Who is this?' She gave me a look of disgust and then picked up Tony's glass and took a drink out of it. Bitchy!

I saw Julie Gold sit back in her chair. She was going to enjoy this, seeing how I coped with Tony's women. I stood up and held out my hand to shake hers. 'I'm Francesca, and I'm standing in because Roxy was busy tonight.' Fortunately for me, I had dealt with a lot of strippers in my time, and some of them could be the bitchiest women you would ever want to meet. This woman was just trying to prove a point – that she and Tony had been lovers. Big deal! Come to think of it, so had we.

At last, I thought, I may have done something right, because behind Mr Lambrianu's blush at one of his girlfriend's being there, he actually smiled at me. In the meantime, while I was talking, I hadn't noticed Julie call over one of Ralph's bodyguards. And with a whisper in his ear, the woman was escorted out of the room.

Then Mr Lambrianu asked me to dance. It was the final one of the evening, so everyone was on their feet for the last waltz. I felt very awkward. Unlike the others, who seemed a little tipsy and were draped over each other, we were stood at arm's length. He pulled me closer to him and the slow waltz continued. I thought back to when I had been in his arms once before; it seemed a lifetime ago now.

'You have done very well tonight Francesca, thank you. And just in case you thought I hadn't noticed, you look beautiful.'

I was mesmerised by Tony, and I was shocked that he'd thanked me. My heart skipped a beat.

Before I knew it, the lights were being turned up, indicating the end of the evening and breaking the moment between us. The band had stopped playing and everyone was saying their goodbyes. Tony, Jake and Sharon walked with me to the car.

That was it. It had been hard and stressful, but now it was over.

At last I was back home in my own living room. Chris had left, and I went into Bobby's bedroom to check on him.

Now I needed a good long shower to wash away the evening. In the morning, I would ring the agency and get my old job back as promised. And I had paid off my debt to Mr Lambrianu, which meant I would never have to see him again.

8

THE PROPOSAL

I had no feedback from my night with Tony, so I figured it must have gone okay. I was therefore surprised when I walked out of a pub one day, and parked outside was a familiar Rolls-Royce. I carried on walking towards the bus stop, when the window of the car opened.

'Get in.'

The words were not an invitation, but a demand, and so I did as I was told.

Jake was alone in the car, and he congratulated me on the ladies' night, even telling me how beautiful I had looked. That made me feel uneasy. It was obvious he wanted something.

He then told me that I was to do it again and make another success of it. He sat there smiling at me, like it was the most natural request in the world. My jaw dropped, and I had been about to say no when he told me he would pay me 2,000 pounds.

'Surely, Francesca,' he said, 'that would buy you some old banger of a car to get around in.'

Two thousand pounds! Just to sit at a table and eat and drink? It all sounded too good to be true. He informed me that it would just be the six of us and that this time I should hold my tongue. They would cover any clothes expenses and send the car for me as before.

While he was talking, my brain ticked over. This was a smaller event, more intimate, and it wouldn't have the same overwhelming atmosphere as the previous event. Before I realised it, I had shaken hands with Jake, agreeing to the deal. Then Jake sat back in his seat and handed me an envelope. Looking inside, I saw that it contained the money as promised.

This time, under Sharon's influence, I wore a black lace cocktail dress, knee-length. My long, wavy hair trailed loosely down my back. Julie Gold was in a white satin trouser suit and, of course, a gold top. Wearing something gold seemed to be her signature and she gave me a warm welcome and a kiss on the cheek.

Ralph had asked me about my son and informed me they too had a son, Joshua, who was at boarding school. Once again, I noticed Julie drinking glass after glass of wine, while I stuck to my lime and soda water. I explained to Julie while she seemed intent on filling my wine glass, that, I didn't particularly drink, and I wanted to keep a clear head.

When all was finished, and we stood up to leave, Julie said the unthinkable, changing the course of history forever. 'So, Francesca, when are you going to make an honest man of Tony and marry him? Ralph and I would love to host your engagement party.'

What a bombshell! It had shocked everyone into silence. Although the dinner had been informal, they had still been testing us.

I blushed and looked to the others for help.

Tony took the initiative. He cleared his throat and jumped in quickly. Giving his most charming smile and sweeping his wispy fringe away from his face, he spoke. 'Julie, you of all people should know that the more you push a woman, the more time she is going to want to make up her mind.' Again, he smiled, showing a perfect row of white teeth.

What the hell was he saying? More to the point, what had he already said? Somehow I found my voice.

'That's very generous of you,' I said. 'But I'm not rushing into anything just now.' I felt like a politician. I had evaded the question without actually answering. They all laughed at my answer, and Ralph told me to keep Tony waiting – woman's prerogative and all that!

Time for a hasty exit. We all got into one car this time and the journey was silent; everyone seemed to be thinking over what Julie had asked. When they got out at the club, I was driven home, alone.

While in the shower, I mulled over the events. There was a lot more to this than met the eye. Tony, Jake and Sharon were doing their utmost to influence this man, Ralph, and he seemed to be doing his best to trip them up at every turn.

* * *

A few days later, I had a telephone call requesting that I go to their office. This time, it was more of a polite invite, which even included a thank you. I hadn't seen or heard from any of them since the lunch date, but my curiosity made me want to go.

Jake, Sharon and Tony were sitting in the office. I was nervous, but they all seemed pleased to see me. After the usual preliminaries, asking how I was and so on, I sat waiting with the coffee they had poured me as they told me why I was here.

As they did so, I stared at them in stunned silence. They were prepared to pay me to marry Mr Lambrianu? Women were falling over themselves to be the chosen one. Why on earth would he want to marry me?

They explained that now the Golds had met me, it was too late to turn the clock back and find someone new.

Mr Lambrianu opened his desk side drawer and took out some sheets of paper and laid them out. 'This is a contract I have had drawn up, should you decide to go through with this marriage. You get a house by the seaside, all paid for, but you don't get the deeds until one year is up. As I say, the contract is for a year only. You can move in straight away. I will be responsible for the bills, and I will give you one million for your trouble. There will be many charity functions and parties to attend, and all dress expenses will be paid. You are to be at my beck and call for all of these – no arguments. In fact, you will be an employee like any other, and the house comes with the job.'

I couldn't believe my ears. A house and a million pounds? Stunned, I waited for them all to burst out laughing, as though it was some April fool's joke. I looked at the contract. It had a solicitor's header and stamp on it and appeared to be some kind of prenuptial arrangement.

Now it was time for me to find my voice. 'What's in it for you? If I were to consider this proposition, I would like to know why you are doing this. I have one failed marriage behind me. Why would I want another? And what about my son? We come as a package, you know.'

Sharon spoke up, trying to iron out the wrinkles. 'The difference is, neither of you are in love. So there would be no claim on anything else when the marriage ends. As for your son, Francesca, we know you come as a package. But think of it, Fran – a house you would own. You would get him off that rough estate, and he would go to a better class of school. And of course, there is the money. You could give him security. The Golds have met you and checked for any skeletons in your closet. It's a stay-at-home job, allowing you to be with Bobby by the seaside, with all the benefits.' Sharon had a way of putting it from a female angle – the soft touch, you might say.

Still staring at their faces in wonder, I saw that Jake and Mr Lambrianu approved of Sharon's heartfelt speech. I asked again, 'But what's in it for you?'

'Business and money. And as for us wanting you to lie and act your head off, you already have. You're up to your neck in it as much as we are.' Those blue eyes seemed to burn into me.

There he went again, making this sound like a threat. 'I'm not up to my neck in anything. I could just tell the truth,' I snapped, 'that you paid me to do it.' I grinned.

The smiles dropped from all of their faces.

'If I am to be an employee, I would want employee's terms, including four weeks' holiday to do as I please. And as an employee, there would be no sex involved. I have heard stories about you and your women.' Now I was feeling brave and a little angry at their assumption that I would just go along with this.

Mr Lambrianu sat back in his chair and gave me a smug grin. 'Don't flatter yourself. I don't want to have sex with you... Believe me, my diaries are quite full in that department.' He laughed at me, like the very idea made him squirm.

I just looked at him, remembering the time when that hadn't seemed so absurd to him. It stung a little. 'Then you wouldn't object, Mr Lambrianu, to a clause in that contract stating that, if you ever sexually harassed me in any way, the deal would be over, and I would be able to walk away with the deeds of the house. Also, as for my son, you keep your distance from him. He's had one father walk out on him, and I don't want him getting attached to you, for you to do the same in a years' time.'

Mr Lambrianu took my hand. 'If that is what you want, then fine. Like you say, you would be another employee. Although my life and women friends would carry on as normal, and you would be the good monogamous wife and mother. I like your style, Francesca. You're seeing it as a contract deal and discussing it properly, without emotion.'

He seemed sincere and kind, and for a moment held my gaze. I could feel myself being swallowed up by those blue eyes. His very touch made me tingle and remember our night together.

Swallowing hard, I moved my hand away. 'I'll think about it,' I said. 'Also, none of your women friends would be anyone I know, and you wouldn't humiliate me in public with them. I don't want to be made a laughing stock of. I've been married to a cheating liar before. I really don't relish the idea of going through that again, whatever the price.'

Mr Lambrianu listened intently and seemed to be looking into my very soul. His voice softened, and it seemed like there was only us two in the room. 'I promise you, Francesca. For the record, I wouldn't be a cheating liar, because you already know what to expect without any emotional involvement. If I were to fall in love and want out of the deal, I promise you, you would be the first to know.'

The conversation went on for some time. Each time I brought something up, they had an answer for me. I was no expert businesswoman, but even I could see there was a lot riding on this, and they wanted it badly.

When I told them again that I would think about it and stood up to leave, Mr Lambrianu opened his desk drawer and laid a set of keys with a label attached to them on the desk.

'Go and take a look at the house. Maybe that will help you make up your mind. The address is on the label.'

I picked the keys up and put them in my bag. 'This doesn't mean I have agreed to anything. I'm just looking, okay?' And with that I turned and left them before they could dismiss me.

On the journey home, my mind was weighing up all of the pros and cons of this offer. There was only one person I could talk this through with: my mam.

'I've heard of Ralph Gold,' she said. 'Nasty piece of work by all accounts. People who offend him usually go missing without a trace. I also know he is a very wealthy, influential man.'

God, she knew more about him than I did.

'Your Mr Lambrianu is small-time in comparison, Fran. No wonder they want to do business with him. But he won't work with just anyone. He has too much at stake.'

I told her about the contract and that I also wanted a no-sex clause included, and she just laughed down the telephone at me.

'What on earth would he need you for, Fran? Don't get me wrong. You're my daughter, and I love you. But have you seen the women he is famous for going out with? They are on the television, in the newspapers, and God knows what else. No, you're definitely safe there, Fran.'

As much as I agreed, I was still a woman, and the fact that everyone kept telling me I wasn't in his league still hurt, especially when I knew I had been his choice once. Or had I just been his bit of rough?

'Go and see the house he is offering you. See what you think. It could be awful and that would make your mind up. But with a million pounds in your pocket, you could make it your own. A million pounds for one year's work and some nights out in posh restaurants and posh dresses. What do you have to lose?'

Both my mam and Sharon were right. Think what I could do for Bobby with that kind of money. We would have no debts and no worries.

I caught the train to see the house, not knowing what was waiting for me.

9

THE HOUSE

The seaside was a little breezy, and the seafront stretched for miles. There were all kinds of amusements and shops selling buckets and spades, and it was indeed a lovely place. I looked at the address on the label and just about walked the full length of the seafront, with all of its bed and breakfast houses, as I looked for the house.

My feet ached and I began to wonder if this house actually existed. Then I saw a policeman and asked him if he knew the address. He pointed towards the very end of the promenade and told me it was the house on the hill. Again, I walked, until eventually I saw a giant mansion with wrought-iron black gates and high walls.

It was like a hotel. I walked up to the gates and found they were locked. I fumbled with the keys I had been given, although none of them fitted. It seemed like I had come all this way for nothing. Either that, or it was the wrong house.

As I looked through the gates, I noticed a huge circular gravel driveway, with a cherub fountain in the middle. The driveway went all the way up to six columns at the front of the house. It was beautiful. He was really going to give me this?

No, I must be mistaken. There must be a small cottage around the back or something. Maybe it was private apartments. Suddenly, as though by magic, the gates slowly began to open.

I walked down the driveway to the huge wooden double-fronted door. It opened and a middle-aged woman, around my mam's age, stood there. She was dressed in black trousers and a flowery blouse. Her hair was tied back in a bun. She gave me a huge smile. 'You must be Francesca. I heard you were coming,' she said.

'How did you know I was here?' I asked, frowning.

'The cameras, my dear. The monitors are inside.'

Curiously, I watched the woman as she opened the doors wide and, with a smile on her face and a sweep of her hand to show me in, she said, 'Welcome home.'

I nervously stepped into the hallway. A huge chandelier hung from the ceiling and on the far left side were the beginnings of a huge wooden spiral staircase. Again I looked at the woman, confused that she was even there. 'I'm sorry,' I said as she was taking my coat. 'Who are you? I was led to believe the house was empty.'

'I'm Elle, the housekeeper. I don't live here. I live farther down the road, but I will be popping in on a daily basis to help out,' she said, very matter of fact.

'I don't need a housekeeper. I'm perfectly capable of running my own home, thank you. Although I suspect, if I were to move in here,' I added a little more sarcastically than I should have, 'that you're here to spy on me for Mr Lambrianu.'

I could see that I had offended her the moment the sarcasm left my lips. I could have bitten my tongue. She had been warm and welcoming. Obviously, she had been informed I was coming to view the house and was making the best of it. If anything, I was the intruder.

She ignored my comment and walked down the huge hallway. 'I'll put the kettle on, shall I?' she asked pensively. 'You must be tired, driving all the way here.' She rambled on about the weather and the traffic, trying her hardest to make some connection with me. But I resented her being there and what she stood for.

I explained that I didn't have a car and that I had travelled by train. She seemed surprised that Mr Lambrianu, or Tony as she referred to him, hadn't given me one of his drivers to bring me to Southend-on-Sea. I was shocked that, being the housekeeper, she very casually called our mutual employer Tony, as though she was used to it.

I followed her into an enormous kitchen, the size of my whole house. It was beautiful, like something from a film. A huge stainless steel breakfast bar with a shiny black worktop dominated the centre of the room. It had a double range oven and a huge double-doored American fridge freezer, which still had the plastic and cardboard on it.

The large patio doors, which were the full length of one wall, led into the garden. The kitchen itself had obviously recently been designed and fitted with loads of cupboards and cabinets and a beautiful marble flooring. Good God! He was going to give me this?

I was curious now to see the rest of the house.

My thoughts were interrupted by Elle, who was asking me if I wanted tea or coffee. She could see I was impressed. 'Do you want to start upstairs, Francesca? Or would you rather I leave you alone to look around?'

'Before we start, can I ask you: how come everything is brand new?' Even the windows still had the plastic tape on them glaziers used to prevent breakages.

She gave out a huge sigh. 'It hasn't been used, and more is the pity. It's a beautiful house, but it has no life in it. Tony just hired the designers and the decorators to do everything. I think he has stayed here once, maybe twice at most.' She looked almost downhearted as she surveyed the room.

It was a shame that a house like this had been neglected in such a way. We both agreed on that! Now, I was as intrigued as anyone would be. 'Why did he buy it then, if he never intended to use it?'

She shrugged her shoulders. 'Why does Tony do anything? Shall I lead on?'

There was indeed a lot to get through. The house had ten bedrooms, all with en suites and each one as glamorous as the last. The master bedrooms, as she called them, were opposite each other. Each consisted of a supersized carved wooden four-poster bed.

The main master bedroom had patio doors leading out onto a balcony, where you could look out and see the seafront. It was more like a hotel than a home. There were dining rooms and lounges, all fully furnished, with dust sheets covering them. The large chesterfield suite still had the labels attached.

The only obstacle was the colour scheme. Every room was magnolia! He really hadn't taken an interest and had just gone for the safe option. The place had no warmth. It was a house, not a home – almost museum-like.

After three hours of trying to take everything in, I had to leave and get home to Bobby. I explained this to Elle, who was still chatting about all the different features the house had, including the gardens and excess land. Elle walked me back towards the front door and said, 'Do come and live here, Francesca. You and your little boy could breathe some life into it.' She seemed very sincere.

Suddenly, realisation was dawning on me. 'You know everything, don't you? You know my name, about my son, and obviously the offer Mr Lambrianu has made me. Who are you really, to be taken into such confidence by him? None of his other employees are,' I said.

'Just a very old friend, who is always on hand to help – nothing more and nothing less. Yes, I do know about the offer and the circumstances. I'm not going to start off by lying to you. I would be here to help you sort out this place and turn it into a home.' She waved her arm around the hallway.

I said my goodbyes, shook her hand, and left. When I stood outside the front gates, I couldn't help but look back at the house. It was truly beautiful. All of this could be mine and Bobby's, but it was very overwhelming too.

I had a lot to think about. On the surface, it seemed very easy to say yes. But the upkeep of that house alone would cost a fortune. As I walked along the seafront, I gazed out at the speed boats and fishing boats. The air was clean. The sandy, pebbled beach would be a fantastic spot in the summer to have picnics with Bobby.

Stop! I was getting way ahead of myself, imagining the life we could have here. But I knew in my heart that Bobby would love it.

On arriving home, my mind was still thinking things over.

Bobby ran to me. When I looked at him, I pictured him on the beach, with all that fresh air, and living in that house. If I acted out my role as wife properly, the deeds would be all mine. To never again be threatened with eviction letters... It was tempting, sorely tempting.

I knew that, by now, Elle would have let Mr Lambrianu know that I had been to the house. He would be waiting to hear from me and, hopefully, get my answer. Before I telephoned him, I would telephone my mam and tell her. She too would be waiting to find out about the house.

She sounded very excited when I told her about the place. It crossed my mind that with all of those bedrooms, my mam and brothers could come and stay for a holiday at the seaside.

It seemed as though I was thinking about everyone but myself. What about me? What would I have to do? Day in and day out, I would have to live a lie, always be on my guard. I wasn't sure I could do it.

'You lived a lie with Luke,' my mam reminded me. 'Day in and day out, you let people think you were happy, and all the while, you knew you were not.' Her tone was matter of fact.

Ouch! That hurt. But the truth always does, doesn't it? 'What would you do, Mam, if you were in my position?'

I knew it was a stupid question, and the answer was simple. 'If I was ever to be in the same position as you are now, Fran, surrounded by wealth and security for Bobby – all for a year of my life, and all I had to do was strut around like the lady of the manor – I would bite his bloody hands off.'

* * *

I let the days roll into a week. No one contacted me. My mam was right, of course. But I felt the ruse would be a lot harder than it sounded.

I did a shift at one of the local pubs, and during the shift, a fight broke out. One of the men involved had a broken bottle put into his face. Glasses were being smashed, while shouting and threats were exchanged. The landlord indicated to the DJ that he should turn the music up louder to drown out the noise of the fight. We watched as the landlord picked up the telephone and I presumed he was calling the police.

But within a few minutes, six black-suited men walked through the doors and immediately started to throw punches at the troublemakers.

One man, totally out of place with his black suit and tie, walked up to the ringleader, who was still holding the broken and now blood-smeared bottle in his hand; took out a handgun; and pointed it towards him.

The ringleader shouted, 'Come on, city boy. You wouldn't dare.'

It was obvious this man was on something, because he couldn't see that the man in front of him with the gun meant business.

With a strange smile on his face, the suited man pulled the trigger, shooting the other man in the arm, and then in the foot. He remained poker-faced all the while. The gun had a silencer on it, so there was no real noise. And the music drowned out the cry from the ringleader, who was now on the floor, shouting in pain and covered in blood.

The patrons, upon taking in the scene, jumped to their feet and ran towards the doors in droves in panic and fear. Two other men in suits were standing by the door. Each, in turn, stopped the men leaving and said, 'This never happened, and you were never here. Or we will find you.'

The man who had been shot was still writhing and screaming on the floor, covered in blood. At the other side of the room was the man who was bleeding from the face after being attacked with the glass bottle. The cuts looked deep.

I was frozen to the spot. It was like something from a horror movie. 'Aren't you going to call an ambulance?' I said to one of the girls standing beside me. I shaking with shock.

'Don't be silly, Fran. These are Mr Lambrianu's men. That is what the landlord pays protection for. This place would have been trashed, and there would have been more casualties if they hadn't have come.'

Two more men walked through the door. They were not wearing suits but, rather, large decorating overalls. They walked up to the man who had been glassed in the face, who by now had passed out.

'Drop him off outside the hospital,' one of the suited men

instructed. 'And him' – he pointed to the man on the floor writhing in pain – 'get rid of him.'

Both men were carried out through the back doors. The man with the gun turned to us girls behind the bar. We stared wide-eyed at him, waiting to see if we were next.

'Show's over, folks.' With that, he calmly put the gun into the inside of his jacket and walked over to the landlord. 'Close up for a couple of days while the place is being redecorated.'

With that, they all calmly walked out, leaving us in a shocked silence. The landlord reached for the brandy and poured everyone a drink. Even the landlord's hand was shaking as he gulped his down. Two of the girls beside me were crying. I was rooted to the spot. My legs wouldn't move. The carpet and the walls looked like a bloodbath.

'What are you going to do about this?' I asked.

'You heard them.' The landlord picked up a bar towel and wiped the sweat off his face. 'Two days from now, you won't recognise the place. God, that Lambrianu and his men are some nasty scary bastards.' He turned towards the till and took out some money. 'Here, girls. Here's twenty pounds each. Now go home and forget what you've seen.'

Although I felt my legs wouldn't carry me, I walked towards the door with the other girls, stepping over the bloodstained carpet and broken glass on the way out.

One of the other girls offered me a lift in her car. Once inside, I burst into tears.

'Look, Francesca, I know you're upset, but that could have been you or me with that glass in our faces! Then where would we be? No one gives a shit about a couple of strippers involved in a pub fight. What would happen to your kid if you'd been on the receiving end of that drugged-up greasy bastard's attack, even if you had survived? Forget it, Francesca.

It's over. And those hoods are the only people on our side. Enough said?'

I looked at her and realised she'd made a very valid point. It had never dawned on me that, each day, I could be risking my own safety. What would happen to Bobby? Oh, I know my mam would look after him. But how would I ever work again, if I were to be scarred badly, or worse?

I had been offered a 'get-out', with security and cash, even if it meant working for a dangerous psychopath. At least I would be on the right side – well, for now anyway.

Mr Lambrianu needed me for the time being. So if I followed the rules and acted out my role, I would be safe. And more to the point, so would Bobby!

* * *

After that night, I dreaded going to work. I was always looking over my shoulder for something bad to happen.

There was only one thing for it. It had been a few weeks now since Mr Lambrianu had made his offer, and I hadn't heard anything since. Maybe he had changed his mind or got someone else to take my place. Maybe I had left it too long?

Well, there was only one way to find out. I dialled the number on the card I had been given and was surprised when Mr Lambrianu picked up the telephone straight away, and in that smooth, charming voice of his said, 'Francesca, how lovely to hear from you. What can I do for you?'

His velvety, calm voice didn't make me feel at my ease. If anything, it made me nervous, so I just blurted it out. 'That offer you made me, is it still on, Mr Lambrianu? If it is, I would like to accept it, with a few tweaks to your contract.'

'I'll see you this afternoon around 4 p.m. We will talk then,

Francesca. I am sure we can discuss your tweaks.' With that, the
line went dead. I had been dismissed again!

Only Mr Lambrianu and Jake were at the meeting. The
contract lay on the table. Jake asked me what changes I wanted to
make to the business deal. I informed them that I wanted to make
it clear that I didn't like the idea of Elle, the housekeeper, spying
on me and that I was perfectly capable of looking after myself and
Bobby. I told them I appreciated there would be times when we
would have to look like a married couple, but when not in the
public eye, there would be no pretence.

I also wanted to make it clear that they were hiring me for the
year. They didn't own me or my son. They both looked at each
other, and you could see them thinking about what I had said.

'The East End pubs are a dangerous place to work at times,
very seedy. So I can see why you would want to work for me again.'
Mr Lambrianu looked at me; his blue hypnotising eyes held my
gaze. 'We heard that you were involved in an unfortunate incident.
But that's life without protection. Are you okay?'

Jake let out a slow whistle. 'You were lucky to get out of there
alive. It happens a lot and it could have been so much worse. It
could have been you.'

Noticing the furtive glance between them, I felt there was more
to it and wouldn't be surprised if they had staged it all to frighten
me into a decision.

He was right, of course. I had felt safe when I'd worked for him
in his clubs.

He reached over his desk and, with his well-manicured hand,
held mine. His face portrayed a genuine warm smile. 'We don't
mean to treat you like some prostitute for hire, Fran. May I call you
Fran?' His voice was tender and warm, almost reassuring.

I smiled at him, and our eyes locked. I suddenly remembered

being locked in a gaze with him once before and how nice it had been.

'This, Fran, is purely a business deal – hopefully, one that could benefit us both. We will have to appear intimate at times, but I agree with you – nothing more, nothing less. Elle stays, though. She can help you, guide you, and be there for you when things get tough. You can confide in her and let off steam when you think it's all getting a bit stressful.'

I was mesmerised by his speech, and thinking of everything that was on offer and how insecure I had felt lately, I decided to take a chance. I turned the hand hold he was still maintaining into a handshake.

'You have just got yourself a wife, Mr Lambrianu.' Once I had said it, I felt better. It was as though a weight of worry had been lifted off my shoulders.

This was a whole new adventure. I was finally leaving the past behind me. I explained to Bobby that we were moving to a big house near the seaside. He seemed a bit confused by it all, but I knew he would understand more when he saw it.

10

THE FUTURE

The club was decorated in banners, ribbons, and balloons, all with 'Congratulations' and 'Engagement' written on them. Our engagement had been a headline in the local newspapers, and of course there were photographers and journalists wanting to get all the information on Mr Lambrianu, club land's most eligible bachelor, deciding to marry at last, and to some woman they had never heard of.

Julie and Ralph Gold had arranged everything as promised. Caterers and waiters filled the room, and the champagne flowed. God, if this was the engagement, what would the wedding be like? It had never occurred to me that the newspapers would take such an interest.

Mr Lambrianu had got his chauffeur to pick me up, and then I was told to go directly to the office. I walked down the long hallway and knocked on the door. Tony and Jake were both waiting for me. As always, they were together.

Julie Gold had sent me a pink, spangled halter neck dress. It was beautiful. I left my hair down, letting the wavy curls fall across my left shoulder.

Mr Lambrianu actually looked embarrassed when I walked in. His face seemed slightly flushed beneath his suntan. 'From now on, Francesca, you call me Tony, okay? And you will need this.' He handed me a small red velvet square box. Puzzled, I opened it. Inside was an oval-shaped diamond ring. It took my breath away.

I looked down at the huge diamond. It sparkled, a rainbow of different colours, as it caught the light. Never in my wildest dreams would I have thought I would own something like this. I took it out of the box and slipped it on my finger.

'It's beautiful, Mr... er, Tony.' I blushed and smiled at him. I really didn't know what to say. Normally, when you thought of getting engaged, you pictured the man of your dreams down on one knee proposing and you throwing your arms around him, full of love and happiness. Was this to be my fate, two loveless marriages? The ring was part of the deal and I'm sure he had bought his many girlfriends jewels before. My heart sank when I looked at it – it meant nothing.

'If you don't like it,' he said, 'I can change it.' He was looking down at his desk, avoiding my eyes. This was obviously a conversation he was not comfortable with.

'No, it's perfect. Thank you.' I could almost feel tears brimming my eyes, and there was a lump in my throat.

Jake opened the office door.

Tony took my arm, and the three of us walked towards the mayhem of the party that was already in full swing.

We didn't get a chance to spend any time together as we were both monopolised by well-wishers, each one carrying a gaily-wrapped parcel and placing it on the table at the back of the room, which was already overflowing with presents of all shapes and sizes.

I wasn't used to being the centre of attention like this and was overwhelmed by it all.

* * *

It was very late when the crowd started to leave.

Tony walked up to me and tapped me on the shoulder. Then he bent forward towards my ear. I thought he was going to kiss me. But instead he whispered, 'The car is outside waiting for you. You can leave now.'

I felt sick to my stomach. I really had got carried away by all the well-wishers. I was so stupid. This wasn't real, and this was how things were going to be.

His head turned to a corner of the bar where a woman with long blonde hair was sitting waiting for him. I was being sent home so he could enjoy the rest of the evening. What a bore this must have been for him.

I obeyed my orders, immediately sobering up to the situation, and said my goodbyes. Once in the car, I looked down at the ring on my finger and wanted the club out of sight. All that glittered definitely wasn't gold. I had made my choice and agreed to this deal. This would be my life for the next year.

* * *

Since the engagement party, I had come to expect the evening dismissal after some charity ball or party night. I had learnt to rein in my feelings, knowing that I had only been picked because I was dull and boring. Wasn't that what Tony and Jake had said? No skeletons in my closet and no unexpected surprises that would cause embarrassment.

My wedding was supposed to be in two months! Some people planned their wedding a year in advance. But no – Julie Gold had turned up at the house a day or two after the engagement party, to get things started. She was beautifully turned out as always, wearing a bright red skirt suit, which matched her blonde bobbed hair to perfection.

'Surprise!' She smiled at me as I opened the door in my jeans and soiled T-shirt.

As I looked up, I saw another woman getting out of the car and walking towards the door.

Julie pushed a large black folder into my chest and arms. 'This is Maria,' she explained excitedly. 'She is your wedding planner.'

'What?' I almost shouted at her. Not only was I surprised to see her, I hadn't been informed of any of this.

Julie pushed Maria past me into the house, and they both left me standing on the doorstep to close the door.

Elle was in the kitchen cleaning out cupboards and opening new boxes that contained brand-new high-tech kitchen gadgets.

'Get some glasses, will you, dear? We have a lot of thirsty work to do.' Julie spoke to Elle as though she was indeed the housekeeper.

Elle did as she was told, and the wedding planner opened her bag and took out a couple of bottles of champagne. Within minutes, the champagne flowed, and folders and magazines were laid before me, displaying wedding dresses, enormous wedding cakes, and menus.

'Tony told Ralph it had to be a Catholic church, so now we have to choose one,' she said.

Tony was a Catholic? Now, I did find that funny – the very thought of him confessing his sins. It must take an awfully long time.

'I don't want a big fuss,' I explained shyly, taking a sip of my first drink. Julie was now already on her third glass. 'Just something simple, nothing extravagant.' I looked towards Elle, who could see I was drowning in a sea of wedding plans.

Julie looked offended and disgusted. 'So Mrs Lambrianu-to-be, what do you want? A buffet of sausage rolls and an off-the-peg dress? There will be over a hundred guests filling that church, and even more at the reception. You have to look your best, Francesca. And we're here to help you.' She sounded more excited than I was. 'As it will be near Christmastime, we are going to have a winter wonderland theme – lights everywhere. If it doesn't snow, we'll buy a snow machine.'

I simply nodded, not knowing what to say.

Julie and the wedding planner went through the books and folders and were soon arranging cake and food tasting sessions. The country manor she had chosen was lovely indeed, but I couldn't help feeling nervous and twitchy. 'Shouldn't Tony be choosing some of this?' I asked.

Julie, already opening another bottle of champagne, looked bored. 'Francesca, Tony has already told Ralph that whatever you want you can have. He also mentioned you would be a little shy about it all and would indeed need some help. That's why I'm here. Didn't he tell you?'

So, this was just another clever ploy of his to get Julie and Ralph onside. He had obviously told them a lot more than he'd told me. Another businesses discussion, I presumed.

An hour had already passed, and although I could see their lips moving and their fingers pointing at photos of brides, I wasn't really taking in what they were saying.

Julie, who by now looked a little tipsy, clapped her hands together, bringing back to the moment. 'Okay, Francesca, best bit now. Wedding dress time.'

I forced a smile. 'No meringue dresses with loads of under-skirts,' I said, stopping her before she got carried away.

The wedding planner eyed me up and then flicked through a folder and showed me a picture of a dress. It had a lace sweetheart neck with pearls sewn on. The A-line shape of the long satin dress with its small train looked simple, but classy and elegant. I smiled at her and nodded. She certainly knew her job and had chosen the correct dress for me.

'Right then, all sorted,' Julie slurred as she stood up. Her eyes were glazed and she had obviously enjoyed her afternoon.

I was still holding my first glass of champagne. I couldn't wait to put the kettle on.

As Julie and Maria walked down the hallway towards the front door, Julie turned on her heels, looking around. 'Next, Francesca, we have to sort this bloody house out – give it some colour and taste.'

With that, they walked out, and I shut the door behind them. Phew!

I ran quickly to the hallway window and watched the wedding planner struggling to get Julie in the back of the chauffeur-driven limousine.

This truly was another world, wasn't it? Within a few hours, my winter wonderland wedding had been planned, my dress had been chosen, and the church had been booked. Maria had informed me that my mam and brothers would be contacted and told where to go to get measured up properly for their wedding clothes.

Now it was all a matter of bridesmaids! I didn't really know anyone. I couldn't ask a bunch of strippers who were also Mr Lambrianu's employees to be my bridesmaids.

Candy would obviously be on my list. But who else? I knew Chris wouldn't want anything to do with it, although I made a mental note to invite her.

Elle, who had watched me intently during the proceedings, made me a cup of coffee. She began clearing away the glasses that Julie and Maria had left. Then she picked up her coat and was about to leave when I stopped her. I had my own personal 'to-do' list, which didn't include wedding dresses and cake.

'Where are the local schools around here, Elle? Do you know any? I'll also need to register at a doctor's surgery.'

She actually looked pleased that I had asked her. We hadn't found our middle ground yet, and I was still wary of her. She seemed to be always there, floating around, tidying up and making Bobby little treats. I knew I had offended her when I'd told her Bobby was my son, and I would look after him. Bobby was just an innocent in all of this and nothing to do with her or Mr Lambrianu. And even though I felt that I was being taken over, and everyone was organising my life for me, I was adamant this wasn't going to be the case for Bobby – I wouldn't let him be used.

* * *

A short drive away from the house was a very quaint modern primary school. I took Bobby with me and went to speak to the head teacher. She informed me that the school did have a place if I wanted it and Bobby could start straight away. The school was bright and cheerful and a far cry from the school on our old estate. Bobby was very excited looking at all of the pictures painted by the children on the corridor walls.

Next on my list was to register at a doctor's. When I walked through the door, I stood shoulder to shoulder with a queue of people rolling their eyes and complaining. I pushed my way through the crowd and saw the poor receptionist sitting on her own behind a desk on the telephone looking flustered and stressed. It seemed as though the patient on the other end was sharing their life story!

I didn't know what made me do it, but seeing the situation and listening to the crowd, I walked to the front of the reception desk and lifted up the shutter that let staff in and out.

'Who's next please?' I asked.

The receptionist tried stopping me and had a worried look on her face, while still locked in a conversation with the person on the end of the telephone. When she saw that I was checking people in for their appointments and giving out prescriptions, she looked relieved.

The patients nearly cheered that they didn't have to wait much longer, and there was the usual moan of, 'about time too.' Finally, the receptionist was able to put the telephone down at long last.

'Lisa.' The receptionist held out her hand and shook mine. 'Thank you. We've had two colleagues telephone in sick today, and it's been manic.'

A large woman in a black suit came out of a side door and instantly looked me up and down in disgust. She wanted to know who I was and what I was doing. I apologised and explained that I'd just moved into the area and had come to register myself and my son at the doctor's.

With a snotty look still on her face, she handed me the paperwork to register, which I filled in and handed back. I nodded to Lisa and walked out. I was sure that manageress would go out of her way to make sure I never got an appointment!

When I got home Elle was in the kitchen and I could smell something delicious cooking in the oven.

'How did you get on?' she asked nonchalantly, obviously noticing something was wrong.

I gave Bobby a drink and put the kettle on, while telling her all about my ordeal at the doctor's. Bobby noticed some chocolate buns on the worktop and instantly walked up to them, pointing and asking for one.

I looked at Elle. It was blatantly clear that, while I had been out, she had baked the buns especially for Bobby, and a casserole was slowly cooking in the oven. It had been a long time since I had come home to a homemade meal especially made for me. I felt a pang of guilt at the way I'd been treating her.

'Julie called and said that everything was in hand and you're not to worry. She will telephone you later.' Elle raised an eyebrow and gave me one of those looks that spoke a thousand words!

'Why is she taking over everything? I feel like her new project. Surely a woman like her has other things to do.' I made a coffee for us both. It was a kind of peace offering. At this moment in time, apart from my mam, I felt Elle was the only person on my side.

'Maybe so, Francesca. But maybe she's lonely. Her husband is a busy man who throws money at her like it's going out of fashion. She also drinks far too much, considering she has everything money can buy. In my opinion, people drink too much either to forget or out of boredom or both.' Elle was a wise woman, who had watched Julie carefully and made up her own mind about her.

We were interrupted by the telephone ringing and to my surprise, it was the manageress from the doctor's surgery.

She apologised for her rudeness and then went on to ask how I knew so much about reception work. I told her that I had trained in business and administration, and one of my work experience jobs had been at a doctor's practice. She then asked me if I would like to work for her on a temporary basis. I couldn't believe my ears.

Thinking quickly, I knew this wouldn't affect Tony's nights out. And it was only part-time, wasn't it? 'Yes, I'd like to,' I answered.

Quickly ending the call, I informed Elle that it had just been the doctor's surgery needing more information. This was my business – something for me to organise. A job meant a little more security. This would keep me going, when the year was out.

* * *

As a man of his word, Tony had put the money he had promised me into my bank account. I had never seen so many zeroes after numbers in my life. For the first time ever, I could send a substantial amount home to my mam. That felt good.

The next day, I looked at my watch and realised it was nearly time to get ready for work. But I didn't have a childminder! Elle was still at the house but as uncomfortable as I felt, I told her I was having to go to the doctor's for some kind of induction and asked her if she would look after Bobby for me. I explained that I would try and find a childminder locally, as I would need someone permanent, especially as I would be out most weekends.

Elle agreed to look after Bobby, but she seemed disappointed that I would be organising a permanent childminder of my own. I left her with Bobby watching cartoons, while she busied herself in the kitchen. Yet again, I was leading a secret life. It was silly really, but I knew Elle would relay everything to Tony. Off to work I went, feeling very happy and pleased with myself.

When I eventually got home four hours later, Bobby ran towards me excitedly, holding a huge painting he had done.

Paint pots, brushes, and paper were scattered over the kitchen table. He had obviously had a great time in my absence. Elle made her excuses to leave, and I thanked her for looking after Bobby so well.

Hanging my coat up and tidying around, I noticed the answering machine flashing. When I pressed the button to listen, the first message was from Julie telling me she would be picking me up tomorrow for a dress fitting. My goodness, this woman could rule the world. The second and third messages were from Tony. The first time he asked me to call him back. The next message wasn't so polite, and he demanded that I telephoned him immediately. Why hadn't Elle answered the telephone and explained?

I nervously dialled his number, knowing he would be angry that it had taken me so long to answer his messages.

'Francesca.'

His calm sultry voice hadn't been what I had expected. I started to ramble on with my excuses about where I had been and he just started laughing.

'You're not a prisoner Francesca. You can do as you please, as long as you are there when I need you. After all, like any employer, I like to know that I can rely on you. Has Julie been in touch about the wedding arrangements?' he asked.

I explained that she had it all in hand and had completely taken over everything, with her wedding planner in tow.

'That's okay then. I will see you Saturday night as arranged.' He went on to tell me what time I would be picked up and then hung up.

What a day it had been!

I decided to run myself a hot bubble bath and soak the day away. I was just about to get in when I heard a knock at the door. I wrapped my dressing gown around me and went downstairs.

Tony's chauffeur was standing beside a large Range Rover, and behind that was a black Jaguar. I looked at him, puzzled by the scene before me. The chauffeur held out some car keys in my direction. 'Compliments of Mr Lambrianu.' I took the keys in my hand and watched him walk to the Jaguar and open the door. 'Wait!' I shouted to him. 'Are these keys for that Range Rover?'

'Yes. The documents are in the glove compartment.' He opened the passenger door and got in alongside the driver. I stood in the doorway and watched them both drive away. Then I looked at the car in front of me.

It was bright red and shiny with tinted windows. It must have cost a fortune. Bobby was running around it excitedly in his pyjamas. I opened the car door and saw the red leather seats.

Bobby got into the car and jumped around. I was totally gobsmacked.

Back in the hallway, my mind in turmoil, I picked up the telephone and dialled Tony's number. He answered in his usual velvety smooth voice, and I told him I had just received the car. 'I can't accept it,' I said. 'I can buy my own now. I appreciate the gesture. But, well, I don't know what to say.'

I heard a deep sigh on the other end of the telephone line. 'Do you like it, Francesca? If you like it, keep it. If you don't, well, that's up to you.'

I could sense his impatience. It obviously wasn't the call he had expected. I supposed he had expected me to be gushing thank yous down the telephone, like his girlfriends did when he bought them something. But this was different, wasn't it? I felt uncomfortable.

'Look, Francesca, this is all very entertaining,' he barked at me down the telephone. 'Your coyness does you credit. So just accept it with good grace, eh?'

With that, he put the telephone down.

The next morning, I took Bobby to his new school and decided to try the car. It was indeed luxurious, unlike anything I had ever driven.

When I looked up at the rear-view mirror, I noticed two fluffy dice hanging from it. A sticky note was attached. It read:

From one gambler to another, TL

TL – Tony Lambrianu. I hadn't seen it last night, and so his joke had gone amiss. No wonder he'd been a little angry when I'd telephoned him. Apart from me thanking him, he had expected me to laugh at his joke, not sound ungrateful. It warmed me to think that he saw me as a person and not just an employee. Maybe we were making a connection? I didn't know; my mind was all over the place. My fiancé had bought me a car, or my employer had let me use the company car. Which was it?

I felt a little deflated when I took Bobby to school, as he was instantly distracted by some boys playing with a football and went to join them.

The teachers came out to line up the children and nodded to me. 'He'll be okay,' one of the teachers said, smiling reassuringly.

I drove to the town hall, picked up a list of registered childminders, and went home to find Julie Gold already sitting in the kitchen, while Elle was filling the dishwasher. I had forgotten she was coming. I put the folder on the table. Elle, seeing my sullen face, asked how Bobby had got on.

Julie grabbed my arm. 'Never mind that now. We have a fitting. Come on. We have bridesmaids to sort out, too.' She almost pushed me out the door.

I was driven into the heart of London, near some very exclusive shops for the fitting of my wedding dress. All the while Julie constantly talked about the next things we had to do. She even had a notebook with everything listed!

I was back in time to pick up Bobby, but totally exhausted. Bobby was full of excitement and chatter, telling me all about his day and the new friends he had made. Elle had gone home, and for once, the house was empty. I ordered some pizzas and after watching some cartoons, there were no arguments from Bobby when it was bath and bedtime. He was shattered.

For once, I was going to take advantage of that enormous Jacuzzi bath, and as I soaked in the bubbles with the jets flowing, the warm water around me felt amazing. Meanwhile, I read through the childminders' list. On the third page, I stopped and looked again. Elle's name was on it. I felt it was strange that she had never said anything. I circled a few of the others and decided to call them tomorrow.

Feeling refreshed, I rang my mam and gave her an update on what had been happening. She knew most of it, especially the wedding arrangements, but at long last, there was something I could tell her she didn't know. I had a job at the local doctor's surgery. She was really pleased when I told her. She felt everything was coming up roses!

* * *

Saturday night arrived, and another charity dinner was ahead of me. I had not seen Tony for a few days and had not spoken to him since the car had been delivered. I was excited, but wary of seeing him. I knew I was slowly slipping under his spell, but I couldn't help it and all of this time pretending to be a couple was making my mind run wild.

Elle was at the house and offered to make Bobby's dinner while I got ready, as I was being picked up at 6 p.m.

The telephone rang while I was putting my make-up on. It was the childminder I'd arranged informing me that she would have to cancel. She apologised and then promptly put the telephone down. Elle had heard the conversation, so I told her that I would have to ring Mr Lambrianu and cancel.

'I could stay if you like,' she said. 'I don't think Tony would be too pleased if you cancelled at such short notice.' She nodded her head towards the clock on the wall. 'The chauffeur will already be on his way.'

'Why didn't you tell me you were on the childminders' register, Elle?' I asked.

'Why would I, Francesca? I know you don't like me interfering or looking after Bobby. But I can tonight if it helps. I have no other plans.'

She made me sound harsh. Maybe I had been a bit full-on. All she had ever done was help me. And I really didn't fancy having to tell Mr Lambrianu that I was going to have to cancel and face his wrath.

'Thank you, Elle. I would really appreciate it if you would look after Bobby tonight for me.'

I felt easier when I saw the big smile cross her face. Maybe she too was lonely. No sooner had I thanked her, than the chauffeur was knocking at the door and it was time to go and meet Tony. I felt like an excited kid on prom night. In my black taffeta ball gown, which Julie had chosen for me, I was driven off to meet my prince charming. I secretly hoped he would feel the same way.

* * *

Walking into the club foyer, I saw Julie waving at me to attract my attention. She linked my arm in hers and walked us both through the crowd to the bar, which was roped off for VIPs. Ralph, Jake and Tony were standing with Sharon having a drink. Tony held a glass of champagne out to each of us. Julie drank hers in one.

He held out his arm to me to pull me closer and kissed my cheek. I could feel myself blushing. 'You look beautiful,' he said and put his arm around my waist.

I saw Julie watching with a scowl on her face and wondered what was so wrong.

'Well, Tony, if Francesca here looks so beautiful and you're about to marry her, what kind of a welcome kiss is that?' She laughed at her own joke and kissed Ralph on the lips to prove her point.

I saw Tony look at her and then at myself. 'You're right of

course, Julie.' Still with his arm around my waist, he pulled me closer to him and placed his perfectly formed lips on mine. I felt my cheeks go bright red and pulled away as quickly as possible. Fortunately, the lights at the bar were dim and before anyone could say another word, a bell was rung to indicate it was time to go into the function room. Taking Tony's arm, I walked towards the door. I could still feel his lips on mine. And as much as I would like to think of myself as lady-like, the thoughts going through my mind at that precise moment were far from it.

Tony was very attentive and made a point of taking my arm to dance the last waltz with me.

'Did you like your dice?' he whispered in my ear.

I looked up at him and smiled. 'I didn't notice them until the next morning.' I breathed in his aftershave as we danced slowly; it wasn't overpowering, but it suited him. And smelt so good.

All too soon, the lights started to come on, indicating the evening was over. Looking over, I saw a very tipsy Julie dancing with, or, rather, being held up by, Ralph. Jake and Sharon were dancing and very engrossed in each other. To anyone watching, we all looked like the perfect couples. But it was a farce, all of it. People see only what they want to. I felt ashamed of living a lie, but it was too late now.

Ralph had won some award for a charity contribution. When he accepted it, he introduced Tony and Jake as his new business partners. The smiles on their faces were a picture. It seemed they were achieving their goal.

Ralph walked them around the room, introducing them to some MPs and other influential businessmen who Ralph had in his pocket. Tony and Jake were both on cloud nine and looked like two little boys who had got what they wanted for Christmas.

Later, Tony walked me to the car. The chauffeur opened the door, and I was surprised when Tony got in.

'I need a lift back first, and then Graham will drive you home. Is that okay?'

I nodded and smiled at him.

It amazed me how quickly he could change. One minute he was holding me around the waist and whispering into my ear, and the next he sounded bored at the prospect of having to share a taxi with me.

As we pulled up outside the club, it did cross my mind to wonder who was waiting for him in his apartment above it; it hurt more than I wanted to admit thinking about it.

The chauffeur got out and opened the door for him. Tony turned towards me, and for one brief second, I thought he was going to kiss me. But that was what too much champagne did to you!

'I will see you in church. Don't get cold feet now.' He smiled. 'Goodnight Francesca,' was all he said as he stepped out of the car and walked away. He turned around as the car started up again and watched us drive away.

I didn't know why, but I felt a heavy ache in my heart. After such a nice evening, I felt discarded, almost a burden to him. But that was what I had signed up for. I had got what I wanted, and it seemed both Tony and Jake were getting their hearts' desire too.

11

THE WEDDING

Stepping out of the white Bentley with my mam, I noticed ushers were standing outside the church in their grey tuxedo tails and top hats. Some photographers with journalists were outside too, taking pictures as I got out of the car and shouting my name to attract my attention, so that I would turn around and they would get a better photo. My main concern was not tripping up in front of them. Now that really would have made the front pages.

I was nervous, trembling inside. Julie was in the car behind me, and I had decided to ask her to be my maid of honour, considering all the hard work she had put into this day. Candy and Sharon had agreed to be my bridesmaids, and Julie had picked the other four. Apparently, they were wives of some very influential men who did business with Ralph and would now be doing business with Tony and Jake.

Julie definitely had her head screwed on and knew how to keep the equilibrium.

The bridesmaids were all in full-length red bustier ball gowns, with little shoulder-length red capes trimmed in white fur. Of course, this had nothing to do with the fact that it suited Julie's blonde hair perfectly!

Julie had all of us 'girls' at the beauty spa the day before being tanned, waxed, and God knows what else. Elle had been given the job of looking after Bobby and my brothers while all this was going on. My mam had loved it. She had never been so spoilt in her whole life. Then again, neither had I.

Julie had insisted that I wear a tiara and had chosen the biggest one she could find, which looked more like a crown and was very heavy. Flowing from the tiara were layers of white netting, creating a full white veil, which seemed to make me a foot taller. It was beautiful, the stuff that dreams were made of. I felt like a princess.

My bridesmaids were all in place outside of the church, and all I needed to do now was put one satin shoe in front of the other and start walking down the aisle. The church was an old one with stained-glass windows and a huge bell tower, and was such a far cry from my first wedding!

My mam, dressed in a rose-pink suit and hat, took my arm, which I was grateful for. 'Are you ready, Fran? Take a deep breath,' she said, holding my arm tighter.

Standing at the back of the church, I saw all of the people awaiting my arrival. It was packed to the hilt and I slowly started walking, clinging on to my mam much more tightly than I should have.

I was glad the veil covered my face. I was nervous and feeling quite shy with all of the attention. As I walked closer to the front, I saw the priest fully adorned in his finery. I had asked about Tony's parents and thought that maybe I should meet them before today. He had just told me not to worry about that. There wasn't anyone I should meet. So again I was dismissed. I wasn't even good enough to meet my in-laws!

Looking through my veil, it was only then that I saw Tony. He looked very handsome. His grey morning suit and tails, with his red cravat, enhanced his blond hair to perfection. He took my breath away.

We knelt before the priest to start with a Catholic mass.

When I stood up again, slightly aching because the prayers seemed to go on forever, I turned towards Tony. He was smiling at me with those intense blue eyes of his, which made me blush.

During the vows, which I nervously stumbled through, I discovered his name was actually Antonias! How ridiculous was that? I was marrying a man whose name I didn't even know. And then it dawned on me. He was Italian! Of course he had wanted a Catholic wedding.

At last the proceedings came to an end, and the priest pronounced us man and wife. It was now time to 'kiss the bride'. Tony turned and slowly lifted my veil up from my face and over the top of my tiara. Playfully, he looked at the crowd and smiled and then turned towards me and kissed me with those perfectly formed lips of his. I felt on top of the world. I was Mrs Lambrianu and he loved me, didn't he? My imagination was in overdrive, but I didn't want to believe anything else. This was my wedding day after all. The guests clapped their hands and cheered, possibly glad the long Catholic ceremony had finally ended. Their bums were probably numb!

As Tony took my arm to walk back up the aisle to the exit, we were met by people reaching out to shake our hands and wish us well. All I could do was smile.

As we walked outside of the church, confetti flowing through the air, the wedding photographer snapped away with his camera.

Other photographers and journalists called out the names of their magazines, wanting photos of us both. 'Come on, Francesca, over here,' they shouted, all in good spirits. Ralph's and Tony's bouncers let them take their photos and then politely pushed them out of the way.

The snow machine Julie had promised started pouring out white flakes of fake snow. At the end of the path was a white carriage drawn by four white horses!

What a perfect setting. It truly was a fairy-tale wedding, but it was a circus and Tony was the ringmaster. He escorted me into the carriage, and I turned to look at the crowds of people throwing confetti and some of the fake snow towards us. I saw Bobby and my brothers running around catching the snowflakes. We waved to the crowds like royalty as the horses took us to the large manor house where the reception was being held.

I looked down at the gold ring on Tony's finger. I was surprised he had chosen to wear one, considering it might put off his lady friends. Obviously he was arrogant enough to know it didn't matter to them. I supposed, if anything, it would create more of a challenge: taking the newly married Tony Lambrianu from his dull wife!

Sitting back in the carriage, Tony took my hand and kissed my wedding ring. 'Would it be inappropriate, Mrs Lambrianu, if I told you that you look beautiful,' he said, smiling at me.

'Would it be inappropriate, Mr Lambrianu, if I told you that you also look beautiful.' I laughed.

It was an odd moment. He didn't have to act now. No one could hear or see us. Maybe he too was caught up in the moment.

I was glad when the carriage stopped and the door was opened for us to get out. We were greeted by the wedding photographer, who promptly carried on taking more photos, while all of the cars and guests arrived.

The manor house was lit up outside with fairy lights everywhere. The waiters came out to greet us with silver trays of champagne, before ushering everyone inside.

We were the last to enter the great hall. Then I heard the strange announcement, which made a tingle go down my spine. 'Ladies and gentlemen, please rise for the bride and groom, Mr and Mrs Lambrianu.'

Everyone rose and started clapping and cheering as we were led to the top table.

Christmas trees bejewelled in baubles and lights adorned the room. Red and white balloons flew in the air. In front of each lady's seat was a present waiting on the table for her. Each gift contained perfume or whatever Julie knew the woman liked. At the side of the room was the four-tier wedding cake. It must have all cost a fortune!

They had even organised a room especially for the children, full of bouncy castles and games so they didn't get bored during the proceedings.

I felt a little sad because none of this was real, and I had to keep reminding myself of that. Something like this was for people in love, not some contracted business deal. And as beautiful as it was, I wanted the day to be over with.

The extravagant meal was served, and the speeches commenced. Obviously, Jake, as best man, had the perfect speech. I learnt later on, though, that he actually had an earpiece in, and the wedding planner was telling him what to say!

Julie, already worse for wear, was more than tipsy before the evening disco had begun. She came over and started bitching about the ridiculous hats some of the women were wearing. Not funny I know, but some of her descriptions made me and my mam laugh out loud.

'Ladies and gentlemen,' I heard the DJ announce, 'it is now time for the first dance. Please, Mr and Mrs Lambrianu, step onto the dance floor.'

First dance? I hadn't chosen anything. I looked up at Julie and asked if it was another one of her surprises.

'No, Fran. This is all Tony's choosing. Even I don't know what it is.' She pulled me out of my chair, and I saw Tony walking towards me.

He took my hand and walked me onto the dance floor. I could see he was more than a little tipsy himself, what with everyone wanting to share a toast with him. He guided me onto the dance floor, and the music began. It was Dusty Springfield, singing 'The Look of Love' and the words of the song haunted me. We were waltzing, and then suddenly, he took hold of my arms and pulled them around his neck. He was so close. We were cheek to cheek, with his arms firmly wrapped around my waist. My heart was pounding, and I felt like crying, my emotions taking over.

As I looked over his shoulder, I noticed a woman in the crowd watching us dance. It was one of the women I had seen him with at the club. He had his girlfriend or girlfriends at his wedding. I looked around and wondered how many more of them there were watching this farce! I felt bitter and angry, and suddenly this fairy-tale seemed tacky and ugly.

'You're mine now, beautiful Francesca,' Tony slurred into my ear.

Hell, just how far was this guy prepared to go to get business deals? Did he have no morals? I couldn't help it. I pulled my arms down from around his neck and looked him in the face. 'Just for a year, boss. Let me know when you want me to leave, Mr Lambrianu. Then you can enjoy the rest of your evening.'

The music finished, and I was about to walk away when he caught my eye and followed the direction I was looking in. When people saw the tears brimming in my eyes, they thought it was love and emotion. They didn't know I was embarrassed and humiliated!

I walked off to where my mam and Julie were sitting and left

Tony alone on the dance floor. He didn't seem to care. He joined his friends and carried on drinking. My mam instantly knew there was something wrong.

Suddenly, there was a loud crash and we all turned to see that Tony had collapsed onto one of the tables, sending it flying across the room. People were laughing and joking, while Jake and Ralph each took one of Tony's arms and placed them around their shoulders, trying to walk him away from the crowd and towards the lift. Someone said they were taking him to his room to sleep it off.

I felt that was my cue to leave. People were laughing and commiserating with me about my 'wedding night' or, rather, lack of it, because Tony was so drunk. No one seemed to care really. Everyone was allowed to get drunk at their wedding. It was all taken in good fun.

I saw Jake come back into the room and walked up to him. 'He's okay, Fran. Don't worry.' He smiled.

'I wasn't worried,' I said. 'Can you get one of the drivers to take me and my family home please?'

Jake looked at me, rather puzzled at my lack of concern. 'If that's what you want. I'll have a car around the front in five minutes. What about your husband?' he added sarcastically.

'What about him, Jake? He's safe with you, isn't he? He's alone in the honeymoon suite. When he wakes up, I'm sure he'll find somebody to share it with. Now, I've done my bit, and I would like to leave.'

Jake organised one of the limousines to take us home. At least that way, the children, who were all tired and sleepy, could lie down and sleep. Jake was standing by the car as everyone was getting in.

'Don't think badly of him, Francesca. He's just had a little too much to drink. I'll get the boys to get all your stuff packed up and send it on, okay.' He touched my arm.

When everyone was in the car but me, I turned to Jake. 'I've already seen my replacements at the reception Jake. I'm sure even you know by now that it's time for me to leave. I've served my purpose. Tell him to let me know when I'm needed again. Goodnight, Jake.'

I got into the car, and as it drove away, I could see Jake frowning as he stood on the driveway.

I was glad to see home again. Yes, that was how I was beginning to think of this enormous mansion. The chauffeur helped us get the kids into the house and upstairs. The wedding seemed a world away now, and I tried not to think about what was happening in my absence.

It was the early hours of the morning, so I just let my dress fall to the floor and pulled on my pyjamas, falling asleep as soon as my head hit the pillow. The worst was over now. I could get on with my life.

* * *

Late the next day, there was a knock at the door. Jake stood there with his chauffeur and together they emptied the contents of the car of all our baggage that I had left at the hotel. He told me the wedding presents would follow in due course, as there were so many of them. My mam was due to stay another day, and Jake told her that, whenever she was ready, he would organise a car to drive them all home.

'Aren't you going to ask me how your husband is this morning?' He looked at me with a discerning look that seemed almost challenging.

Without thinking and still a little tired from the day before, I said, 'Luke? Why would I ask about Luke? I haven't seen him in years.'

The moment it left my mouth, I knew what I had said. He had meant Tony!

Looking very angry and staring daggers at me, Jake shouted, not caring who heard him. 'For fuck's sake, you haven't been married twenty-four hours, and you have forgotten Tony is your husband! I knew this wouldn't work,' he snarled, walking towards me.

Out of habit, I cowered, waiting for the first blow as I had always done in the past. Tears were rolling down my face, and I was shielding my head.

Jake stood back and stared at me. His shock at my behaviour seemed to stop his anger. 'My God, Francesca, you thought I was going to hit you, didn't you?' His voice seemed to soften as he spoke again. 'Is that what your first husband did, Francesca? Use you as a punching bag?' Jake held out his hand and raised my face up to look at him.

The room had gone silent.

'What a bastard! Just wait until Tony hears about this!' Jake said, venting his anger as he left.

I was wiping my face now, embarrassed to look at my mam after this revelation.

She got up and walked into the kitchen to put the kettle on, giving me a chance to pull myself together. Fortunately, all the children were upstairs and hadn't witnessed the scene.

We began the long process of clearing away and unpacking the clothes, when another knock sounded at the door.

'Surprise! I knew you wouldn't feel like cooking, and I wasn't sure what you fancied. So I've just brought a mixture of everything.' Julie Gold stood there, dressed to perfection as usual, while we all looked weary and tired in our pyjamas. There was every takeaway you could think of: curries, burgers, fries, and even pizzas.

The kids started tucking in, and my mam, trying to be polite in front of Julie, got some plates out.

'Go on, you lot, get stuck in. I've brought my own, Fran,' she added, smiling at my mam. We both watched as Julie undid the cork on her champagne bottle and started pouring.

'I'm going to have to get Tony to fill the cellar with wine. I can't keep bringing my own. Whatever would people say?' Julie gave out a loud cackle – as if she cared what people would say!

Cellar? I didn't even know we had a cellar. And why would Julie need it stocked up? The wedding was over. She had no reason to keep dropping in on a regular basis now. I would have to discuss this with Tony. Just how many spies did he think I needed? However, I liked Julie, she was funny, even when she was being bitchy. Sharon had warned me that she played the fool, but she was far from it. Even Elle looked forward to the familiar knock on the door and all of the inside gossip about the women at the parties. Julie was fun!

Julie picked at the food but drank more and then eventually staggered into the back of her car and left. I smiled to myself as I watched her. Julie Gold – what a legend!

* * *

The next day, my mam decided it was time to leave. After a few tearful farewells and promises that Christmas was only a few weeks away and I would be home as usual to enjoy the festivities with them, it was time to see them off.

Tony hadn't been happy about me taking Christmas off. But when Sharon reminded him that Christmas was one of the club's busiest times, he had relented, on the condition that I was back for the big New Year's Eve party that all wives – including me – were expected to attend.

Elle came around, bringing with her a mini bus, which was full to the brim of wedding presents. There were chandeliers, works of art for the walls, Persian rugs and custom-made plates. I hadn't known it at the time, but Julie had set up an account at Harrods and made a list for everyone to choose from. Of course, everyone had wanted to impress and buy the best. For the time being, we put them all in one of the bedrooms, until it was time to go through them properly. After all, I wasn't sure where I stood on these presents. Were they mine, ours, or Tony's? It had been clear in my contract that I took only what was given and nothing else. I presumed they were his and he would take them home. After all his home wasn't mine! We needed to discuss this; it was so confusing.

* * *

The next morning, there was a knock at the door.

Elle, who I had asked to join us for some of her own home-made cottage pie, got up and answered it. I looked up and saw her leading Tony into the kitchen.

'Hello, Tony.' I stood up to greet him. I wasn't sure why he was here and felt a little nervous. We hadn't seen each other since the wedding.

'Francesca.' He nodded towards me, and then there was an awkward silence.

Elle saved the day. 'Have you eaten, Tony?' she asked him and, without a word to me, promptly put another plate on the table.

He sat down and tucked in, listening to Bobby chatting on as we ate. Small talk followed, and then Elle steered Bobby away into the lounge so that Tony could tell me the real reason he was here.

'Francesca, I have been busy over the last few days, thanking people for coming to the wedding and so forth. Sorry if I caused you any embarrassment at the wedding. You really didn't need to pack up your family and leave. Surely, you could have waited until the next day.' His voice was as calm as ever, but I felt an underlying tension in his tone.

'I suppose I could have, but I wanted to come home. I had served my purpose, and it seemed like you were going to be busy entertaining.' I dropped that in, both of us knowing exactly what I meant.

He flashed a big smile at me and shook his head. 'Not a chance in the condition I was in.'

I tried to sound professional. 'I suppose you've dropped by to add some more dates to the diary. Oh, and there's a host of wedding presents for you to decide what you want to do with.'

'What I want to do with?' Tony looked confused. His brows were furrowed, and he gave a shrug. He put down his coffee cup and looked at me straight in the face. Again, I saw his eyes cloud over, which I had learnt by now meant he was losing patience or just getting plain angry.

'I tell you what, Francesca, if you don't like them, give them to charity.' With that, he pushed back his chair and stood up, walking towards the hallway.

'I didn't mean to offend you,' I said hastily, walking behind him while he marched ahead.

'You never do, Francesca. And yet, you always manage to.'

'Stop! Wait a minute. Before you go, you haven't forgotten I am going to my mam's for Christmas, have you? I also wanted to ask you about Julie Gold.'

This seemed to stop him in his tracks. 'No, I hadn't forgotten about Christmas, as long as you are back for the New Year. When are you leaving?'

'Christmas Eve,' I answered. I urged him to sit back at the table and made a coffee for him.

He gave me one of his friendlier grins. 'You have a good memory, Francesca. Now, what about Julie Gold?'

I told him how she was constantly coming around, even now when there was no need to. Even this morning, there was a message on my answer machine informing me of when she would be popping by so we could go shopping. I explained that I appreciated she was being friendly and that she had organised the wedding, but surely now that we were married, Ralph Gold no longer felt the need to look for more skeletons in my cupboard and spy on me, did he?

Tony listened. He seemed genuinely puzzled by all of this and seemed to not know why Julie was making arrangements with me now.

'I'll speak to Ralph about it,' Tony assured me. Even he seemed concerned that Ralph didn't trust him.

12

HOME FOR CHRISTMAS

Bobby gave Elle her Christmas presents before we left and she had organised a Christmas tree with him. I hadn't planned to put a tree up, as we wouldn't be there, but I had come home one day to them both dressing one with tinsel and ornaments. I did feel a twinge of jealousy watching them. But then, I also had another twinge – this one of guilt because I hadn't done it for Bobby.

I kept promising myself I would make this house our home, but there never seemed to be enough time. My life at the moment was one big merry-go-around. The New Year was the time to get organised.

Bobby and I packed up the car with lots of presents and treats, said our goodbyes to Elle, and drove off to face the Christmas traffic.

Opening my mam's front door was amazing. It brought back so many childhood memories. The lounge was lit up by the Christmas tree lights. The television was on showing that old classic: *A Christmas Carol*. My mam still had an open coal fireplace, and the flames warmed the room. The smell of oranges and home-made mince pies wafted through the house. Now this was home.

Bobby burst in first, shouting to my mam and parking himself on the sofa beside my brothers. My mam walked through from the kitchen. As usual, her hands were covered in flour from baking. Leaving the boys to their movie, I went into the kitchen where she was just taking the last lot of mince pies out of the oven. I made a coffee for myself, and my mam had a nice cup of tea.

The kitchen was warm and cosy, and Mam had baked enough sausage rolls, jam tarts, and mince pies to keep us all going till next Christmas. By the time we had stuffed ourselves with all kinds of sweets while watching a movie, we were ready for bed, knowing tomorrow morning would be a very early one. The excitement of all the parcels under the tree was almost too much for the boys to bear. Fleetingly, I wondered what Tony was doing this Christmas or who he was spending it with. I doubted he was thinking about me. I was surprised at just how often he popped into my head and sorely wished I had sent him a Christmas card. Looking out at the December night with fairy lights in every window, it reminded me of our Christmas wedding.

* * *

At 6 a.m. on Christmas morning, the boys burst into my mam's bedroom, which I was sharing with her.

'Has he been?' they all screamed in unison.

They ran downstairs; it was like a stampede. They were kneeling down in front of the tree, looking at the names on the labels.

'Wait!' shouted my mam. 'Before anything else, I am going to make some tea, and then we will sit down and take it in turns opening the presents. Okay?'

I had brought some of Bobby's presents with me. Those, combined with what he'd got off my mam, would suit him until we got home. I had explained he would have two Christmases and be able to open up the other presents at home, especially as Santa knew our new address. A couple of hours later, the floor was covered in Christmas paper. Everyone was playing with cars and Lego. Christmas annuals were strewn on the sofa to read later. It felt good. I had been able to buy extra special presents this year, as well as give my mam some extra money towards all expenses. That alone made this business deal of a marriage worth it.

* * *

It was a great day. Christmas dinner was cooked to perfection, as always. Crackers were pulled and the table was filled with warmth and laughter.

At one point, I found myself wondering what Tony was doing. Then I reminded myself that he would probably be having a Christmas lunch somewhere with one of his lady friends. My mobile bleeped; it was a message from Tony. Smiling, and some-what surprised, I opened it.

Merry Christmas Mrs Lambrianu. See you at New Year.

I text back quickly, wishing him a merry Christmas too. I couldn't help grinning. When I looked up, my mum gave me a wink. I didn't need to tell her who it was from.

The next few days passed in a blur. The snow was now turning to slush, and my mam and I discussed Bobby and me leaving before it got worse on the motorways.

When we arrived home, the house was cold. I put the heating on and started unloading the car. Bobby ran indoors with one of his presents. Then I heard a loud scream. It was deafening. 'Mammy!'

I ran indoors to see what was wrong. Panic gripped me as I heard Bobby scream out again. My mind was in turmoil. What on earth had happened? Running into the living room, I stopped short.

Bobby was holding the handlebars of a black bicycle with the yellow Batman logo on it. My jaw dropped. Where on earth had that come from? My first instinct was Elle. But she had already given Bobby his Christmas presents. Then I saw the label. It was from Tony. When had he been?

Instantly, Bobby wanted to take the bike onto the drive and ride it. He wobbled and fell off a few times but was determined to get the hang of it. It was Bobby's first grown up bike, unlike the little plastic baby ones I had bought him when he was younger. Wincing inside, I remembered watching my younger brothers learning to ride their first bike and how many bumps and scrapes they had got when they had fallen off! Bobby was determined to get the hang of it, so I felt it was better that I leave him to it. You can never concentrate and do something properly with people standing over you, watching you, can you?

After a couple of hours, I could hear Bobby talking away. When I looked out of the patio doors, I saw Elle with him in the drive. She was watching him ride his bike up and down the drive and shouting encouragement.

After a while, she came in. 'Phew! It's cold out there. I was driving past and saw the lights on. I thought I'd pop around. Is that okay?'

'Who brought the bike around for Bobby?' I asked her directly and poured some coffee.

She looked down at the floor and then back up at me. 'Tony brought it, but you had already left. I let him bring it in to save him taking it back with him. Was that okay?' She looked a little sheepish. I knew she was being pulled in all directions and couldn't do right for doing wrong. Mentally, I wondered why he would remember a little boy at Christmas and buy him a bike. I was touched and surprised by the gesture. No one would have known if he hadn't bought Bobby anything.

'Well, Tony could have rung if he wanted to drop something off, and I really don't need him involving Bobby in all of this.' I didn't know what to say. I hadn't expected this. Then I looked at Elle and could see she felt uncomfortable with the situation.

'Sorry, Francesca. I didn't mean any harm. It's Christmas, and I thought it would be okay to leave it here. Tony seemed sorry to have missed you...' Tailing off, she held out the key ring to me. 'You can have your keys back if you like.'

'No, keep them. It's just that this is supposed to be my house, and I get to say when people walk in and out of it.' I sat down and put my hand to my forehead. 'Sorry, Elle. It's been a long journey and a busy few days. I'm just a bit tired.'

'Why don't you have a relaxing bath, and I'll rustle up something to eat for you both. Have a little time to yourself.' Elle always felt better when she had something to do. And to be honest, I was grateful. Tony Lambrianu was a complex man. But beneath the hard surface was clearly a very different person.

13

NEW YEAR'S EVE

Julie turned up the following day, glowing with her suntan. She looked beautiful and well turned out as always. Not one to break a habit of a lifetime, she opened her bag and took out two bottles of champagne. Elle, now knowing the routine, put a glass in front of her.

She gossiped on about her trip and how exclusive it had been.

'While we were away' – she smiled playfully – 'I bought you this. This will get that husband of yours gagging for it.' She laughed at her own joke and handed me a large box.

The name on the front was obviously designer and she was eager for me to open it. Those brightly red painted lips of hers held a smile that seemed to cover half of her face.

'Why do you think I need to get my husband "gagging" for it?' I smiled back at her, all the while moving my hand towards the box.

'Oh, Fran, love, anyone can see he's desperate to grab hold of you. But you're so reserved about it all – shy, I suppose. Never really been something I've suffered from – shyness.' She was bubbling with excitement like a young girl.

Stunned by Julie's playful banter, I laughed, but was shocked by what she was saying. She thought Tony was gagging for me? I couldn't believe it. Could it be true? Did he fancy me?

Julie went on. 'Anyway, I've had a great idea. You never had a honeymoon, and Ralph and I have a villa in Italy. Why don't we all go, including the boys of course? I know you wouldn't want to go without Bobby. What about you, Elle?' She looked up to where Elle was busying herself. 'Are you up for a holiday in Italy?'

I was about to untie the red bow around the box when Julie took a large gulp of her drink and put her hand over mine. 'Actually, don't open it until you're ready to wear it at the New Year's Eve party. I know what's in it already, and you will lose your nerve. Let's say it's a little risqué.'

Now I was worried. Knowing Julie, I didn't dare think what would be in that box. I had already bought my dress for the party and I knew it wouldn't be in the same league as what was in that box!

'This isn't some clown's outfit or something, is it, Julie?' I had begun to get the measure of Julie's sense of humour, and I had seen a lot of wives being the brunt of Julie's jokes.

The smile she wore became serious, and a frown crossed her brow. 'Don't be silly, Fran. It's beautiful, really it is. But I know you might find it revealing. Promise me, Fran, you will wear it.' She wagged her finger and, draining her glass, got up to leave. 'Let Tony see what a beautiful woman he's married, eh?'

Julie really did have a heart of gold. Her concern for my marriage touched me and she'd spoken as if she had seen right through my sham of a marriage. Did we look so estranged to the outside world?

Reaching over the breakfast bar, I held her hand. 'Are you okay Julie? You look after everyone, but who looks after you?'

Squeezing my hand, she smiled. 'You do Fran. You and Elle here. That's what friends do isn't it?'

I liked having Julie for a friend, and I was sorry that I had complained to Tony that she kept popping around. Each day she came over was funnier than the last, even if my table looked like a wine bar!

I walked her to her car.

She shouted to me, 'Think about Italy, Fran. See you tomorrow.'

When I returned to the kitchen, Elle put the kettle on. Then she picked up Julie's empty bottles and started to clear away. 'You know, Francesca, when I was a girl, you used to get money on the bottles you took back to the shop. Maybe that's where Ralph made his fortune.'

We both burst out laughing.

* * *

The morning of New Year's Eve brought snow and the usual winter gale-force wind. Bobby wanted to play outside, so we donned our hats and coats and went for a long walk on the beach. Although it was cold, we enjoyed ourselves, drinking hot chocolate and eating doughnuts. Some people were walking their dogs along the seafront.

'Can we have a dog, Mammy?' Bobby suddenly asked, totally out of the blue.

'Dogs are a big responsibility, Bobby. They have to be walked every day and looked after properly. Maybe someday, but not right now, okay?'

I saw the disappointed look on his face, but I just didn't think the time was right.

When we got home, Elle was still there, busying herself with the ironing. Bobby burst in and told her he wanted a dog. I stood behind him, looking at Elle, waving my arms, and shaking my head no. I needed her to agree with me on this.

'Well, you do both go for walks on the beach every day. But dogs need a lot of looking after, Bobby.'

That really wasn't a lot of help. I supposed she was trying to appease him, but all she had done was raise his hopes. I decided I'd talk to her about it more tomorrow once I was back home. Elle was going to be staying over, as she was looking after Bobby while I was at the party.

I took a leisurely bath and pondered the evening ahead of me. What a difference from last year. Here I was, lying in a large Jacuzzi bubble bath in a mansion house, while the housekeeper cooked my son's dinner. Crazy or what? The car was to pick me up around 7 p.m. I decided to put my hair up and just leave a few ringlets on the side of my shoulder. I still hadn't seen the dress. Now it was time to open Julie's magic box.

I pulled at the ribbon and took the lid off. Layers of tissue paper covered the material. I parted it all, and all I could see was chiffon netting.

Pulling out the dress, I had my first chance to take a proper look at it, although it just looked like thin layers of chiffon. Where was the dress? It was so oddly-shaped, I couldn't fathom what went where. I shouted for Elle. When she came up, I showed her.

The colour was 'nude', a sort of beige coffee colour. It had a long halter neck, which seemed to start from the waist up. Fortunately, the front had bra cups inside the material. The material was thicker from the waist to just below the thigh, and then it stopped. From there, it was four long wide strips of see-through chiffon. It looked like a long dress. But when you walked, the four panels came apart and showed an awful lot of leg.

'Oh, my goodness, Elle. I can't wear this.' My heart sank. The dress was very erotic, in its own classy way.

I saw Elle eyeing it up. She didn't give the horrified response I had expected her to give. 'It's very feminine. Apart from the halter neck straps hanging down your back, there is no back until it reaches your waist. Those lovely long panels will swirl around your legs. In fact, you can see a lot, but you can see a lot of nothing. It reminds me of one of those Egyptian princesses from the Old Testament, like Salome or something.' She laughed, shaking her head.

Panic rose inside me. 'I'll have to tell Julie it didn't fit.' I walked to the wardrobe to get out the original black cocktail dress that I had bought for the occasion.

'No, Fran. You said yourself you don't want to upset anyone, do you? I have to say, in comparison to that' – she pointed at my black dress – 'it's beautiful and very feminine. And you can't tell her it didn't fit. It's been made specially for you. Look at the name on the label. She has even bought you matching shoes.' She put her hands into the box and pulled out a pair of high-heeled shoes in exactly the same colour as the dress. Julie had outdone herself.

Putting on the dress, with its soft chiffon panels against my body, made me feel sexy – sexier than I'd ever felt when I had been a stripper.

'You look beautiful, Francesca. The colour suits you, and those shoes make you look even taller than you are, like some Roman goddess. Julie really does know her stuff.'

A Roman goddess, I mused, as I twirled around in front of the mirror. I felt different: confident, sexy and ravishing. Well, if Mr Lambrianu was gagging for it, tonight he would be on his knees begging for it. I laughed to myself.

When I eventually arrived at the club, we were nearly an hour late and it was packed to the hilt. All the men were in their best suits, and all the women had donned their diamonds and designer dresses. The club looked fantastic. The dim lighting set the scene and the bar was covered in silver buckets, with champagne bottles resting in ice. The music was loud, and everyone was looking forward to seeing the New Year in with style.

Julie was the first to spot me. She flung her arms around my neck and kissed my cheek. Then she stood back to take a good look at the dress. 'Do you like it, Fran? Say you do.'

There had been real warmth in that hug. This wasn't some bitchy joke, as I had presumed. Looking around the room, I could see some of the other wives looking shocked at Julie's display of affection. She had always come across as the ice maiden. To me, she had become just Julie. She made me laugh and I looked forward to seeing her. Who would have thought it: me and Julie Gold, friends?

Blushing, I hugged her back. 'It's lovely Julie. I hope I do it justice.'

The waiters handed us both a glass of champagne. Julie linked her arm through mine, and we walked through the crowd towards Ralph. Julie's dress was straight, white, and stopped just above the knee. From the low cleavage hung row after row of gold tassels. It suited her to perfection. 'You look beautiful, Julie. And thank you for my dress.'

'I got them both in Italy. Come on, Fran. Let's go and see what the three musketeers are up to.' She pushed her way through the crowds of people standing near Ralph shaking hands and wishing season's greetings.

Then a dark suited bouncer approached me and told me that Tony wanted to see me in his office at once. I had been summoned.

Walking into his office, I saw Tony sitting in his large leather chair, swivelling it back and forth. As always, he looked very handsome in his dinner suit and bow tie. He reminded me of James Bond. When he saw me, he stood up and held out his hand to indicate that I should sit on the chair in front of him. Why did he always make me feel like a schoolgirl sitting at the head teacher's desk?

'Evening, Francesca. I hope you enjoyed your Christmas with the family.' There was a warmth in his voice and a smile that showed a perfect set of white teeth.

I sat down before him, feeling a little nervous. 'You're going to complain about this dress, aren't you? Is that why you've summoned me in here?'

He walked around his desk towards me and put his hand into the inside pocket of his jacket, pulling out a long rectangular box. 'Did Bobby like his bike?' he asked, ignoring my comment. He held out the box.

Taking it, I looked up at him. 'Yes, he did like his bike. But as you know, I would rather you didn't buy him things. I don't want to sound ungrateful, but he already had one father walk away from him. And after all this is over, you're going to do the same. I know some of the kids at school have asked about his new dad. I've explained to him that you are just Tony, Mummy's friend. It will make things easier when all of this is over.'

I could see my speech didn't please him much, but he nodded in acknowledgement. 'As you wish, Francesca. This is for you. I couldn't give you it at Christmas because you had already left when I called round to the house.'

Inside the box was a large gold locket. Again, I looked at him, a little confused.

'For God's sake, Francesca, take it out of the box, will you? It won't bite.' He was losing his patience now. He could lose his temper at the flick of a switch!

Holding up the heavy gold chain, I looked at the large oval locket. It was engraved with FL. Tony took it from me and opened the locket. Inside was a wedding photo of the two of us. On the opposite side was a picture of Bobby and me.

It was beautiful, and the photos in it brought a lump to my throat. Bobby was in his little suit and tie. Absolutely lovely. 'Oh, I see. You want me to wear this to show the other wives my Christmas present? What's FL mean?' I asked.

Tony ran his hands through his hair and gave a deep sigh, while staring up at the ceiling – possibly looking for inspiration.

'F and L,' he said through gritted teeth, obviously trying to hide his frustration, 'are your initials: Francesca Lambrianu! No, it isn't to show the wives what I bought you for Christmas, but for you. I thought you might like it.' I could see he felt a bit embarrassed.

Now I felt stupid. What a fool. Of course FL were my initials. I just hadn't got used to thinking of myself as that. He took the locket from me, undid the clasp, and told me to stand up. I moved my hair so he could fit the chain around my neck. I had my back to him and could feel his breath on my neck. Goosebumps were rising on my back, and I could feel myself shiver.

The locket lay comfortably between my breasts. Tony was still standing behind me. I let my hair drop to one side and turned to face him. Our eyes met and for some stupid reason, I raised my hand and traced my thumb along the cleft in his chin. My heart was pounding. I felt as though he was going to kiss me. I looked at his lips and remembered them kissing me on my wedding day.

The door burst open, and Sharon walked in with a large cloth bag, presumably full of money.

'Here, Tony.' She passed him the bag with some of the night's takings in it. 'Put this in the safe, will you? Hi, Fran. You look nice. Come on, Tony, it's heaving out there, and people are asking for you.' She seemed totally oblivious to the scene before her.

The moment was gone. Tony snapped out of it, and it was business as usual.

'Of course, Sharon. It looks like it's going to be a good night.' He kissed the bag jokingly and put it in the safe.

I headed out with Sharon. I felt my face burning with embarrassment as I walked out into the dimness of the club. What the hell had just happened in there? I reached up and touched the locket and walked towards Julie in the VIP lounge.

Tony was more than attentive when he joined us all for a drink, his arms around my waist and his hands on my bare back. It made the hairs on the back of my neck stand up. He leaned forward in the dimness of the club and whispered into my ear. 'As for the dress, Francesca, I think you look very sexy and very beautiful.' The tip of his tongue touched my earlobe teasingly. Fireworks seemed to go off in my body and I could feel myself trembling at his touch, making me almost gasp.

I looked over at Julie. She had a big smug smile on her face and gave me the thumbs up. She obviously felt her dress had done the trick and was satisfied.

During the course of the evening, Tony didn't leave my side. We danced together, flirted together, and laughed together. He truly was a handsome man and made me feel very special indeed.

At one point, Julie turned towards Ralph and slurred, 'I think Fran and Tony should come to Italy with us, don't you? I mean the kids as well. But tell them, Ralphy, my love. They have to come.' She was giving Ralph her best puppy dog eyes and even threw in a kiss for good measure. It was obvious; he couldn't refuse her anything. Julie was the jewel in his crown, and for such a gangster-like man, he was putty in her hands. He adored her, and it was clear that Julie was not only his partner in love, but in business too.

'Yes, and let's not forget Jake and Sharon. Let's make it a big holiday to start the New Year with.' Ralph was in high spirits. He loved his wife and was lapping up all of the attention she was giving him. The atmosphere was electric. Everyone was enjoying themselves and having a great time!

Lots of the other men's wives came up and joined us for a

drink. I knew a few quite well by now, and they were all taking an interest in my locket. I showed them the photos inside and told them that Tony had bought it for me for Christmas. They all admired it. I felt like a princess, with a handsome prince beside me.

Julie and I went to the ladies' room. It would soon be midnight, and she wanted to touch up her lipstick. I was in the toilet cubicle and when she shouted at me to hurry up, because it was nearly time for the countdown. I told her to go on ahead of me. It was hard going to the loo, lifting up all of those panels to get to my underwear. I heard some women come into the ladies', and they were laughing and chatting.

'When Tony gets rid of that wife of his, the party can begin,' I heard one say.

There was drunken laughter from a few women. Hearing Tony's name, I stayed in the cubicle, not daring to make a noise.

'Roxy,' I heard one of the women say, 'you know Tony adores you. She's not a patch on you. Did he marry her to make you jealous or something?'

'What did he get you for Christmas?' They were all joining in, firing questions at Roxy about Tony.

'That would be telling,' I heard the woman tease her friends. 'But I definitely got my present: from Christmas night all the way into Boxing Day, if you know what I mean.'

There was an eruption of laughter, and then I heard the women leaving and the door close.

I sat there, stunned. Tony had spent Christmas and Boxing Day with this woman and was flirting with me just a few days later, just to please Ralph! I had fallen for it again. I had got caught up in the moment. My eyes brimmed with tears, and I could feel them fall down my cheeks. Everyone knew this marriage was a sham, and I was a joke!

I had to compose myself. I stood in front of the mirror and started replacing my make-up the tears had washed away.

Julie came swaggering in. 'For goodness' sake, Fran. I thought you had fallen down the loo. Come on.' She dragged me by the arm back into the club.

While Julie was pulling me through the crowds, I couldn't help but survey the room. Who was that woman I had heard in the toilets? I looked around. Then I heard the name Roxy being shouted. It wasn't a common name, and so I looked across the room.

My eyes stopped at a group of women, all laughing and drinking champagne. In the middle of them was a woman sitting on a high chrome bar stool, answering to her name. Although she was sitting down, she still looked very tall, with long legs. Her straight long blonde hair fell down her back, and the mini sequinned dress she was wearing showed off her suntan and her very expensive boob job. She was everything I wasn't. We couldn't be more opposite.

Tony had had a large television screen installed in the club so that everyone could watch London's famous Big Ben clock chime in the New Year. Julie was still chatting away, but I wasn't listening. My eyes were fixed on this beautiful leggy blonde waiting for my departure, so that she could be with my husband!

The crowds in the club were standing around, waiting for the clock to strike twelve. I felt Tony behind me. He put his arm around my waist and I felt sick inside. He was holding me a little too tightly and pressing his body against me. I was sure I could feel his growing arousal pressing against my thigh. I wasn't imagining it. I stepped forward, creating some distance between us. Bloody cheek. Was I the warm-up act before he spent the night with his girlfriend? No way!

Thankfully the club was dark. So I made a point of stepping a little closer into the crowd, while they were all shouting out the countdown from ten. Then Big Ben struck midnight and everyone cheered.

Without being noticed, I moved aside. I took out my phone and dialled my mam's number. I wanted to hear a friendly voice.

* * *

'Where the hell did you disappear to? I turned around, and you were gone.' Tony couldn't understand what had changed so suddenly – what had made me want to leave his side.

He was interrupted by Julie. 'Francesca, come here.' She flung her arms around my neck and kissed my cheeks. 'I love you, Fran.'

Ralph was hot on her heels. Holding her up, he steered her to a chair, before she fell down.

Tony shook his head. Ralph clearly had his hands full.

'I think we had better call it a day, Tony,' Ralph said. 'You don't mind if I take Julie home, do you?'

Tony shook his head again and smiled as he pulled me to the side. Then the questions started. 'What's wrong? Why did you walk away? I wanted to see the New Year in with you first.'

'I'm surprised you even noticed I'd gone. Anyway, I wanted to telephone my mam. And I'm also ready to leave if you will tell the driver. Then you can enjoy the rest of your evening.'

Tony frowned. There was a moment's silence, which seemed to last forever. He reached his hand out for mine, and I pulled it away.

'I don't do games, Francesca. Obviously something is wrong. So just spit it out, will you?'

'You promised me that you wouldn't humiliate me,' I said. All the love I had felt turned into anger. I was hurt and I wanted to hurt him. I had been blind, falling for his charming smile, stupid even. Just another notch on the bedpost as it were. 'But you have tonight. Your girlfriend Roxy over there' – I waved my arm in her direction, and Tony's face was set in stone – 'was in the toilets, boasting to all of her friends about getting rid of me so that you can both enjoy your evening – you know, like you did on Christmas night and Boxing Day.' Without realising, I had started shouting, but I had started, and I was damn well going to finish. 'You're not humiliating me, you're humiliating yourself. You buy a wife, you sleep around when your wife doesn't want to spend Christmas with you. You're the clown, not me!'

Tony's face went red. Whether with embarrassment or anger, I didn't care.

'Stay at arm's length in future, will you? And keep control of whatever that was pressing into my thigh.' I pointed to his trouser crotch. 'Here, take this.' I pulled the locket from my neck and put it into his open hand. 'Your employees must love you, Mr Lambrianu, giving away Christmas presents like this,' I snapped. I felt my own face flush with anger.

Tony grabbed hold of my arm and nearly pulled it out of the socket while he frogmarched me through the crowd to his office. No one seemed to notice, but I knew I had gone too far.

He just about threw me into the room. 'Firstly,' Tony shouted, 'don't ever shout at me in public again. And secondly, who is humiliating who? This is a club. Roxy can come and go as she pleases. Yes, I spent Christmas night with her. I don't deny it. What is your problem? I didn't know she was going to shout it out to all of her friends, did I?' He was angry, and he was shouting. His blue eyes seemed to change colour and darken.

'The locket,' Tony rasped, 'was a genuine present. But I don't expect you to wear it, like your bloody wedding rings discarded on a window ledge in the kitchen. I see you remembered to put them on.' He was breathing heavily, and his face was red with anger.

I looked at him oddly. He must have seen my rings when he'd brought Bobby's bike into the house at Christmas.

There was a moment's silence. We were both taking a breath, and I was trying to take in what he had just said.

'My wedding rings feel like a uniform, something I only need to wear when I am out with you. And I always wear them when Julie comes to the house.' I spoke in a low soft tone. This argument was going nowhere. Too much alcohol and too much hype. Now we had both sobered up a little, it seemed silly. There were no promises between us, and he had never lied. Even now, he admitted he had been with Roxy.

Tony had his back to me. Standing in the corner by the door, I waited for him to turn around and speak.

At last, still with his back to me, he said, 'You don't like me very much, do you, Francesca?' Although his voice was calm, it was dripping with sarcasm. 'Well, I remember, Francesca, when the thought of me touching you wasn't so abhorrent. Oh, yes, Francesca, I remember you. Did you really think I didn't? I also know that you recognised and remembered me. Or do you make a habit of finding yourself in beer gardens having sex with strangers?' Tony turned slowly to face me. He looked me directly in the eyes. He had a smug expression on his face.

This felt like some cruel joke at my expense. He had known all along. I didn't know what to say. There were no words. He had wanted to hurt me and had saved this up for this very moment to put me firmly back in my place. This was his best weapon yet.

'Why? Why did you want me to go through this charade, Mr Lambrianu?' I felt it only right to address him properly. This was all I could muster up. My throat was dry, but I was determined not to cry in front of him. I opened the door and walked out of the office. I walked quickly, ignoring everyone as I made my way to the front entrance, where I knew the car would be waiting.

Once in the back seat, the tears flowed. He'd remembered my stupidity that night. So why had he chosen me to do this? For all of my moral judgement on him, I was no better than him or any of his women. I had shown myself to be an easy cheap tart, and he knew it.

I could see the chauffeur looking at me through his rear-view mirror, and then the car stopped. The chauffeur got out and went to a nearby roadside caravan that sold tea and coffee. He walked back to the car, opened the door, handed me a plastic cup of coffee, and shut the door again.

When he started to drive off, I took a sip of the coffee, and my mobile phone began to ring. I looked at the number. It was Tony's. I ignored his call. There was nothing more to say.

I couldn't sleep that night. I needed answers, although I wasn't ready to hear them yet. I had sounded like some bitter jealous wife, and he obviously thought I had got above my station. Eventually, something would have to be sorted out. Where did we stand now? My telephone rang constantly through the night, with Tony leaving messages on my answerphone asking me to call him back. When I looked at my mobile, it was full of text messages asking the same thing.

I wanted to unwind and spend New Year's Day with Bobby and gather my thoughts, so I unplugged the telephone and switched off my mobile.

14

REVELATIONS

Busying herself and avoiding my eyes, Elle asked for perhaps the hundredth time, 'Have you spoken to Tony yet?'

I looked at her. She knew I hadn't. I could only presume Tony was now turning the pressure on Elle to keep asking me to call him.

'You're both as stubborn as each other,' she sighed. 'It's been a week; surely you've both had a little space and time to cool down?'

'I know whose side you're on Elle, but you don't know all the facts. And there's nothing left to say.'

Elle looked directly at me in that motherly way she had. 'Maybe I do know the facts, which is why you need to clear the air.'

Sometimes, it annoyed and confused me that Elle was Tony and Jake's confidant who knew everything. But, truthfully, since New Year I hadn't thought of much else. Each time I closed my eyes I could see that smug expression on his face and the sarcasm dripping from his mouth about me having sex with strangers in beer gardens. He had played me from the very beginning, and I had fallen for it. Why had he mentioned my name to the Golds when they'd asked if he had a steady girlfriend? The more I thought about it, the less it made sense. It worried me slightly that he could terminate our contract and I would be homeless. The year wasn't up, so where did I stand in all of this?

'I'm not on anyone's side Francesca, but, from my point of view you've argued and he's trying to discuss it with you and you're ignoring him, which can only mean one thing.'

'What? What does it mean Elle?' I hated the way she made me sound like a sulky child.

'He will come here Francesca; you're forcing his hand. If you don't want that, then call him.'

'What do you think he'll do?' Gripped with fear, I stared at her. My old demons of Luke being angry frightened me. Now, I didn't know what to do.

Seeing the horror on my face, she patted my shoulder. 'Nothing sinister Francesca, but he will come, believe me.'

I was due to work at the doctor's this afternoon, and was glad of the time away from Elle. Who needed a telephone when Tony had his own spy in my kitchen?

I was surprised when Lisa, the receptionist, handed the phone over and said it was an emergency. Instantly, I thought it was the school and Bobby had been in an accident.

'Francesca, I'm sorry to bother you, but Tony is on his way to the doctor's surgery.'

'What?' I couldn't believe what Elle was saying to me. My heart pounded. How did he know I was here? How did Elle? I had always made up excuses for why I was out, preferring to keep this job as my little secret. 'How do you know about me working here?'

'There has been a lot of talk about a new receptionist and I wanted to warn you.'

My heart sank. Well, I mused, it had been nice while it lasted and now Tony was coming to spoil it. As an afterthought, I felt it was only right to Elle to apologise for my deceit. 'I'm sorry Elle, I should have trusted you.'

'No matter now love. The bottom line is, he knows you're working and that doesn't look very good for a man in his position. Jake told him to give you some space, but we both know he couldn't hold back his impulsive ways forever. He came to the house looking for you. He thought you had packed up and left.'

I was trapped and didn't know what to do. 'Thanks for the heads up Elle, I appreciate it.'

Walking out into the reception area again, I was stunned. There was Tony, leaning over the reception desk, smiling and chatting to Lisa. 'Lisa, that's a lovely name. Now could you let me know if Mrs Lambrianu is here?'

Lisa blushed and smiled and looked quite flustered, then she spotted me. 'Fran, do you know a Mrs Lambrianu? I can't find her on the system.'

Tony turned and looked at me in my uniform. I wanted the ground to swallow me up. Walking over to the desk, I did my best to smile. I must have paled somewhat, because Lisa asked if I was okay. Ignoring her, I looked up at Tony. 'Hello Tony, how nice to see you again.'

Taking my lead, Tony smiled. Thankfully, he hadn't come to cause a scene or he would have done so by now, and he could see how nervous I was. 'It's good to see you Fran, maybe we could have a catch up when you're finished here.' He grinned. Now I knew he was toying with me. I could see Lisa staring at us both, and thankfully the telephone rang and she had to answer it.

I pulled Tony out of earshot and in a low voice, said, 'Please will you go and meet me at the house? I finish in an hour. Please Tony, not here.' My face was burning with embarrassment as the patients looked on. Tony glanced at his watch and nodded, and was interrupted by an elderly female patient holding out some chocolates for me. 'Sorry son, it's pension day and I have to go. These are for you Fran, thank you.' Then she turned to Tony. 'She's been very good to me, sorting out my piles and she gets all my medication delivered to my door. If you need looking after son, Fran is the woman you want.'

I almost laughed when Tony choked at her comment. That was far too much information for him. His grin was wide and he gave a little chuckle. 'Thanks for the tip.' He winked. He waited while I took the chocolates. I felt the old lady had eased the tension. 'Well, Florence Nightingale, I will see you later.'

When he left, I breathed a sigh of relief, but each minute seemed like forever as I waited to leave. When I got home, the house was empty which surprised me. Where was Tony? More to the point, where were Elle and Bobby? I changed out of my uniform into my jeans and T-shirt and then I heard the car.

Bobby ran in. 'Mammy! Tommy has met my dad and we had ice-creams. He didn't believe I had a dad, until Tony came to the school with Elle.'

Tommy was the popular kid at school everyone wanted to be friends with, and he had also become the thorn in my side. He was forever telling Bobby about his own dad and the fun they had together, while reminding Bobby no one had ever met his dad, and that he doubted he had one. Poor Bobby had looked crushed and disappointed when he had told me this. They only answer I had was, 'Everybody has a dad Bobby.' He'd accepted it, but I felt that I hadn't made him feel any better. What could I say? Your dad, Luke, abandoned you when you were a baby and didn't want you in the first place!

Angrily, I looked up at Tony. What had he been saying to Bobby and this friend of his? Filling his head with all sorts. 'Bobby love, I have told you before, Tony is not your dad.'

I instantly felt sorry for my outburst. Bobby looked like he was going to cry.

'Was that necessary Francesca?' Tony barked at me. 'Didn't you know he's been teased at school for not having a dad like the others? I showed that kid Tommy and his bloody mother too, nosey cow. Whether you like it or not, I am your husband and that makes Bobby my son.'

Excited, Bobby carried on. 'I showed Tony the dogs on the beach Mammy, and me and Tommy stuck our heads out of the car window and waved to all our friends.' It didn't matter what I said, Bobby was happy to have had his 'dad' pick him up from school and it seemed Tony had enjoyed it too. I supposed it had given them time to talk and get to know each other better, and no, I hadn't realised just how much Bobby was being teased at school by Tommy and his elite gang. It seemed Tony had found out a lot more about him in a short space of time.

As we glared at each other, Elle intervened, and knelt down and put her arm around Bobby. 'Bobby love, why don't you get changed and we'll go out for a burger, then we can see if there are any dogs splashing around on the beach.' To me and Tony, she added, 'We're going out for tea and will be about an hour. Try and play nice children, eh?' Glaring at us both, she left the room.

Tony sat down and swept his blond wispy fringe back, which I had learnt was a habit of his. No matter how hard he pushed it back, it always came flopping forward, making him look even younger. 'Well, Francesca, where do we start?'

I sat on the sofa opposite him. 'Let me start first, then it's your turn. Don't interrupt me. I've been playing this over in my mind all week.' He nodded and I took a breath. 'We made a business deal. I don't know if you want to continue, but I am happy to if you are. I don't know why you chose me to be your pretend wife, it all seems so ridiculous now. New Year's Eve stung a little. Roxy thinks I'm a fool and you're already tired of me. I can see why, she is beautiful. Why not use her in your scheme to please Ralph and Julie Gold?'

Tony sprawled on the sofa with his arm resting over the back of it. With every word I spoke I could see he wanted to interrupt, but he let me carry on, watching me with those blue eyes.

'Yes, Tony,' I sighed, 'I do remember our encounter in the beer garden. I sincerely hoped you hadn't. I was at a low ebb and Luke was divorcing me. Everyone was in couples enjoying themselves and I stuck out like a sad, single woman. I didn't want to go to that party, but my future bookings depended on it. You know how it is. I didn't know who you were, and I'd had one too many glasses of wine. I have regretted that foolish moment ever since.' I saw a frown cross his brow. 'That's not who I am, but, that night I wanted to feel needed. Luke didn't want me, but, you did.'

I could see him watching me, waiting for me to finish, but he clearly realised I needed to get this off my chest.

'I presume your ego doesn't like me working, but I will need a job at some point. As quickly as you have come into my life you will be gone, and I doubt we'll ever meet again.' I hadn't realised how much that idea hurt until now. Never to see him again. It seemed so final.

'Your turn.' I smiled. For once, I felt like his equal.

'Well, Francesca, what can I say to top that? Okay, I'll give it a go. I have never lied to you Francesca. I like sex, and I have a lot of women friends but I don't have relationships. I am sorry that you regret our night in the beer garden, but I need you to know that I did enlist Jake's help to find you. He calls you Cinderella for running off like that.' He grinned, trying to make light of it. 'I don't know why I tried to find you, I just wanted to know if you were okay. I didn't want to go to that party either, but we were like kindred spirits, lost in that shithole, until we found each other.' Seeing Tony blush at his own words warmed my heart. 'I like Roxy,

I always have and there is no denying she is beautiful, but as you have found out for yourself, she has a big mouth. She likes sitting in the club and lording it over her friends. I don't know why.' He shrugged and smiled sheepishly. 'I've slept with most of them, so she is the misguided one.'

I was surprised by his honesty, even if it hurt a little.

'That was the point, Francesca. Roxy would have enjoyed being my wife too much and would have held me to ransom with Ralph. When it was over she would want half of my empire, which I have worked bloody hard for, and I wouldn't be able to get rid of her. I felt you would stick to that deal. And I too would like this deal to continue, and I feel it can now that we're being honest. From my point of view, it has all been worth it.' Looking up at me he grinned. 'As for your job, I can't say that I am overjoyed, but you saw an opportunity and grabbed it. That is what I like about you Francesca, you're level headed. If we carry on with the arrangement, I am prepared to compromise. It does hurt my pride, people thinking that I can't afford to keep my wife. Christ, what would Julie say?' He laughed. Putting his hand in his pocket, Tony pulled out the locket he had given me. 'This is yours Francesca Lambrianu. I am proud to call you my wife. Everyone knows you don't fool around.'

His voice softened, almost sadly. 'You loved your first husband, didn't you Francesca? I had to pay you to marry me.' His shoulders seemed to droop a little and it saddened me.

The room was silent and the skeletons were out of the closet. I stood up and held my hand out to him to shake it. 'Let's carry on then shall we? Is it okay if I decorate?'

Grinning, Tony stood up and hugged me. 'Make this yours Fran. After all, this is your house.'

'Thank you for the locket, and Bobby loves his bike. What are we going to do about Ralph and Julie and their Italy trip? Newly-weds sleeping in separate rooms?'

Tony held my hands. 'We should have talked like this in the beginning Francesca; we will sort out Ralph and Julie. Let's just play it by ear shall we.' I could see his brain ticking over and even he didn't have the answer to that one. We hugged again, and this time it was genuine.

The kiss he gave me on the cheek sealed it. This was another side to Tony I hadn't seen before, and I must confess, I liked it. I liked it a lot. We walked to the front door as he was leaving like old friends.

'Bye Mr L,' I joked. I was sorry to see him go; it had been the first real conversation we'd had on our own and it had gone better than I'd ever expected.

Later, as I was washing Bobby's hair, it dawned on me that I hadn't seen Julie this week either. The house seemed empty without her sitting on her usual stool at the breakfast bar, opening a bottle of champagne. I made a mental note to call her.

I telephoned her later that evening, but on hearing my voice she seemed cold and distant. When I asked her what was wrong, the hurl of abuse that followed was something I wasn't prepared for. Unknow-ingly, I had hurt her when I had told Tony after the wedding that Julie was still popping around and I didn't know why. Ralph had told Julie that I had complained to Tony, saying that I thought she was spying on me. I could tell she was deeply offended, because she was angry.

'You know Mrs fucking Lambrianu!' she screamed down the telephone. 'I just thought you might need a female friend, espe-cially someone that your husband hasn't slept with, and believe me, that's a hard woman to find,' she spat out and slammed the telephone down on me.

My heart sank. I supposed I deserved that. I understood that she wanted to hurt me the way I had hurt her. I tried calling her back, but she wouldn't answer. So I sent her a text saying that I needed her help. Tears ran down my cheeks. I had hurt her, and only time would tell if she could forgive me. She had always been on my side and I had been too blind to see it.

15

DECORATING

I left Julie alone for a couple of days, hoping that she would calm down a little and call me back. But she didn't.

I needed to do something about this and quick. After all, this was the kind of bad feeling that Tony had wanted to avoid.

I rang Tony. 'Hi. Is Ralph with you?'

He seemed very surprised that I was asking for Ralph. 'Is everything okay, Francesca? What's wrong?'

I told him again that I needed to speak to Ralph. He could obviously sense the urgency in my voice, and I could hear him talking, and then Ralph answered the telephone.

'Ralph,' I blurted out, 'it's Francesca. Will you get Julie to telephone me, please? I was wrong, Ralph. Really, I was. Ask her to call me, please. Tell her the kitchen's not the same without her.'

Ralph listened as I told him what had happened and assured me he would talk to her.

When Julie did eventually telephone, she still seemed a little cold but was prepared to listen. I told her that I had missed her and that I was sorry for being paranoid. Then I let it slip, accidently on purpose, that I was thinking about decorating and wondered if she wanted to help me or at least offer some advice. I knew that would be the carrot tempting the rabbit!

Of course, she was far too busy to help me and had lots of things to do. She would see if she could find a slot in her diary and let me know. Well, I had tried.

Elle and I went about our usual business. She had become Bobby's childminder now, unofficially. It was obvious, though, that he liked her a lot, and she enjoyed spending time with him. I didn't object. If it wasn't broken, why fix it? At least I could tell her now when I was working and didn't have to hide it any more.

Within two hours, there was a knock at my door. When I opened it, there stood Julie. She pushed past me in an offhand manner and walked into the kitchen. She put her designer bag down on the table and put her hands on her hips.

'Thank God I've come in time,' she declared, looking at Elle. 'God knows what this place would look like if I left it to her.'

I couldn't help but smile. I was forgiven. Julie made out that this was a big inconvenience and she was doing me a big favour, for which I should be very grateful. She took out a notepad from her bag and started writing. Elle automatically put a glass in front of her, waiting for her to take out her bottle of wine.

'You live in this bloody kitchen, Fran. I don't even know what mine looks like. So as big as it is, even with that conservatory, were going to need an extension. After all, you have the land.'

'Extension?' Panic began to rise inside of me. 'I meant just a few colour charts and painting.' Building works? I wasn't expecting this.

Julie looked at Elle again, and then she shook her head. 'See what I mean, Elle? I have come just in time. Let's get stingy Tony to put his hands in his pockets, shall we? God knows he can afford it. Anyway, use your credit card.'

She was bossing and in her element; it was good to have her

onside again. Then I had to explain to her that I didn't have a credit card.

'Well, that is the first thing that goes on my list. Did I call him stingy Tony? What I meant was old tight-arse Tony.' She burst out laughing at her own joke and poured herself a drink.

Later that evening, when Julie had left, I rang Tony. I started to explain what had happened and all of the plans that Julie was making.

The warm velvety voice that greeted me assured me all was well. 'Francesca, you're a little late. Julie has already been in touch.' Although his voice was calm and eloquent, you could hear the laughter in it. 'I already know that I'm a penny-pinching prick. Do what you want, or rather, what she wants, Francesca, and I will sort out your credit card. Maybe I could pop around tomorrow and discuss it.'

'I am sorry, Tony. I didn't mean to cause you any trouble.'

The laughter on the other end of the telephone was infectious. 'Tomorrow, Francesca. Bye.'

Tony arrived early the next morning, which meant he must have left London even earlier to avoid the rush hour traffic. I made him a bacon sandwich and a coffee and then shouted for Bobby to get up. Even though it was early, Tony was still immaculately dressed in his suit and tie, and the waft of his aftershave dominated the kitchen. I felt frumpy. I was still in my pyjamas!

We talked about Julie and her plans, and I told him that I would pay the bills and it would be our little secret. Let her think that Tony was paying for all of this. As for the credit card, I didn't need one, especially one that he would be paying for. Again, I apologised about Julie criticising him.

Bobby interrupted the conversation. 'What's that noise coming from your car, Tony?' Bobby was looking out of the window while eating some toast.

'Oh that, Bobby. It's just something I am doing for a friend – something I have to drop off. Why don't you go and see for yourself?' Tony had an uninterested, bored expression on his face.

Bobby ran out of the door, and instantly I was alarmed by his shouts and screams. 'Mammy, Mammy, come see.'

Running out of the door like a shot, I saw that the car window was down to the maximum, and Bobby had his head inside it. I walked up and looked through the window to see what all of the fuss was about. Inside was a little Labrador puppy, barking and wagging its tail. I turned to look at Tony, who was nonchalantly standing in the doorway watching the scene before him.

'Whose dog is it?' said Bobby. His eyes were wide, and he was laughing excitedly at the little dog inside the car. The chauffeur got out and opened the door, so the little puppy could be released. It instantly left a puddle on my driveway!

Folding his arms, Tony announced. 'I'm dropping it off at the homeless dogs' kennels. No one wants it.' That look on his face said it all. The dog wasn't homeless. I knew exactly what he had done. How could I say no now?

'Can we have it, Mammy?' Bobby asked. 'We could look after it and take it for walks, couldn't we?' The pleading eyes, not only from Bobby but also from the puppy, doubled my guilt. I had been well and truly conned.

'No. Sorry, Bobby, but it has to go to the dogs' home to find a family. You can't expect your mum to take in a poor homeless little puppy with nowhere to live,' Tony replied and although he was doing his best to sound stern in front of Bobby, I could tell he wanted to burst out laughing.

I watched as Bobby's eyes filled with tears. 'Please, Mammy. No one loves it. Please can we keep it?'

I had been beaten. All I could do was nod my head. 'Well, Tony, do you think we could have the puppy and save you the journey of dropping it off at the dogs' home?' I let the sarcasm drip from my voice. I wasn't angry, though. And watching the schoolboy grin on Tony's face made me smile.

The chauffeur started taking a dog's bed, food, and toys out of the boot of the car. Amazing... For a puppy that was going to a kennels for homeless dogs, it had a lot of luggage. Tony had bought that puppy especially for Bobby and had enjoyed every moment of watching me squirm. Knowing Bobby wanted a dog, Tony had gone out of his way to please him. Tony had a really thoughtful side to him, although he hid it really well! He never wanted to show weakness; I suppose that was part of his job, but I enjoyed the friendly banter now between us. Behind the man was the mischievous schoolboy.

All of the dog's things were brought into the kitchen, while Bobby played with his new friend, apparently now called Susie. I poked Tony in his well-ironed shirt. 'You, Mr L, are one sneaky underhanded polecat. Julie is right. You are going to pay for this. Homeless dog, my arse. It has more luggage than I do.'

Tony picked up the other half of his bacon sandwich and pushed it into his mouth. He nearly choked he was laughing so much.

'Bye, Fran,' he shouted as he made a hasty exit to the car. I could hear him laughing out loud as the car went up the driveway.

I looked down at Susie, who was emptying her bladder again. 'Come on, Bobby. Let's give her some breakfast.' I couldn't help smiling to myself.

Mr Lambrianu – what was I going to do with him?

* * *

No sooner had Julie started her plans, than chaos began. When she walked in later that morning, she looked down at Susie. 'What the hell is that?'

'That, Julie, is Tony's joke of the day. Apparently, it's a little homeless puppy, with a shipload of luggage and dog food.'

The sparkle was back in Julie's eyes, and she put her hands on her hips. 'Homeless dog? Sounds like one of Tony's ex-girlfriends to me.' With that, we both burst out laughing. 'That's him playing good cop, is it? Father of the year. And you would be the Wicked Witch of the West if you had said no. Well, Fran, we're going to make him pay for his jokes.'

It was good to have Julie back onside.

Julie sat at the breakfast bar in her usual place, mobile phone in one hand and notepad full of builders' telephone numbers on the table. There were numbers for interior designers and decorators, too. Oh goodness, this wasn't what I had in mind. She pointed her pen at me and asked if Tony was sorting out the credit card. I nodded.

Elle popped round and looked down at the puppy. 'What is that and where did it come from?'

'I tell you what that is, Elle,' said Julie, holding the telephone to her ear and waiting for someone to answer. 'That little joke has just put another 10,000 pounds on Tony's bill.'

'Tony,' was all Elle said.

I nodded. 'Apparently it was homeless.'

We both looked at each other and smiled.

Elle thoroughly enjoyed the proceedings and kept interrupting Julie with ideas about the house and the garden. That would give Julie another idea, and she would start making a list, one of which included landscape gardeners.

'Julie,' I confessed, 'what you're planning is going to cost a lot of money. And I also need to tell you that I won't be here all the time, because I have a job.'

That definitely silenced her. Julie put the telephone down and listened to what I was saying. She seemed shocked.

'Tony's making you work? You have a job: being his wife.' She was astounded. It never entered her head that I might actually enjoy my work.

'Tony's not happy about it, but it's something I want to do. I'm working at the local medical centre as a receptionist.'

Julie stared at me in disbelief and then looked at Elle, who was nodding her head to confirm what I had said.

'I thought you were a stripper?' Julie looked confused and so poured herself another glass of wine.

'Yes, I was. And now I'm a receptionist. The point I am making is that I won't be here all the time to let the builders in, but—'

Before I could continue, Julie interrupted. 'You're full of surprises, aren't you? Oh well, that means I can do it freelance. I will just have to manage it all myself, Mother Teresa.'

I looked at Elle. I felt I had just made a bad situation worse. Julie had now appointed herself fully in charge.

'Just one thing, Julie. I don't mean to be rude, but cut down on the drinking please. I want you sober when you're choosing things for my house. In fact, no, Julie. Cut it down full stop. You don't need it, and you're going to be very busy. The last thing all of us need is you falling over on this building site you're planning.'

I could see I had hit a nerve, and the smile dropped from both Julie and Elle's faces. I had said the wrong thing again.

Julie looked me directly in the face. The laughter had gone. 'Okay, Mrs Receptionist, but maybe just a small brandy after dinner, eh? I will cut down my drinking, Fran, if, after all this, you come to Italy with me. I want to show you the villa, and you will need the break.' She was looking at me with the same excited

puppy dog eyes I had seen earlier that morning from Bobby and
Susie.

What could I say? I reached out my hand to shake hers. 'Deal,
Mrs Gold. Italy, here we come.'

* * *

The next morning after dropping Bobby at school and arriving
home, I saw an army of men in the driveway. Trucks were parked
everywhere. People were taking photos of the house and garden.
No one even noticed I was there.

Julie was inside at her usual place at the breakfast bar talking
to some people. There were drawings all over my table, builders
were measuring up, and surveyors were walking around.

'Fran.' Julie waved me over. 'Come and see this. It's a great idea.'

The builder and the architect had decided it was pointless to
make the bottom of the house larger. It would look odd, and so
they had decided to build a full extension all the way up, including
another couple of bedrooms.

When I looked stressed, Julie just laughed it off and waved me
out of the way. The one thing I did notice, though, was, apart from
one empty bottle of wine on the table, there was also a coffee cup
at Julie's side. She was keeping her promise.

Work was underway. And to be honest, I was glad to go to work
and be out of it, unlike Julie. She relished it all. Julie even stayed
over some nights so she could be there bright and early the next
morning, organising the proceedings like a site manager.

Ralph was a little perturbed. Julie had told him she would be
staying at my house more, and he had accepted it. But I'm not sure
he believed it. If she wasn't there and hadn't been spending nights
at my house, then where was she?

One day the men surprised us all and arrived at the house unannounced. Elle opened the door and let them in. In they walked, like the three musketeers. Julie wasn't to be seen, and Ralph looked uncomfortable.

Then, as if by magic, they could all hear her voice coming from upstairs, shouting at one of the builders. The look of relief on Ralph's face was a picture, even though some of the language wasn't lady-like.

When Julie eventually came down and saw Ralph, she looked surprised but seemed to understand why he had come. Sometimes you don't need words, and she had been known to disappear before apparently.

She took his arm and walked him towards the scaffolding, showing him all she was doing. Even though it looked an absolute mess, he seemed interested, not in what was going on but to hear his wife all worked up about her new project.

Then she told him that, in a few weeks, we were all going to Italy.

I looked at Tony. Out of the blue, he picked up the dog lead and suggested we go for a walk on the seafront. We walked along casually, like old friends, with intermittent stops while Susie emptied her bladder. Tony seemed to be enjoying himself.

We stopped and bought two coffees from a stall on the seafront. Sitting down on a wooden bench looking out at the sea, we drank our coffees while Susie ran around.

'We have to go, you know,' he said, looking straight ahead. 'To Italy.'

'I know, but don't you think they're going to sense something is wrong when we don't share a bedroom? I thought you said you were going to come up with something. We can't pretend to argue all the time just so one of us can sleep on the sofa.'

I could see he was trying to think his way out of this, but there wasn't a way out.

'Can't we just be adult about this, Francesca, and share a room? I can sleep on the floor or couch or something. I don't know until we get there and see the layout of their villa. Do you fancy some chips?' He gave a weak smile and went to get some.

When he came back with the open bag, we both sat watching Susie and shared the chips. Soon enough, we were laughing and chatting like old friends, about normal day-to-day things, even my job. It was nice. It was one of those rare times we had spent together, just getting to know each other. I enjoyed his company. He held my hand as we got up from the bench and headed back to the house. It felt like the most natural thing in the world.

I knew we shouldn't have been holding hands. But after all, we were friends, and Julie was always putting her arm through mine and giving me a hug. There was no harm, surely?

Over the next few weeks, in between my shifts at work, Tony became a frequent visitor. We got into a routine of walking the dog, with or without Bobby, and sitting on 'our bench' and drinking coffee. I found myself looking forward to seeing him, hearing his warm laughter, and seeing his hair blow around in the wind. I was also disappointed on the days he didn't come.

I kept reminding myself that it was only friendship. And on our usual evenings out at some party or dinner, I left him to his own devices around midnight. It still tormented me, though, wondering what he was doing once I'd left.

The house was coming together brilliantly, and it looked great! I telephoned my mam and gave her daily updates on how things were going and did a little soul-searching along the way.

One day, Julie came in waving airline tickets. 'Here are yours, Tony's, and Bobby's. We leave on Monday.'

Tony had sorted mine and Bobby's passports out. It seemed we were set to go.

Julie certainly hadn't given us much time to change our minds. Today was Thursday, and she wanted to shop and buy a whole new wardrobe for the trip. In the meantime, my credit card had arrived, and Julie decided it needed a good spending spree to break it in.

I had never been abroad before, so the prospect was a little daunting but exciting at the same time. Bobby had boasted to all of his friends at school that we were going to Italy, even though he had no idea where it was.

Italy with Tony, I mused to myself. A belated honeymoon. It sounded too good to be true. The excitement bubbled away inside me regardless. 'Italy,' I said out loud. 'What magic will you bring...?' This was an adventure of a lifetime.

16

ITALY

Bobby loved flying. We travelled first class, which seemed to make all the difference. Julie and Ralph had their son Josh with them, too, and explained that he had a few learning difficulties, including a bad stammer. He was quiet and shy but watched Bobby, looking at his books that were far too young for him. He would point things out to Bobby and correct his reading. They seemed to be on a level, although Josh was six years older than Bobby.

A chauffeur was at the airport to pick us up in an open-topped Rolls-Royce. The sun was hot, and as we drove to the coast, Julie pointed out places in the area she thought might be of interest to me. I stared, open-mouthed. Everything was beautiful.

What Julie had said was a 'villa' was more like a castle. I supposed I should have known better. It had a cook, a maid, and a nanny. The swimming pools were enormous and surrounded by marble. I had never seen anything like it. On arrival, we were met by the butler, who welcomed us and took our bags. You had to admit, Julie Gold did things in style.

We settled in and were told to pick our own rooms. I saw Tony and Jake look at each other. They had obviously discussed this.

Looking in the rooms, we found there was no need to worry. The rooms were more like luxury apartments, with corner sofas that unfolded into beds. And then Julie saved the day.

'Personally,' she said, 'I like my own bedroom. Ralph snores, and I like my own dressing space.'

I agreed and was given my own room too. Apparently, it was the modern thing to do!

There was a strange awkwardness surrounding Sharon and Jake. They seemed to be bickering a lot, and you could sense something off in the atmosphere. We left them to it while we went to explore outside.

Bobby wanted to go into the pool, so we all got into our swimwear. Josh sat at the side with his feet in the water. I must confess, when we all sat at the poolside and Tony got out of the water after playing with Bobby, I saw for the first time the golden hairs on his chest that led all the way down to his stomach. The drops of water seemed to glisten on them, making me thankful I was wearing large sunglasses; the fantasies I was having when I saw him weren't exactly lady-like! I could feel my face going red with embarrassment.

* * *

The next few days were a whirlwind of swimming, eating out, and clubbing. We took the boys to a water-themed fun park and did the whole sightseeing thing. Of course, Julie stopped at all of the well-known designer shops and bought herself yet another wardrobe of clothes. Sharon had declined the shopping trip and just seemed to sit around the pool. It was obvious she didn't want to be there.

When we arrived back at the villa one day, I noticed the men were raising their voices in some sort of debate. When we walked into the lounge, they stopped talking. Julie and I, along with the boys, made ourselves scarce. There was something definitely wrong, and I felt a sense of foreboding. The Italian sunshine seemed to cloud over, reflecting the mood.

Sharon eventually gave in to the awkwardness between her and Jake and made her excuses and left Italy. Once she'd gone, the atmosphere seemed better. Jake even perked up a little, enjoying himself in the pool and on the excursions Julie had arranged. She even took us to Rome to see the Vatican.

It was past midnight one night when I went to get a drink from the kitchen. I noticed the swimming pool lights were on. I opened the patio doors and walked out to find Tony lying on a sun lounger wearing a bathrobe. He had a drink in his hand, and I could see he was deep in thought. When I walked up to him, he didn't even notice me until I spoke.

'Are you okay, Tony?' I felt like I was intruding.

He gave me a well-rehearsed smile and told me he was fine. I started to leave when he spoke again. 'Don't go, Francesca. Stay a while. Take a seat.' He pulled one of the sun loungers closer to him, and I sat down.

He reached his hand over the arm of the sun lounger and held my hand while we sat in silence.

'I have to go to Naples tomorrow,' he said in a low whisper. 'Would you come with me, on your own I mean? This isn't some indecent proposal. I'm just asking if you'd like to come.'

I could hardly see him under the umbrella, but I felt this was not the time to ask why. So I just said, 'Yes, I would like that. The nanny can look after the boys, and I think Julie wants a day with Ralph on their own anyway. So yes, I would like to come with you.'

Tony released my hand, and I felt that was my cue to leave. I stood up and left him sitting quietly by the pool, deep in thought.

I got up early the next morning, showered, and was ready to go.

When I walked into the kitchen to make some coffee, I was surprised to see Tony. He too was dressed and ready to leave.

It was still cool when we left, although the sun had risen. We chatted but not about where we were going or anything important. Eventually, we turned into a lane surrounded by lots of green fields, farmland even. At the end of it was a large house. If we had been in France, I would have called it a chateau.

My curiosity was rising. Tony turned into the driveway. I could see groups of people standing in the nearby fields, busily working. Suddenly it dawned on me. This was a vineyard. Had Tony really brought me all this way to buy some expensive wine?

The door to the house opened before we got to it, and a middle-aged woman in a blue dress and white apron stood there with a big smile on her face and threw her arms open wide. Tony walked into them, returning her a hug, and immediately started speaking fluent Italian. The woman then put her arms around me and stood aside for us to enter.

Tony had perked up massively. He had a beaming smile on his face and seemed to know exactly where he was going in this large house. We walked into a small lounge. Sitting in a rocking chair near the mantelpiece and dressed in a black lace dress was an old lady with white hair.

She immediately broke into a smile and stood up. 'Antonias, my boy, come here.' He was immediately enveloped in her arms.

It was strange. When I looked at this very smart lady, possibly in her seventies, I saw she had Tony's blue eyes. This was family.

They both spoke excitedly in Italian for a few minutes, and then she beckoned to me. 'Sit down, Francesca. You must think us very rude. But it has been a long time.'

I sat on the pretty floral sofa. The sitting room was bright and airy, but I was perplexed. This woman seemed to know who I was.

Tony had his arms around her shoulders and was kissing her on the cheek.

'This, Francesca, is my grandmother.' He seemed quite excited, like a young boy.

She walked towards me and put her arms around me. I was shocked, because he had never mentioned he had a family. I didn't even know he could speak fluent Italian. But then that was silly. He was Italian, so of course he would speak Italian. Being in Italy was like a busman's holiday to Tony. He had come home.

The lady who had greeted us at the door, Rosanna, came in with coffee and cakes. She was not only the maid but also a sort of housekeeper-cum-companion. I was very confused. It seemed Tony's grandmother owned the vineyard and was known to sell famous wines to all well-known outlets. She knew an awful lot about me and asked about Bobby. She assured me that she spoke to Tony often on the telephone, and she apologised for not being at the wedding. She had arthritis and didn't travel well.

Rosanna cooked us lunch, and we sat chatting. I sensed Tony would want to spend some time alone with his grandmother to chat, so I asked if I could look around her gardens. I could see Tony was grateful that I had made my excuses.

The roses were in full bloom, and the perfume that came off them filled the garden. I walked around in the sunshine and then noticed a small church. It had half a dozen windows, all stained glass with biblical saints on them. I waked into the cool entrance. There were half a dozen pews and, before them, an altar with a large brass crucifix and a statue of Jesus Christ. It was beautiful, peaceful, and calm. The stained-glass windows filled the church with a rainbow of colours as the sun shone through them.

Suddenly, I heard a cough. When I turned, I saw Tony and his grandmother standing there behind me. I felt I should apologise for going in without permission. His grandmother walked towards me slowly, resting on her walking stick.

'You should wear something on your head when you come in here,' she said. Her voice warm and friendly. 'Here, take this.' In her hand was a white headscarf made of lace. She handed it to me and then put one on her own head.

She sat down in one of the pews and held her hand out to me. 'Do you like my little church, Francesca? Goodness, when I say your name, you sound more Italian than I do. Francesca Lambrianu.' She nodded and looked at Tony. When she said it in her Italian accent, it sounded completely different.

'It's beautiful,' I said, looking around. 'I could get married here. It feels special.' Then, I looked at them both and blushed. That had been a stupid thing to say.

She seemed very pleased and then explained to me that she had got married in this church. 'You should come back on your anniversary, Antonias, and have a blessing here. Then I can watch you take your vows.'

I actually felt sick to my stomach lying to his grandmother – and in church as well. We wouldn't be together on our wedding anniversary; our year would be up. I noticed Tony blush slightly and look down at the slate floor.

Tony left me chatting away to his grandmother, who insisted I call her Miriam, or Nonna. She was a lovely, warm and friendly woman, who obviously adored Tony. She caught my stare as I looked at the numerous photo frames on the mantelpiece. There was a photo of a pretty woman holding a baby in her arms, standing near a man.

'Antonias' mother and my son,' was all she said as she looked at the photo herself.

I knew I shouldn't have, but now the subject was brought up, I couldn't help myself. 'Where are Tony's parents? Do they live here as well?'

She paused and then answered, 'Both in heaven, my dear. Has Antonias never told you?' She seemed surprised. 'My son died first. And then Annette took Antonias away. I never heard from her again.' She stopped herself to think for a moment. 'I searched for my grandson for years and eventually found him in England. Thankfully, he had been fostered by Elle, who had also fostered Jake.' A tear fell on her cheek, and she wiped it away.

I secretly hoped she hadn't noticed the stunned look on my face and my jaw dropping. Elle was Tony's foster mother? Now that made a lot of sense. I remembered she had been on the official childminding register.

My brain was spinning. Tony had been fostered?

This was earth-shattering news and revealed a totally different side to the man I had come to know. Tony presented himself so confidently in his clubs. Yet his history was a different story. No wonder he trusted Elle and she was so familiar with him. She was his mother figure. Today was turning out to be an insight into the man behind the mask.

When Tony came back into the room and interrupted us, Miriam fell silent. 'Antonias,' she said after a moment, 'why don't you take one of the mopeds and show Francesca around the vineyard? Take a picnic while I have a nap.'

I told her we should be leaving and if she was tired, then we should go. But she seemed a little perturbed by this and apologised for being an old woman who got tired quickly.

'This is your home, Francesca. Why leave because I am going to have a nap? All of this will be yours one day, maybe even your children's.' She looked at us both and paused.

Tony assured her that we would stay a little longer, and he would show me around the vineyard while she took her nap.

When we were alone, I told him that I didn't like pretending in front of her. It didn't feel right.

He smiled and nodded. 'I know. Believe me, Francesca, I don't like it either.'

We got a small moped out of one of the garages. Sitting behind him with my arms around his waist, I could feel his well-muscled body. He had changed from his shirt and trousers into a white vest and jeans. He looked more Italian than ever. I had to keep reminding myself he wasn't mine, and this wasn't real.

Workmen and women in the fields shouted to Tony, and he would steer the bike towards them and speak to them, introducing me as his wife. They all seemed so pleased to meet me. As nice as this day was, it was full of deceit and lies, and I hated it. I was starting to wish I hadn't come.

Back at the house, he hugged his grandmother and Rosanna. He held my hand as they walked us to the door.

'My Antonias, what a beautiful couple you make. Make sure you both come back soon,' his grandmother said with a tear in her eye as she bid us farewell.

He kissed me on the cheek and then went towards his grandmother and gave her another kiss, saying something to her in his native tongue.

Driving back, he hardly spoke, and I dozed off. It had been a long day. When I woke, I realised I was lying against him, and he had his arm around me as he drove. I sat up and apologised; he said nothing.

The scent of his aftershave on me made me smile and I realised how much I liked Antonias. He was a beautiful, warm, friendly man. Unlike Tony Lambrianu, who could seem very cold and calculating sometimes. I felt closer to him now, than I ever had. In fact, dare I say it, I felt like his wife.

17

IRELAND

The men had left on business before I got up the next morning. I felt it was a shame Tony hadn't felt the need to say goodbye after our trip to see his grandmother. But that was him all over. I felt deflated; our bond was over too soon. After a day in dream land, I had been brought back to earth with a bang. Stupid Francesca, always daydreaming. I meant nothing to him, and nothing was going to stand in the way of business. Now he was being Tony Lambrianu again.

Julie, the boys, and I just carried on as normal. Until the night that changed everything...

I remember the next few days as if they were yesterday. They were a whirlwind of emotion and upheaval. I had been kept in the dark and Julie had deserted me and so had the men in our lives. As I found out later, the stark truth was earth shattering.

I recalled how Julie had burst into my bedroom. 'There has been some trouble at the business meeting, and I have to go.' She hadn't said where she was going. 'I'll ring you as soon as I can. Francesca, do you trust me?' She had seemed very serious and unlike the Julie I had come to know.

'Yes, I do, Julie,' I'd answered.

She had nodded. 'Good, because I need your help. When I call you, tell the staff they can have a couple of days off for all their hard work. Call Elle and ask her to come and look after the kids. Trust me, Fran. I will be back.' With only that for an explanation, she had left.

I'd waited for her telephone call. I was worried and nervous, and the clock never seemed to move. Eventually, the telephone rang. 'We're on our way home. Get rid of the staff, like I said. And when you're out by the pool, shout for Ralph, Tony, and Jake. I know this sounds crazy, Fran. But I'm relying on you.'

Firstly, I had telephoned Elle and asked her to come and help out with the boys. She hadn't asked any questions, for fear of being overheard by the builders. And to be honest, I didn't have any answers. I'd told the staff we were all going sightseeing, so they might as well have some time to themselves, instead of hanging around here. I'd hoped I sounded convincing. So there it was, just me and the boys.

I sat there with the television turned up loudly, the boys shouting around the pool, and me shouting to an imaginary Ralph, Tony and Jake. It seemed ridiculous.

Thankfully, to break the monotony, Elle had turned up later that afternoon. We went into the bedroom so we could have some privacy away from the boys, and I explained to her what I knew, which wasn't a lot.

'Well, let's get things sorted, shall we?' she'd said in a matter-of-fact way. She went into the kitchen and started cooking up a meal for the boys. Bobby had been pleased to see her and had lots of things to tell her. By then, I'd been frantic. There had been no more telephone calls from Julie, and my imagination was getting the better of me.

'Stop pacing, Fran. You will make yourself ill,' Elle had told me.

'You knew they were no angels, and they have got into a spot of bother. Let's just wait and see.' She'd seemed quite offhand about it all. But I could see she was concerned. After all, Tony and Jake were her sons, weren't they?

At last, they had all turned up, covered in blood. I hadn't expected anything like this. Once back at the villa, Julie had the car parked as closely to the doors as possible, and I saw Tony and Jake get out quickly. Then I watched them carry Ralph on a sunbed, using it as a stretcher. Tony looked as though he had been to hell and back.

When I saw them, I paled. What the hell was this?

'Take him into the bedroom,' said Julie. 'Fran, did you get rid of all of the staff?'

'Yes, I did as you said and gave them a couple of days off. Elle is here.' I looked at Tony. 'Are you okay?' I didn't know what to say, other than I was relieved to see him.

I took in the sight before me. Ralph was bandaged and covered in blood. Tony was also bandaged and both he and Jake were bloodstained. Julie was barking orders at everyone. Apart from that, everyone smelt of fish!

Tony looked up at my worried face. 'I'm just tired. I need to lie down.' He walked off in the direction of his bedroom. Suddenly, he turned. 'Where is Elle? Is she here?' He didn't wait for an answer.

Julie organised for a doctor to come and see Ralph. The doctor checked him over and gave him some more morphine. 'The wounds are clean, but he has lost a lot of blood. It's best to keep him sedated.'

Julie lit a cigarette. I had never seen her smoke before. 'Will he live, doctor?' She was sitting in the lounge, waiting for the prognosis. Good strong Julie – she had held all of this together. She must have been shattered.

'Yes, Mrs Gold, he's out of the woods now. Now he needs time to heal. Call me if you need me.' The doctor left some medication and left.

After a shower and a hot meal, Julie, Tony and Jake had their own meeting. They were all feeling a little better now. I guessed the surroundings helped. Elle was in charge of the boys, keeping them busy. They seemed oblivious to everything that had happened, and Elle never mentioned what was going on under her nose.

Tony came to see me. He looked battered and bruised, but he was alive at least.

Everything seemed surreal.

He put his arms around me. 'I'm sorry, Francesca. I'm sorry for dragging you into all of this,' was all he said.

'Do you realise, Tony, you never even said goodbye to me? That could have been my last memory of you.' I don't know why I said it, but I was upset and had been worried sick. 'I want to know what happened, and I mean the truth. You all know, yet I am expected to just accept it and ask no questions.' My worry and anxiety were boiling over into anger. He didn't trust me, no one did, and yet I felt like a puppet when they needed me. 'No lies Tony. I am your wife and you tell me the truth or I am on the next flight out!'

I realised that when I had seen him deep in thought, that night by the pool, and he'd asked me to go and visit his grandmother with him, Tony had already accepted that he might not return from the excursion he had undertaken with Ralph. He had known all along it was going to turn nasty and how serious it was. He had gone to say his goodbyes. The very thought made my blood run cold. He had travelled all that way, for a last goodbye to his grandmother, but he had never thought to say goodbye to me. I felt heartbroken and now I was up to my neck in it along with Julie.

'You're right Fran.' Holding onto his ribs, he sighed and rolled his eyes to the ceiling. 'You deserve an explanation. We walked into an ambush. If it wasn't for Jake following Ralph's orders about calling Julie if we got into trouble, we wouldn't be here. She saved us all Fran.' Tony rubbed his face with his hands. 'Ralph has an old partner in Ireland who has been sort of running things out there for him. But, in Ralph's name, he has been creaming his percentage off the top and selling hard-core drugs to patrons of his clubs. It needed sorting; it was getting out of hand. That's what we were discussing the day you and Julie walked in. Ralph had to go and insisted it was his problem and he would sort it. Jake and I argued that we were partners, so we should all go. And thank God we did Fran.' Reaching out for my hand, Tony squeezed it hard. I heard a choke deep within his throat.

I saw Julie's cigarettes on the table and lit one for Tony, who looked as if he needed one. 'Go on Tony, I'm listening. What happened next?'

Exhaling the smoke into the air, he gave me a weak smile. 'Fortunately, Ralph wanted to hold the meeting at some office building he owned, and on arrival this Paddy bloke was sat at the head of the table with four or five henchmen. He had come for a fight and they were tooled up with guns.' The shocked look on my face must have spoken volumes because he smiled again. 'We had guns too but we were outnumbered. After their preliminary talk, Ralph accused Paddy of drug dealing in his name. Paddy knew who I was and took great delight in calling me pretty boy. He pissed me off big time,' Tony spat out. 'Next time it will just be him and me.'

I took a sharp intake of breath. 'You're not going back?'

Tony gave me a reassuring smile, which meant nothing. 'Do you want to hear this or not Francesca?'

I nodded my head and waited for the worst of it.

'Paddy was the first to pull out his gun and I jumped in the way to protect Ralph, but the bullet caught his arm. Jake took out his gun and fired it at one of Paddy's men. I shot two of the other men in quick succession. It was becoming a blood bath, an absolute massacre. Blood was pouring from Ralph; he tried reaching for his own gun, but he couldn't get up, that was when Paddy held a gun to my head and told me to drop my own. He also had a knife and said he was going to slice me up and spoil my pretty face, the bastard! Jake, as always' – Tony half smiled – 'came to my rescue and pointed his gun at Paddy. Instead of firing at me, Paddy shot Ralph in the leg. Almost immediately, his suit turned crimson with blood. I pushed Paddy, taking my chances and reaching for my gun, but he fired first. Thankfully it missed me and he shot one of his own men. Then I heard a shout from one of Paddy's men, saying that he could hear police sirens. Paddy hit me with the gun across the head so hard I fell to the floor, then they started punching and kicking me. I fell unconscious. They ran for it, leaving Jake behind to face the music with two unconscious men and several dead bodies.' Tony took another drag on his cigarette, and I felt sick inside. Although I didn't want to hear any more, I urged him on. I hadn't been married a year and now I had very nearly become a widow! 'Ralph had told us to call Julie if things went wrong, and to be fair Fran, we thought that was a stupid idea. What the fuck was she going to do? We were in Ireland. But, with nothing to lose, Jake did. Years ago, Ralph had had a secret lift put in to take him up to a helipad on the roof. No one but him and Julie knew about it, not even Paddy. And to open the lift door, you pressed the dimmer on the light switch... Clever bastard, Ralph Gold.' Tony shook his head and smiled in admiration.

'Clever! For getting you all nearly killed,' I snapped. 'I don't call that clever, Tony.'

'Shush, they'll hear you.' Putting his finger to my lips to stop my outburst he smiled again. 'It's our line of work. You knew I didn't work nine to five for Christ's sake and sometimes it involves risks. Let me finish.'

I felt like crying but wanted to remain strong. My emotions were all over the place.

Squeezing my hand again, Tony carried on. 'No sooner had Jake telephoned Julie than she sent a helicopter for us all! Poor Jake had to drag us into that lift. How he did it is anyone's guess. Fear and adrenalin I suppose. He'd fastened his belt around Ralph's leg to stop the blood flow. Jake told me that the helicopter flew us to a private aerodrome and who should be there but Julie, wearing a black wig by all accounts!' Tony tried making light of it, but I wasn't interested in joking around.

'She had a doctor there, who took the bullets out of Ralph and saw to me. Then a captain of a trawler called Roland came in; Julie seemed to know him well and he brought us all back to Italy on his fishing boat.' Tony laughed and held his ribs. 'I've spoken to Julie about the mess we left behind and she says there is no mess. Apparently the man who shouted to Paddy that they had to leave was Ralph's man on the inside. Once we were all in that helicopter, that bloke threw two hand grenades into the place to blow it up. We had to get back to Italy and leave the way we came, through the airlines. It was our only alibi. The rest you know Francesca. Thank you for helping. Thank you for saving us all.'

My eyes brimmed with tears. I had wanted the truth and I'd got it. Part of me was pleased that he'd told me but the other half of me was angry. I might never have seen him again and would never know what had happened. I overcame the sick feeling in the pit of my stomach. If Julie could be strong, then so could I. The only difference was she'd obviously had more practice.

'I'd better go and see how Ralph is getting on.' Standing up, I could feel my body trembling, and my legs felt weak after listening to this horror story. Tony looked confused when I left him sitting there, but there was nothing else to say.

* * *

Julie and I stayed by Ralph's bedside over the next couple of days. We mopped his feverish brow during his delirium and took turns nursing him. Elle kept the boys busy and cooked all the food. She gave everyone time to rest and gather their thoughts.

Late in the evening, when the boys had gone to bed, Julie came into the lounge where we were all sitting. Ralph seemed over the worst and had opened his eyes. Elle was spoon-feeding him her special broth.

'Right, listen up.' Julie, again, was taking charge. 'We all have to go home now. Here are my plans, and I want no arguing. We need stronger alibis than we have, and I have to get Ralph through customs with two bullet holes in his body.' She sat down and lit a cigarette.

I reached over and squeezed her hand. 'No arguments, Julie. Whatever you say.'

She smiled and squeezed my hand back.

The plans seemed simple enough. Jake was to fly back to England to make up with Sharon and host a very large charity party at the club. Then she looked at Tony and me.

'I need you two to be arrested,' she announced very calmly.

'Arrested? No way. This has nothing to do with me. What about Bobby?'

She didn't seem to be listening. 'I want you to go to the night-club area opposite the beach in town, where all of the young tourists go for the half-price booze and the night life. The police are always patrolling there.' She looked at Tony, who was listening closely to what she was saying. 'I want you to have sex on the beach. Make as much noise as possible. Grab the attention of the crowds, which, in turn, will attract the attention of the police.'

I stood up. This was going too far. She wanted us to have sex in public so not only the drunken crowds could see and hear us, but the police would also arrest us?

Tony put his hand up to stop my outburst. 'Go on, Julie. I like it,' said Tony. He was nodding at her, and I could see he was thinking. 'Listen Francesca, if we're arrested, then we're still in Italy and have been the whole time. Who can argue with that?' Tony had a smug expression on his face.

'Excuse me, you two, what about me? Why can't I go back with the boys like Jake? I can't have sex in public. No way.'

It seemed neither Julie nor Tony were listening to me. Their minds were made up.

Julie lit another cigarette and blew smoke into the air. 'Do you want your husband to have an alibi, Fran?'

My husband? I looked at Tony, waiting for him to say something. But he was silent. I could see the pleading look in his eyes, begging me to go along with it.

'Come on, Francesca. You wouldn't be the first tourists to have sex on the beach while a little drunk.' She laughed.

'What if we get thrown into prison? What about Bobby?' I pleaded. Panic was rising inside of me.

'Trust me,' said Julie. She handed me a bottle of vodka and told me to go and get dressed into something that would make it look as though I was on a night out.

'What? You want us to do it tonight? Now?' I asked.

Julie told me to take a large gulp of the vodka. I did as she said. It tasted horrible.

I looked up at Tony. He was already following her instructions to get dressed as though we were having a night out.

Once ready, we got into the car, and the chauffeur took us to the other side of town. It was full of cheap hotels and people still in their teens and early twenties on holiday having a good time. The clubs were all lit up, and they had bar staff on the pavements offering passers-by free shots of alcohol if they went into their club.

It was loud. People were standing outside the clubs, smoking, drinking and gathered around in groups talking. Some were even singing football anthems. As we drove along the main high street, each club looked the same, full of people partying the night away.

'This will do.' Tony indicated for the chauffeur to stop the car. I was frightened and still holding on tightly to the bottle of vodka Julie had given me.

Across the road from the clubs was a wall, with steps at the side of it leading down to the beach. This was probably where all the partiers came to sleep when they had drunk too much.

Tony led me onto the beach and walked along it near the sea. 'Take another large sip, Francesca.' I knew he was nervous and possibly felt awkward asking me to do something like this.

It was dark, but the beach was lit up by the lights from the club. It was the early hours of the morning, yet it was warm. I took a large gulp of the vodka. It seemed to burn my chest. I watched as Tony knelt down on the soft dry sand. He held out his hand for mine. When I knelt down beside him, he took off his jacket and discarded it, and started undoing the belt on his trousers. I watched him closely. All of this meant nothing to him. All he cared about was saving his own skin.

'I can't do it, Tony. I'm sorry.'

18

THE ALIBI

I took another sip of the vodka. I felt sorry for him. In fact, I felt sorry for all of them. They were all relying on me now, after everything they had been through.

'Believe me Francesca, if you don't want to do this, that's fine, I understand, I really do. Sit here beside me.' He smiled up at me and I knew I was sunk. 'It doesn't matter Fran, I'm sure we can come up with something else.' His words were said in a hushed tone. This wasn't a lie or an alibi; we were together, and he needed me.

The vodka must have started working on me because I sat down and looked up at him, staring into those blue eyes. He leaned his head close to mine and rubbed my nose with his. The vodka was making me feel light-headed and giddy. Dawn was approaching, and the gentle lapping of the waves on the shore held an atmosphere all of its own.

He kissed my lips, gently at first, and then again. I put my arms around his neck, running my hands through his hair. 'Antonias, my beautiful Italian gladiator,' I said.

He looked down at me and our eyes met. This wasn't pretence, this was passion.

This time, the kiss was ardent. Everyone in the distance seemed to disappear and everything I had felt but held back came pouring out. We were locked in each other's arms, kissing each other with wild abandon. Tony nuzzled my neck and started to speak in Italian. I knew *amore* meant love, but that was as far as my Italian went.

My dress was pulled above my head, and I felt my breasts tingle against the golden hairs on his chest that I had admired what now seemed a lifetime ago by the poolside. Clothing was flung in every direction. Nothing mattered any more. I had nearly lost him, and we were hungry for each other. Our bodies were doing the talking. He was kissing my breasts, and suddenly, I felt the full force of his manhood.

My whole body trembled and shook, I could feel his excitement growing, and I was responding to his every movement. This was pure heaven. We were like wild animals, hanging onto each other, afraid to let go. I wrapped my legs around his waist and felt my body tense. Then, it felt like fireworks had gone off inside of me, and I heard myself cry out. Tony flung his head back, trying to gasp some air back into his lungs. We were both panting when I heard a noise.

I looked over Tony's shoulder; standing there were two policemen.

They shone a torch at us, directly into my face. I shielded my eyes from the glare with my hands. They instructed us both to get up. I reached for my dress and put it on, while Tony pulled his trousers up. There was a huge cheer from the football supporters I had seen earlier.

The two officers were smiling and it seemed as though they were just going to let us off with a slap on the wrist. Thank God.

But Tony went out of his way to aggravate the situation, arguing with them like some drunk and asking them why they were spying on us like a couple of perverts. Didn't they have anything better to do?

I started to feel cold and shivered slightly. More people from the nightclubs came out. Obviously they had been told what was going on. A few drunks were waving their arms about and shouting about us being arrested for doing it on the beach.

Tony wouldn't let the matter drop. He put his arm around my shoulders to keep me warm and told them to get lost.

One officer knelt down and picked up the vodka bottle. They both looked at each other and then started to read us our rights. They handcuffed Tony and led us both to their police car. Tears were streaming down my face. All the people from outside the nightclubs were booing and hissing at the police officers and telling them to let us go. It was a nightmare.

At the police station, we had to state our names and have our fingerprints taken. The charges seemed to go on forever. Tony had really annoyed the two policemen, and they were throwing the book at us. Drunk and disorderly behaviour, public indecency, insulting police officers, and they even included littering the beach with the vodka bottle! All of that for a moment of passion?

We were both taken away in opposite directions and interviewed by the police. Once our statements had been made, we were put in cells for the night until they could confirm the address we had given them. We were also informed that we would be up in front of the local magistrate in the morning. I felt sick. My head was swimming, what with all the vodka I had drunk. That was the worst part. I felt sick, and suddenly I started to vomit. Then I noticed I was doing it all over the police officers' shoes!

The duty solicitor advised me to admit what I had done and apologise. That was all. I stood in court side by side with Tony. It was the first time I had seen him since last night. While I had lain on the bed in my prison cell, I'd thought back to Tony and me on the beach. I knew we'd had to make it look real to get arrested, but the emotions involved had surprised me. It had been so spontaneous, and our feelings had got the better of us.

I had feelings for Tony – possibly even love. I remembered how I had felt when Julie had said they were in trouble. I had been sick with worry. I knew now that I had felt like this for a while but had fought it, knowing Tony didn't feel the same.

Having sex on the beach with me had meant nothing to Tony. I had been an alibi with benefits. For me, being in his arms and feeling his kisses had been a magical experience.

I looked over in the courtroom and saw Julie. She gave me a little wave and a smile. It made me feel hopeful, but I was nervous about the outcome of all of this.

The magistrate waited while the charges were read out. He didn't look too pleased.

After listening to the charges, the magistrate then turned to either side of him to speak to two other magistrates. Apparently, we could appeal the charges and ask for someone from the embassy to represent us, or we could have it dealt with now. We both agreed to not prolong it any further.

Before judgement was given, the magistrate asked if there was anything we had to say. He looked at me first.

I lowered my head, ashamed. 'I'm sorry,' was all I could think of.

Now it was Tony's turn. Having heard the name Lambrianu, the magistrate had asked him if he was Italian, because the name was familiar. Given that the magistrate looked to be in his seventies and balding, I didn't imagine he was part of the club scene.

Tony gave a heartfelt speech, speaking in Italian. I would learn later that he apologised to the magistrates and then turned to the police officers who had arrested us and apologised to them. He told the magistrate that we were newly married, and he had wanted to bring me to his beautiful homeland. He waved his arm around the room, adding that it was the most beautiful and romantic place in the world. I could see everyone in the courtroom smiling and agreeing with him. Tony said he was sorry for disgracing himself and tarnishing the reputation of this beautiful place, but given the surroundings, the alcohol, and his beautiful wife... He paused.

I looked around the courtroom. I couldn't understand what Tony was saying in Italian, but his obvious remorse was clearly affecting everyone in the court.

The duty solicitor had said we might be deported. But after due consideration, the magistrate decided not to do so, as we were leaving anyway. He didn't want a fellow Italian being thrown out of his own country. Tony Lambrianu could talk the birds out of the trees. No wonder so many women – including myself – had fallen for his sweet talk!

We were given a large fine and two months suspended sentence if we were ever caught acting unlawfully in Italy again. Tony seemed to breathe a sigh of relief. The other option would have been to throw us out of the country, never to return. At least this way Tony could always go back and visit his grandmother.

Julie was waiting outside in the car for us. She was all smiles and looked really pleased with herself. 'Well done you two.' She laughed out loud. 'Bloody hell, Tony, that was one expensive moment of passion.'

Bobby ran to me when we got back to the villa. I decided there and then that I wanted to go home. Julie understood and agreed.

Once I'd packed everything, I went to the kitchen.

Tony pulled me to one side. 'I'm sorry, Francesca. I also mean thank you.' He looked embarrassed, and it was obvious he didn't know what to say.

Thankfully, Julie interrupted him. 'We're all booked on flights for tomorrow,' she announced, looking pleased with herself.

'Why not today?' I asked. 'I want to go home today.' I started to cry, what with everything that had happened.

Julie told me to take a moment by the pool to calm down. She got Tony to go into Ralph's bedroom with her and instructed him to help her carry Ralph out to the side of the pool too.

Ralph's arm was in a sling and healing okay. When he had his shirt on, you couldn't see the bandages. The main problem was his leg. He couldn't walk, and that would mean a wheelchair. How on earth were they going to explain that they needed a wheelchair?

As Tony laid Ralph by the poolside, Julie came out into the blazing sunshine holding a cricket bat and a bottle of whisky. We stood there in silence, confused. 'Okay, Ralph,' said Julie, very matter of fact. 'Here is one for the team and your alibi out of Italy.' She raised the cricket bat and hit Ralph on the leg, just below the knee. Tony and I heard the loud crack as the bone broke.

Ignoring us both, Julie shouted out for Elle to call an ambulance. I looked down at Ralph. He was howling and rolling around the floor in pain. When the ambulance came, Julie was crying and making a song and dance about Ralph being drunk and slipping.

The ambulance crew put Ralph on a stretcher, and Julie and I went in the ambulance with him. I was still in shock. Julie was as hard as nails and very devious. The hospital did X-rays and confirmed what we already knew: his shin and ankle were broken.

They put his leg into a plaster cast. I was amazed that the X-ray department never looked any higher than his shin, and they didn't need to take off his trousers because he was wearing shorts. Another one of Julie's well-thought-out plans. They gave him some painkillers and sent him home.

Julie telephoned the butler and informed him we were leaving, so he had better come back and close up the villa. Tony and I didn't really have time to talk. Personally, I think watching Julie break Ralph's leg without remorse had sent cold chills down his spine.

Ralph was given a wheelchair and was put on the aeroplane by the airport staff first. He had all the legal travelling documents to fly from the hospital. Even I had to admit, Julie had really pulled the rabbit out of the hat this time. No one questioned why Ralph couldn't walk and was in a wheelchair. His broken leg would heal, and it hid a million lies!

Walking out of the airport, we were greeted by a host of flashing lights in our faces. People were shouting out our names. The airport was full of reporters. They had heard all about Tony and me being arrested for having sex on the beach, and that caused a lot of innuendos and laughter.

They were taking photos of us both, and then they saw Ralph in his wheelchair, being pushed by a member of the airport staff. Julie made a point of moaning to the journalists how 'that drunken old fool Ralph had spoilt her holiday.' The reporters were lapping it up. This was the perfect newspaper story. Tony took my arm and marched me through the airport to the chauffeur waiting for us.

It was time for us all to go our separate ways. Julie and Ralph went in their car, while we got into ours. I couldn't believe it had all been so easy. Julie had obviously been in similar situations before. She was so calm about it all.

Tony and I couldn't discuss the last couple of days because Bobby was there. Maybe that was for the best. After all, what was there to say?

Seeing my house and familiar surroundings again seemed like heaven. Elle got out first, taking Bobby upstairs for a nap. I got out and Tony stayed in the car while the chauffeur was carrying the luggage in.

'I'll be in touch, Francesca. Get some rest. You look tired,' was all Tony said once the chauffeur got back in the car.

I was stood on the driveway, looking at him through the half-open car window. 'Where are you going?' I asked him, surprised.

'Home of course.' He smiled at me curiously, as though I had said something stupid. Of course he was going home. Where else would he be going?

'I thought you might like to come in for a while, Tony, have a coffee or something.' I felt embarrassed. It had been a stupid thing to say.

'Not now, Francesca. We'll speak soon.' He looked worn out and tired, and he still had a few fading bruises on his face.

I watched the car disappear through the gates. 'Goodbye, Antonias,' I said to myself.

* * *

Normality resumed. Except the whole scenario wasn't normal, was it? Bobby was back at school, telling everyone about his holiday and what a great time he'd had.

I was working back at the surgery, though things were a little awkward. The staff and the patients had all seen the photos in the newspapers of us all walking through the airport – me with my mysterious and famous husband, Tony Lambrianu. I think they thought I had deceived them and wasn't to be trusted. Why did I need the job, when there were other people out there who genuinely needed the money? I supposed they had a point.

The office where the staff had tea breaks went silent whenever I walked in the room. After a week of this, I'd had enough.

'When I started to work here,' I began, watching their hostile faces, 'I wasn't married to Tony. I wasn't Mrs Lambrianu, okay? I wanted you all to get to know me, Francesca. Yes, I know what they say. He's a womaniser, a club owner, and has some dodgy friends. I know he has money, but I'm an independent woman, much to his disapproval. I haven't changed. Only your opinion of me has changed.' There, I had said my piece. The rest was up to them.

I went back to the reception area and started working. Sure enough, things calmed down after that. The patients were too wrapped up in their own problems to care about me and who my husband was and the jibes from the other staff subsided; I was included in their tea breaks and gossip again. What is it they say? Today's news is tomorrow's fish and chip paper!

Julie had telephoned but had said nothing about the recent events in Italy. She'd just updated me on Ralph moaning on and how she was expected to wait on him hand and foot.

I didn't hear a word from Tony. He had obviously put it all behind him and was carrying on as before. Was it just me who was feeling the shock of what had happened? Although it felt like a lifetime away, it had been only a couple of weeks.

I carried on for Bobby's sake, and soon enough, Italy became a distant memory. The building works eventually finished and the house looked amazing.

A couple of days after the builders and decorators had left, an envelope came through the letter box. When I opened it, it was the deeds to the house. I was only supposed to receive these at the end of the year when the contract was over. This large brown envelope spoke volumes. Our deal was over. Tony had said that it might not take the full year, as things had gone so well with Ralph.

So that was his way of ending our marriage, was it? I would have thought he would have told me to my face. I was gutted and couldn't stop staring at the paperwork. After everything that had happened in Italy, this was my reward. How could he? Where was my Antonias?

I was of no use to him now and I accepted my fate. It was over. I had been wronged by a known womaniser. It wouldn't shock anyone if I divorced him, would it? Luke had divorced me when I was the innocent party. I was damned if I was going to let that happen again.

19

THE FINAL HURDLE

'Trust me, Mrs Lambrianu, you could come away from the divorce with a very nice settlement. Obviously, I know of your husband, and it's my job to advise you that you are being a little naive. You are entitled to some sort of settlement. What surprises me even more is that your husband never set up some kind of prenuptial arrangement. He was badly advised. Personally, I would have insisted on it.'

The solicitor I had employed to start my divorce proceedings was quite exasperated with the fact that I wasn't demanding half of everything Tony owned.

Sitting opposite him at his desk, I watched as he seemed to go on and on, instructing me in all kinds of ways that we should have a meeting with Tony's solicitors or at least take it to court.

'Mr Sanderson, I do understand what you are telling me. But I assure you, I know what I'm doing. As for wanting more out of my husband, I have my house and money in the bank, and I also have a job. It would be unfair and greedy of me to want more. After all, we haven't been married very long, and my husband has built his empire and worked very hard to make any money long before I came along. Also, as you say, he trusted me. And I am not prepared to abuse that trust and look like a gold-digger.'

Mr Sanderson let out a deep sigh of despair. 'Very well, Mrs Lambrianu. Let's get this straight. You have the deeds to your house, and Mr Lambrianu is to make no claim on the marital home. You are asking that he pay the legal fees for the divorce and to inform him that you will be changing your name back to your previous surname. Was that your maiden name?'

'No, Mr Sanderson. It is my previous married name – the same name as my son. I have been married before. And Tony would be more than generous letting me keep my home and money. He would be leaving me without debt.'

I watched as Mr Sanderson eyed me up. He couldn't quite make me out. I was either hell to live with or there was something very wrong with me to have two failed marriages in such a short space of time. I wasn't sure if he pitied me or thought my husbands were well rid of me!

'Very well, Mrs Lambrianu, I will get this all written up and write to Mr Lambrianu advising him to instruct a solicitor of his own. That way, we can start proceedings immediately, if that is what you really want.'

I stood up and shook his hand. 'Thank you, Mr Sanderson. I'll wait to hear from you.'

There, I had done it. Tony had said that I was to file for the divorce when the time came, preferably for adultery, because that would be quicker, and he would take all of the blame.

I had the deeds to the house, and Tony had said that I would only receive them when the contract was over. As it had been a month since I had heard anything from him, I guessed the contract was over.

It saddened me that Tony hadn't felt the need to say something or even shake my hand goodbye. I don't know what I expected, but it had just come to a standstill. I was back to square one; only this time, I was a lot better off than I had been with Luke.

All the decorating was finished, and the place was completely transformed. The kitchen alone was the size of a house and led through to a full circular conservatory. The garden at the side of the conservatory, which was smaller and more intimate than the others was a basic square lawn with surrounding borders full of little rose bushes in an array of colours. At the very far corner was a cherry blossom tree for shade if needed. I had wanted my own little bit of garden just for myself to potter around in, and this was what they had come up with. Beautiful.

The rest of the extension had included another bedroom en suite and walk-in dressing rooms. The house had always been beautiful. But all this, even down to the soft pink chiffon curtains Julie had had the designers put around my four-poster bed, made it look even more feminine and relaxing.

Bobby's bedroom had gone beyond all expectations. The designers had installed a black carpet with the yellow Batman logo on it and all the walls had been painted with wipe-clean paint. You could wash and wipe away all those fingerprints without washing the paint off. He had walk-in wardrobes, so no clothes were scattered all over the place. Of course, the pièce de résistance was the large double bed with a Batman headboard.

They had even organised a playroom, so all his car racing tracks and Lego buildings didn't have to be dismantled and put away. A large television was on the walls and had all of Bobby's consoles fitted around it.

Julie had gone that extra mile and had one of my bedroom walls fully mirrored. She had stated, tongue-in-cheek, that it was easier seeing your evening dresses from all angles. Then she had given me one of her cheeky smiles and a wink! All in all, it was a show house.

The cellar was huge, and I hadn't really known what to do with it. Julie decided to get the builders to halve it so that one half was filled with racks of expensive wines and champagnes, something I was never going to use. It would take me years to get through all of those.

Julie had been like a naughty schoolgirl when it came to the other half of the cellar. It was apparently a secret, so much so that I wasn't allowed down there. When the workmen had finished, I was led down the stairs by Julie who gave a loud triumphant round of applause and left me to gaze upon her creation.

She had got the designers and builders to turn it into a men's drinking room. It looked almost like a pub or a gentlemen's club. There were pool tables, a fully stocked bar, lager pumps, and even barrels underneath the bar. A large television dominated one wall with all of the sports channels you could possibly dream of. Consoles were fitted up and scattered around. There were tables and chairs and even a poker table. This was a man's paradise. It was amazing. But there was a problem, wasn't there? I didn't have a man to put in paradise.

She had been all excited when she had chatted on about it being somewhere for Tony and the guys to relax when at home, without being under our feet. She had drummed her fingers on her lips with a pensive look on her face. She couldn't decide whether to show Tony now or make it into a birthday or Christmas present for him. Then she had asked me the unthinkable. 'By the way, Fran, when is Tony's birthday?'

I had been rooted to the spot. It was such a simple question, but it was one I didn't have the answer to. How ridiculous. Dear God, I was married to man, and I didn't even know when his birthday was. Even if he had mentioned it, I didn't remember, what with everything else I had to think about. I knew how old he was. He was exactly ten years older than me, but the month and date?

Blushing slightly, I had made my excuses about needing the loo and ran upstairs. Searching through a folder that I kept all of my personal paperwork in, like mine and Bobby's birth certificates, I had found what I was looking for: my marriage certificate to Tony! Phew! There it was: his date of birth in black and white. Relief washed over me.

Quickly flushing the toilet, I ran back downstairs and composed myself. 'Sorry about that, call of nature. You were saying about Tony's birthday?'

'Blimey Fran, when you need to go, you really need to go, don't you?' She laughed. 'Yes, I was asking when Tony's birthday is.'

'August the 15th; he's a Leo,' I said triumphantly.

Julie smiled. 'The lion, eh? Leader of the pack. Well, I'm a Virgo the virgin!' She burst out laughing. 'So all that astrology stuff counts for nothing, doesn't it.'

I laughed along with her and mentally, I was relieved I had just dodged another bullet and got myself out of an embarrassing scrape.

I recalled how, during all of the building works, Tony and I had started to talk properly, how we'd walk along the beach with Bobby while walking Susie – anything to escape the dust, noise, and Julie barking orders at the workmen. It seemed to me only I had seen those times as special, because Tony had not wanted to do it since we'd got home. I knew I was in a confused state. I had developed feelings for him, but I wasn't sure if it was out of habit from seeing him so often or if I fancied him like so many other women.

Tony had spent all of his life being charming. It had all become second nature. He probably didn't even realise how it affected the women in his life. Or if he did, he didn't care.

* * *

Julie came to see me. Only this time, I noticed she wasn't her usual bubbly self. She looked slightly agitated, as though she had something on her mind. Elle, who was there baking Bobby's favourite cakes, cast a glance towards me. It was obvious to both of us that something was wrong.

'Okay, Julie. What's wrong?'

'Oh, Fran. Is it that obvious? Well, Ralph hasn't noticed yet. He's too wrapped up in himself. He gets chauffeured back and forth to see Tony and Jake.' She stopped, clearly thinking. 'Oh God, here goes. I'm going to say it out loud. I'm pregnant.' Julie looked at us both, waiting for our reactions.

Elle looked at me. She took her hands out of the mixing bowl full of flour and butter and started wiping them on a towel. We were both stunned. Whatever we had imagined was wrong, this wasn't it.

'For God's sake, you two, say something,' Julie shouted at us both. She looked like a woman in despair.

I trod carefully. 'Is this good news or bad news, Julie? How many months do you think you are?'

She didn't look any different. She hadn't put on any noticeable weight, although now I thought about it, she hadn't been drinking at all. She hadn't even mentioned she'd been to the club.

'It's a bloody disaster, Fran. For a man who said he couldn't get around quickly, he moved pretty sharpish when I gave him the nod towards the bedroom.' Now she was strutting around the kitchen like a chicken without a head. She was standing by the breakfast bar, in her white trouser suit and high-heeled shoes. She decided to sit down. It seemed all the fight had left her.

'I can't have children, Fran – bad ectopic pregnancy when I was younger. Josh isn't my son.'

I felt this conversation was going to take some time. This was real soul-searching. And for everything Julie had, it seemed she only had me and Elle to tell. Having her confide in me this way felt like an honour.

Elle pulled up a stool.

We both sat there and listened to Julie's story about Josh being her dead sister's son.

She put her hand on top of mine and looked at me. 'Don't let this freak you out, but' – she paused and looked apologetic – 'her name was Frances. You're not a replacement or anything. But you have been the only friend I have had since her. You too, Elle.' She looked over at Elle.

'Is that what drew you to me Julie?' I actually felt a little hurt by this.

'Oh God Fran no, no way.' Shocked, Julie held her hands up in her own defence. 'It was just fate Fran. Weird really. Anyway, I used to call her Frankie. Don't take offence Fran, it's not meant to be offensive, that's why I didn't tell you.'

I squeezed her hand. 'No one can replace a sister, Julie. It is a big coincidence that we almost share a name. Weird, yes, but that's life. As for Josh, it's a beautiful thing you and Ralph have done. Does Josh know?' I thought I already knew the answer to that.

'No. And he doesn't need to – well, not yet anyway.' She pulled her hand away and looked at us both seriously. 'Not one word, do you both hear me?' She pointed her finger at us both. 'I won't have all those bitches at dinner parties gossiping about me or Ralph. Do you hear what I'm saying? One word, and we're finished.'

I could feel the panic rising. She had said far more than she had intended to and was now beginning to regret it.

It was Elle who spoke up first. 'That goes without saying. Nothing leaves this room.' Somehow, her words seemed like those of a mother, assuring Julie. 'Come on, how do you know you're pregnant? Have you taken a test?'

For the first time ever, I saw Julie cry.

'Don't you think I've checked?' she sobbed. 'Even the doctors are amazed. But yes, it's only a month and a bit in, and the doctors aren't sure if it's going to stay put, which is why only you two can know about this. If I told Ralph about this and then had a miscarriage, he would be devastated. Come to think of it, so would I.' She started crying again.

I had hold of one hand, and Elle was holding the other. 'Then we have to make sure you take it easy and rest up. Let's keep "little Ralph" safe.' Elle nodded towards Julie's stomach and smiled.

Through Julie's tear-stained face and smudged mascara, she smiled. She had been carrying this burden for weeks. You could see the relief on her face – relief that at last she could tell someone. She felt and looked better. We all had a lot to think about.

* * *

Bobby and I were taking our usual walk along the beach with Susie. It was a beautiful sunny Saturday, and the area was full of people visiting the seaside for the day. Susie ran into the sea for a swim, and as Bobby and I chased her, I bumped into a woman. At first, with the sun in my eyes, I just apologised for my clumsiness and was about to walk on when the woman spoke.

'Is it you, Francesca?'

I didn't recognise her at first. Then it dawned on me. My jaw dropped. It was Emma, who Luke had run off with. She was holding the hand of a little girl. I knew the child was Luke's instantly because she had his eyes. I looked around. Somewhere among all of these people sitting on deck chairs and enjoying themselves would be Luke.

'Hello, Emma. How are you?' I really didn't know what to say. It had been a long time, and I just wanted to get away.

Many times in the past, I had rehearsed what I would say if I were ever to see her again. But now she was standing in front of me, I couldn't think of anything worthwhile.

'I'm sorry, Francesca – for the way things turned out I mean.'

I could see she felt as awkward as I did. Bobby was shouting for me and throwing the ball for Susie, who by now was barking and chasing the waves on the sand.

'Is this your son?' she said, as though trying to think of something to say.

'Yes.' I looked down at the little girl. 'I take it this is yours and Luke's daughter?' I still felt bitter. We had once been friends, and I had confided in her. And all the while, she had been sleeping with my husband.

She nodded.

I glanced nervously around.

'If you're looking for Luke, he's not here,' she said, as though reading my thoughts. She seemed older than I remembered. But then so did I. Years had passed. 'Luke's dead.'

My head was spinning, and I was finding it hard to take in what she had just said. 'Dead? How? When?' I stood there looking at her, and even though it was a warm day, I felt myself shiver.

'It's been a while now. He just disappeared one day. And after a lot of investigation into him as a missing person, the police eventually found him washed up on a beach in Wales.' She looked sad as she looked down at her little girl.

'I'm sorry,' I said. I really didn't know what to say. I was shocked. It seemed strange. Here stood two women on the beach, both widowed by the same man and both of us with Luke's child.

'Some people say I got my just deserts, after what happened. Luke ran me ragged and worked his way through my savings – forever living beyond his means. Eventually to get out of some gambling debts, he got in with the wrong crowd, and things went downhill from there.'

So Luke had treated her in the same manner as he had myself, except she had more to lose. She held out her hand and indicated a deck chair at the side of her own. I sat down, watching Bobby play with Susie and the little girl on the sand.

Emma seemed to want to unload all of her troubles, and so I listened. It seemed Luke had enjoyed living in her house, with a decent sum of money in the bank. He had spent as much as he could get his hands on, and she had trusted him with her finances. This all sounded very familiar.

Luke had forged her signature and used her house as collateral against some hare-brained money-making scheme, which, of course never came to anything. She'd had to let her parents help her out to save her home. They had argued. And she hinted that there had been other women.

I could see her embarrassment as she confessed this, but I didn't comment. I knew exactly what she had been through.

She told me how well I looked and that she had seen in the newspapers that I'd married Tony Lambrianu. She was inquisitive about how I had met him, but I just told her it was through a friend. We were talking civilly, but we were not friends. And there was no reason to go into detail.

After a while of listening to her problems, I decided it was time to move on and so started to make my excuses about Bobby wanting something to eat. She was even more surprised to learn that I lived here, and when she asked me where, I pointed to the large house on the hill overlooking the sea. The enormous mansion stood out and looked impressive, very different to the barely-furnished little flat she knew I had shared with Luke.

My ego was inflated as I saw her eyes gaze at my big house. She had thought nothing of taking everything away from me and had even robbed Bobby of a father. I no longer hated the woman, but I did like the idea of letting her see that I had dragged myself up out of the mess Luke had left me in and done very well for myself.

So now I had closure. Luke was dead, and it was time to move on. No longer did I feel I had to look over my shoulder in case he turned up. There were no more ties to the past. I said my goodbyes and got up to leave.

Emma looked very sincere as she apologised again for everything that had happened and reached forward and kissed my cheek.

It felt strange seeing her again after all of this time. She had known me as a young girl training as a secretary, and now I was a grown woman with a young son. There was no point in feeling bitter any more. I must admit, though, that, in that moment, I enjoyed being Mrs Lambrianu, queen of the manor house. It was vain and selfish I know, and I was on the brink of divorce. But from her point of view, I had done well for myself. And Luke leaving me was the best thing that could ever have happened.

20

BOBBY'S BIRTHDAY

My baby boy was growing fast, and Julie and I had decided to throw him a big party for his birthday. I had organised a magician to entertain the children and to give the adults a break.

The sun was shining. Bouncy castles filled the gardens, and we had put a large pool out for everyone to cool off in and swim if they wished. Julie had organised an ice cream van to park in the driveway. Personally, I felt that was a true recipe for disaster and an awful lot of the children's parents would curse her when they were up during the night with children with stomach aches. Elle had spent the day filling party bags and organising balloons and banners.

I had invited my colleagues from the doctor's surgery and their children, and Bobby had invited most of his school! Josh was to come, which pleased Bobby, as they had got on so well on holiday in Italy. Julie had arranged pizzas and burgers to be delivered, and I had ordered a birthday cake with a Batman logo on it. The day was to be alcohol free. Apart from the adults not drinking in front of the children, it saved a lot of questions being asked about Julie not drinking.

Bobby had got up extra early, and the time couldn't pass quickly enough for him before the party began. The party theme was superheroes, so when the gates were finally opened, we welcomed assortments of Spiderman and the Hulk walking through them.

Obviously, Bobby was Batman and Josh was Robin. Julie, not to be outdone, came as Wonder Woman.

It was hectic. We were so glad when the magician turned up and entertained the kids in the gazebo. We could actually have a coffee and have five minutes to ourselves. Although Julie had made her entrance, Elle made a point of sitting her at the soft drinks table, pouring the drinks for the children. This way, she could sit under an umbrella and be off her feet. We looked after her as best as we could, even to the point where she would stay at my house for a few nights. Ralph accepted this now. He knew she would be with me, and he was welcome to turn up and check if need be.

I could hear Bobby shouting towards the kitchen, where I was putting the candles on his cake.

'Mammy! Come and see Batman and Robin. They are here! They are really here!' Bobby ran into the kitchen all excited, and pointed out of the kitchen window.

When I went outside, I saw that Bobby was right. There was Batman and Robin – otherwise known as Tony and Jake. My jaw dropped. All I could do was stand and stare at the two figures before me. Julie was in hysterics, laughing out loud at them both. Why did Tony Lambrianu do things like this? It had been months since we had spoken, let alone met. He didn't need me for his charitable balls any more and I was prepared to get on with my life, even with a heavy heart. But, here he was, floating back into my life looking even better than ever. God I'd missed him! What a beautiful thing for a man in his position to do for Bobby. It almost made me want to cry – Tony always did the unexpected! I moistened my lips as I saw the bulging muscles of his arms through the T-shirt he was wearing. I felt almost everything else go moist as well.

Tony was wearing black trousers and a black T-shirt with the yellow Batman emblem on it, along with a mask that actually made him look more like a highwayman. Poor Jake had drawn the short straw. His T-shirt was red, with a large black R for robin on it. He too was wearing a highwayman's mask. Ralph was wearing his normal trousers and shirt, but he had joined in by wearing a mask, and they were all wearing capes! Dear God, if the newspapers could see them now.

Julie was quickly snapping photos of them, while laughing and shouting threats that she was going to sell them to the newspapers. All the children thought it was great fun watching the three of them. Susie wagged her tail and ran up to Tony like an old friend. He bent down and gave her a stroke. He then picked up Bobby and wished him a happy birthday. The three of them had really made the effort.

I tried to compose myself. I was dressed as Catwoman, all in black with a headband that had cat's ears high up on it and a long tail hanging from my black Lycra trousers. It wasn't exactly the way I had wanted to look if I ever saw Tony again. I had wanted to look elegant and sophisticated, definitely not wearing ears and a tail.

Julie's outbursts of laughter seemed to drown out everyone else. She shouted over to Ralph from the drinks table, 'Who have you come as?'

Ralph was smiling. It was obvious to anyone that he felt it had been worth turning up and making a fool of himself just to see her laugh like that.

'I'm Commissioner Gordon, Batman's friend,' he said while limping over. We all saw him look down to where Julie was sitting at the drinks table. A frown crossed his brow. He was obviously noticing the absence of her champagne glass.

'Only soft drinks today, Ralph. This children's party is an alcohol-free zone. Do you want an orange juice or something?' I said. I could see the relief in Julie's face at my intervention. This stopped her having to make up an excuse about not drinking.

'There you are, Commissioner Gordon, alcohol free. More's the pity.' Julie put on her best disgruntled face at not being able to drink, and that seemed to satisfy him. It was so unusual to see Julie without her bottles of wine or champagne, she actually had to make an excuse for not drinking!

In the garden, Tony and Jake were surrounded by the children, who seemed to be circling them and showing off their costumes.

Tommy, now one of Bobby's best friends from school who had met Tony before and wanted to show the other children that he knew everything, announced to them all, 'It's not Batman. It's Bobby's dad. I've been in his car.' He seemed to enjoy his moment of glory, lording it over the others.

His words stung me. Bobby's dad? We were in the middle of getting a divorce.

It was Jake who came over to join us first, glad to escape everyone. 'Fran,' was all he said. Short and sweet I know, but I felt as awkward as he did.

'It's good to see you, Jake, and looking so stylish,' I said, breaking the ice and making it obvious he was welcome.

Julie was enjoying herself immensely. 'Come on, you lot. Group photo time – something to show our grandchildren, eh? Hey, Jake, what does the R on your T-shirt stand for? Rsehole?' She waved Tony over and gave one of the other parents her camera. This really was one for the album!

Tony eventually spoke to me. 'How are you, Francesca?' He seemed a little subdued. He gave me that familiar grin. 'I hope you don't mind us turning up like this.'

He waited for my reply, but I never got the chance. Elle had lit all the candles on the cake and was wheeling it out on a large trolley. Everyone began to sing 'Happy Birthday'. I scurried behind her with paper plates for the cake. A sea of hands from the children reached out and grabbed them, one by one.

Josh had been watching everyone playing. His socialising skills were not up to all of the chaos surrounding him, but he did his best. Bobby had made him go on the swings with him but he'd made a hasty retreat back to his own chair.

I saw him pick up a drawing book and pencils that one of the children had bought for Bobby's birthday and start to draw. We left him to it, and he was having his own good time. I went to check on him a few minutes later, and when I looked down at his drawing I was amazed. It was a drawing of Bobby. You could tell who it was instantly.

Although Josh had his problems, he had been given a gift. He shielded his picture from me, and I pretended I hadn't noticed and walked away.

Sitting next to Julie and Ralph, I couldn't help asking, 'You never told me that Josh had an artistic flair.'

They both looked at me curiously. But then, Josh spent so much time away from them at school, how could they know?

Julie glanced over at Josh concentrating on his drawing. Ralph was just about to walk over to him when Julie stopped him. 'Not now, Ralph, leave him to it. Let him show us, in his own good time.'

Suddenly there was a lot of shouting and laughter. We looked over, and Tony had thrown Jake into the pool. They were both laughing and splashing each other. Personally, I got the feeling they were enjoying this party more than the children. Thankfully, it was a large deep pool that had taken hours to fill, because all the children started jumping in as well. Susie followed suit, doing her doggie paddle.

Elle went indoors and grabbed an armful of towels and started to hand them out. Fortunately, it was hot, and everyone dried off quickly. I couldn't help but look at Tony's damp blond hair in the sunlight and think how handsome he looked. Seeing his body reminded me of Italy, when we had set aside our secret longing and the raging tide I'd felt inside was held no more. I desperately wanted to feel his kisses again, but that was the past and this was just a good will gesture I supposed.

Party bags were given out as parents came to pick up their children and although there had been a few children running to the bathroom to be sick from all the ice-cream, it had been a great day for Bobby and an exhausting one for me and Elle.

The sun was going down, but it was going to be a nice evening. Tony, Jake, and Ralph were lying on sun loungers drying off, complaining about how wet they were and then laughing because they had caused the water fight. Elle was laughing and smiling with them. It seemed to make her happy watching her two sons relaxing and laughing with each other like school kids; after all, they were still her little boys.

We all heard a noise and turned around. Josh and Bobby were in the bouncy castle together, jumping up and down and laughing. I turned and looked at Ralph and Julie. They were watching Josh joining in and having fun. I thought I saw a tear in Ralph's eye.

'Well,' said Tony, standing up, 'we had better be going.' His T-shirt was still clinging to him, and I had to admit unladylike thoughts were going through my mind.

'Thank you for coming.' I shouted over to Bobby to come and say goodbye to Tony and to thank him properly. I tried avoiding eye contact. I really didn't know what to say. There was so much left unsaid.

'Thanks, Tony Dad,' said Bobby and gave Tony a big hug around his waist. Then he turned to Jake and did the same. A lump rose in my throat. It was heart wrenching and I brushed a tear away quickly without anyone seeing.

'Walk with me, Francesca.' Tony took my hand and started towards the car.

'I got your solicitor's letter. You didn't let the grass grow under your feet, did you?' said Tony. He wasn't laughing or smiling now. He was serious, and I really didn't want to get into deep conversation or an argument now. The day had been too exhausting, and it wasn't over yet.

'Not now, Tony. But for the record, how long should I have waited?'

We were standing at the side of his car now and his chauffeur got out and opened the door for him. I stood there in silence, which seemed to be deafening. It was like one of those awkward first dates.

'Nice cat's ears. You really do have nine lives, don't you, Francesca? You start from the beginning time and time again.' With that, Tony got into the car with Jake following not long after.

I couldn't help myself. On impulse, I knocked on the car window. 'If you're ever passing by, the kettle is always on.' I don't know why I said it, but I just didn't want it to be the last time I saw him or Jake. That thought saddened me. They had both made a huge effort for Bobby today. It deserved to be acknowledged in some way.

'Thank you. I'll keep that in mind, Francesca.' With that, Tony indicated for the driver to leave.

Julie and Ralph's chauffeur turned into the drive, and it was their turn to leave. Josh was carrying his party bag and looked very pleased with himself. Ralph walked along with his arm around Josh's shoulders.

'Bye, Aunty Fran,' Josh said shyly. It was a lovely statement from such a shy boy, although he wasn't ready for me to give him a hug yet.

Ralph and Josh got into the car. And I must admit, it did make me laugh that, after all this time, Ralph suddenly remembered his bad leg and started complaining about it aching. Julie had told us he used it for sympathy.

'Are you okay, love?' Julie whispered into my ear as she leaned in to kiss me on the cheek.

I nodded. 'I'm fine, but you're not. You have Ralph moaning about his leg all the way home.'

Julie raised her eyes up to the sky and got into the car. Bobby and I stood there, waving them off. I bent down to him. 'Come on, sleepyhead, bath time. Happy birthday, love.' I gave him a kiss. All in all, it had been a great day, albeit a very busy one.

21

AN EYE FOR AN EYE

A week had passed since Bobby's birthday, and I hadn't heard a word from Tony. I'd given up hope of seeing him. I'd made the offer of friendship and told him my door was always open, but he hadn't come. Maybe I'd just sounded desperate.

Julie was constantly at the doctor's. They were keeping a close eye on her. Not only were things delicate, but they also classed her as an older woman having her first child. That hurt her vanity more than anything else.

Ralph was still in the dark about all of this, though he must have found it strange that she was keeping away from the night-club scene and preferred to come to my house instead. He possibly thought she was giving me moral support, as they both now knew about the divorce.

Julie announced one day that she had decided to take Josh out of his boarding school and have him somewhere closer to home. She said she and Ralph had talked it over, and maybe now was the time to try him in a mainstream school if possible.

Now they had seen for themselves that Josh had a flair for sketching, Ralph had indulged his talent and bought all kinds of paints and pencils for him to work his magic with. They had seen he could mix with other children, and by socialising more he would get better with time. He had limitations, but the very fact we ignored his odd little ways seemed to take the pressure off him and make them unimportant.

Now was the time to let him make friends and be accepted for who he was.

My solicitor had asked to see me. When I went, he informed me that everything was going along smoothly and that Tony had signed all of the papers and agreed to pay all the legal expenses. 'No hiccups,' was how he had put it. So I had to accept, whatever I had hoped, that Tony didn't want me, and he wasn't going to fight for me. Things were changing.

I poured two cups of coffee and sat at the table. 'Elle, we need to talk about things. Or rather, I need to talk about things.'

She turned from the sink and looked at me. I think she knew what was coming and could probably tell by the look on my face it was going to be a serious conversation. She wiped her hands on her apron and sat down.

'You're the closest person Tony has to a mother,' I began. 'Obviously, your loyalties are with him. You know the divorce is imminent, and so you don't have to come around any more. I don't know what your arrangement with Tony was. He wanted you to be the housekeeper.' I felt bad saying this and watched her sad face as I carried on. 'What I'm trying to say, and badly, is that I don't need a housekeeper, Elle. But I do need a childminder, and if you don't want to do it any more, can you recommend anyone?' It had sounded clearer in my head when I'd rehearsed it. Now it seemed a jumbled mess.

'Well, I don't know what to say, Fran. I suppose I knew this was coming, but I don't know what you want me to say.' She picked up her cup and took a drink.

My face must have shown disappointment. It seemed crazy, really. I hardly knew anything about her, but I felt close to her and she had become a close friend. I could see she was thinking and I didn't want to push her too hard. But I needed to know where I stood.

'I would, of course, like to continue looking after you and Bobby,' she began. 'Even Julie has become family to me now. But I do realise I am here a lot and you're more than capable of looking after things yourself. You needed me when you were constantly out with Tony at the weekends, and I must get under your feet at times. As for Tony...' She let out a deep sigh, rested her elbows on the table and put her head in her hands.

'He is his own man, Fran, and does as he likes. I would like to continue looking after Bobby for you. You've both filled a gap in my life. I didn't realise how lonely I was until I met you both.' It seemed to me Elle had her own speech prepared and was now clearing the air. She carried on, and I listened to her heartfelt words. Poor Elle. She had been dragged into this by Tony, and now he was leaving her to sort his mess out.

'So yes, in answer to your question, I would like to continue our arrangement when you're working if you want me to.'

This was a conversation I felt we should have had a long time ago – cards on the table as it were. It was the first proper talk we'd had about the situation we were both in.

'If that's the case, Elle, then I would like to pay you for all the childminding – put things on a proper footing if you like. It's time I stood on my own two feet again.'

Elle thanked me and nodded. She stood up and continued making herself busy at the sink. I couldn't be sure, as she had her back to me, but I thought I saw her brush a tear from her cheek. I walked away to give her space. The air seemed solemn, as though someone had died.

A few minutes later, I heard her shout to me, 'I'm off now, Fran.'

She stood in the kitchen, car keys in hand, ready to leave. I could see I had been right. She had been crying. Her eyes were red. I almost felt like crying myself. I didn't know why she was leaving so early. But I understood she wanted time on her own to think.

Sitting at the kitchen table, I looked around at the walls. I hadn't wanted to hurt Elle. I had come to rely on her a lot, and she had become some sort of surrogate grandmother to Bobby. She was family and I knew my words hadn't come out properly. She was Elle, she could come and go as she pleased. God, what had Tony done? He had affected so many people's lives. I would speak to Elle again, when she didn't feel so sad. Maybe I could make her understand I didn't take her for granted. I loved her.

* * *

Julie came round the next day, full of her usual gossip. Ralph, Tony and Jake were having a new supersized club made – all VIP lounges. The building works hadn't started yet. It was still in the architect stages. It all seemed very glamorous and part of a world that I wasn't involved in any more.

Ralph was still walking with his stick, which was why Julie had taken to calling him Charlie Chaplin. The pair of them seemed to express their love in the permanent banter they had, forever complaining about each other. Odd, but it worked for them.

Elle wasn't due to pick up Bobby today, so she wasn't here. It was unlike her. Then it dawned on me. She was starting her new routine already. Julie was also surprised, and I had no option but to tell her about the conversation.

'I see your point, Fran. But she must feel like her family is being taken away from her. And she has no legal rights to see Bobby. You're not related or anything. Give her a ring and tell her to come over. No. Better still, I'll telephone her and tell her I need some hot baked scones. If you do, she will think it's out of pity.'

Poor Julie. She had enough on her mind without sorting out my mess.

Within minutes, Elle was there, the coffee was on, and the oven was heating up. Everything was back to normal, or so I thought.

During the conversation, I noticed Julie glance at the CCTV monitors a couple of times over my shoulder.

'Is everything okay, Julie?' I turned in the direction of the monitors. There was nothing to see. Maybe she was expecting Ralph or something.

She just gave one of her quirky smiles. 'Of course. Just my baby brain wandering off. Hey, now Ralph is back on his feet, do you want to go out this weekend? I could do with some fun.'

'I really don't think that's a good idea, Julie, unless it's somewhere away from the clubs. Anyway, the last thing you need to do is go dancing.' I knew she meant well, but I felt awkward. Like Elle, Julie was also in the middle of all this.

'Francesca Lambrianu!' she shouted at me. 'Your name is still above the door. You have as much right as that other Lambrianu to go in there.' She seemed angry that I was prepared to just give up.

Without saying anything else, I put down a glossy magazine in front of her. On page six was a picture of Tony with his arm around some woman's waist. 'No, Julie. It's all too complicated. That's why.'

Again, I saw her glance at the monitors. She seemed preoccupied. I was showing her a picture of a very happy smiling Tony with some glamorous model. He had moved on, and now it was my turn.

Julie looked agitated. 'I have to go, Fran. There is somewhere I have to be.' She picked up her mobile and rang her chauffeur to pick her up. Julie rushed out of the door without a word. I looked at Elle.

'Do you think I offended her, Elle, showing that picture of Tony and refusing to go out with her?' It was strange for Julie to run off like that, especially when she had the opportunity to insult Tony, which was her prime hobby lately. Mentally, I knew something was wrong, but I couldn't put my finger on it. It unnerved me, but Elle brushed it off.

'Hormones probably,' said Elle. 'Well, I'd better go.' I saw her hesitate.

'Stay and have another coffee, Elle. Anyway, the oven's hot now. What about Julie's scones?'

She seemed relieved, but I hated this skirting around each other.

Julie came back half an hour later, looking a bit windswept and walking through the door, making some excuse that her chauffeur was picking something up for her. It all seemed a bit odd.

'Well, I will leave you with Elle, and I'll go and pick up Bobby.' I picked up my bag.

I was about to leave when Julie shouted after me, 'Fran, leave the gates open and don't put the alarm on. My chauffeur will be back in a minute.'

* * *

When I arrived home, I couldn't believe my eyes. My house was in mayhem and the police were there! What had happened? I had been gone just over an hour! Looking across the front yard, I saw Tony, Ralph, and Jake. I held Bobby's hand tightly as I got out of the car and was stopped by a police officer. He could see the horrified look on my face and asked me who I was. I told him this was my house.

'Tony!' I shouted.

He turned and started running towards me. He flung his arms

around me and squeezed me tightly. 'Fran! Oh my God, Francesca, you're safe,' he said over and over again, holding me as though he was never going to let me go. He looked sick with worry and swept his hair from his face. He was panting like he had run all the way here. Taking my face in his hands, he kissed my forehead and then my lips. His blue eyes seemed almost watery, as though on the brink of tears. 'Don't ever frighten me like that again Francesca, I don't know what I would do if anything happened to you,' he rambled on, while holding me close again.

Tony's emotional outburst shocked me. He seemed genuinely frightened and panicked that I had been hurt. Stunned, I looked around over Tony's shoulder. Did Tony really care about me? That shocked me more than the mayhem.

'Where are Elle and Julie?' I asked him.

He raised his head and looked at me and then shrugged. 'Julie noticed that someone with Irish number plates was hanging around the house. She rang Ralph and got you to leave the gates open. I know as much as you do.' Spreading his hands wide before him, he shrugged.

'She left the gates open for a group of burglars to come into my home?' I was astonished. 'Why would she do that?'

'Because it's payback time.' Tony sighed. 'You remember I told you about Ralph's partner in Ireland? Well, this was some opportunists of his that thought they would come to the house. Thankfully, Julie had her gun and we got here as fast as we could, and I don't know how many red lights we went through. For God's sake Fran, you have to believe me.'

'I can't believe this is happening. Why would they come here and why did Julie have a gun?' My mind was spinning. While Tony was talking I watched the police trample over my gardens and through my house. 'They were probably going to kidnap you for ransom Francesca.'

They were going to kidnap me? I felt dizzy, almost faint.

We started walking towards the house. Bobby, who was clinging on to my hand, started crying at the frightening scene. Tony bent down, picked him up and held my hand as we walked towards the devastation.

I saw Julie first, standing outside what used to be my kitchen. There was glass everywhere – the remnants of my former patio doors. 'Julie! Are you okay? Where is Elle?'

Julie started walking towards me and then promptly fainted.

I looked up and saw one of the ambulance technicians. Running towards her, I cried, 'Come on. Help her. She's pregnant!'

Ralph appeared from nowhere. I was on my knees holding Julie's hand and talking to her. The ambulance technicians were giving Julie oxygen. I told them she was pregnant again, and they asked me how many months along she was.

Ralph looked at me. 'Francesca, what do you mean Julie's pregnant? She can't be. I don't know if you know, but—'

I held my hand up to stop him. 'I know, Ralph. I know it all. Believe me. That is why she didn't tell you, in case anything went wrong. That's why she's been staying with me so much and not drinking. We've been looking after her while it's still early days.'

His voice was almost a whisper. 'I'd better go with her; come later if you can. This shock could make her lose our baby.' Then he stopped short, and a thought seemed to cross his mind. 'It's mine?'

'Yes, Ralph, that little bundle of gold in there is all yours. Now stop being silly and look after your wife.'

His eyes brimmed with tears. Then he saw Tony with Bobby still in his arms and composed himself. He turned around and got into the ambulance.

Jake was holding Elle who was visibly shaking and crying. Bobby was wriggling to get out of Tony's arms, and when Tony put him down, Bobby ran towards Elle to comfort her.

Two plain-clothed detectives had turned up and were trying to find out what had happened.

Elle tapped one on the arm. 'Excuse me, officer.' She sniffed, wiping her eyes. 'The man in the ambulance, is he alive?' She looked worried.

'Why do you ask that?' said one of the detectives. He eyed us all suspiciously. After all, this was the Lambrianu house, and seeing that Ralph Gold was there as well – let's just say, we didn't exactly look innocent, did we?

Elle started wringing her hands. 'I confess, it was me. They were going to rape Julie.'

We all looked at her in surprise. She was babbling on and apologising to the detective about how she was guilty.

The detective looked as surprised as we were. 'We will be taking statements in good time, miss. But for the record, just exactly what are you confessing to?'

We were all intrigued by that question.

'I'm the one who hit him over the head with the wok. I had to stop him. He was going to rape Julie, and so I hit him hard with it.' She started crying again.

You could visibly see the detective bite his bottom lip and try to prevent a smile. 'He's alive, miss. But I dare say, he won't be eating any Chinese food for a while.' He turned to his colleague and walked away, possibly so he could start laughing. What a confession!

Jake was the first to laugh out loud. 'You hit him with a wok? My God, Elle, you're lethal in the kitchen.' He looked at Tony, and they both burst out laughing.

The detectives came back over to join us. They informed us that this was now a crime scene, and we couldn't stay there. I asked if I could get some things and when an officer escorted me in to get some clothes, I glanced towards the kitchen. It was covered in glass. The hallway and the stairs had furniture thrown around everywhere. My home had been ransacked, and my friends threatened. How could I ever feel safe here again?

Elle insisted that Bobby and I stay with her, so Tony and Jake drove us to her house. It was a beautiful newly-built bungalow with a garden. I wouldn't have expected anything less. Tony and Jake would make sure she didn't go without anything.

Tony had ranted and raved in the car about how he was going to get the security improved at the house, even to the point of getting security guards! I'd ignored his comments and when we entered Elle's house, Jake went into the kitchen with Bobby and Elle to make some tea, and possibly to escape Tony's wrath.

I'd had enough. I was angry and upset, and all Tony could think or talk about was security guards patrolling my house and getting bigger and higher gates.

I walked up to him, raised my arm, and slapped him across the face hard. I had hit him so hard my hand was throbbing. Tony's head turned sideways, and he staggered backwards.

'Don't you dare make any smart remarks or threats to me, Tony! Don't you dare!' I was shouting, and I was angry. I could see Jake coming through from the kitchen with a tray. He looked at us both and then retreated back into the kitchen.

'Firstly,' I said, waving my finger in Tony's face, 'that is my house you're talking about and I don't want your security turning it into a prison. Trouble seems to follow you, and everyone gets caught up in the crossfire.'

Tony stood there, rubbing his face in stunned silence. It must have been a long time since someone had given him a piece of their mind.

'The only time I am going to feel secure, Tony, is when my divorce comes through, and you can saddle someone else with all of your cops and robbers rubbish. Get out, Tony, and take your trouble with you.' I knew it wasn't my house, but I was angry and wasn't thinking straight.

Tony picked up his jacket and, still rubbing his red face, walked towards the kitchen. He gave Elle a kiss on the cheek and indicated for Jake to follow him.

They both left in silence.

Elle and I didn't discuss what had happened, but I thought she must be mentally exhausted and need to rest. I got Bobby something to eat, and soon, he was playing happily with Susie in the garden.

After a while, I went to see Julie. Ralph was still at her bedside. I poked my head around the door and saw her. She looked pale.

'Fran, come in.' Julie held out her hand to greet me.

I gave her a kiss on the cheek while Ralph made an excuse about going for coffee.

'Before you ask, we are both fine. They are just keeping me in for observation. How are you and Elle?'

'Elle's fine, Julie. But what happened today? Who would burgle Tony Lambrianu's house and live to tell the tale? Who would be that stupid, Julie?'

'Oh, come on, Fran. One of those guys thought he was going to put his dick in my mouth, and if he had done it, I would have bitten it off.' She tried giving me one of her best smiles, but she looked weak and tired.

I could tell she was putting on a brave face for me. At some point, I might actually get the truth, but not now.

Two policemen came into the room, asking if Julie was okay to make a statement. She agreed. She wanted to get it over with while what had happened was still fresh in her mind. Ralph, who'd returned with coffees, objected, saying she wasn't well enough, but she wouldn't listen.

Her story was very short and sweet. I had gone to pick Bobby up from school. She was with Elle having a coffee, and then they heard a loud crash. There was banging and crashing and a lot of glass flying around. I had left the gates open because the chauffeur was due. That was Julie's story. Everybody had an alibi.

'Well,' I said to them both once the officers had left. 'You have told the police a good story, now I want the truth.' I saw them cast furtive glances at each other, and shaking my head, I headed for the door.

'Don't go Fran,' Julie called after me. Looking across at Ralph, Julie gave a weak smile. 'I'm going to break the code Ralph and so are you. She doesn't know why Tony has been away. She doesn't even know he has, or why he sent her the deeds to her house. It's time to tell her.' Ralph lowered his head and nodded.

Julie patted the side of the bed. 'Sit down, Fran. After that Italy business Tony knew Paddy would want to finish them all off once he knew they were still alive, so Tony took it upon himself to go to Ireland. Only Tony and I knew that. Not Ralph or Jake. It was Tony's choice and I helped him. Paddy was a massive heroin addict, who had hidden himself away, but we have friends in Ireland.' Julie smiled. 'Paddy had already organised for those two idiots to come to England and finish us off, but Tony got there first. I organised a gun in Ireland for him to pick up, but instead he gave Paddy a massive dose of heroin to finish him off. No suspicious circumstances because everyone knew of his addiction.' She shrugged, with a sneer on her face.

I looked at Ralph curiously. No one had told me Tony had gone to Ireland again. This lot were like secret squirrel, you were either on the inside or not and I was definitely not!

'The two men who came to your house were pissed Francesca, they had drunk the ferry dry. It was probably the first time they had been to England. Sure, they had a job to do, but greedy Paddy wouldn't pay them much and so they wanted more. Seeing the house, they knew there would be money and jewellery so they wanted a bonus. My chauffeur is a hit man; I warned him the minute I left your house and he was armed and waiting for them. It got rough and they tied me up and were going to screw me. I was scared, Fran, believe me...' Julie tailed off.

'Julie, anything could have happened. What if you couldn't get hold of Ralph in time?' I had a million questions but, she had all of the answers.

'Ralph and I both have two mobiles Fran. One is for emergencies. It doesn't matter where we are, or what we're doing, if that mobile goes off it means trouble. It always gets answered.' Julie grimaced. 'What I'm saying Fran is, that old fool Tony does love you. He made a will before he went to Ireland and sent you the deeds to the house. His first thought was of you. Maybe give him a little breathing space eh? He did what had to be done and we're all safe.' Julie patted my hand and smiled. Looking over at Ralph, they both nodded to each other. It seemed like they had their own code for love.

The police obviously thought two gangland bosses like Ralph and Tony must have had something to do with what had gone down, but their alibi was rock solid. When their driver had sped up at Tony's request and gone through a red light, they had been caught on surveillance cameras. They had turned up at the house when the police were already there in the same car that had been seen on camera.

Tony, Ralph and Jake could swear on a stack of Bibles that they didn't know what had happened and didn't know the men involved. This was all true.

Ralph stressed the fact, albeit very calmly, that he would not put his pregnant wife in danger under any circumstances. The police had to accept the incident was just an attempted burglary by two idiots who didn't know any better.

All that was left now was to take statements from the men involved. Obviously, only one could be questioned; the other was still in hospital with head injuries. The police were interested in why the two had come from Ireland. Again, the response was all apparently rather vague. They had come to England for a holiday. No wonder the police were confused.

The police knew that Ralph had Irish connections and that, lately, an old friend of his, Paddy, had taken an overdose of heroin and choked to death on his own vomit. Ralph and Julie had contacted the widow, whom they both knew, and paid for the funeral. They had also given her a large sum of money to help her out.

Paddy's widow couldn't have been more grateful. And, when the police had spoken to her, she couldn't speak highly enough of Ralph and Julie. There was nothing to connect Tony and Jake with Ralph's deceased friend, because they had never met. So the case seemed cut and dry.

22

___

CONFESSION TIME

Ralph insisted Julie stay in hospital for a few more days under observation. As it was a private hospital and Ralph was paying, there was no shortage of beds. He was angry Julie had been threatened, but now their unborn baby had been threatened too, he was fuming.

Julie's worst fears were coming true. Ralph was wrapping her up in cotton wool. He didn't want to celebrate the pregnancy until Julie was feeling better and the investigations were over.

I knew Julie was afraid. She didn't want all of Ralph's happiness to come crashing down if she were to have a miscarriage. I felt I was to blame for blurting out the truth at the scene of the crime. But seeing her faint like that, what else could I have done but raise the alarm?

When I went to visit Julie, she was sitting up in bed and putting on her lipstick. She kept telling me she was sick of Ralph treating her like a patient, so she thought a little bit of lipstick might just convince him she was okay.

She held my hand and squeezed it tight. 'I'm sorry I deceived you, Fran. But let's just say I have had more dealings with scumbags like that than you have.' She started to cry, and apart from being hormonal, I knew those tears were for what she had been through.

She wiped her stained face and blew her nose. There, at last she had let her fears out. She had felt vulnerable and weak, and she didn't like that feeling. It brought back bad memories.

'So, tell me about you and Tony,' she said. 'Are you still going through with the divorce? Or has all this made you realise that you still love each other?' She was smiling, but it was through smudged mascara.

I had come to love Julie. She was a good friend and confidant, and now she had risked her own life to save me and Bobby, I didn't want to lie to her any more. 'Tony and I couldn't be further apart, especially since the break-in. We had a hell of an argument. Or rather, I did. Our divorce has always been on the cards, Julie, from day one. We're not in love, and we never have been.' I lowered my head, embarrassed at my confession.

Julie looked at me strangely and raised her eyebrows suspiciously. 'You're wrong, Fran. I know how much he thinks of you, and I also know what you think about him. Has he cheated on you or something?'

I patted her hand. I didn't want her getting angry. 'You know he has someone else, Julie. You saw the picture of him. I've already been replaced. Marriage isn't for Tony; he isn't a one-woman man and I'm done with sharing my husband with other women.' Tears started to roll down my face. I had kept this secret from her for long enough. It was eating away at me.

I started to leave; I didn't want to upset her. Now was not the time for me to unburden myself. She pulled my hand tighter towards her so I would sit down again. 'What are you saying, Fran?

Tell me and I promise you it will never leave this room. Just you, me and baby makes three.' She gave a weak smile and waited.

What had I to lose? Ralph was more than happy with Tony and Jake. They had become even closer these days, and Ralph treated them more as partners. He knew he owed his life to them both. They could easily have left him behind to die in Ireland, but they hadn't. This had cemented their friendship as far as Ralph was concerned.

'It's all been a lie, Julie. Everything has been a lie. I'm sorry.' Once I had started, it all came pouring out. 'Tony and I made a deal. He wanted a wife so that Ralph would do business with him. He knew Ralph didn't want a playboy but a respectable married man. Don't get me wrong, this is not all of Tony's doing. He has been very generous, the house being one of the ways. Given I'm a single parent who worked as a stripper and stole from Tony for my family's sake, he's been very lenient.'

She listened as I poured out my heart and told her the whole sordid story from beginning to end, including how I had first met him and then worked for him. Saying it out loud sounded awful.

She took a deep breath and lay back on her pillow. I could see she was thinking, and I was afraid I had gone too far. Sometimes honesty was not the best policy.

'It's Ralph and me who are at fault. We pushed you both into this while testing Tony. You were both desperate, Fran. I have been destitute and schemed to survive. I'm sorry, Fran. We shouldn't have pushed you. And what about me? Are you such a good actress that you have fooled me twice?' She sounder a little harsher now, and I could tell she meant our friendship.

'Julie – our friendship. I was a little wary of you in the beginning. I thought you were spying on me all the time. Why would anyone as high class as you want to spend time with me? But you're my friend, Julie. Well, I would like to think that you're still my friend.' I looked at her for reassurance. 'No, you're my family, Julie. Sometimes I don't know what I would do without you.'

She held her arms out for a hug. The door opened, and Ralph walked in. Seeing the emotional scene before him, he stopped. 'Oops, women's business. I'll get some coffee.' He walked out again.

We looked at each other and burst out laughing. From now on, Ralph was going to blame everything on Julie's hormones!

I wiped my face and stood up to leave. 'I'll leave you in Ralph's care.'

'Stop! Wait, Fran.' I turned to see what was wrong. 'Tony loves you more than you know. In fact, he loves you more than he knows. And I know you love him. Trust me, Fran. Neither of you are such good actors.' With that, she blew me a kiss.

Julie's words haunted me as I left the hospital. The very idea of Tony loving me seemed impossible, but as for me loving him, well that was a different matter. Ralph was right – Julie was hormonal.

* * *

The all-clear was given by the police, and I was informed I could go back home. I was concerned about being alone when Bobby was at school. I didn't think Elle would want to step foot back into the place, considering all the bad memories it held for her.

I was therefore surprised when Elle insisted on coming with me to the house. When we drove through the gates, things actually looked worse than I had remembered.

Where the patio doors had once been were enormous boards the police had put up to secure the place, and all of the broken windows had been boarded up. There were strips of discarded police tape flying around on the floor, blown by the wind. It looked like a dark ghost house.

'You don't have to come in, Elle.' I could see had gone pale and her breathing seemed heavier. I thought she was going to have a panic attack.

She took a large breath and nodded. 'I'm ready, Fran. Come on.'

We held hands and walked slowly to the door. I took out the key and opened what was left of it. I didn't need the key. It just swung open.

The scene that greeted us was like a bomb site. Doors were open in the hallway. All the furniture seemed to have been thrown around. We both stood there in stunned silence. I was glad I hadn't brought Bobby with me. We wandered down the hallway to our newly-built kitchen. I saw Elle take a breath and close her eyes for a moment.

'We need to contact a glazier, Fran,' she said, trying to compose herself.

I thought for a moment, and a smile crossed my face. 'Elle, we have all the telephone numbers for builders that we need. The builders we used for the extension – they can sort out everything, even those bullet holes in the wall.' I was trying to make light of the situation, although I didn't feel like it.

The bullet holes were hard to miss. The police had circled them with a large red pen. I looked down at my feet and could see dried blood on the floor, where the man Elle had hit on the head had fallen. It was the first time I had seen the house since the burglary had happened. I had briefly been in to collect some clothes from upstairs, escorted by a police officer. But this was reality.

Elle found the builder's number, and the supervisor assured us someone would be there within two hours to take measurements and see what needed doing. Of course, as it was short notice, it would be more expensive!

'That's okay,' I said. 'Send Mr Lambrianu your bill. I'm sure he will go through all of the details with you.' I had intentionally sounded sarcastic, and I knew the builder realised it. Tony would definitely have something to say if he thought this builder was going to try and make some money out of our misery.

Elle got out the sweeping brushes and handed me one. 'Come on. Let's make a start and get rid of this glass.' She then handed me a pair of rubber gloves and some bin liners. 'I think your builders will come a lot sooner now that you have mentioned Tony's name.'

Elle made some coffee, and we started the big clean-up. It looked like the police had made more mess than the burglars. It hadn't helped having no windows in and the wind blowing all the dust up from the driveway.

While sweeping the floor, I saw the magazine with the picture of Tony with his arm around a woman's waist. I picked it up and threw it in the bin.

We were making some headway when I heard a noise in the driveway. The builders had arrived!

A couple of men jumped out of the back of the open truck and surveyed the damage outside. 'That driveway is going to need relaying, Mrs Lambrianu. You're never going to clear all of that glass, and we don't want you falling on it or bursting your car tyres.'

'Just sort out everything, and redecorate the kitchen. You know where to send your bills.' Tony had done this, so as far as I was concerned, he could bloody well pay for it.

'I've ordered a skip, Mrs Lambrianu, and the men are going to collect some windows for you. They should be back later on this afternoon. That's a whole wall of windows.' Albert, the supervisor, took off his cap and brushed back his thinning hair.

Elle made everyone a drink and she even opened up the biscuits, which made Albert smile.

As the skip was backing into the drive, Elle went to see where they were putting it. Then the strangest thing happened. I was sitting alone at the breakfast bar, taking a moment to myself, when Albert came and sat alongside me. 'That Mrs Elle, is she your mum?' He paused, waiting for my answer.

I shook my head; he was definitely fishing. 'No, she's my mother-in-law.'

Again, I could see him thinking, wondering what to say next. The air was tense but funny. 'She's Mr Lambrianu's mum, is she?'

'Why do you want to know?' I asked him.

And then the penny dropped. I could see where his questions were leading. 'Will your father-in-law be coming later to help out?' Albert looked down and dipped another biscuit into his tea and put it in his mouth.

Standing up, I picked up the sweeping brush again, smiling to myself for making him wait for my answer. 'No, Elle's not married. She's free and single.'

I had said enough, and Albert seemed happy now he had found out what he wanted to know.

Elle walked back into the room, and I looked at Albert and watched him turn a very light shade of pink. Love turned up in the strangest of places.

I left and picked up Bobby from school. He'd had a busy day, telling everyone about the burglary, even though he hadn't been there. On the way back I bought lots of fish and chips, not only for ourselves but also for the builders. They had worked really hard and had been very kind and helpful in the process.

As I drove along, I passed the bench that I used to sit on with Tony. It made me feel sad. People were walking children home from school. The sun was shining. And everyone was getting on with their lives. I looked at the old, battered bench again. It was empty. It seemed lost without me and Tony sat there, bringing it to life with our laughter.

When I got back to the house, I was surprised to see everything was looking in order. The workmen were hard at it, and their faces beamed when I showed them the bag of food I had with me.

'When are you going to inform the insurance company, Mrs Lambrianu?' asked Albert.

Insurance? I hadn't even thought about that. Of course the house would be insured. Only I didn't know with who or where the paperwork was. Tony had sorted it all out. I was going to have to contact him and get the details.

I waited while the workmen were sitting in the kitchen. Elle had buttered them some bread and butter and made more tea. I checked that no one could overhear and dialled Tony's number.

He answered immediately. 'Francesca, how are you?' He seemed pleased I had called him.

'Tony,' I stammered. 'I'm back at the house with the builders. They are sorting out the windows and stuff.' I felt nervous talking to him. 'The builder wants to know if you have informed the insurance company.'

There was a pause on the other end of the line. 'Well, not yet, but I will get on it right away. Is there anything else you wanted to talk to me about?' He sounded almost hopeful.

'No, that was all. I would like the paperwork if possible. Would you post it to me?'

Again, Tony told me he would sort it.

'I'm sorry I slapped you, Tony. I shouldn't have.' I felt like a silly schoolgirl trying to think of something to say, trying to break the silence.

'Goodbye, Francesca.' And with that the line went dead; he had put the telephone down on me. At least I knew he was back to normal and dismissing me again.

* * *

The doctors had decided that, while Julie was in hospital, it might be a good opportunity to take matters into their own hands and make sure her pregnancy went smoothly. It seemed her womb was weak, and she could still miscarry. The doctors had decided that a small operation, which would include putting a small stitch into the neck of the womb, would secure things. Julie had agreed – anything to keep the baby – but I could tell she was afraid, although full of bravado.

When she was taken to surgery, I waited in Julie's room. It was full of flowers from the wives of the men who worked for Ralph. It looked like a garden. Ralph was sat in a chair beside the bed. His head was down, and he was looking at the floor. He looked older than his years. Stress and worry were written all over him. Ralph looked around the room at the flowers. I felt awful because I hadn't brought any and apologised immediately.

'This, Francesca, this is all show.' He waved his arm around the room. 'You're here. You care about Julie.' He held my hand tightly. 'What do you think Julie would rather have? A hollow gesture or her best friend at her side? And you are her best friend. It's been a long time since she's had someone like you.' Ralph patted my knee, and we both sat there in silence.

Eventually a doctor came into the room. It seemed like we had been sitting for hours, but it hadn't been that long.

'Everything is okay, Mr Gold. She's still in recovery, and she'll be brought back to her room soon. Everything has gone very well indeed.' The doctor smiled reassuringly.

Ralph, at last, smiled. He shook the doctor's hand. 'Trust me, doctor, there will be a nice bonus in this for you.'

The doctor looked embarrassed and glanced at me. 'There's no need for that, Mr Gold. You can see her soon.' He quickly left the room.

Ralph hugged me. 'She's going to be all right, Fran. Julie and our baby are safe.' He looked as if he was going to burst into tears of relief.

I nodded and smiled. There was nothing to say. Julie was okay, and that was all that mattered.

I picked up my telephone and rang Elle. I knew she would be waiting for the news.

'I will let the boys know,' said Ralph. 'I know its women's business, but they will be pleased to know that Julie is okay.' Ralph was smiling. It seemed all the worry lines had cleared from his face.

I sent Ralph home. I knew he had things to do, and so I reassured him that I would stay with Julie and telephone him as soon as she was awake. Although Julie was still asleep, I knew she knew I was there.

The next morning she was fully awake. She asked how things had gone, and when the doctor assured her everything was okay, you could see the weight lift off her shoulders.

She lay back on her pillow and asked where Ralph was. When I informed her that I had sent him home, she seemed relieved at that as well.

'Ralph must be shattered,' she said, not caring about herself. 'He has been so worried, and he can't cope with all of this. Thanks, Fran. You did right to send him home.'

Within two days, Julie was home herself. She was still a little sore but back on her feet, wanting to know all the gossip. I had asked Ralph if Julie could come and stay at Elle's with me so we could look after her. Poor Ralph. Showing his emotions didn't come naturally, but the hug he gave me said it all.

Fortunately, Elle's bungalow was big enough for all of us and more if needed. Julie thoroughly enjoyed lounging on Elle's sofa, being waited on hand and foot, while I told her all the juicy gossip about Elle's new admirer, Albert.

Ralph and Jake visited, but there was no sign of Tony. He had obviously decided to keep his distance.

'You have to talk to Tony sometime, Fran, if only for my sake,' Julie said while we were having one of our heart-to-hearts. 'Ralph wants to have a low-key party to celebrate, but I know he will drive me mad, fussing around me all night. If you come, Fran, it will take the pressure off him, knowing you're there. That means you too, Elle,' she shouted through to the kitchen. 'Maybe you could bring a plus one.' Julie gave me a little wink and a smile.

'I tell you what, Julie, why don't you and Ralph make it a baby shower?' I said. 'That would give the party a theme, wouldn't it?' I looked at Julie and Elle, who had now come into the lounge to see what Julie was talking about.

Julie clapped her hands and smiled. 'Oh yes, Fran. That sounds great, doesn't it, Elle? Well, Fran, it's your idea and your party arrangements. You can tell Tony all about what kind of party it's going to be.' Julie really was a minx. She loved organising everyone's lives, although we all knew she meant well.

I waited till I was on my own to telephone Tony. It seemed to ring forever, and I was just about to end the call when he answered. Before he could say anything, I just blurted it out. 'Hi, Tony, just calling to let you know Julie wants the party to be a baby shower if you want to make any special arrangements and let people know. Also, Julie has asked me to come to the party. Would that be a problem? I don't want to make things awkward for you.' I waited for an answer, which seemed to take forever.

'No, Francesca, there will be no awkwardness from my side. I promise you.' With that, he put the telephone down. Well what was that, if it wasn't awkward?

I hated the uneasiness between us. I really wanted to see him;

my only hesitancy was wondering who he would have on his arm.
Pursing my lips together, I toyed with the idea of not going, but
knew that wasn't an option. Whatever happened, it would be nice
to see him again. I hadn't realised how much I'd missed him until I
heard his voice.

23

THE PARTY

A couple of weeks after my very short telephone call with Tony, the house was finished. At last I could move back in, although I felt a little nervous about it, considering what had gone on there.

Ralph was elated because at last he could announce Julie's pregnancy to everyone and boast he was going to be a father. The party was to be a dinner and dance, but Baby Gold was the theme. Julie wasn't wearing maternity clothes yet, but she wore a loose pair of pink trousers and a designer T-shirt. On the front of it, across her bosom, in black capital letters was the word 'baby'. A black arrow pointed to her stomach.

Julie had outdone herself with her hair and make-up. She looked stunning. 'I'm telling you, Fran. Those bitches at that party are going to wait for me to look fat and haggard. Well, they will have to wait a long time,' she had shouted down the telephone to me. Secretly, I thought she seemed a little nervous. Here she was, the ice queen Julie Gold, pregnant. That would really give them all something to gossip about.

I wore a black trouser suit and, under Julie's guidance, had my hair and make-up done. I felt it was like an armour I could hide behind. I really didn't want to go to the club and see Tony dancing and drinking with whomever.

I thought about wearing my wedding rings, but then decided against it, considering my divorce was looming, and everyone knew it.

Julie picked me up in her car, and we went together. I must have looked pensive because she commented on it. 'Don't look so frightened, Fran. You're coming to my party with me. You're not walking into the lion's den, you know. Anyway, it wouldn't surprise me if someone we both know felt just as nervous as you do.' Julie gave me that knowing look of hers and patted my hand.

When we arrived, the club seemed to be already full. The place looked bigger than I remembered. It seemed strange that, in such a short space of time, things had changed so drastically. I really had punched above my weight marrying my boss.

The whole place was adorned with balloons and all the cocktails were named after baby items. I stayed on the soft drinks with Julie, although I must admit, I felt like downing the large glass of champagne that was on offer. I looked around. I saw Ralph, Jake, and even Sharon, but no Tony. I didn't want to look too obvious and ask, but I was curious. Surely he wouldn't miss Ralph and Julie's big night?

Ralph was shaking everyone's hands and beaming, and his happiness lit the place up. Then he spotted Julie. She walked over to him and hugged him. Everyone gave them a round of applause. Ralph leaned over to me and whispered into my ear, 'Will you go to the office and tell that workaholic husband of yours to stop whatever he is doing and come for dinner? I think he might appreciate the gesture from you.'

What Ralph meant was: go and break the ice, Francesca. I walked down the corridor to the office. I gave a slight knock and opened the door. I was taken by surprise to see a young woman sitting on the edge of the desk, talking to Tony. It wasn't the woman I had seen in the magazine. She was wearing a blue sequinned mini dress. Her dark hair was shaped into a short bob.

Tony was sitting at his desk. He wasn't wearing his suit jacket, which was over the back of his chair. I surveyed the scene and felt like an intruder. Obviously, I had interrupted something. They were still smiling at some joke they had shared before I had entered. Ignoring the woman and trying to hide my embarrassment, I concentrated on Tony, who was now looking up at me. He didn't flinch or show any embarrassment. I could feel my face burning red.

Clearing my throat and trying my hardest to appear calm and nonchalant, I spoke up. 'Sorry to interrupt. Ralph asked me to let you know dinner's about to be served.'

'Okay,' said Tony with a wave of his arm, 'I'll be out in a minute,' and those smooth dulcet tones of his filled my ears. He looked at me with indifference. In fact, they both sat there waiting for me to leave. The woman smiled at me with her bright red lipstick, like the cat that had got the cream!

Closing the door behind me and walking back into the corridor, I took a moment to catch my breath and put a smile on my face before I walked back into the party. We all sat down to dinner, and Tony came out alone and took his place at the top table beside me. I couldn't stand to be near him. No awkwardness? He had known I would be here, and he had gone out of his way to humiliate me again.

I could hardly eat anything. I felt sick to the stomach. I wondered who the woman was. I had half expected her to be at his side, but she was nowhere to be seen. Strange. I supposed Tony hadn't wanted to start gossip about his new lady friend, taking the shine off Ralph and Julie's party.

Tony hardly looked at me. He was being his old self, laughing and joking with Ralph about changing nappies and being the host with the most. When the dinner ended, and we were ready to go into the disco room, there were two large thrones for Ralph and Julie to sit on. Ralph didn't want Julie standing for too long. This way she could observe in style.

Eventually Tony leaned over to me. 'Are we divorced already then?'

I followed his gaze as he looked down at my empty wedding ring finger. I felt a sense of achievement, knowing that he had noticed I wasn't wearing them. 'It would seem so,' was all I said.

Julie and Ralph were holding court and doing the rounds in the room, laughing and chatting and thanking everyone for their very expensive gifts. Julie beckoned to me to come and sit beside her in Ralph's chair. I was glad to escape and get away from the crowds and their knowing looks.

'What's going on, Fran? What has Tony said to you? Tell me. I can tell something's wrong. I know you too well by now.'

'Nothing to worry about tonight, Julie,' I said. I longed to tell her but felt I should hold my tongue.

I could see people talking about me, and the women's voices seemed to drip with sarcasm when they told me how surprised they were that I was at the party, given the circumstances. No one dared say the word divorce. But reading between the lines, I knew what they meant, and so did Julie.

Hormonal and angry, Julie snapped at them. 'Why the hell shouldn't she be here? It's Francesca's name above the door, and you're in her club, drinking her booze for free.' That seemed to stop them. Pregnancy hadn't changed Julie. She was still fighting the good fight.

The night dragged, and I just wanted to go home. Ralph and Julie did a slow waltz together. It was obvious to the world that their little baby had been the icing on the cake between them.

Eventually the evening came to a close. Julie was tired and even more so than she would have normally been, having had to watch everyone but her have a drink and dance the night away.

Ralph was going to drop me off en route to their house, which was more than out of their way. I had no option but to accept, which made me feel guilty. I was pleased and surprised when Jake came up to us and offered to see me home or at least let me use his chauffeur to drive me.

Jake could see I appreciated this, and I couldn't thank him enough as he walked me to his car and kissed me on the cheek. 'Goodnight, Fran. It's been good to see you.' Jake always seemed to be the peacemaker.

Tony was nowhere to be seen. Although I had a feeling where he might be, there was no point in dwelling on it.

Well, why shouldn't Tony have a girlfriend? I reasoned with myself. We were divorcing. It didn't matter any more, did it?

Tears brimmed again. Yes it bloody did matter! I was tired of being reliable Fran, understanding Fran. What about Francesca the woman who was boiling with passion for a man that was doing everything I craved with another woman. Well, she could have him, all of him, but I had his name, I was Francesca Lambrianu and she couldn't take that away from me!

When I arrived home, Elle was dozing in a chair. It was obvious she had stayed up to see how things had gone. Like a comforting mother, she made a hot chocolate drink and listened to the evening's events. I told her about the baby shower and how Julie had really enjoyed herself under Ralph's watchful eye.

'What about Tony?' she finally interrupted. 'How was he? Is everything okay between you?'

'Tony was with his new girlfriend,' I said nonchalantly. 'I didn't catch her name and she didn't stay for the party.' I felt like Elle could see right through me. She knew I was making light of it. But the truth was I was gutted and hurt.

* * *

Julie came around the next morning with a great big smile on her face and announced that Ralph wanted to take her away on holiday. Both Elle and I felt that was a good idea. The rest and the sunshine would do Julie a world of good. Ralph had suggested a cruise, possibly because the ship had a doctor on hand night and day.

They were to leave in a few days, and Josh was going with them. It would be a real family holiday, even if the baby was undercover!

Julie had some things to sort out first: the usual packing, shopping, and more shopping. She asked if I wanted to go with her, and I said I would, but my heart wasn't in it. Everything in Julie's golden garden was smelling of roses, while mine was full of weeds. As much as I loved her, her happiness made me feel worse.

At around six, after hours of shopping, we decided to call it a day, possibly because the chauffeur couldn't fit any more bags in the boot in the car. By the time I got home, Elle, Bobby and Albert were all sitting around the table having a cup of tea and some homemade apple pie. It looked like a very happy family scene.

I went upstairs to give them some space to themselves. I could hear Albert getting ready to leave, hoping that Elle would see him to the door. She did, but with Bobby in tow, using him as a shield.

'You tease that poor man, Elle. You know he likes you,' I said once he'd gone.

She became defensive, acting as though she didn't know what I was talking about. 'He's had no encouragement from me, Fran. He is only hanging around until your insurance money comes through.' She avoided my eyes and busied herself upstairs, running Bobby's bath.

I had to laugh to myself. You could see she enjoyed Albert's company. And by all accounts it had been a while since she'd had male company. She had never said much about herself. But when I'd stayed at her bungalow, I'd seen photo frames full of pictures telling different stories about her past.

What had first caught my eye was a photo of Elle with two teenage boys, one with blond hair and the other one with dark hair. Guess who? There were also lots of pictures of children; I guessed these were all the children she had fostered in the past.

And as much as she loved all the children she had cared for, it was obvious to anyone that Tony and Jake were her boys and held a special place in her heart.

She had spent her life taking on everyone's troubles. But now she had an admirer, and as offhand as she was with him and as much as she spent her time bossing poor Albert around, it was clear she liked it.

Good for her. It was time she had something for herself.

I felt lonely sometimes, even though my life, on the face of it, seemed full with Bobby and working at the doctor's surgery. I enjoyed the chatter of the women I worked with and listening about their families. Julie kept me busy with all of her gossip about the other wives whose husbands worked for Ralph. But I missed having Tony's male company, even when he had Jake in tow.

I wondered what Tony was doing. I knew he would be at the club or the casino, but with whom? Night after night I would toss and turn thinking of him. Once I had found out which very expensive aftershave he wore, I had bought a bottle and would hold it to my nose, or even spray my pillow with it – I was becoming obsessed, but I couldn't help it. I wanted my own true love. My own fairy-tale.

* * *

The morning Julie set off on her holiday, an official envelope was
delivered to the house. I opened it and stared. It was my divorce
papers. The divorce had gone through a lot faster than I had imagined, but there it was in black and white – decree absolute.

I was no longer Mrs Lambrianu.

24

DECREE ABSOLUTE

The divorce had been in the newspapers and a local celebrity magazine. There was an old photo of me and Tony at some party dancing together. The magazine had drawn a big zigzag line between us. It looked like a bolt of lightning. 'Lambrianu's Split,' the headline read.

I must confess, I wasn't prepared for it. And when I saw the magazine on the way to work, I knew by the way everyone looked at me that they had seen it too. The sympathetic looks were more than I could bear.

By lunchtime, I'd had enough. I stood in the middle of the staff canteen where the staff were all gathered. 'Yes, Tony and I have divorced,' I announced. 'End of story.' I never went into any more detail. I didn't need to. They could read it all for themselves. Tony had been fooling around with other women. There were no head-lines about me getting some big cash settlement or anything. All it said about me was that I was the wronged wife – a very familiar story. Bad news travelled fast, and today's news was tomorrow's fish and chip paper. Right?

Tony hadn't been in touch or visited, and the only time I had seen him privately was when I had gone to his office the night of the party – when he had been with a woman. That was not the time to discuss money, not in front of his girlfriend. But he had mentioned my wedding rings and that got me thinking. I really should hand them back to him – they weren't mine to keep any more.

By the time I had finished work and picked up Bobby, I had made up my mind. The rings were Tony's to do as he pleased with. I bought one of those bubble wrap envelopes on the way home. And much later on, when Bobby had gone to bed, I picked up the square jewellery box and put the rings in the envelope. Then I wrote a cheque for 30,000 pounds. I wasn't sure how much the extension had cost, but at least I could give him something towards it.

I took the locket he had given me for Christmas. He had assured me he had bought it for me, but I still felt it had been something to show to all of the wives who were eager to see what Tony had bought me for our first Christmas. It was really over, wasn't it? It hadn't seemed real until now. I had hoped Tony would come on his white charger and claim me as his love, but no. That only happened in movies. If I left my job at the doctor's surgery, I would hand in my uniform and keys. This was the same thing. The last link between us.

I popped a note inside the envelope explaining the contents.

Mr Lambrianu,

I am returning my uniform in lieu of our divorce.

I also enclose a cheque towards the extension. If any more is required, please let me know.

I know you haven't used the study that you have in my house, but I wondered if there was anything you would like out of it before I clear it out.

Please let me know what you decide. And thank you for everything.
Francesca.

The following morning, the sun was shining through my bedroom windows. In three weeks, my mam and brothers would be here having a holiday by the sea. I was looking forward to it. Although we spoke every day or so, it wasn't the same as having them there in the flesh.

I took Bobby to school and saw some of the other mothers stop their conversations when they saw me. Hopefully, the gossip would be over soon, and that would be the end of it. Bobby kept asking me why Tony didn't come around any more. All I could say was that he was busy. This was what I hadn't wanted – Bobby to get used to having Tony around and then lose him. This was all very confusing for him, and he had been dragged into it. It was all my fault.

At least unlike my former divorce, Bobby and I had come out of this with some security for our futures. This had been the plan all along. It made me think back to when I had received my divorce papers from Luke. That had been the night I'd met Tony. Could you believe it? Well, I had done it before and I would do it again. Brush myself down and start over. This time, I wasn't struggling to pay bills and had a lot to be grateful for. It had been a good chapter in my life and I knew I would never experience anything like it again. So, I decided to keep it as that and move on.

25

A STRANGER IN THE NIGHT

It was the early hours of the morning, and I had gone to bed early. I saw headlights flash near the drive, but in my sleepy state, believed I was dreaming. Then I had an awful thought. What if it was more burglars? I got out of bed and stood on the landing. Maybe I should call the police. Then I heard my name and banging and shouting.

'Francesca! Francesca!'

I looked towards Bobby's bedroom door. He hadn't got out of bed. Nor was he shouting for me. As I ran downstairs, the banging continued. It was coming from the kitchen. I walked through, switching on all the lights in the conservatory, as well as all the outside lights too.

That was when I saw Tony and Jake. Tony was leaning on the glass, his fists against the windows, shouting out my name. He looked dishevelled, not his usual immaculate self. His face was red and you could see he had been drinking. Why the hell was he banging at my door in the middle of the night? Jake stood at his side looking sheepish.

I was just about to give him a piece of my mind, when he

almost fell through the door. He was very drunk, swaying as he walked and slurring.

'What the hell are you both doing here at this time? Keep the noise down. Bobby's in bed.'

'Sorry, Fran.' Jake looked apologetically at me. 'I tried stopping him, but he insisted on coming.'

I looked at Tony, my hands on my hips. 'Well, you drunken fool, what do you want?'

Tony fumbled in his jacket pocket and pulled out the envelope. I recognised it instantly.

'*Grazie per I gioielli, l'anello, cara.*' Being drunk, Tony had slipped into his native Italian. As he continued to try and speak, he was going back and forth between English and Italian.

I looked up at Jake. 'I presume you know what he's saying,' I said, 'because I certainly don't.'

Jake nodded. 'Thanks for the jewellery, the ring, dear.'

Tony staggered towards me, pulling me roughly outside the patio doors. Tony kissed the rings, which were in the palm of his hands and threw them in the air into my garden. I was stunned. I looked at Tony's face. He wore a satisfied smirk. I couldn't believe what he had just done.

I turned to Jake. He looked as shocked as I was.

I raised my hand to my face. 'Oh, Tony, why did you do that?' I felt my eyes brimming with tears, and I was regretting my impulsive decision to send them to him. He didn't want them, he'd proved that, but even now, my fingers felt empty without them. How could he?

He banged on his chest like some ancient caveman. '*Il capo, sono in controllo. Sei mio.*' Then he started to laugh.

I looked across at Jake. He looked embarrassed and obviously didn't want to repeat what Tony had said. 'He's the boss, he's in control, and you are his.' Jake shrugged his shoulders.

'Get out, you drunken idiot. Get out and leave me alone.'

Tony put his hand inside his jacket again. He pulled out the divorce decree. Again, I watched as he made his big gesture. '*Mia moglie, tu non sei niente. Tu mi odi.*' Now Tony turned his head towards Jake and waved his hand at him to translate for him.

'My wife, you are nothing. You hate me.' Jake's awkwardness was showing through now.

Tony held out the divorce papers, tore them in half, and threw them towards me.

I'd had enough. I grabbed the arm of his jacket and pulled him to where his car was waiting. 'Take your bits of paper, boss man. And don't forget, I am not your wife any more. And you too,' I added, glaring at Jake. 'Fancy letting him come here in this state.'

Jake shrugged. 'What can I say? It was better I come with him, wasn't it? If nothing else, I translated. I thought he would pass out in the car, Fran. He's not right in the head these days. He beat up a publican and smashed the place to bits over a thousand pounds. It was ridiculous and cost me more to have the place redecorated. Fuck knows what Tony's problem is, but I will put money on it being you. You're always tormenting him and teasing him. One minute you laugh and joke, the next you're sending jewellery through the post. He never knows where he stands. You didn't exactly fight for him did you Francesca? The year wasn't up, but you couldn't wait to see the back of him. Well, fuck you! I'm glad he's getting it off his chest. Maybe now things can get back to normal. He just works and drinks; I doubt he could even raise his dick for another woman, all he talks about is you.' It seemed Jake too was fed up with the situation, but I was shocked hearing his slant on things. Was this how I seemed? To be toying with Tony and using him?

'*Mi dispiace. Mi manchi mio cara.*' Tony was waving his arms, looking like the stereotype of an Italian and walking back to where I was standing. I looked at Jake and waited.

'I'm sorry. I miss you, my dear.'

Tony was saying he missed me, but this was not the romantic setting I had fantasised about. It was a nightmare. Tony reached out and grabbed a fistful of my hair and pulled me towards him. I put my hand up to the back of my head to stop him pulling out the roots.

He tipped my head back, and I really didn't need a translator for this. '*Baciami, bella. Ti amo.*' He roughly put his mouth on mine and started to kiss me. It wasn't a gentle kiss or even a passionate one. It felt like my face was being swallowed up.

I tried pushing him away, but the more I struggled, the stronger his hold became on my hair. I shoved Tony back and put my hand to my mouth. It was bleeding. He had kissed me roughly and had bitten my bottom lip.

Jake stepped in and grabbed him. 'Enough now, Tony. Let's go, for Christ's sake. Leave her alone. Look what you've done.'

I wiped my mouth. It was throbbing. Tears filled my eyes, but from pain not sorrow.

Out of the blue, Tony reverted back to English. 'You didn't always hate me, Fran. In fact, you loved the way I made you feel. Say my name,' he demanded. 'Say my bloody name!'

'Antonias,' I said, my voice a hushed whisper. I looked at this drunken mess before me. 'You were Antonias to me, not Tony Lambrianu.'

'I still am, Fran. I will always be Antonias.'

Tony looked at Jake and then at me. His eyes were glazed. He looked as though he had run out of steam. When he started to walk towards me again, he collapsed into a heap on the floor. He had at last passed out.

Jake knelt down beside him. He was slapping his face and

saying his name, but there was no response. Tony was out cold. Jake looked up at me. 'Well, at least that's all over. Sorry, Fran, I didn't mean to shout. It's just been a stressful time. I feel like his childminder stopping him lashing out at everyone all the time. I'll get the driver to give me a hand getting him into the car.'

'Do you think you can manage to get him to one of the bedrooms upstairs?' I asked. 'Let him sleep it off here. You will only have to try and get him out at the other end. You can stay too if you want to.' I looked at Jake and then at the driver.

Jake seemed almost relieved. 'Are you sure?'

'He's only going to sleep anyway. I think I'm quite safe, don't you? He's out cold, Jake. Go on. Get him upstairs.' Tony was lying there, lifeless and snoring his head off.

Jake had his shoulders and arms, and the driver had the worst of all jobs, grabbing his legs. Tony was out cold and flopped around while they were trying to carry him. In the end, they managed to drag him up the stairs, scraping him and banging his body as they went.

As they placed him in the bedroom opposite mine, I heard a noise. It was Bobby coming out of his room. He was rubbing his eyes and walking towards me.

'It's okay, Bobby. Go back to bed. I'll be there in a minute. It's only Uncle Tony going to bed.' Poor little mite. He must have wondered what had happened. There were two men puffing and panting with sweat on their foreheads trying to drag Tony into the bedroom.

I got Bobby back into bed and reassured him that Tony was okay and he nodded and turned over, drifting off to sleep.

When I walked back into the bedroom, Jake and the driver were both standing there catching their breath. They had their hands on their hips. 'God, he's a heavy son of a bitch, and those stairs don't help. Couldn't we have just left him downstairs and thrown a duvet over him?' said Jake.

'Stop moaning, Jake. You're just as responsible for this, bringing him here. It would have been worse if you'd have had to get him in and out of the car, wouldn't it?' I snapped.

Jake held his hand up. 'Sorry, Fran. You're right. I owe you one.'

We both looked down at Tony. He was lying under the duvet, fast asleep. The lamp in the room seemed to make him glow.

'He is sure going to have a hell of a headache in the morning,' said Jake, walking down the stairs quickly. It was obvious he was eager to leave.

After they had left and I switched the downstairs lights off, I took a bucket and a bottle of water upstairs with me and walked back into Tony's room, where he was sleeping. I put the bucket at the side of the bed and the water on the bedside table, just in case. The last thing I needed after all this was Tony being sick all over the floor. At least the bedroom had an en suite.

Going back to my own bedroom, I sat on the edge of the bed and looked at the clock. It was three in the morning! I climbed into bed and lay in the dark bedroom. I played over in my mind some of the things that Jake had translated to me. Some were flattering. The rest was just bravado. I smiled to myself thinking about him waving his arms around to stress his point, like a typical Italian; everyone knew they talked with their hands.

I wondered how many other women had seen that side of him. The more I thought about him being just across the landing from me, the more restless I became. I couldn't sleep. I decided to get up and check on Bobby. Opening the door, I saw that he was fast asleep.

Then it occurred to me that I should check on Tony. After all, I was just seeing if he was all right, I reasoned with myself. I opened the door gently, just in case he had woken up but found him still in the position they'd left him in.

Impulsively I bent down as I had with Bobby and kissed his forehead. He looked so helpless. It was then that I noticed that his shoulders were bare. I pulled back the duvet and saw that they had undressed him. All they had left him with was his black silk boxer shorts. I pulled the duvet back further and marvelled at his suntanned masculine body. He was beautiful, statuesque.

Golden blond hairs were on his chest and went all the way down to his stomach. His legs had the same blond hairs, like golden fluff. The frame of his body was pure muscle. I had never seen him properly, apart from beside the swimming pool on holiday.

A thought occurred to me. I had never shared a bed with my husband. The two times we had been intimate, it had been outdoors and in the dark. I don't know what possessed me to do it, but I dropped the straps from my nightgown and let it fall to the floor and gently eased myself in beside him.

I raised my hand and let my fingers trace the outline of his perfectly formed lips. I leaned over and gently kissed them. I let my fingers trail down from his lips to the cleft in his chin and the square jaw it rested on. I could feel myself becoming aroused. It was time to leave, but I couldn't.

I knew it was wrong, taking advantage of someone unconscious like this, but I wasn't doing anything wrong. Was I? No harm was being done, I reasoned with myself, and decided to stay just a little longer. I let my hand slide down to his stomach and felt the muscles beneath the flesh.

I lay closer to him and rested my head on his chest. I let my tongue flick over his nipple, and I raised my leg and rested it over his stomach and thigh. I could feel my breathing increasing. He was still unconscious. He hadn't stirred one bit this entire time. I carried on stroking him and then began rubbing my breast against him. I raised myself up slightly, letting my tongue trace the outline of his lips. It felt wonderful; I pulled the duvet back and could see his body, and I instinctively started moving my own against his. This was pure lust, and I didn't care.

Taking his weak hand, I placed it on my breast gently, so as not to wake him. I moved his hand around them, feeling his caress. Breathing heavily now and trying to compose myself, I stopped. I lay my head back on his chest and drifted off into a deep sleep – warm and safe in the arms of the man I loved. It would be the last chance I would ever have of holding him in my arms again. What a night to remember. It was my secret.

Tony turned over in the middle of the night and pulled me closer to his body. 'Francesca,' he murmured in his sleep.

I woke with a start. My God, what time was it? I looked at the bedside clock and saw that it was around six. Oh no, I had been there for hours. I was lying on my left side, and Tony was lying behind me. We were like two spoons in a drawer, his head resting on my shoulder.

Lifting his arm up gently, not daring to breathe, I edged myself out of the bed. Carefully, I reached for my discarded nightgown on the floor and put it on, all the time not daring to take my eyes off Tony in case he woke.

I tiptoed to the door and slowly turned the handle, glancing backwards to make sure Tony hadn't stirred. I went back to my own bedroom, sat on the edge of the bed and took a breath. What had I done? My heart was pounding. I messed up my own duvet cover on my own bed and thumped the pillows as though I had slept there. Then I pulled on my dressing gown and went downstairs.

I switched on the kettle and started making some coffee. It was nearly time to wake Bobby for school. As though on autopilot, I set out the breakfast things. When I sat down to drink my coffee, wanting to take a moment to myself, it stung. The hot liquid hurt my mouth. I reached up to touch it and remembered that was where Tony had bitten me when he had kissed me.

I touched it again. It was sore, but it was a nice memory. I brushed my hair back and tightened my bathrobe around me. It was time to wake Bobby. He was half awake when I went into his room.

'Come on, Bobby. Time to get up.' I put my finger to my lips. 'Shush. Tony is still asleep. Come on, quiet as a mouse now.'

Bobby smiled and was enjoying the little game. He stifled giggles as he walked past Tony's door.

Downstairs, Bobby asked me why Tony was sleeping at our house. I told him he had been passing and didn't feel well, so he had come here. That seemed to satisfy his curiosity, and he returned to eating his breakfast and watching television.

I put my coffee cup on the breakfast bar. Now, it was time to make noise. Bobby had to go and get washed and dressed, and anyone who knows children knows they cannot do it quietly.

I wasn't at work until the afternoon, so I was surprised when Elle came in. I must have looked guilty or something, because instantly, she asked me if I was okay.

'Yes, I'm fine, Elle. It's just that Tony's upstairs, fast asleep.'

I saw the look in her eyes, and a wry smile appeared on her face.

'Oh no. It's not what you think,' I added quickly, feeling my embarrassment.

'It's okay, Fran. I know,' she interrupted me. 'Jake rang me and told me about Tony turning up drunk last night.'

I told her I didn't think he was awake, as Bobby had been up and down the stairs stomping around, and that was enough to wake the dead. I told Elle I was going to take a shower while she watched Bobby for me. I saw her look at my swollen mouth, but she didn't say anything.

Waiting for Tony to wake up felt like a nerve-racking death sentence. I needed to know if he remembered anything about his drunken stupor. No, I really needed to know if he remembered anything about me... and what I'd done to him last night.

* * *

After dropping Bobby at school, I walked back into the kitchen, avoiding Tony's stare. He put down his knife and fork.

'Morning, sleepyhead. Do you want some more coffee?' Still avoiding his gaze, I started pouring coffee into his cup.

He grabbed my arm. 'Who did that to you, Francesca?'

'You did, Tony,' I said light-heartedly, 'right after you threw the wedding rings out of the conservatory doors into the garden.'

His face drained of colour. 'Are you saying I hit you, Fran?' He stood up in a wild panic. He was looking at my swollen lip.

'No, Tony, you didn't hit me.' I smiled at him to ease his guilt. 'You tried to kiss me and ended up sucking my face off and doing this instead,' I added, with a hint of sarcasm, just for the hell of it.

Slamming his fist down on the worktop and knocking over his coffee, he shouted at me, 'If I was so bad, why did you let me stay here?' He was angry, though not really at me. It was himself who he was angry with. It was clear last night was a complete blur to him.

'Calm down, Tony. You were out cold. It was easier to let you stay here to sleep it off.' Then I thought I would subtly question him about my own guilt. 'Do you remember anything about last night?' I asked him. I needed to know if he remembered anything about our encounter.

With his elbows resting on the worktop and his head in his hands, he said, 'Let me think, Fran. Just give me a minute.'

Elle decided to make herself scarce and went to strip the beds upstairs. I sat before him, waiting to see what would pop into his brain first.

'I admit, Fran. I was angry that you sent your wedding rings back and wanted to clear the house of me, and then you sent me a cheque for the extension. It was my birthday, Fran. I got my divorce papers. And well... I don't know. It all sounds a mess I know. But I'm sorry about everything.' He looked very sheepish, like a young boy with his hands caught in the sweet jar.

I was confused. Why would Tony react like that over the divorce papers? That was what he'd wanted and we'd both known it was coming. So why did he care? None of this made sense.

'I'm sorry, Fran. Can I have a shower and then I will leave you in peace?'

Tony walked into the hallway. He telephoned his driver and then went upstairs to take a shower.

Elle was on her way down with the bedding she had taken off. 'Well, Fran, I think you have made him feel as badly as you possibly could. Don't you?' she said. She looked a little stern, but I dismissed it. 'It's a shame you didn't tell him that Jake must have dropped this under the duvet while he was getting him into bed.' Her voice dripped with sarcasm.

This time it was me who felt guilty. She held up my earring between her finger and thumb. I could feel my face burning with shame, taking the earring out of her hand and thinking up an excuse.

I laughed it off and told her that it must have come off during the struggle of getting Tony into bed.

She gave me a look that said she didn't believe me at all. I immediately felt defensive.

'What are you implying, Elle?' I snapped. 'I didn't ask for some drunk to turn up in the middle of the night, throwing diamond rings out of the window and insulting me in Italian, did I?' I picked up Susie's lead and headed for the door. I needed to get out of there quickly.

Elle had seen straight through me. She knew I wasn't as innocent as I was making out.

I walked along the beach. It was going to be another beautiful day. I made sure I was out of the house for a good couple of hours. I mentally timed how long it would take for Tony's driver to pick him up. I wanted Tony gone when I got back, and I was crossing my fingers that Elle hadn't told him about my earring.

When I eventually got home, Elle was making herself busy tidying around, and she informed me that Tony had said thank you and left feeling guilty. 'Oh, he told me to give you this.' Elle held out the cheque I had written. 'He said he would pay for the extension, and he meant it.' Her voice was still a little stern, and she was making her point.

I made some excuse to go out into the garden. Out of curiosity, I wondered if my rings would be anywhere to be seen. I looked around, spreading my hands over the soil. There was nothing. They had gone. I hoped that, maybe when I cut the lawn, they would get caught in the blades, and I would find them. It would be a shame if they were lost forever.

* * *

As soon as Julie got back from her holiday, she came round, baby bump first, with a handful of designer shopping bags. 'Prezzies, girls, from abroad, courtesy of Ralph's credit card.' She laughed out loud.

It was good to see her. We had both missed her. She was full of gossip about all of the sights she had seen. She moaned relent-lessly about Ralph being overprotective and boring, though Elle and I could both see she had enjoyed it. She had put on a little weight, but as far as she was concerned, she looked like a beach whale!

She told us all about Josh and what a pleasure it was seeing him enjoy a holiday for once – probably because Julie had been sober and Ralph hadn't spent all of the time on the telephone. It must have seemed like a real family holiday to Josh.

Julie enjoyed asking Elle about Albert and how things were going. She loved tormenting and teasing Elle about the new man in her life. For once, I could watch Elle squirm and look embarrassed.

'He's not my Albert, Julie,' Elle said indignantly. 'He's just a friend. That's all.' She poured Julie some orange juice and didn't mention Albert again.

'Well, you have had my gossip. What's yours? Anything exciting happen?' Julie looked back and forth between us, waiting for one of us to speak up.

Elle got in first. After Julie's teasing, she wanted to get her own back. 'Tony stayed over,' she said. And then, having purposefully dropped her bombshell, she hurriedly made herself scarce, going upstairs to dust something.

Julie's eyes widened with expectation. She picked up her glass and took a sip. 'Well, well, Francesca. Come on. Give me the dirt.' She made herself more comfortable on her chair and waited.

'Oh, there's nothing to tell.' I explained what had happened.

Apart from being shocked and then bursting into laughter about his foolish behaviour, she looked at me oddly. 'What is it, Fran? What is it you're not telling me?' She gave me that cheeky wink of hers and waited.

Of course, I denied there was anything more to tell and brushed her suspicion off.

She waved her finger at me. 'You're hiding something, Fran. Spit it out.' Julie was a wise woman, and she could see straight through me, unlike Elle, who wasn't sure. Julie could see my guilt and wasn't going to stop probing until she got the truth. Now this was the kind of gossip she enjoyed.

I got up to close the kitchen door and made my way back over to the breakfast bar to where she was sitting. I saw the frown on her brow. Now she knew there was something, because I didn't want Elle hearing it.

'I may as well tell you because I know you won't leave it alone. But before I do, Julie, you have to swear not to tell a soul. Promise me, or I won't tell you. I mean it, Julie, if you ever say a word, our friendship is over.'

She could see I was serious and was taken aback at what I had said. She folded her arms. 'Okay, Fran, I swear. Has he hurt you? Because if he has, I will strangle that son of a bitch with my bare hands.' I could see Julie's anger rising.

I shook my head. I didn't want to raise her blood pressure. Then I poured out the whole sordid story from beginning to end. I could see the shocked expression in her face, and little by little, her jaw nearly fell onto the breakfast bar. She stayed quiet and didn't comment until I had finished.

I was glad to tell someone. I had felt it was loving and warm at the time, but now, the more I thought about it, it sounded disgusting. When at last I finished my confession, I looked at her, waiting for everything I had said to sink into her astonished brain.

Suddenly she burst into laughter – large howling laughter. Tears were coming down her face, and she could hardly speak. So much for not raising her blood pressure. 'You saucy minx. Are you telling me that while he was unconscious, you were groping him and getting off on it?' Again she burst into laughter, wiping the tears from her eyes with the backs of her hands.

'It wasn't like that, I swear.' I could feel my face burning. I hadn't expected this. I thought she would have taken it more seriously.

'Tell it to the judge Francesca. Oh my God this is hilarious.'

'Shut up, will you. Elle will hear you.' It had felt good telling someone and getting it off my chest, but her reaction made me curse myself.

'You promised me, Julie. Not a word. Not a word to anyone. You promised.' I was desperate now and could feel my panic. Why had I told her? What had I done?

'You know what, Fran, love. I almost wish I hadn't promised now. Do you realise he would be suicidal if he knew? In fact, I don't know a man in the universe who wouldn't be kicking himself. There he was, in body, if not in spirit, and a gorgeous young woman climbs into bed with him and starts groping him, and he doesn't remember. Are you sure he doesn't know?'

I let out a sigh of relief. Thank God Julie could see the funny side of it. 'I think I covered my tracks,' I said and then burst out laughing with her.

Although we were laughing like two schoolgirls now, I still regretted telling her.

26

A FAMILY HOLIDAY

At last my mam and brothers were coming for a holiday. It was nearly the end of the summer and the only time my mam could get off work. Nothing was going to spoil this holiday. I had looked forward to it for weeks. I met Mam and the boys at the train station. I had hired a minibus for the week.

After loads of hugs and kisses at the station, we all, including Mam's horrible boyfriend George, piled into the minibus. He had decided to come after all, and I had decided to make a valiant effort for my mam's sake. But I could see the pound signs in George's eyes when he saw the house.

I suggested a walk on the beach, and the seafront was in full swing, people enjoying their holidays. The caravan parks were packed to the hilt with families enjoying the weather and all the seaside pleasures. The queues for the theme park were long, so I suggested we go back later or another day. After all, I lived there. We didn't need to stay and do it all in one day, did we?

Watching my brothers and Bobby paddling around in the sea and building sandcastles warmed my heart. I had got all this through my deal with Tony. There had been times when I had wondered if it had been worth it, but seeing them all enjoying themselves confirmed it. It had all been worth it.

It was nearly five by the time we got back. I didn't think anyone would want to eat much, considering they had eaten fish and chips, ice creams, and doughnuts. As predicted, the boys weren't hungry, so it was upstairs to the bathrooms to shower off all of the sand. They all looked tired, and obviously they just wanted to relax, possibly watch television. Then it would be time for bed.

It was a warm evening. So they all wanted to sit outside in the garden with their drinks, their faces red from the sun and bearing that tired look that comes from a good day. It was time to discuss what we would all do tomorrow.

It was at this moment that George finally got his backside off my sofa and came out to join us, beef sandwich in one hand and a can of lager in the other. He really had made himself comfortable. 'What about meeting the big man himself?' he said, looking at me directly.

I looked at George, waiting for him to say what he meant.

'That husband, or should I say that ex-husband, of yours. When are we going to visit his fancy club?' The smug expression on his face made my blood boil, and my mam could see it.

'What he means, Fran,' she said in that peacemaker voice of hers, 'is that it would be nice during the holiday to have an adult's night out. Maybe visit the club we have all heard about.' She was defending George's shallow comments. That was all he had come for, to meet Tony and possibly have his photo taken with him to impress all of his friends down at the local pub.

'Anyone is welcome to go, George,' I said through gritted teeth. 'The entry fee is around 100 pounds. In fact, I don't mind babysitting while you take my mam out. That would be nice, wouldn't it?' I knew he had no intention of spending that much money on an entrance fee.

That really didn't go down well at all. He gave me one of those disgruntled looks I had come to associate with him and took another gulp of his lager. He didn't say any more on the matter.

My brother told me when I took them all upstairs to bed that George had told all of his friends at his local pub that he was best friends with Tony. God, what an overbearing man. I felt I might need some help during the course of George's stay. So I telephoned Julie and asked what she was doing over the next couple of days.

Thankfully, like the cavalry, Julie turned up the next morning, all guns blazing. She had everyone make a list of where they wanted to go and put all of their bits of paper in a bowl and shook it. She took out one piece of paper and read it. That was the plan, and over the next few days, it was how we decided what we'd do.

George had at last had his bit of excitement. He had met Julie Gold. He sat at the breakfast bar with her, and his eyes lit up. 'You're Julie Gold,' he said, stating the obvious. 'I've read about you and that husband of yours. He's a bit of a lad, isn't he?' I think he was waiting for some silly stories to come out about Ralph so that he could pass them on to his friends. But this was Julie he was talking to.

Julie looked at me and then at George. She gave her best smile and walked up to him with all her feminine charm. It reminded me of the first time I had ever met her.

'I am glad you've heard of Ralph, George. Just thank your lucky stars he hasn't heard of you.' She tweaked his chin for good measure and sat back down again.

George's smile dropped. If he had read anything about Ralph, this thinly-veiled threat from Julie spoke volumes. She had put him in his place without an argument or a cross word.

What had happened to my mother? Had she lost her tongue or something? She never stopped him bossing my brothers about or pretending to be the man of my house.

Julie kept a lid on things. 'It's their business, Fran. He's not hitting the kids or anything, is he?'

'No, he's not hitting them. It's just his attitude towards them, Julie. And you've heard the way he speaks to my mam sometimes, like she's his servant.'

She opened her arms and gave me a hug as best as she could, considering her bump. 'Fran, love, I have met these kinds of men. They want status. He has boasted far and wide that his girlfriend's daughter is a Lambrianu, divorced or not. While he's doing his best to impress his friends, they are buying him free drinks and making his ego bigger. He sees you as the golden goose.'

Julie made good sense. George was afraid of losing face in front of his friends and become a laughing stock.

* * *

The next few days passed in a blur. Julie stayed over with Josh. It was easier than coming and going. Elle helped with the boys and even took them to the arcades. We had done all of the London sights, including the London Zoo. Julie happened to know what time the changing of the guard was at Buckingham Palace. I wanted her to take it easy, and Ralph was in constant touch, but she seemed to be enjoying herself. And with her pregnancy, she was glowing.

Julie talked George into taking some time out and popping down to the local pub for a few drinks. She took a twenty-pound note out of her purse and told him to have one for her.

He was out of the door as quick as a flash. I know I had wanted my mam to myself, but I also felt it would have been nice if he had asked her to join him. But this was our chance to discuss with Mam about buying her house for her. Mam wasn't sure.

'Listen to me,' said Julie in her usual authoritative manner.

'We're going to buy that house of yours, something bigger if you wish. And it's going to be in Fran's name. That way, you will always have a roof over your head and a bit of security for your boys.' She spoke to my mam in a wise, worldly manner – woman to woman, so to speak.

At last, my mam let Julie's words sink in and agreed. 'I get lonely sometimes, Julie,' she said, reaching for Julie's hand. 'It's nice to have someone around to help out – an adult conversation, someone to hug me for a change and listen all about my bad day.'

'I know, love,' said Julie, putting her arms around my mam. 'Come on, Fran. Group hug. Girls united.'

I smiled at Julie over my mam's head. She really was a problem-solver.

* * *

All too soon, it was time for them to leave. The boys were all slightly tanned from the sun. They had really enjoyed themselves. But you could see by their lack of enthusiasm for another day out that they were tired.

Julie, in the meantime, had not let the grass grow. She had already contacted the lawyers who worked for Ralph, saying she felt now was the time they earn their money. They had contacted Mam's landlord, and plans to buy the house were all set in motion.

Julie had been amazed at the difference in the price of houses from London to Yorkshire – so much so she'd insisted we use the money I had in my budget to build a small extension on the back of Mam's house. There she went again, organising everything. It was all a dream to my mam; but at last she seemed happy. And so I was happy too.

27

FRIENDS WITH BENEFITS

I was getting ready to work the afternoon shift when I heard the familiar chime on my mobile that indicated I'd received a message. It was from Tony.

Have dinner with me, Francesca

I read the message again. I didn't know what to say. Why would he want me to go to dinner with him?

Instinctively, I texted back:

Why and when? And if it's at the club, the answer is no.

I pressed send and nervously waited for a reply.

My mobile chimed again.

You choose where and when.

There was no answer to the why, but I was tempted. I put my mobile down on the worktop. I confess, my pulse raced, especially after remembering my last encounter with him. But the nagging thought was why? We had nothing to discuss any more. What bombshell was he going to drop on me? Was he getting married? I wasn't sure about it.

Julie broke the silence and ran into the kitchen where I was still standing. looking at my mobile.

'Have I got some news for you!' She was beaming as she took her usual place at the table. She put down her bag, still smiling. 'Ralph and I have decided to move. It's going to take a while because a lot of work needs doing. The place needs rewiring and has no central heating. Oh no, I forgot to tell Ralph that bit,' she said, putting her hand over her mouth.

'Where are you going, Julie? Abroad or something?' I was pleased for her, but selfishly my heart sank. What about me?

'Well now you mention it, Fran, have you seen that little church nearby?' Julie bowed her head a little, and I could see a pale pink flush in her cheeks, highlighted by her blonde hair. 'It's not that far from here, and it means less travelling time, plus Ralph will save a fortune on petrol, tight fisted old git.' She smiled. 'It makes sense, don't you think? What with me being here most of the time...'

It felt as if she was asking for my approval. She didn't want to invade my space. For once, I could see the hesitant, almost shy side of Julie.

My smile couldn't have been wider, which I could see made her feel better. 'I think that's a great idea Julie; I would like that.' I beamed. 'But which church, where?' I asked. I couldn't recall one, apart from an old building that resembled a church, with a great big steeple, about ten miles away.

'What, do you mean that old derelict church that hasn't been used in years?' asked Elle. 'It's an eyesore. Shame though; it used to be beautiful.'

'That's the one. And I'm glad you said that Fran, as Ralph and I have just bought it.' Julie glanced at me slightly sheepishly. 'It's going to cost a fortune, I know, because we can't pull it down – registered building or whatever they call it.' She was laughing now.

'Julie,' said Elle in that motherly way of hers, 'that is going to take a lot of work. It's a listed building and hundreds of years old. It's a building site.'

Julie wouldn't be put off; in fact, Elle's protests made her more determined. 'Yes, I know. But Ralph has enough money. It's about time he started spending it. And it's not a building site, Elle. It's my building site – lock, stock, and steeple.'

Her excitement was infectious. She started telling us all of her plans for the church and how she felt like Lady Chatterley having a gamekeeper's cottage on the grounds. After a couple of hours of details on how the building firms and architects were already working together and making up blueprints for approval, at last she took a breath.

'Now then, what about you?' she said when Elle had decided to hang the washing out, still dazed by Julie's announcement. 'Come on, Fran. Have you got over your night of illicit passion yet?'

Now it was my turn to tease her. 'Oh, nothing exciting: work, Bobby, shopping. And, oh yes, Tony texted me asking me out to dinner.' I grinned at her with a casual air.

Her eyes widened, and her jaw dropped a little. 'Well, when are you going? Come on, when? Or have you been already and tucked him in again.' She was laughing now. She was never going to let me live that night down.

'No, I haven't.' I gave her wrist a gentle slap. 'I wish I had never told you about that now.'

'Come on, Fran. I'm a pregnant woman who is starting to balloon out. Ralph has gone into celibacy, and this is the closest I have come to sex in ages. So when you going and what are you wearing?'

'I'm not. I've decided there's no point. Why does he want to have dinner with me? We have nothing to discuss. He's not short of dinner parties, or women to have dinner with, so what's the catch? I just feel like some substitute for a quiet night.'

Stupidly, I went to the loo, leaving my mobile in full view. Julie, I would learn later, had seen my mobile charging on the worktop. Her mischievous brain had gone to work again. Once I returned, Julie said, 'I've been thinking, Fran. Next week's your birthday, isn't it?' She smiled at me and then at Elle.

I had secretly hoped her baby brain would make her forget. 'Yes, it is, Julie. But I don't want to go to the club. I'm just going to stay here and have a quiet one, okay.'

'That's fine. Let's face it, Fran. I'm not exactly in a position to have a good booze-up, am I?' Julie pointed to her stomach. 'I tell you what. Thursday I am busy, but why don't we have dinner on Saturday at that Italian place in town, just us. What do you say?'

'That's a lovely idea. Thank you, Julie. Do you want to come, Elle?' I said. 'After all, we could take Bobby with us.'

Elle was emphatic. She couldn't come because she was going to babysit and let us have a girl's night out. That was the end of that.

Julie popped around in the week. She had brought my card and present. She'd left earlier than normal. But as she'd left, she had given me a kiss and said, 'You do know I would never do anything to upset or hurt you, don't you, Fran? You're my family, and I just want you to be happy.'

She had gone all sentimental and tearful. I could only presume it was hormones. I gave her a hug. 'Of course I do, Julie. Girl power, eh?' I tried making light of it. I didn't know where she was going with this, but there was real affection in her hug.

She sniffed and wiped her damp eyes. 'See you Saturday at seven. I'll meet you there. You can wear my present. The little

Italian restaurant. After all, you like a bit of Italian, don't you?' She winked and walked out of the door.

I was a little perturbed. 'Elle, do you think Julie is okay?' I walked over to the dress box Julie had brought with her. It was the famous little black Chanel dress. It was beautiful and very expensive. I held it up and looked at it.

'She's pregnant, Fran, and that is beautiful. You know she loves you, although I must say you couldn't be more different. They do say opposites attract, don't they?' Elle laughed. Obviously she knew something I didn't.

My mam and the boys had sent me some slippers and some books they knew I wanted. Elle had bought me some earrings from herself and Bobby. It was a nice birthday, and in the evening we had a takeaway. Bobby fell asleep, and I carried him to bed halfway through a movie.

There wasn't a word from Tony. I was a little disappointed; I had to admit it.

* * *

I had been looking forward to Saturday night with Julie. It had been a busy week, and with one thing and another, I felt I deserved a treat. I made a real effort. I left my hair curly, and it hung down my back in ringlets. I put black sparkly combs in it so it would sweep to the side and down my left shoulder.

Elle had bought me some diamante earrings. So I thought I would give them an outing. Julie had not only bought my dress, when I looked in the box properly, I saw there was another Chanel box inside containing high black velvet court shoes. You had to hand it to Julie. She knew how to dress.

Elle was looking after Bobby for me, and I told her I wouldn't be late. But she waved her hand in the air and told me to take as long as I wanted. I decided to drive to the restaurant. Julie wouldn't be drinking, so neither would I.

I got to the restaurant fifteen minutes early. I was surprised when I said there was a table booked in the name of Gold and the restaurant staff had no knowledge of the booking. In the end, I told them to try Lambrianu, and yes, they found it. How strange.

I waited for what seemed forever. Directly at seven, I got a text to say she had been delayed and couldn't make it. Her text was full of apologies and promises of how she would make it up to me and telephone me later. Damn it. I was all dressed up with nowhere to go. I had bent down to pick up my bag when I heard my name.

'Francesca, you look stunning.' I looked up and saw Tony standing there.

Oh no, what on earth was he doing here? He looked stunning too, though, as if he had just stepped out of a James Bond movie. He was wearing his tuxedo. His blond hair shone, and his fringe swept across his face.

'Tony,' I half stammered, 'how are you?' I didn't know what to say. In the back of my mind, I wondered who he was having dinner with, having made such an effort. I scanned the room quickly, looking for a lone beautiful woman sitting at a table, but I couldn't see anyone.

He sat down opposite me at the table. He was all smiles and charm. I watched as he placed a little present bag on the table, and I ignored it. He motioned to the waiter to come over and then asked me what I wanted to drink. This was weird, but I presumed he was just being polite and killing time before his date turned up.

'No thanks. I was just leaving.'

'You're leaving? Why? I'm not late.' He looked at his watch and then back at me. He looked confused and then saw the confused looked on my face. 'What's wrong, Francesca? Changed your mind, have you?'

'Changed my mind about what?'

'Changed your mind about having dinner with me, of course. The very least you could do was text me and tell me.' He started to sound upset and angry, as though I had played some awful trick on him.

'I was having dinner with Julie for my birthday,' I stammered. 'She has just texted me to say she can't make it.' I took out my mobile and showed him the message.

Then Tony held up his mobile, showing me the text I had supposedly sent him asking him out to dinner. Julie!

Tony's face paled underneath his suntan. 'You didn't send this text, did you, Francesca?' He looked down at the table. He was starting to go a little red in the cheeks – possibly from embarrassment or anger, maybe a little of both. I shook my head and told him I had no knowledge of the text. I knew the minute I left he would rant and rave at Ralph and possibly Julie.

'Right then,' he said, standing up. 'I will leave you to it. Sorry about the mix-up, Francesca. Bye.'

I reached out my hand to stop him. I had to do something, as silly as I felt. I knew he would take Julie to task over this, and his words would be harsher than mine could ever be. Now I knew what she'd meant when she had said she wouldn't do anything to hurt me. She'd planned this and was probably shaking in her boots right now.

'Tony,' I half whispered, 'we could have a drink together before you go. After all, we're both dressed up and have nothing else planned, unless you have other plans of course.'

He looked at my face and slowly sat down again.

'I don't have any plans, not yet anyway. So we could, if you want to. It seems your friend Julie not only has a lot of explaining to do but she has put a lot of trouble into her deceit and lies. Sorry, Francesca.'

Looking at him, I realised he had gone to an awful lot of trouble just to meet me.

'This'– he handed the little Chanel bag to me – 'is for your birthday.' He made a point of looking nonchalant and bored with the whole thing. He wasn't a man who liked to look a fool in front of a woman, and goodness knows who or what he had turned down to come and meet me here this evening.

In the bag was my favourite perfume. I couldn't help smiling. 'This is lovely. Thank you, Tony. How did you know Chanel was my favourite perfume?'

Tony just shrugged and told me he had smelt it the other day, and it had reminded him of me for some reason. He looked puzzled at the thought.

Now it was my turn to feel embarrassed. I had been wearing it the night he had come to the house. Before I had gone into his room, I had given myself an extra spray of it. No wonder he looked puzzled, somewhere in the back of his mind, he was having flash-backs to that night. I dreaded that he would remember everything one day.

I opened the perfume and gave myself a spray, which seemed to please him and put the smile back on his face. The waiter, now noticing we were staying, came back to the table to take our drinks order.

He started asking about Bobby and Elle and then telling me about the club and Jake. The conversation flowed. It seemed we both felt at ease with each other and had a lot more in common than we had ever realised.

'Do you want to stay for dinner, Francesca?' he asked me in those beautiful velvety tones of his. He looked relaxed now and was laughing at my silly stories of my days at the doctor's surgery. He had a warm heartfelt laugh. It suited him and made me feel good about myself.

I saw other women sitting at their tables casting sideways glances at him. And why not? If I had been in their seats, I would have looked at him too. The candle in the lamp seemed to flicker in those blue eyes of his. I nodded that I would like dinner with him, and we ordered.

This was a fun restaurant. That was why I liked it. The entertainment was the staff. Every now and then, they would burst into song. They were very good and very funny. The chef, dressed in his white chef's hat, black trousers, and a large white linen apron wrapped around his large stomach, came out and gave us a rendition of Pavarotti. Everyone was cheering and clapping. The atmosphere was electric.

Suddenly, the chef looked across the room and saw us. He pushed his way through the crowd. 'Mr Lambrianu, Antonias my boy.' He held up his arms and Tony stood up to hug him. They seemed genuinely pleased to see each other.

They talked and laughed in Italian for a few minutes, and then Tony introduced me. 'This is Francesca.'

I held out my hand to shake his, but he ignored me for a moment and turned to Tony and spoke in Italian again. I could see Tony looking slightly embarrassed, almost like a schoolboy.

The chef put his enormous arms around me and gave me a hug. 'You are the lovely Francesca we have all heard about.' He was nodding and smiling. 'Even your name sounds Italian, my beauty.' He kissed the back of my hand and turned to speak to Tony again. He carried on, shaking Tony's hand and chattering until eventually he left.

'I take it he's a friend of yours then?' It was nice to see Tony looking so relaxed in front of old friends he obviously knew and trusted.

'A family friend, an old family friend, Francesca. Sorry I didn't mean to be rude and speak Italian in front of you like that. It's been a long time.'

I asked what Tony had ordered, and he took a forkful of his food and steered it to my mouth. I opened my mouth and tasted it. We were sharing each other's meal. It was a real fun night out, and I was enjoying myself enormously.

When we had finished eating, the waiter cleared the table, and the chef came out with a trolley. On the trolley was a large birthday cake, in the shape of an F. The candles were a fire hazard, and it had sparklers on the top that seemed to light up the room. I couldn't contain my pleasure.

Tony looked at me. 'I ordered it a couple of days ago, when I thought you wanted to have dinner with me,' he said. I couldn't help thinking, *No wonder women love him. He really does think of everything.*

'What a lovely thought, Tony.' I leaned over without thinking and gave him a gentle kiss on the lips. 'Thank you, Antonias.'

It seemed to cause a tense moment. He looked at me, and I couldn't quite make out what he was thinking. In my excitement, I had got carried away. Maybe I had overstepped the mark.

'Are you okay?' I asked him. His mind seemed to be wandering, and he looked a little confused.

'I'm fine. In fact, I am very good.' He smiled. 'That perfume suits you. You should wear it all the time.' He grinned at me.

The waiter interrupted us and gave me the knife to cut the cake. I cut one slice while everyone in the restaurant sang 'Happy Birthday' to me. I insisted everyone have a slice of the cake to celebrate. This was met by huge applause.

I ordered a soda water, and Tony ordered a brandy. 'Take a sip,' he said. 'Have you tried it before?'

I shook my head. I wasn't a drinker. He knew that, though. I had the odd glass of wine now and again, but nothing as hard-core as brandy. Taking the glass from him, I took a sip. It was nice. I handed the glass back to him.

'You know,' he said, 'you should never drink brandy out of a cold glass. You should always drink it warm. It tastes better.'

He moved his chair around the table next to me, almost sitting on my knee. He took a sip of the brandy. I was slightly puzzled. Then he held my chin and moved closer to my mouth. He leaned in to kiss me, and I opened my mouth. It seemed like the most natural thing in the world.

Gently kissing me, he shared the brandy from his own mouth. It felt warm. A little dribbled down my chin, but the warm golden liquid filled my mouth and warmed my throat and chest as I swallowed. We pulled apart. Some of the brandy was on his own chin, and he wiped it with a napkin. The feeling was electric. Suddenly, I felt like I was in the restaurant alone with him. I couldn't see anyone else but him as I looked into those blue eyes. I raised my hand and swept his fringe away from his forehead and smiled.

Stupidly, I opened my big mouth and broke the moment. 'Tell me, Mr L.' I grinned at him. 'Do you spend all your days thinking up seduction tricks to impress your lady friends?' I started to laugh, but then I realised it wasn't funny at all.

The mood changed instantly. I looked around the room and saw people looking at us. Tony moved his chair back to his side of the table. Those blue eyes of his seemed to go darker, and I knew I had upset him. What a stupid woman I was, and what a ridiculous thing to say.

'For God's sake, Francesca, you know how to kill the moment, don't you?' he snapped at me.

I reached my hand out across the table and laid it on his. 'Sorry, Tony. It was a joke. I didn't mean it like it sounded.' I felt awful. There was nothing I could do or say to take it back.

'No, Francesca. I'm the joke, aren't I? You always throw my past in my face. I have never denied I like women. And some, you may be surprised to learn, actually like me.'

Now I could tell he was angry.

'Nothing can compare to that lovely husband of yours, can it? You know, the one who you loved and adored until he treated you like rubbish, used you as a punching bag, and dumped you,' he spat out at me.

I knew he was getting his own back with the only weapon he had. Still, I felt the dig was the lowest of the lows and my eyes brimmed with tears. I hadn't meant to ridicule him. And of course, he only spoke the truth about Luke; that was the worst part.

He took out his wallet, pulled a pile of money out of it, and put it on the table. He indicated to the waiter that it was there and started to stand up.

The manager came over and picked up the money and handed it back. 'Your money is no good here, Tony. I hope you enjoyed your evening. Come back soon, eh?' Then he spoke a little in Italian to him, and they shook hands.

I looked on, feeling foolish and embarrassed at my stupidity.

Tony looked down at the table where I was still sitting. I felt like crying. 'I will walk you to your car if you wish. No seduction tricks, just a gentlemanly gesture.'

I nodded and stood up.

Fortunately, my car was just outside, so there wasn't far to walk.

'Thank you for a lovely evening, Tony. I'm sorry I spoilt it.' I was waiting for absolution.

'Goodnight, Francesca.' He walked to his car and left me standing on the pavement.

I started my car and drove off. After a couple of minutes, I pulled over and put my head into my hands and let the tears fall. I had ruined everything. I wiped my faced and drove on home.

It was quite early when I got back and Elle was still up. 'Is that you, Fran?' she called to me. She came down the hallway and saw my face. My mascara was smudged, and my nose was red. It was obvious I had been crying.

'What's happened, Francesca? Why have you been crying? For goodness' sake, what has Tony done now?'

Elle hadn't realised what she had just said, but it was obvious she had been in on this date with Julie. Otherwise, how would she know that I had seen Tony?

I walked into her open arms and told her what I had said and done. She hugged me, but I saw her eyes roll up to the ceiling, and she sighed. I could tell she wasn't pleased with me. On asking her, she confirmed she had known from the beginning that I would be meeting Tony for dinner. She had laughed at the time when Julie made the date, and now she wished she had talked her out of it, or at the very least told me not to go.

We had a coffee and she decided to go home and not stay over. I felt she was also angry with me. Who could blame her?

I texted Tony and apologised, but he didn't answer.

My mobile rang, and when I looked down, I saw that it was Julie. I was sorely disappointed, but I answered anyway. I wanted to give her a piece of my mind. This was all her fault. She never should have interfered.

'Are you alone?' she whispered down the telephone. 'Did you have a good time, Fran?' Her voice was filled with excitement, and she stopped, waiting for my answer.

'No, I bloody well didn't. And it's all your fault. Just keep your nose out in future, will you, Julie?' I knew I was using her as the whipping boy, and I could hear the hurt in her voice when she tried apologising and wanted to know what had happened.

Once I had calmed down, I told her about the evening. She seemed pleased with how it had gone, and then I told her what I'd said. I could hear the exasperation in her voice. I had upset three people in one evening. Yet the truth was, I was to blame.

There was nothing else to do but turn off the lights and check on Bobby before going to bed. Looking in the mirror, I saw my tear-stained face black with mascara and watched Bobby as he slept without a care in the world.

I texted Tony, hoping he had calmed down a little. But I knew it was pointless. Even when I rang him, there was no answer. So I just left a message for him to ring me back. I knew I wouldn't be able to sleep, but once I had taken off my make-up I went to bed anyway, putting my mobile phone under the pillow and hoping it would ring. It didn't of course.

28

THE COLD LIGHT OF DAY

Tony didn't reply to any of my texts. Even though I went through the motions and spent Sunday with Bobby, my evening out and what a nice time I'd had kept going through my mind.

Monday was back to work. Bobby was at school, and life carried on as normal. When I got home to Elle and Bobby having dinner before he did his homework, Julie turned up.

'I know you think it's all my fault, Fran. But it wasn't, was it?' she said, pointing out the obvious. 'You said yourself that you enjoyed it. The rest was up to you.'

I put down a mug of coffee in front of her. There was nothing more to say, and it wasn't worth arguing about it. She was right, though. I had enjoyed myself, and then I had opened my big mouth and blown it.

The next day I woke with a start. Something had woken me up, but I didn't know what it was. I had heard someone call my name in the darkness of the bedroom. I jumped out of bed and turned the lights on to illuminate the room to the fullest. I went into Bobby's room to see if he was okay, but then a thought occurred to me. Bobby wouldn't call me Francesca. I had heard it as clear as day. Tentatively, I crept downstairs, but there was no one around. I had a feeling of dread but couldn't explain it.

It felt spooky, eerie to say the least. Maybe I had been dreaming? My name had been said so clearly it sounded like someone was in the same room as me. It made me shudder.

I went back upstairs but couldn't settle. Leaving the bedroom lights on, I lay back. I had this strange feeling of foreboding. I waited in the silence to see if I could hear it again.

I couldn't sleep. So I got up again and turned on the television and started to make some coffee.

Eventually, it was time for Bobby to go to school and when I got home, I was surprised that Elle wasn't there. She usually came early. I telephoned her, but the call just went to her answerphone. And then Julie called.

'Fran, listen to me. Tony's been in an accident on the motorway. An articulated lorry on the other side of the motorway crashed through the barrier and into Tony's car. Tony is in a critical condition and his chauffeur is dead. Ralph and I have just left the hospital. Tony is in a bad way. He went into cardiac arrest in the early hours of this morning, but he's alive. I'll keep you updated.'

My eyes filled up, and panic gripped my chest. I was listening but the words weren't sinking in. I had to go to him, nothing else mattered, but Julie warned me away. Sobs wracked my body and my head was swimming, while I listened to Julie and watched the news at the same time. It looked horrific. Tony's last memory of me would be me sounding like a bitch! 'Does Elle know?'

Julie informed me that Elle had been there all night. 'I'll explain more when I see you.'

So that was why I hadn't heard from Elle. I'd been in total ignorance all morning about what had happened to Tony. I turned up the volume on the television, and there it was. The motorway was covered with fire engines and police. There were parts of cars scattered along the road. Then I heard the unthinkable. 'Tony Lambrianu, famous nightclub owner and playboy, was believed to be involved in the accident. His condition has been reported as critical.' It was official. Tears fell down my face. I didn't know what to do.

Suddenly, a strange thought occurred to me. Something serious had happened to Tony in the early hours of this morning, around the time I had woken with a start. I wasn't a great believer in superstition, but it seemed to coincide with when I had heard my name being called. No, that was ridiculous, wasn't it? Had Tony said my name this morning?

Later that night, there was a knock at my door. I ran downstairs and opened it. Standing before me was one of Ralph's drivers. I presumed he had come to give me some bad news about Tony. His face showed no emotion.

'Mrs Lambrianu, Mr Gold has sent me for you.' That was all he said, and then he walked to the car and opened the back door for me.

What was I going to do? It was late, and I had no one to look after Bobby. Elle was at the hospital. I was just about to tell the driver I couldn't go when a friend of Elle's, Minnie, came walking down the driveway.

'Fran, love, Elle has sent me to look after Bobby for you. It seems I came in the nick of time, doesn't it?'

'I don't know how long I'm going to be, Minnie. Are you okay with that?' I asked.

'Take as long as you need, Fran, love,' Minnie called. 'I'll look after Bobby and see that he gets to school in the morning. Go on.'

The drive was long. It took forever getting there, but at last we arrived. All the time I didn't know what to expect, and the driver said nothing. Had Tony died? I was nervous, but grateful that Ralph had sent for me. I needed to keep my emotions in check.

The driver rang Ralph when we arrived, and Julie came out to meet me. She gave me a big hug. 'Thank God you're here, Fran. He's asking for you,' said Julie.

I stopped. 'Tony's awake?'

'No, Fran, just in and out of consciousness. But he said your name. In fact, he's said it twice now. Tony wants you there. Be prepared to face the firing squad. Jake's angry because you hurt Tony and he's just found out that Sharon is having another man's baby.' Julie was full of gossip as usual, but this time my head was spinning. Sharon was pregnant? I had some catching up to do!

'Here, Fran.' Julie took her lipstick out of her bag and put some on me. It was bright red and didn't suit, but I was past caring. 'Do you have any perfume, Fran? Here, take some of mine.' Julie put her hand in her bag.

'No, Julie,' I said. 'I have my Chanel Tony bought me. He will know I'm here when he smells this.'

Jake was standing outside the hospital room waiting for me. 'One sarcastic remark out of you, or if you upset him, and I will strangle you with my bare hands. Have you got that?' I knew Jake didn't hate me; he loved his brother and at this moment he wanted a whipping boy. He opened the door for me and let me go in alone.

I walked in and saw Tony lying in a hospital bed. I could hardly recognise him. His face was black and blue, and his arms and leg were in plaster casts. Walking over, I bent over him and planted a kiss on his lips. Then I sat on a chair at his bedside. I looked on in shock.

'Antonias,' I whispered. 'Please don't leave me. I'm sorry for everything.' Tears streamed down my face. I took his hand and held it. Then I felt that wasn't good enough, I needed to be closer to him. I had nearly lost him. Nothing else mattered now. I knew how I felt about him.

I took off my shoes and then carefully, so as not to disturb anything, lay beside him, lying my arm across his stomach. I could hear his breathing. It felt comforting, and I hoped he could sense me too. There was a dim light on in the room. For a moment, it felt like there was just me and him in the whole world.

I must have dozed off because when I looked up, a nurse was there, to check on his drips and take his blood pressure. I apologised for lying on the bed, but she shook her head at me, smiled, and told me not to worry about it.

I decided to get up and see where the others were. When I opened the door, I saw they were all sitting awkwardly in chairs, dozing.

Julie opened her eyes. 'Everything okay, Fran?' She blinked, trying to wake herself properly. 'We need some of that rubbish coffee from that machine. Come on.'

'You need to go home, Julie. You need your rest,' I said.

Tony had some good friends. Each and every one of them had stayed by his side.

'I wouldn't sleep anyway, would I? Anyway, you need someone to keep Jake from biting your head off, don't you?' She made an attempt to laugh, but it fell flat. 'Anyway'– she winked at me – 'I had to stay for Tony's sake, what with you creeping in bed with him when he's unconscious.' She smiled at me and stood up.

She was never going to let me forget that, was she?

When we got back with a lot of coffees, the others were waking up. I went back into Tony's room to see how he was. The medical team had put Tony into an induced coma because of the swelling on his brain, and they wanted to keep him as still as possible. What if he didn't wake up? The very thought made my blood run cold. I needed him to wake up. I needed him.

* * *

Days passed into weeks and Tony finally woke up. He couldn't speak through his swollen lips, but he was going to be okay. Ralph and Jake had organised for Tony to be moved to a local private hospital in London when it was safe enough. Being closer, I visited as often as possible but left time for Jake and Elle to be alone with him.

The last thing Tony remembered was his driver talking to him about a lorry coming towards them and driving erratically. That was all he knew. He had been very lucky and vowed never to travel again on a motorway without a steel-plated car. It had saved his life. When the story eventually unfolded, we got more information. People had been thrown from their cars and killed. The lorry driver had died. It was suspected that he had been drinking the night before, and the alcohol was still in his system. Then he was speeding to try and make the time up for his delivery.

Tony was sorry he had missed the funeral of his loyal driver and friend, John, who he had known for years. He felt John's death was his fault. But everyone reassured him that John had driven down the motorway a million times in the past; it could have happened anywhere. Even John's grieving wife came to see Tony and told him it wasn't his fault.

But Tony had insisted on paying for John's funeral and making sure his wife was suitably well off financially for the future.

I usually went to feed Tony his dinner. It was still soft baby food because he could hardly swallow with his sore throat from the tubes and he couldn't feed himself with two broken arms.

Jake wanted Tony to go home so that he could look after him, which caused another argument. Elle insisted that he go home with her because she had a bungalow, and that made more sense.

Tony declined both offers for now. He spoke slowly but insisted he had some pride left and wanted to keep his dignity. He had two broken arms and, in his own unique way, said, 'Who's going to wipe my arse and hold my dick when I need to go to the loo? I can't even feed myself. I'm staying here.'

'I will,' I said. 'Come home to me, Tony, whenever you are ready.'

But he declined my offer as well. He did ask Ralph to get him a bigger bed, though, in case I stayed over again. I had lain with him many nights, sometimes just for a few hours and other times all night, while Elle looked after Bobby for me.

Although it had been an awful time and still was, it was a good time, because, for once, Tony and I had all the time in the world to get to know each other. There were no business meetings, no club events, no charity nights, and no one butting in when I wanted to talk to him.

We spent time sharing our likes and dislikes. I read to him, and we watched television together. Sometimes, we said nothing at all. We just held each other.

Julie, who, given the circumstances, could never ignore a bit of juicy gossip, kept nudging me and whispering when she saw Jake and Sharon together. They seemed deep in conversation these days. And, Julie stated, it was only a matter of time before they got back together. 'The grass isn't always greener, Fran. Sharon thought she could just have had a quick affair and be done with it.' All in one go Julie blurted out Jake and Sharon's problems. 'Apparently, she's been cheating on Jake with some bank manager or something. Met him when she took the takings from the club. Usual stuff Fran, she felt neglected by Jake being a busy man. Really shitty though, because did you know Jake can't have children because he had mumps as a kid? Well anyway, this manager she divorced Jake for has given her a bun in the oven and gone without trace to a better job in a better land and he didn't leave a forwarding address.'

I was astonished. She was like the secret service – she knew everything.

When I visited Tony one day, he seemed in a more sombre mood than usual. 'I think it's time we talked properly, Francesca, don't you?'

I didn't know what to expect, but he had been looking a lot better during these couple of months. The swelling had gone down, and his bruises were fading. They looked more of a yellow than black and blue.

Nervously I asked, 'What do we need to talk about, Tony? Can't whatever it is wait until you're feeling better?' I was afraid he didn't need me any more, and I had enjoyed being with him, even under the circumstances. Life was going to carry on as before, and all this would be forgotten.

'I'm feeling better, Francesca,' he said. 'Now I want to talk to you. There are things I need to say.' Tony knew he'd nearly died, and now in the cold light of day, he could see clearly for the first time in his life.

'Marry me, Francesca. Put me out of my misery and marry me.' There was a pregnant pause.

I was shocked. It wasn't what I had expected. 'Tony, we've been married, and this is not the time to ask. You've been traumatised. Why don't we shelve it for now, and if you feel the same when you're up and your old self again, you can ask me again when you're thinking properly.' Although it was what I would have liked, it was the wrong time to ask. He was at a low ebb and needed someone. I wanted him to be sure and not asking me out of gratitude.

He looked disappointed. 'We have never been married, Francesca, and I will ask you again. I promise you that, okay. You have to be sure too.'

These were the words I had longed to hear. I desperately

wanted to shout yes. Niggling at me was the fact that he hadn't mentioned love. He was still unwell, and not thinking straight. I needed him to love me, not need a nurse.

* * *

Julie came to see me at home. 'Fran, can I ask you something personal?' she said. 'Would you be my birthing partner?' Julie was nearly due and was obviously trying to get things in order. 'I know I should ask Ralph. But he will probably faint, and I need to give him a get-out clause. If I tell him you will do it, it will let him off the hook.'

We both laughed at the thought of Ralph fainting at the sight of blood, but I knew what she meant. Ralph would do it if he had to but was prepared to stand back if he could find someone else for the job.

'Of course I will, Julie. I would be honoured to. But are you sure about Ralph not wanting to be there?'

'You have to be joking, Fran. He's seen too many movies. He's going to spend all of his time shouting for towels and hot water, although God knows what for. Anyway, how are you and Tony getting on?'

I told her he'd asked me to marry him, and the grin on her face said it all, until I told her I had turned him down and my reasons for doing so. Bit by bit, I saw the smile disappear from her face.

'Don't be silly Fran. He's not brain-damaged. Crazy maybe, but he wouldn't have said it if he didn't mean it. He has never asked anyone else to marry him.' She seemed shocked that I had turned him down.

In a way, I felt she was right. But I had to be sure. Once he was back at the club and living his own life again, I didn't want him to feel like he had made a promise he didn't want to keep.

Julie left it at that. After her hundredth time of going to the loo, she left, leaving me to think about Tony and his offer.

* * *

Tony was getting better every day. We occasionally walked around the hospital gardens to have some fresh air, even though it was late autumn and very cold at times. Apart from bruising and an ankle sprain, he was getting about okay. His plaster casts had been taken off his legs and the physiotherapist said the exercise would be good for him.

But Tony was getting back to his old self, even now flashing that famous charming smile of his at the nurses, making them giggle and blush as they walked up the corridor. His plaster casts on his arms were soon due to come off too.

Julie said that he was milking it now for the attention, and Elle more or less agreed with her. They pointed out that he could walk, talk, and breathe for himself and they both thought Tony liked playing the patient, knowing I would plump his pillows for him and feed him.

I supposed they were right, but to be honest, I enjoyed it too. I liked him needing me. I knew he could do a lot for himself, but we kept up the pretence because it suited us both, and every now and then, he would wince in pain or tell me he was tired so that I would comfort him.

I also knew that he hadn't stopped working. He was using his hands-free mobile to do business, and Ralph and Jake were taking him in accounts and paperwork to look over. He seemed to be enjoying being away from the public eye for a while, but I also knew he would soon get bored and long for his old lifestyle back.

I felt sad when I thought that I would be surplus to requirement. It seemed inevitable that he would soon forget all the things we'd shared and slip easily back into his old way of life, with women to welcome him back into the fold.

One day, I was in bed when the telephone rang. I was half asleep when I answered it and thought it might be Tony. Selfishly, he had got into the habit of ringing me late at night to say goodnight or just to chat because he couldn't sleep. Some days, I walked about like a living zombie after we'd been on the telephone for two or three hours.

'Fran! Fran! Help me. I'm dying. My body is being ripped apart.'

I recognised the screaming voice down the telephone instantly. It was Julie. And by the sounds of it, she had gone into labour.

'My waters have broken, and God damn it, I'm in pain. I need drugs, Fran, lots of drugs. Help me.' The shouting got louder and louder as she tried telling me that she was making her way to the hospital and asking me to meet her there right away. I heard another scream down the telephone, and then she put it down.

I immediately telephoned Elle, who within moments was on her way to look after Bobby.

As I drove through the empty streets to the hospital, the thought of Julie in labour and only having Ralph to shout at made me laugh. Poor Ralph, she was going to make him suffer tonight.

When I arrived I was informed that she wasn't fully dilated yet, but the nurses were monitoring her. It was going to be a long night.

'Fran, oh my God, you're here. Come here. Hold my hand.' Julie was very emotional.

As I walked past Ralph, he leaned towards my ear. 'Don't hold her bloody hand, Fran. She has a grip like a boxer when those pains start.' I could tell he was trying to make light of it, but he was worried.

Ralph looked relieved to see me and could now take a back seat. He didn't know what to do, and Julie wasn't helping him. She kept shouting and screaming until it was time to push. She did as she was told and took breaths. We were breathing together.

Ralph was looking on and panting with us. Julie gripped his hand tightly. 'Does that hurt, Ralph?'

Ralph winced and nodded.

'Good, because now you know how it bloody feels,' she said. Even at a time like this, she was funny. And oh my, the things she was going to do to Ralph when all of this was over, including taking him down to the vets and getting him 'done'. I had to smile.

Julie pushed and pushed, until eventually the midwife went to get a doctor. Apparently, the pushing had been going on for too long and the baby was in distress. Ralph kept looking at me for reassurance. I did my best to hide my own concern, but I too was a little worried.

The doctor checked Julie over and then decided to take her down to theatre for an emergency caesarean. Both Julie and the baby were tired.

'Stay with me, Francesca. Look after my baby, Frances,' she whispered to me through breaths.

29

DIANA

'I'm not going anywhere, Julie Gold, and you're going to give birth to that baby of yours and look after it yourself. Now go with the doctors and make me an aunty, Julie.'

The porters wheeled her bed out of the room and down to the operating theatre.

She had told me and Elle one day that she was afraid of giving birth. The last person she had seen in childbirth had been her sister, and she had died.

Ralph was almost tearful. It had been a long worrying sixteen hours, and now this. 'You're the only person apart from her sister she has ever loved. She would do anything for you, Francesca.'

I linked my arm through his and kissed his cheek. 'You're wrong, Ralph. Julie loves you very much. You're her world. She just doesn't want you to know it. But believe me, Ralph, you're everything to Julie.' I squeezed his arm and smiled.

Tears fell down his cheeks. We were alone in a side room waiting for news.

The doctor came into the room and took his mask off. 'Mr

Gold, you have a beautiful baby daughter.' Although the doctor was smiling, Ralph didn't move.

'What about Julie, is she okay?' Ralph asked. It hadn't quite sunk in what the doctor had just said yet.

'Mother and baby are doing fine, Mr Gold. Come with me and meet your daughter.' The doctor led the way.

The look on Ralph's face on entering the room was indescribable. Suddenly, all the sorrow and the worry left the room. He pulled on my arm, and we walked in together to see Julie holding a little bundle wrapped in a pink blanket.

'Here you are, Daddy.' She smiled at Ralph, reassuring him she was okay. He picked up his daughter and held her close to him. To Ralph, his daughter was pure gold!

The nurses were busying themselves in the room and checking everything was okay. They informed us that the seven-and-a-half-pound bundle was in perfect health, and she proved it by screaming her head off.

Ralph left the room to tell the whole world he was a father. When he came back I was holding the baby while Julie was having a well-earned hot cup of coffee. She was tired and needed some rest. I felt I should go and leave them to a private moment, but Julie wasn't having it.

Ralph was taking photo after photo of his beautiful daughter, and even at a time like this, Julie made me put some lipstick on her and informed me she had taken the precaution of wearing water-proof mascara.

'Well, you two, any ideas on names yet?' I asked.

'Diana,' said Julie. 'Diana Frances Gold, after Ralph's mum and my sister.' Julie held Ralph's hand.

He had tears of joy and sadness rolling down his face.

After a few more minutes, I said I was going to leave. Julie told

Ralph to go as well. She was going to get some sleep. All the adren-alin that had filled us all was now draining away, and little Diana was hungry.

Ralph was reluctant to leave but Julie insisted on it. He gave in and promised he would come back later. Ralph may have been tired, but he was definitely not going to sleep. He was walking on air.

I had to admit, as I drove home, I felt a twinge of envy. Julie had really turned her life around, and now both she and Ralph had a fresh start and a new baby. And Josh had a baby sister. It seemed they had their whole future before them.

By the time I got home, it was after six in the evening. Elle had made a cottage pie and was sitting with Bobby having dinner. They both looked up when I walked in, and Bobby ran towards me with open arms. We cuddled and kissed while Elle got out another plate.

'You look shattered, Fran. Why don't you have something to eat and then have a lie-down?' said Elle, in between Bobby giving me all of his news.

I texted Tony and apologised for not visiting him that day; all I'd got back was a text saying, 'No problem.' After dinner I tried ringing him, but he didn't answer. Surely he wasn't angry with me because I hadn't been able to get to the hospital to see him. Maybe he would telephone me tonight. But as the evening got later, I realised he wasn't going to.

While I lay in bed wondering if Tony would make one of his midnight calls, it occurred to me that next week would have been our first wedding anniversary. How much had changed in a year. I had money and security. Bobby was doing really well at school and was happy. It was more than I could ever have dreamt of.

The next morning I wanted to go and see Tony at the hospital.

Something wasn't right between us, and it unsettled me. I needed to sort out the problem.

When I arrived at the hospital, the nurses seemed surprised to see me. As I walked down the corridor to Tony's room, one of the nurses stopped me. 'Mr Lambrianu went home this morning. Didn't he tell you?'

I was stunned. Tony had left the hospital and gone home? I felt foolish in front of the nurse and tried covering it up as though just remembering. 'Oh yes, of course. Sorry. Baby brain. Mrs Gold had her baby last night, and I've been with her.' I hoped that I sounded convincing.

The nurses knew Julie, and she gave me congratulations to pass on. Smiling through gritted teeth, I said that I would and made a hasty retreat.

While I was in town, I popped in to see Julie. Ralph was already there. Julie looked a lot better now that she'd had some sleep.

'Thank heavens you're here, Fran. Father Ralph here, who knows everything about babies, is giving me advice, although he hasn't offered to change a nappy yet.' Julie was rolling her eyes at the ceiling, while Ralph completely ignored her comments. Nothing was going to spoil his happiness.

I mentioned that Tony had left the hospital that morning. Ralph turned to me while still holding Diana in his arms. 'I know. He rang me to tell me to take some time out – paternity leave if you like – and that he would take the reins again.'

It seemed everyone had known but me. Tony hadn't thought that I mattered enough to tell me. So that was it then? Just like last year, I had been dismissed again. I stayed a while longer and then made my excuses to leave. It was time to go and get my life back, although I didn't know how. So many weeks and months had been taken up with Tony. Now my life felt empty.

* * *

A week later, I still hadn't heard anything. Julie was going home, and I was back at work. It was time to do some Christmas shopping. It was only a couple of weeks away, and the shops were bursting at the seams with all kinds of Christmas treats. Bobby was practising for his school play. He was going to be one of the three shepherds.

My wedding anniversary came and went, as though it had never happened. I had a glass of wine that evening and toasted myself.

'Happy first wedding anniversary, Mrs Lambrianu,' I said out loud. It sounded silly, but I felt there should be something to mark the occasion.

As I walked Susie along the beach later the next day there was hardly anyone around. The sand was damp, and the tide was coming in. Suddenly I thought I heard my name being called.

'Francesca! Francesca, up here.'

I looked up at the metal bars that separated the beach from the seafront and saw Tony.

'Francesca,' he shouted again.

I was rooted to the spot, and my heart skipped a beat. He looked like his old self again. I raised my hand and waved at him to acknowledge that I'd heard him.

I felt my body tingle with excitement. I had missed him, and there he was standing as large as life in his grey suit, pink shirt, and long camel overcoat. He started to walk down the steps leading down to the beach. He stood there and looked at me. Then he opened his arms wide and shouted my name again.

As much as I had agonised, night after night, wondering who he was with and what he was doing when he had so coldly cut me off after leaving the hospital, my heart was now ruling my head. I didn't want to think about any of that any more. There he stood in front of me, his arms wide open and smiling that charming smile of his.

'Tony, oh Tony.' I ran towards him, and he walked faster towards me.

I fell into his arms and felt them envelop me and pull me closer. His mouth met mine, and we kissed. It was explosive.

Tony didn't stop kissing me. He kissed my neck, my face, and my mouth. His hands were underneath my coat and were roaming over my body. At last, when we did part, I saw him looking around. Then he took my hand and started to walk towards the little caves at the side of the beach. These were popular for when people wanted to change out of their clothes and into their swimwear.

Tony led me in and took his coat off. I knew what he had in mind.

It was dark in the cave, just a little daylight coming in from the opening we had just walked through. He threw his coat down on the floor. Then he held my face and started to kiss me again with wild abandon, pulling me down on the sand and using his coat as a blanket.

I put my hands through his hair and pulled him closer. I wanted him. I had missed him, and it was pretty obvious that he wanted me too. He pulled my leggings down and undid his belt. Suddenly, he was on top of me, and it was flesh against flesh. I gasped, but Tony seemed to be in a world of his own. He was saying my name over and over again. It was fast and furious. He was panting, and with every stroke of his body, he felt my ardent response. Then he slumped on top of me and tried to catch his breath.

'I'm sorry, Francesca. Oh, God, I'm sorry.' He kept apologising.

'I needed you, and I wanted you so much.' He was apologising for climaxing so quickly. It was all over in a flash. 'I will make it up to you. I haven't been that quick since I was fifteen.' He was kneeling up now and buckling up his belt. Then he looked down at me and gave a warm deep laugh and pushed his hand through his hair. We held each other.

'Come on, Antonias, my love. Let's go home.' I got dressed and held his hand as we walked out of the cave. I adjusted my clothing and brushed the sand off me. Tony did likewise and put his sandy overcoat over his arm.

Susie was waiting outside the cave for us to come out and wagged her tail. Tony put his arm around my waist, and we walked along the beach to the steps that would take us up to the seafront. Tony's driver was patiently waiting and drove up to meet us.

At home, I opened the front door, and Susie ran directly towards the kitchen, knowing that Elle would have left some treats for her. Tony pulled me towards him and kissed me again. He threw his coat on the bottom of the stairs, and those hypnotising blue eyes looked deep into mine. That velvety voice that sent chills down my spine filled my ears while he was nuzzling my neck.

'Come on, Francesca.' He took my hand and led me up the staircase. 'I said I would make it up to you, and now I intend to.'

We walked into the bedroom and shut the door.

My whole body felt as though little electric shocks were shooting through it. Our passion and hunger for each other were at last free to express themselves. I felt like putty in Tony's hands as he teased my nipples with the tip of his tongue. I arched my back, pulling him closer towards me. It was heaven. He manipulated and positioned my body underneath him until I felt my body tense and tighten, making my head swim.

Wrapping my legs tightly around him, I welcomed him

between my thighs. With every thrust, my body trembled and yearned for more, until I felt a slow explosive release for us both. Each time Tony reached out for me again, it felt more exciting and arousing than the last time. At last, we both collapsed in exhaustion on the bed and fell into a contented sleep in each other's arms.

I woke up later that afternoon, looked at the clock and saw that it was nearly three. Oh no. I had to pick up Bobby.

I jumped out of bed, leaving Tony still sleeping soundly, and pulled on my jeans and T-shirt. I ran downstairs and out towards the kitchen where the garages were. Then I noticed a piece of paper on the worktop in Elle's handwriting.

I will pick up Bobby. Me and Albert are going to take him to see the Christmas lights and have dinner out. Elle x

I breathed a sigh of relief. How could I have fallen asleep and nearly forgotten to pick up my son? Thank goodness Elle was on hand. In my moment of illicit passion, I had let myself be swept along by it all. What kind of mother did that make me? I had put myself before my son, and what must Elle have thought of me when she realised I was upstairs with Tony? Now I was embarrassed.

I switched on the kettle and made two cups of coffee and took them upstairs. Tony was awake and lying in bed with his arms around the back of his head.

'What's wrong, Francesca?' Tony looked at me, frowning.

'I nearly forgot to pick up Bobby from school,' I said. I sat on the edge of the bed at his side and handed him his coffee, filling him in.

'Elle's not stupid, Francesca, and you're not a bad mother.' He pointed at the clock. 'You would have made it by now, just in time.'

Tony put his coffee cup on the bedside table and reached out and stroked my arm. 'Now then,' he said, a smile slowly appearing back on his face. 'Did you say Bobby is having a great time seeing the lights and having a burger somewhere? Then come here. I need you again.' Tony pulled back the duvet for me to get in, and I did so willingly.

It was just after seven when Elle got back. Bobby was bouncing with excitement. Tony had been right. He'd had a great time. They had sung Christmas carols with the Salvation Army and looked at all of the shops. Bobby had a bag with him containing a new box of Lego, which he was desperate to open.

'I'm sorry, Elle,' I said. 'I shouldn't have put you in that position. I was on my way to pick up Bobby when I saw your note.' I could feel my face growing red with embarrassment.

Elle ignored my comments and put on the kettle. 'It's getting cold out there, Fran. I'll make us a drink. Is Tony coming down or has he gone already?' she added, smiling at me. 'You always put everyone else first. But if you remember, Bobby was staying late anyway to practice his play. Don't worry about it.'

I breathed a sigh of relief. Of course Bobby was staying late. I had totally forgotten. 'Tony, well, he,' I began. I didn't know what to say. Yet again I felt my face flush.

Then Tony walked through.

'Tony is here,' he said, wearing a bathrobe and sitting himself at the breakfast bar. 'I'll have one of those, Elle,' was all he said, as if it was the most natural thing in the world.

'Are you coming to see me in the Christmas play, Tony?' Bobby asked. Although he had been out for his dinner, he was now eating his way through Elle's apple pie.

Taking the cup of coffee Elle poured him, Tony smiled at Bobby. 'Of course I am, Bobby. I have to see my superstar in action.' He reached his hand out and ruffled Bobby's hair.

'That's if Tony's not too busy,' I interrupted. I didn't want him making promises he couldn't keep. I looked at Tony.

He ignored me. 'I will be there, Bobby, no matter what. I am never too busy for you.'

Bobby grinned at Elle, and I could see by the look on both of their faces Tony had said the right thing. My heart sank as I watched Bobby's excited face. Tony had the best of intentions, but would he be able to keep that promise, or even remember it? Bobby would be devastated if Tony broke his promise. I couldn't bear the disappointment and tears.

Tony listened to Bobby while Elle and I made something to eat. He seemed a natural with children, considering he didn't have any. They both opened the box of Lego and started to build the model. Strangely enough, it didn't seem odd at all sitting around the table with Tony having dinner like a family. It felt normal and comfortable. Elle cleared away while I took Bobby up for his bath and story.

When I came down, Tony was sitting in the lounge watching the news on the television and talking to Elle. Was I dreaming?

Tony got his driver to drop Elle off now it was getting dark, and after looking in on Bobby, we went to bed. The following morning, I made sure I was up and awake for Bobby. I got him ready for school, and during the noise of him running up and down the stairs, Tony came into the kitchen. I left him with his coffee and took Bobby to school. I felt a little awkward.

When I arrived home, Tony was showered and dressed.

He cupped my face in his hands. 'I need to get a change of clothes, and then I will be back later,' he said as he gently kissed my lips.

'You don't have to come back,' I said, giving him a get-out clause. 'What happened between us, was just one of those things. Please don't feel that you have to come back.'

Tony scowled at me, his eyes searching my face. He ran his hands through his hair and sighed. Had I said the wrong thing again? I just didn't want him to feel obliged.

'Don't go cold on me, Francesca, not now. This was just the beginning. Don't spoil it.'

Suddenly, there was a hoot from a car horn coming from the drive. It was Tony's driver picking him up. I walked him to the door, and he kissed me and left.

* * *

Later that morning, I went into work. Instead of the usual smiling faces that greeted me, I was met by sly grins and whispers. The other staff were nudging each other and giggling.

'Okay,' I said. 'What is it? What's the big joke?' I waited patiently.

'Have a nice day yesterday, did you, Fran?' one of the girls asked me, trying hard not to laugh.

I looked at her oddly. What a strange question.

She held out the newspaper to me. She had a big grin on her face, and the rest of them waited for my response.

My face drained. There it was in black and white. The headlines read:

Beauty and the Beast Reunited: Francesca Tames Club Boss Tony Lambrianu.

There were photos of Tony kissing me on the beach and then of the two of us emerging half-dressed from the little cave, our arms around each other's waists. It was blatantly obvious what had just gone on in there.

I could feel my face start to burn with embarrassment. I was shocked and didn't know what to say. There were no excuses and no denying it. It was definitely Tony and me. I rushed to the toilets, the newspaper still in my hand, and read the column. It was a full description of us running towards each other, reunited in our love. I couldn't read any more.

I took out my mobile telephone and rang Tony. I didn't know what else to do. This was the ultimate humiliation, and I only had myself to blame.

'Tony!' I half screamed down the telephone when he answered. 'Have you seen what the newspapers are saying about us?' I was panicking. A thought occurred to me. My mam would read it. What on earth would she think about me?

Tony's voice was calm and controlled. 'I have, Francesca, and they are only telling the truth. What's the problem? It's not an invasion of privacy, is it, in a public place.' He didn't care. If anything, during the rest of the conversation, he told me not to worry about it. How could I not worry, when everyone was laughing behind my back?

'Are you going to marry me now, Francesca, and end all of this curiosity?' was all he said.

'No, I am bloody not,' I snapped and hung up.

And then Julie rang me.

'Well, well, you dark horse. Come on. Tell me.' You could actually hear her smug smile over the telephone.

'There is nothing to tell, Julie. It was a mad moment. I hadn't seen Tony for a while. And, well, you know the rest. In fact, everyone knows the rest.' I felt like I was going to cry.

'What the hell do you care what anyone thinks, Fran? Apart from the fact that it wasn't just a kiss, and he looks like he was sucking your face off. If he'd have stuck his tongue any further down your throat, he would have been licking the soles of your shoes.' Julie was used to reporters displaying her life, and she had learnt to ignore it. She couldn't understand why I gave a damn. My confidence was waning. What would people say if he dumped me again? I would be a laughing stock and that was the last thing I wanted.

Then she went on to tell me that Tony and Jake would have to go to Paris for a business meeting as Ralph couldn't go. I had spent all of yesterday with Tony, and he hadn't mentioned Paris once. I didn't say anything. By the sounds of it, she thought I knew already.

Was I making a fuss about nothing? I ended the call with Julie and got back to work. After my colleagues had had their fun, everything went back to normal. When my shift was over, I picked Bobby up from school. We ate and then had the usual bath and bedtime story while Susie curled up on the end of his bed. As I came downstairs I heard a knock at the front door.

When I opened it, Tony was standing there.

'Peace offering,' he said. He was holding a bottle of wine in one hand and a bouquet of yellow roses in the other. 'I said I would see you later, Francesca, and I meant it. Stop worrying about nothing. It will blow over. Anyway, I'm more concerned about who the beauty is and who the beast is.' He was laughing and trying to make light of it for my sake. He put his arms around me, and the day just seemed to melt away.

We opened the bottle of wine and took it with us to the bathroom and luxuriated in bubbly warm water. I was lying with my back against the bath and he was lying with his back to me, resting his head on my breasts. This was pure heaven.

Afterwards, in bed, I laid my head on him and stroked the hairs on his chest. He made me feel safe and loved. He told me he had to go to Paris, adding that Julie was making Ralph move into the vicar's cottage, which was why he couldn't go. It seemed weird, hearing all of the gossip Julie had told me from a man's perspective. I didn't tell him that I already knew.

'When are you going to your mum's for Christmas?' he asked me.

I was surprised he had remembered. 'Hopefully on Christmas Eve. Depending on the weather, it may have to be sooner,' I said.

He pulled me closer to him and kissed the top of my head. 'I know it's selfish, Francesca, but I wish you weren't going. Will you come back in time for the New Year's Eve party at the club?'

His question hung in the air. My mind wandered back to the last New Year's Eve party. It made me wonder who he would be spending Christmas Day with this year.

'If you want me to. But if you change your mind and you're busy, no hard feelings. Okay?'

He kissed me in response.

Over the next couple of days, a new routine was established. Tony would either come home in time for dinner or just after. I always had some dinner waiting for him, and I enjoyed sitting around the table with him and listening to him talk about his day.

My heart skipped a beat when Tony walked into Bobby's school and sat beside me and Elle in time for Bobby's play as promised. Dressed in his shepherd's costume, Bobby waved to him from the stage, beaming with happiness. I have to say, it brought a lump to my throat. Tony was full of surprises.

On the weekend before Christmas, Tony went to Paris. I was due to go to my mam's on the following Wednesday. Bobby was adding last-minute things he wanted to his list for Father Christmas.

Julie was determined that we would have our own family Christmas when I got back. 'The queen can have two birthdays, Fran. Why can't we have two Christmases? You go and see your

mum and brothers, and then we'll celebrate when you get back,'
she said.

We had agreed not to exchange presents until then. Bobby had
put Elle's and Albert's presents under her tree. We had bought a
new cap for Albert and a gold charm bracelet for Elle. She'd
admired it when we'd been on a shopping trip and I knew she'd
like it. We'd bought a couple of charms for it, including a Father
Christmas to mark the occasion.

In the early hours of Wednesday morning, my mobile rang.

'I didn't get a chance to kiss you goodbye, Francesca.' Those
dulcet tones, articulate in every way, floated down the telephone
into my ear. Even though I was still half asleep, just hearing him
made me smile. 'I forgot to trace my tongue over your lips and kiss
you, feeling them open, warm and moist.'

My knees went weak, and my mind was wandering to a very
different sort of kissing. He was teasing me, and he knew it. 'Stop it,
Tony, you're a hundred miles away, so there's no point in saying
such things.' I giggled down the telephone.

'Why don't you go downstairs and open the door?' he said.
Then suddenly the line went dead.

I ran to the window and looked out on to the driveway. The
smile on my face said it all. There was Tony's car.

I ran downstairs and opened the door, throwing my arms
around his neck. 'Why didn't you tell me you were coming
home?' I was hugging him so tightly I nearly squeezed him to
death.

'I'm not home. I just needed to see you. No one knows that I'm
here, Francesca. I have three hours, and then I have to be back in
Paris.'

I took his hand and led him upstairs. He told me he'd been
alone in his hotel room and was thinking about me when he'd
decided to come and see me instead. He hadn't even told Jake. On

pure impulse and need, he had got his driver out of bed and told him to find any flight that would bring him to England.

Well, any effort like that needed rewarding, didn't it? Only when we were in bed, it was different. It wasn't the usual frenzied passion we had shared many times before. It was slow, loving, and more intense. In the darkness of the bedroom, as we reached for each other, he looked down at me lying underneath him. 'I love you, Francesca.'

Reaching up, I put my arms around his neck. It was the first time he had ever said it. My whole body was aroused with deep sensual emotion. The warmth of love overwhelmed me so much I felt a tear fall on my cheek. I cupped his head in my hands. 'I love you, Antonias.'

He lowered his head again and kissed me, kissing away the tears on my cheeks. He trailed his lips down onto my breasts and onto my stomach. My body arched towards him, wanting more.

'Marry me, Francesca,' he whispered in between kisses in the darkness of the room. 'If you say no now, I will never ask you again.' His own voice seemed husky with emotion as our bodies trembled with need.

I stopped and looked him directly in the face. 'I can't, Antonias. This way, we have no promises, no commitments, and no lies. We are together because we want to be, not out of duty because we're married. I don't want you to get tired of me. And when you decide you have had enough, you can walk away. No hard feelings, just beautiful memories.'

Tony looked at me and nodded. I couldn't quite see his face in the darkness, but I could feel his disappointment. I didn't want to spoil this with marriage. We'd done that and it had been a disaster. All I wanted was Tony, as we were now. How could I make him understand that?

The air seemed electric, although slow and calm. And for the first time, I noticed Tony didn't reach for his usual protection. It was his usual practice, no matter what the situation. 'Aren't you forgetting something?' I smiled at him.

He shook his head. 'No, never with you, Francesca, my love. I need to feel all of you. No barriers should ever be between us, ever.'

We had gone beyond our secret longing. Every joyous word of love was spoken. Our bodies fit together like a jigsaw puzzle, consumed in love and passion. I would never forget this night for as long as I lived.

When I woke the next morning, I turned over and reached out for him, but he wasn't there. He had gone and left me asleep and content. My heart sank. It was time to get up and start packing up the car with all the Christmas presents for the family and the long drive ahead.

Today felt great. Each time I thought about Tony and me last night, I couldn't help smiling.

When Julie arrived I didn't mention what had happened. Not only did Tony say he shouldn't have left Paris, but I also felt it was our secret.

'Come and see the Christmas tree at the cottage, Fran. It looks beautiful, all warm and cuddly. That Albert of yours, Elle, is a miracle worker with his hands.' She laughed and gave us one of her cheeky winks. She loved teasing Elle about Albert.

On arriving at the cottage, I saw Julie had been right. Albert had worked miracles. From the main road to the driveway, the drive to the cottage was lined with trees, cherry blossom and willow. In the lounge was a huge pine tree, giving out that beautiful scent from its branches. It was a different place completely, full of up-to-date kitchen gadgets and a slate kitchen floor. It was a farm-house, and it looked lovely.

It was starting to get late. It was time for me to leave so we said our farewells. I knew the drive to Yorkshire would be a long and arduous one, especially with all the other drivers on the road wanting to make it home for Christmas.

After a while, we stopped at a motorway café and had something quick to eat and a toilet break. Everyone was in the Christmas spirit. People who usually ignored each other were actually smiling and wishing everyone well, be it for Christmas or New Year.

We eventually arrived at my mam's. Bobby ran to the front door, and my brothers came out to meet me with shouts and hugs. They also helped me empty the boot of my car, which was full of bags and boxes, hoping to be able to see inside.

Yet again, the house smelled of my mam's baking and her homemade Christmas pudding steaming away on the cooker top. My brothers were full of gossip about school and their friends but most of all what presents they were hoping for.

When all of the boys were in bed and my mam and I put the parcels under the tree, we took a deep breath. Christmas was a nice time of year, but it was also very tiring. It would be only a matter of a few hours before the boys burst into the bedroom and wanted to run downstairs to see what presents they had been brought by Father Christmas.

'How are things going between you and Tony?' my mam asked. It sounded like more of a reprimand. 'I saw the newspaper article about you both. Honestly, Fran, I didn't know where to put my face, all of the neighbours knowing what you had been up to.' She wasn't best pleased.

'I'm sorry you had to read about it like that. Tony and I are okay. We're seeing each other and having an adult relationship – friends with benefits if you like, just like you and George.'

Mam never said any more on the subject. It was as though we had come to a mutual understanding.

Christmas morning came in all of its glory. Soon, there was wrapping paper everywhere. The floor was covered, and we were surrounded by happy smiling faces. Julie had bought them each individual game consoles and a designer handbag for my mam. I knew she would never use it, but she would be happy enough just owning it and showing it to her friends. I had bought my brothers bicycles and had them delivered to my mam's house. She couldn't move after hiding them in her bedroom. Even though the weather was bad and they were in their pyjamas, they still insisted on giving them a go.

I spent the morning setting up car racing tracks and Lego models, and then George turned up. He acknowledged me with a grunt and then settled himself on the sofa and lit a cigarette. He totally ignored what was going on around him and even picked up the remote control and turned over the television channel.

I bit my tongue. It was my mam's business. I needed to keep out of it.

My mam was busy in the kitchen, and so I set about helping her. It got me out of the room if nothing else. I sent a text message to Tony.

Merry Christmas. I wish you were here. See you New Year's Eve.

A text message came right back to me.

Merry Christmas, my love. Remember my coming home kisses are better than my goodbyes. Antonias xx

It was the best Christmas present ever and as my stomach somersaulted, I felt like jumping with joy. I couldn't stop grinning and dare is say it – I wanted Christmas over with and then I could go home and see him again.

Lunch was served, and the turkey was cooked to perfection. We all read out the Christmas crackers with their bad jokes and wore hats. We were stuffed, and then my mam brought out the Christmas pudding!

All in all, it was a good day.

* * *

Before I knew it, it was nearly time for me to leave. The days had flown and it had been a great time.

George was sitting in his usual place before the television, smoking and waiting for my mam to wait on him hand and foot.

'George, can I have a word please?' I said. It was the first time I had ever done this, but I felt this was something I needed to say

He walked over to where I was standing with a curious look on his face.

'I am Francesca Lambrianu, and this is my family. Don't ever upset my family, George. What happens between you and my mother is your business. She is old enough to look after herself. But if you ever harm or upset my brothers, you will rue the day. Tony doesn't like me upset, George. Okay?'

George's face dropped. He knew of Tony's reputation. Maybe this warning would make him cool his heels a little. He would think twice about throwing his weight around in the future. His look turned to disdain, and he eyed me up and down. Yet again he thought he was being clever.

'I thought you were his ex-wife. That's right, isn't it?' The smug smile on his face said it all. I felt like slapping it off, but not today.

'You saw the newspapers George. Did that look like the actions of an ex-husband and his ex-wife? Think on what I've said.'

That line seemed to finish the conversation. For all of George's bravado, he wasn't going to risk upsetting Tony, and my mam and brothers would be safe.

I arrived home the day before New Year Eve. I rang Julie later in the evening and informed her we were back. Then I telephoned Elle. I was tempted to ring Tony, but I thought better of it. I'd said I would see him at the club on New Year's Eve, and I would. But I wanted to look my very best.

Elle came around the next morning. Within the hour, so did Julie, Josh and Diana. Bobby was pleased to see Josh and told him all about his visit to my mam's. He took Josh outside and started building a snowman.

There were still some presents under the tree, and I had told Bobby they were for New Year's Day, which was when Julie and I had decided to have our own Christmas dinner. He had scowled and strutted but accepted it.

'I wanted to know what you were wearing tonight,' said Julie, passing Diana over to Elle. 'God, it's going to be nice to have a drink again.' Then she looked at us both. 'I said a drink, not the whole bloody cellar.'

I ran upstairs and came down with a black velvet dress on its hanger. 'I thought I might wear this. What do you think? Black and slinky.' I was waving it around in the air, and then suddenly I stopped.

Julie's face said it all. 'Elle, my love,' said Julie, looking at my dress with distaste. 'Look after the family, will you? We have some serious shopping to do.' She obviously didn't like my choice. So much for me thinking my black dress looked sexy and chic.

A couple of hours later, we arrived back at the house. Julie had also taken us for a very light spray tan. It was more of a tint than an amber glow. Julie had picked me out a very pale rose pink halter neck dress. It fell just above my knee and was very figure hugging. The high court shoes she'd chosen were the same colour, although they had glitter on them and sparkled. For herself, Julie had chosen a thin-strapped turquoise sequined dress.

'Everybody will be wearing the usual gaudy Christmas colours, Fran, or opt for a black dress. We do it different. That is how we stand out,' she said, getting Elle's approval.

It felt strange, but as much as I loved my mam and my brothers, these newly found friends felt more like family to me these days.

When we arrived at the club, the party was in full swing. We were ushered through the crowds by one of the doormen, who saw us to our private booth. He must have radioed through to Ralph and Tony because, in minutes, they were at our table. My heart skipped a beat. Tony looked beautiful. His blond hair rested on his forehead, and that perfect smile seemed to broaden when he saw me.

Suddenly, something dawned on me. Tony's bow tie was the same colour as my dress, and Ralph's matched Julie's. I looked at Julie, who grinned at me mischievously. Apparently, she had bought them and had her driver deliver them to the club.

Julie was like the big sister who always annoyed you with her naughty ways but who you couldn't help loving. I had almost forgotten that she was the famous 'Julie Gold'. She was just Julie to me now, who sat in my kitchen and drank coffee and ate Elle's scones.

Tony came towards me. I expected a kiss on the cheek, considering we were surrounded by a crowd of people. But he bent down towards me and put his hands on the back of my head, entwining his fingers in my hair, and pulled me towards him, kissing me softly and slowly for all to see. I held up my arms and pulled him closer. The very nearness of him was intoxicating.

Julie gave one of those fake coughs, and we parted. She was

drinking her very first glass of champagne in nearly a year. 'Get a room, you two, will you.' She shook her head in mock disbelief.

Tony beckoned me towards him. I stood up and followed him to his office. I secretly smiled to myself. This was to be our time alone before the evening got well and truly underway. I expected him to hold me in his arms and tell me how much he had missed me. Instead, he sat on the edge of his desk and looked at me oddly. He folded his arms. There was a deadly silence and then he cleared his throat and started speaking. 'I've been thinking while you've been away, Francesca...'

I wasn't sure what to expect. Maybe this was it. He was going to tell me we were over.

'I don't want to carry on with our arrangement. I'm not your bed warmer. I am better than that,' he said. I was about to speak, but he held up his hand to stop me. 'Whatever has gone on between us before tonight is over. I don't wish to carry on with your lack of trust and commitment. Always remember, Francesca, I asked you to marry me, and you turned me down. Twice. I told you I would never ask you again, and I stand by that.'

With that obviously well-rehearsed speech of his, he stood up and was about to leave the room. As was his usual custom, he swept his hand through his hair.

I could feel the bile rising in my throat. I wanted to be sick. I looked at him and could feel the tears brimming.

His eyes looked cold and seemed to be staring right through me.

'Stop,' I shouted. He wasn't walking away from me like this, with no explanation. Had his feelings changed so much in one week? 'You bastard, Tony!' I slapped his face. 'Is that why you asked me to come here tonight – so you could dump me? Don't think, Mr Lambrianu that I haven't seen your little harem of women hanging around waiting for you. Girlfriends of Christmases past and future. Well, you're wrong. You're not dumping me. I turned you down!'

His face was red from where I had slapped him. It was obvious he hadn't expected it, but I carried on.

'Is that why you're doing this, because I turned your marriage offer down?' I was breathing heavily. Tears were streaming down my face. And I was angry.

He stroked his face, listening to me rant on.

He turned and took his handkerchief out of his pocket and handed it to me. 'I know some of my female friends are out there, Francesca. I invited them. We all have some very fond memories of each other, and it's time to wish each other a happy New Year – out with the old and in with the new, and all that.'

He left me alone in the office. I was trembling with anger and shock. I hadn't expected this. Was this his New Year's tradition? Out with the old and in with the new? Like all the others, I was his past lover. How many of them had he asked to marry him in the heat of the moment? We were all a joke to him, and yet my heart was breaking.

Opening my bag and turning toward the mirror on the wall, I started patching up my tear-stained face. I supposed it was my fault. I only had myself to blame. He had asked me to marry him, and I had said no.

I didn't feel like partying now. Rather, I wanted to run out of the door and leave. That would have them all gossiping and possibly laughing at me, knowing that I had been dumped again!

Julie had been looking forward to tonight, so if for nothing else, I would put a brave face on for her. I walked back to the table where Julie was sitting with Ralph and the police commissioner's wife and picked up a glass of champagne from the tray. I drank it in one gulp and then picked up another.

'Hey, Fran, steady on. You're not used to drink,' said Julie. Then she looked at me. 'Have you two been arguing?' A frown crossed her brow.

'Maybe, Julie. But now I am having a good time. After all, it's why we're here, isn't it? Cheers!' I said and raised my glass to her before I drank the champagne. I saw her worried face watching me drinking, but I didn't care.

I made a point of dancing with a few men, who seemed intent on groping my bare back. And I laughed and joked with other people at the table. It was a fun evening. I was letting my hair down and didn't give a damn.

Julie took my arm and almost dragged me to the ladies' toilets. 'Okay, Fran, let's have it. What's wrong?'

'Tony has dumped me. There, are you satisfied?' I snapped. I was a little drunk and snapping at the wrong person. 'That's all, Julie. Another one of Tony's tarts bites the dust.'

Julie folded her arms and insisted on the details. I was surprised that she didn't threaten to go out there and give Tony a piece of her mind. She put her arms around me and smiled. 'Oh, he's just smarting, Fran. He's never been turned down before. Dented ego.'

I felt a bit tipsy. Three glasses of champagne was definitely my limit.

As Julie and I walked out of the loo, a man took my arm and started pulling me towards the dance floor. 'Come on, beautiful. It's nearly midnight, and I feel like dancing,' he slurred.

He was pulling at me, and despite Julie and I pushing him away, he wouldn't leave me alone. Julie walked away to get Ralph. I waved my hand to her to let her know that I was okay and could handle it. This guy wasn't the first drunk who had tried grabbing hold of me. I had worked the strip clubs, and that sort of behaviour went with the territory.

The man pulled me closer to him, and the more I pushed him

away, the tighter his grip seemed to get. I shouted at him but was drowned out by everyone shouting the last-minute countdown to midnight, before the New Year's bells chimed.

Suddenly, the man flew across the room and fell into a table, knocking the glasses to the floor. I looked up and saw Tony. He walked towards the man and grabbed him by the back of his jacket, pulling him to his feet. Tony's fist flew hard into the man's face again and again. Blood poured from the man's face. He looked half unconscious, but Tony didn't stop.

'That is my wife, you sleazy bastard,' Tony roared.

In the end, Jake appeared from nowhere and dragged Tony away.

The bouncers of the club had seen what had happened and hurried forward. Picking up the man between them, they dragged him outside. No one would care. It was just another drunk on New Year's Eve who had had a fight. Once he sobered up and realised who he had been pulling around, he wouldn't make a complaint.

I was fuming. I didn't need Tony to fight my battles; what the hell did he care if a man paid attention to me? His arrogance at calling me his wife annoyed me too. Who the hell did he think he was? It was time to clear the air once and for all. Just how many times did Tony think he could humiliate me? Well, this was the very last time. If I was dumped I was going to have my say once and for all, it really didn't matter any more. Sod him! Sod them all!

* * *

I didn't bother knocking on the office door. I just barged in. Tony was combing his hair back and checking himself in the mirror.

'Who the hell do you think you are, Tony?' I wasn't shouting or snarling but just wanted to make my point. 'I am not your wife any more. So why beat up that man and say that I am? For goodness' sake, Tony, stop it. You blow hot and cold all the time. You don't want me, but you don't want anyone else to have me either. Or am I on your substitute list, like all those other silly women out there?'

Tony had his back to me while he was looking in the mirror. He didn't look at me directly but into the mirror at my reflection. 'I never said that I didn't want you Francesca, did I?' He carried on checking his tie. 'In all of our conversation earlier, did I say I didn't want you?' He turned fully now and looked me in the eyes. His face was still slightly flushed, but he had calmed down.

'You said we were over, that you'd had enough. What else is that supposed to mean, Tony?' I was stunned by this revelation.

'It means what I said, Francesca – out with the old and in with the new. It's a new year and a fresh start. And although things haven't gone quite as I planned, that is what I meant. Think about it, Francesca.'

I shrugged and shook my head. I had no idea what he was talking about. He was probably drunk and didn't know what he was saying. I turned and walked out, heading towards Julie at the bar.

'I'm leaving, Julie. I've had enough. I should never have come.'

Julie seemed to panic a little and encouraged me to have one last drink before I went. She ordered a soft drink. I noticed the club lights were being turned up. It was now fully lit up and everyone was looking around and wondering why the music had stopped.

Tony walked out into the middle of the dance floor. I was curious now, as I watched his lone figure standing there while the crowd looked on. Suddenly the air seemed sombre.

'Happy New Year, friends,' he said to put everyone at ease.

Everyone shouted 'Happy New Year' and started applauding him. He was looking around the room, and when he saw me, he stopped and held out his hand.

'Francesca, come here please.' He paused and held his arm out.

Everyone turned to look in my direction, so I felt I should walk forward to Tony. He embraced me and held me tightly. His mouth was near my ear and he was whispering. 'Think back, Francesca, to the place you once said you would like to get married in. Think of the one place in the whole world where I would never tarnish beautiful memories with deceit and lies. You want commitment, Francesca, this is all I have.'

His lips were warm against my ear. I was trying to think what he was talking about.

He pulled away and addressed the crowd again. 'I have asked the beautiful Francesca to marry me, and sadly, she turned me down.'

You could see the shocked look on people's faces, and I could see Roxy and his army of lady friends sitting at the bar. They were turning their heads from side to side to get a better view.

'Well.' Tony beamed a large smile at them all. 'I told her that I would never ask her again, because this time I am telling her.' He held my hand and brushed a wisp of hair from my face. I wasn't taking any of this in. 'Thank you to all of my beautiful lady friends whom I invited here tonight. Thank you for coming.' He pointed towards the bar where some of them were sitting. 'It's been a real pleasure, ladies. But now everything changes. In two weeks, I am getting married to Francesca. She has walked in and out of my life, and I cannot stand it any more. Enough is enough.'

I was shocked. I looked at Tony and then around the room at the faces staring at us. Everyone seemed as shocked as I was. They must have thought he was drunk, although he didn't look it; he was very coherent. I tried pulling away. 'No, Tony, stop it. Don't do this. You're making a fool out of me.' I turned my back and started to walk away.

At the top of his voice, Tony shouted, 'Do you love me or not, Francesca?' I could hear the impatient anger rising in his voice.

I turned to face him. It seemed like there was only him and me there, although there were hundreds of onlookers watching the notorious Tony Lambrianu declaring his love.

'Yes,' I shouted back at him. 'For what good it has done me, Antonias, I love you with all of my heart!'

He walked towards me and grabbed my arms. 'And I love you too. I think I have since we met at that Christmas party in the East End. That's why it's only right I do this now, at Christmas. I have asked you to think back to a place where I would never lie to a woman or hurt her with my selfishness. Is this public enough for you, Francesca? There are no secrets now.'

I looked into his eyes. Instantly I knew what he meant. His grandmother's church. Tony's grandmother had told me she had got married there. Tony would not use it to play his games. His family church was hallowed ground.

'Your grandmother's church?' I whispered, not wanting everyone to hear me.

Tony nodded and smiled at me. To him, that was the ultimate commitment. He would never take his vows in there unless he truly meant it. He went down on one knee and took a ring box out of his pocket. I looked down at the little square box as he opened it. Inside was a huge diamond surrounded by sapphires.

'I will not give you the chance to say no again, Francesca. You're marrying me in Italy in two weeks' time. I have the airline tickets booked.'

'We need to talk in private, Tony,' was all I said. I didn't know what to do; I was embarrassed and elated at the same time. Stunned doesn't even come close to how I felt that night. This was Tony's declaration of love. I was in total disbelief and my heart was thumping in my chest. It was what I wanted and I couldn't believe it. Was I dreaming? Then I walked towards his office, ignoring everyone around me. I heard the music start up again as I stood in Tony's office and waited.

'Tony,' I began as he walked in, 'you can't just organise a wedding in two weeks, especially in a foreign country. And how come you're so sure of yourself? I don't want that circus wedding we had last year, full of people I don't know.'

He put his arm around me and cupped my face and kissed me on the forehead. 'It's not a foreign country, Francesca. It's my home, where my mother and father lived. It's taken me longer than I expected to arrange it, and your mother has declined to come due to other commitments. There will be only a small number of us: me, hopefully you, and the rest of our dysfunctional family. Oh, and Nonna and Rosanna will be there, too. I have asked Elle if she wants to bring Albert.' He was grinning now at the mention of Albert's name.

'My mother knows about this?' I couldn't believe what I was hearing. She knew but wouldn't come? Everyone seemed to be in on this. 'I need time to think, Tony. Really I do.'

I turned to leave, my mind in turmoil. 'You will marry me, Francesca. I'm not letting you go. You say you love me, and I love you. What more do you need to think about? You drive me crazy, Francesca.' His tone was full of despair.

I turned and left him sitting in his chair and walked out of the club, the crowds watching. I had a lot to think about. All in all, it had been an eventful night. I realised now Tony had put this pantomime on for my benefit, to prove his love.

I presumed he had wanted to ask me to marry him on the stroke of midnight, but with the fight, it had all gone wrong. I now realised, when he had said that he was tired of the way we were carrying on, he meant our little affair. He wanted marriage, nothing less. Inviting his lady friends was some kind of farewell to his past life. He had worn his heart on his sleeve. No one had ever done that for me before and probably never would again.

I didn't sleep very well that night. My mind was in turmoil. Tony had always been in control of things. I'd thought he'd dumped me. He had watched me cry and then announced he was going to marry me. I don't know what had gone through his head. For a level-headed businessman, when it came to love, he didn't have a clue.

I needed to get away from here. Julie was supposed to be coming today for our postponed Christmas. I really didn't feel in the mood for all of that. Elle had stayed overnight while looking after Bobby. She seemed surprised when she got up in the morning and found me up and about. She also noticed Tony's absence. I knew she wanted to know what had gone on last night, but she said nothing.

I decided to get rid of the elephant in the room and clear the air. 'I presume you knew he was going to ask me to marry him, Elle, didn't you?' I asked.

She took a deep breath and nodded at me, sighing. 'What did he do, Fran? What has happened? I told him not to rush in like a bull in a china shop.'

I told her. 'Tony thinks I am just going to go along with his plans. He doesn't care what I think. Why would I get married without my family there, Elle? In fact, why would I want to get married at all? We're happy, Elle. Why change things?'

'That's Tony, love. He will never change.' She laughed, shaking her head. 'I have known Tony for a very long time, and he does everything with a passion – there are no half measures. Now for the first time in his life – and I'm not just saying it for your benefit – Tony has found love, Fran. You have made the mistake of telling him that you love him. As far as he is concerned, there are no more questions to be asked.' She stood up to leave. 'If you tell him that you don't love him, he won't take it easy. But he will accept it. He doesn't scare easily, Fran, but he is afraid of losing you. And this is his ham-fisted way of showing it.' Elle picked up her coat and left.

Why couldn't we just carry on as we were? I was afraid of getting my fingers burnt again, but I was more worried about one big question.

Would Tony and I survive married life this time round?

30

HOME AND AWAY

Looking at the business-class airline tickets gave me an idea. I telephoned the airline company and asked if I could change the flight dates. I was going to Italy today, I'd decided. I needed to get away. Space to take in what had happened, time to myself without everyone's opinion about what I should do. This was my life, not theirs.

As we stepped off the aeroplane, it was still warm and sunny. Bobby had loved the flight and the pilot had let him sit up front with him. I knew where Julie's villa was and that the staff would be there to let me in. But when the driver asked me where I wanted to go, I looked into his rear-view mirror, catching his eye.

'Do you know the Lambrianu vineyard?' I asked him.

'It's a long drive, over an hour. It will cost you a lot of money. Do you know the Lambrianus?' he said.

I could see he was mentally calculating how much he was going to charge me, but I didn't care. I told him to take me there and didn't answer his questions. It was late evening when we finally arrived. I felt silly now. Why on earth had I come here? I told the taxi driver to wait while I went to the door and knocked.

Rosanna, the housekeeper, opened the door and instantly recognised me.

'Francesca!' she shouted. 'Come in, come in, my love.' She seemed very excited to see me. Then she saw Bobby, who was drowsing in the taxi. She argued with the taxi driver and got him to carry Bobby upstairs to bed. He didn't seem at all happy with whatever she had said, but I felt it answered his questions. Yes, I did know the Lambrianus!

In her broken English, Rosanna told me she was going to make Bobby some hot chocolate and take him something to eat. She walked ahead, and I followed her lead towards the lounge, where I knew Tony's grandmother would be. She was waiting patiently for Rosanna to show me in after hearing all of the commotion.

'Miriam, I am sorry for turning up like this.' I walked towards her. I stood awkwardly, not knowing what to expect. She must have thought this was very strange – me and Bobby turning up on our own late in the evening with no advance warning.

'Francesca.' She stood up to greet me. 'I take it Tony has made you run for the hills?' She smiled. 'Where else would you go but here, home?'

I didn't need to explain. She had already guessed. She was a handsome woman with a very warm and welcoming smile.

'No one knows that I'm here Miriam. Please don't telephone Tony and tell him. I need time to think.' I knew this was a lot to ask. Tony was her family.

She came forward and put her arm around my shoulder. 'I understand, my dear.' She walked me to the staircase. She wore a long black lace dress. Her white hair was up in a fashionable French pleat and waved softly around her face. She walked with a stick but was very elegant and very feminine.

I don't know why, but I felt safe here. I went to bed after checking on Bobby and slept. It had been a long day.

The next day I woke early but not early enough, it seemed. When I went down, Bobby was already halfway through a plate of pancakes. I asked Rosanna where Miriam was.

'She is taking Mass in the chapel, Francesca. She always takes Catholic mass first thing in the mornings and then in the evening. Come sit down and have some coffee. What do you want to eat?'

Rosanna carried on fussing around and I realised Tony was right; there was no way he would marry someone in his grandmother's church, where she prayed frequently, unless he truly meant it. Breakfast was served, and the sun was shining. It was a peaceful place.

I heard Miriam's voice behind me. 'You seem to like it here, Francesca. Go outside. Get acquainted with the place. Go and get some sun. You look pale, my dear.' She walked over to the table and waited for Rosanna to pour her coffee.

I wandered out. It was a huge place. Farther down the pathway from the house was a sort of factory. I put my head inside the door.

'Mrs... Francesca, come in.' A black-haired man wearing overalls beckoned to me. 'This is the bottling factory, Mrs Francesca. All the wine is put into bottles here, and then it is stored in the cool cellars to mature. Everything has to be the right temperature. Otherwise, it will be ruined.'

I couldn't help smiling. Mrs Francesca? That was a new one.

He was doing his best to speak in English to me, but most of all, he showed me with his hands. The labelling on the bottles simply read: Lambrianu.

It dawned on me that this was a very wealthy place. Why had Tony worked so hard building all of his businesses and running protection rackets when he had all of this?

When I arrived back at the house, I mentioned to Miriam that I didn't understand why Tony didn't work here.

She didn't give much away. 'He's his own man, my dear. He has worked very hard for what he has, and this will always be here for him. It's his after all,' was all she said.

'I see that you have lots of photos around you of Tony's parents but he has never mentioned them.'

'That is for him to tell you Francesca – respect that.' She had Bobby sitting on the floor beside her chair, holding his book. 'Now Bobby, you can continue reading to me.'

She had totally dismissed the conversation and would not be dragged back into it.

After dinner, she told me she was going to evening Mass. She invited me to go with her. I explained that I wasn't a practising Catholic. 'What does that matter, Francesca? God is God. We all need someone to ask for guidance at times. Here.' She handed me a black lace scarf to put on top of my head, and we walked arm in arm into that beautiful little church, which seemed to look even more beautiful by candlelight.

As I knelt beside her at the altar while she prayed, I looked around. There was something special about this place. It had real warmth, and it was full of memories and happiness.

'Amen,' said Miriam and made the sign of the cross on her chest.

I did the same.

* * *

Over the next few days, Miriam and I got into a routine. Each evening, I would go to church with her, and she encouraged Bobby to come with us. Soon, I had been there a week and it was time to leave. According to his plans, there was a week to go before the wedding. After a long hard think, I decided it was best to walk away now and save myself a lot of pain in the future.

When I told Miriam it was time for me to go, all she did was nod her head. There were no questions. She just accepted it. I had enjoyed my time there, and so had Bobby.

I was upstairs packing when I heard a knock at the door. Rosanna opened it with her usual enthusiasm. 'Antonias!' I heard her shout. 'Come in, come in. Why are you knocking? Your grandmother is in the lounge.'

I froze. What was Tony doing here? I sat on the edge of the bed, trying not to make a noise. I listened as they all broke into their native Italian.

'Speak in English, Antonias. I need the practice,' I heard his grandmother say. I knew she was doing that for my benefit.

'She has gone, Nonna. Francesca, I mean. She has taken Bobby and disappeared. She has left the house behind and everything in it. Julie hasn't heard from her. She hasn't been to work. Elle found a note on the worktop saying that she was okay and just needed to get away from it all.'

'Well, that does take me back, Antonias. It's strange to think life is a full circle.' Miriam's voice was soft and gentle, like the voice you used when soothing a small child. I felt like I was eavesdropping into some private conversation. This house seemed to be full of secrets.

'Tell me, Antonias, how you feel right now? Now that Francesca has gone. It seems to me that you are both afraid of the same thing. You are afraid of losing Francesca, and she is afraid of losing you. She thinks you will soon tire of her if you get married. That would break her heart.' I winced inside, because when I had brought the subject of Tony's proposal up to Miriam she had calmly listened to all of the reasons why I felt I couldn't marry him.

'I have tried to think of everything. I have run out of ideas. You know I would never have brought her here if I didn't mean it.'

I thought I heard his voice break as he spoke, as though he was rying. That was impossible. But then I heard Miriam comforting him, as I did with Bobby when he was upset.

Miriam's voice was calm and soothing. She sounded just like Tony. 'What you need, my lovely boy, is trust. Passion is all well and good, but if you don't have trust, then you don't have anything. You have hidden behind that wall you have built for far too long. Show her, Antonias. She doesn't want grand gestures, Antonias. She wants you.'

I hardly dared breathe as I listened to Tony pouring his heart out, thinking no one could hear him. It felt a little deceitful. 'How can you be so sure, Nonna? What makes you think she would want me?'

I heard him pause, waiting for calming advice.

And then she dropped the bombshell. 'Because, Antonias, my boy, Francesca and Bobby are here. Where else would she go but here, to your home, where she could think away from the hustle and bustle of life?'

I didn't see his face, but I heard him gasp. Then I heard his feet rushing up the stairs.

'Francesca!' he was shouting. 'Francesca, where are you?'

I was standing on the landing. Tony stopped in front of me. His eyes were damp, making those blue eyes shine like sapphires.

We stared at each other for a moment and then fell into each other's arms. Nothing else mattered. I never wanted this moment to end. This was my Antonias, the man other people never saw. He was mine. Pulling myself away, I looked up at him and swept his fringe away from his brow. 'Isn't there something you want to ask me?'

The huge smile across his face told me everything I needed to know and put my mind and fears to rest. His voice was choked with emotion. 'Will you marry me Francesca and give a lost wandering soul some place to call home? I love you, I always have.'

Tears of joy fell down my cheeks and I nodded. 'And I have always loved you Antonias. You are my heart and soul. Yes, I will marry you, not because you're telling me to, but because I cannot imagine being with anyone else. I want to be your wife.' My heart burst with joy. At last, after all of this time, we could actually agree on something. We loved each other; the rest was immaterial.

* * *

It was two days before my wedding date. Julie had come to stay and we had planned to go and buy a dress, but Miriam came into my bedroom holding a large box.

'Take a look at this, Francesca. I thought you might like it. It brought me a lot of happiness.'

Opening the box, I removed the tissue paper. Underneath it was a beautiful white wedding dress. It had a satin underlining, and the rest of the dress was all white lace. It had a high sweetheart neck, and it was calf length.

'Is this your wedding dress, Miriam, the one you wore on your wedding day?' I asked in amazement. Looking at her and then looking back at this fragile white lace dress, I was quite taken aback.

Even Julie stroked the lace and said how beautiful it was. It was unusual for Julie to like a dress someone else had picked out.

I saw the tears fill Miriam's eyes, but she held them back. I told her that I couldn't wear something as precious as this. It was her memory of a beautiful day.

'I understand. If you don't want to wear it, you don't have to. But it would also be a beautiful memory of my only grandson being happy. I am an old woman, Francesca. All I have left is memories, but you must make your own memories, too.' I looked behind Miriam and saw Julie and Rosanna looking at the long full veil. It was beautiful. This was the Lambrianu heirloom, and it meant much more than money and things.

I put my arms around Miriam. 'Thank you Nonna. I would be honoured to wear such a beautiful dress. You have been so kind to me and now you're trusting me with your grandson. I promise I will do my best to make him happy.' For a moment we stood there holding each other and I could feel the wetness of the tears on her cheek against mine. We were the Lambrianu women and we had each other.

* * *

Finally, it was our wedding day. And it was everything I wanted. Tony, Jake, Sharon, and Elle were staying at Julie's villa. Miriam had insisted that I stay with her and not see Tony until my wedding day. Julie, as my matron of honour, was to stay with us too, so she made Ralph stay at the villa with the others.

It was a warm sunny day. The church seemed full of rainbow colours from the stained-glass windows. The family priest stood at the altar, which had been decorated in flowers. Tony was waiting for me with Jake at his side. They were in their grey morning suits. The whole service was beautiful.

We exchanged our vows. Tony's will always stay in my heart. 'You are my very soul, Francesca. I have spent all my life looking for you,' he said.

As much as I told him that I loved him, I couldn't match his words. Emotion overwhelmed me and my heart skipped a beat. I remember how my head swam with love and I could hardly speak. This was the man I was always meant to marry and he was beautiful, inside and out. The look of love on his face as he held my hand, was something I could never describe. I had never been so happy in all my life!

The whole vineyard had been given the day off in celebration, and they had worked hard putting up lots of trestle tables covered in white linen tablecloths. They were full to capacity with food and wine. This was what memories were made of.

'So,' asked Julie, giving me one of her mischievous winks, 'now you are officially Mrs Lambrianu, what are you going to do first?'

'Oh that's easy,' I said, laughing with her. 'The first thing I am going to do is learn to speak Italian.'

Everyone found that funny and clapped, but for me it was insurance. Whenever Tony got drunk or angry or both and started ranting and raving in Italian, at least I would understand.

The others went home, but Tony and I stayed in Italy for a few more days, savouring our newfound love for each other.

When we did arrive back in England, I was surprised at the way everything seemed to slot easily into a routine, as though it had always been that way. Tony came home each evening and left early in the morning. I thought he seemed tired and worn out, running back and forth after playing host at the club.

In the end, it was Jake who came to see me when he knew Tony was busy and explained that he felt Tony was burning the candle at both ends.

'He's afraid not to come home, Fran, in case you think the worst of him. He's finishing work at two in the morning and then coming home around three and then starting all over again. I'm worried about him. He's so tired he isn't concentrating, and when he's in a meeting he's looking at his watch all the time, panicking that he has to come back to you.' Jake looked apologetic.

I was glad he'd told me, because I'd already had my suspicions. 'I can't tell him not to come home, can I, Jake? And yes, it would bother me if he didn't want to come home. But I understand his work is not nine to five. I also understand that his work takes him away at times. But you're right, Jake. If we're going to survive our marriage, it has to be sorted out.'

We couldn't live our lives like this, forever wondering. Eventually Tony would resent me for not trusting him, and I would hate myself for making him feel so guilty. It was a double-edged sword.

After talking it through will Elle and Julie, I had my plan of action.

'He needs to feel secure, Fran, and so do you,' Julie said. 'He's offered to buy you a new house and start again, but you don't want to move. Dynamite wouldn't make you leave this place, but he is like the lodger.'

Tony was bending over backwards to please me, but it seemed to be all on my terms. I rang him and asked him to come home later that afternoon. When he arrived I saw a tired man, dark under the eyes.

'You look tired, my love. I'm worried about you and about us,' I said.

He held my hand reassuringly and dismissed what I had said. Apparently everything was okay, which meant it wasn't.

'No, it's not. You have people who rely on you. It's all your hard work that pays for us to live in such luxury.' I could see him frowning and that worried look appear on his face. 'If we are going to be happily married, we have to stop pretending and be ourselves. Maybe you should stay over at your apartment now and again and get some rest before you're up at the crack of dawn with early morning meetings.'

There, I had said it. As I expected, he went berserk, strutting around and blaming everyone for interfering. He accused me of being tired of him already and not wanting him any more. It took me a while to make him see sense.

Then I had an idea I'd forgotten all about. I waited till he calmed down and stopped pacing before I put my idea in place.

'I am always here waiting for you, Tony. This is our home. I'm prepared to put the deed in both our names if you want, re-decorate, but I don't want to leave. Anyway, Ralph would go bonkers. He only just bought that house for Julie because she wanted to be nearby. Think about poor Ralph.'

At least that made him laugh. He looked a little calmer now, and I could tell he had his own thoughts and ideas about the situation.

'I have something for you, Tony, a wedding present if you like.'

I saw that twinkle in his eye.

'No, not that. Come on.' I took him towards the cellar. During the building works, Julie had had the workmen design a men's room, including a full bar, a games room, and a television loaded with all the sports channels. This would make it his home. This was his place. I had also cleaned and aired out his old study and made it useable again.

He was amazed and bewildered when he saw it and was smiling from ear to ear. This small gesture made it his home, his place. It seemed to cement things between us.

'I have conditions though, Mr L,' I began. 'Firstly, whatever happens, I want you all home for Sunday lunch, and I mean everyone: Jake, Sharon, Julie, Ralph, and so on. Our family, Tony. Secondly, when you're not here and stay at the apartment, a side of your bed stays vacant okay? Lastly, I want one day or night a month that we put aside for each other – date night, if you like.'

It was as though I had lifted a great weight from his shoulders. He accepted my conditions and liked the idea of our monthly date, making time for each other no matter what. And the vacancy in his bed made him laugh.

'That goes without saying, Fran. It's taken me a lot to convince you that I love only you. You can turn up at the apartment anytime you like, night or day, and there will be no cuckoo in the nest. It also goes for you too, Francesca. Your bed stays empty too.'

There, we had got over the obstacles. The ground rules were laid for the future.

Wedding photos were put on the walls. Tony filled his old study with work he could do from home. And Julie bought him a mug that read, 'I'm the boss for as long as my wife lets me.'

Tony brought up the subject of adopting Bobby. It was a lovely thought and another gesture from Tony to make us a family. He was trying hard, and I appreciated it.

Our nights were filled with passion and ecstasy. Life didn't get any better than this.

Time was passing, and I hadn't felt very well for a few weeks. Julie kept going on at me to go to the doctor's and get checked out. I kept telling her I was just tired with all of the recent events and that I would be okay.

Then I saw her look at Elle. 'I'll be back in a minute.' Julie turned and hurried out of the house.

She came back half an hour later and emptied the contents of a shopping bag on the worktop. 'Here, let's get started.'

I looked down at the boxes on the worktop. There were half a dozen pregnancy-testing kits.

After the fifth one, we gave up. None of the others were going to say any different. Each and every one of them was positive. Julie was smiling and hugging me, Elle was beaming, and I was gripped by a state of panic. This was not what Tony had signed up for. We were only just married, and I was going to become fat and ugly – more than enough to make him stay away more.

'You can't keep it a secret forever,' said Julie.

I needed to get my head around all of this first. 'Let's leave it for now. I'll tell him when the time is right.'

But I was worried. Would Tony be smiling if he knew he was

going to be a father with a screaming baby in the house? That would be when he'd wish for his old life back, for freedom and the nightlife. I didn't want to think about it. My blood ran cold when I remembered how Luke had reacted when I'd told him I was pregnant.

After Julie's constant nagging, I decided that it was time to tell Tony. I thought he might have guessed because he had commented about my breasts seeming fuller and rounder and the fact that I was always eating rhubarb yogurts.

In bed one night after making love, with just the glow of the lamplight in the room, I said, 'Tony, I love you. You know that, don't you?'

I felt him squeeze me closer to him.

'I would never want you to feel trapped in this marriage. I am so happy with you, but there is something I have been putting off telling you.'

Instantly I felt his body tense. He moved my head and sat up in bed. Talk about killing the moment.

'What are you saying, Francesca? You're scaring me now. What's all this talk about trapping me? Do you think I have been messing around? Because I haven't, Francesca, I swear.' In true Tony fashion, he started to look annoyed. It was better that I nip this in the bud and not drag it out any longer.

I plucked up the courage. 'I'm pregnant, Tony. I'm having your baby. I know this is not what you planned and it doesn't suit your image, but I thought you should know.'

As quickly as I blurted it out, Tony looked like he had turned to stone. He didn't move. I could see him looking around the room, trying to take in what I had just said. 'You're wrong, Francesca,' he said. That was all.

It wasn't the reaction I was expecting. 'I am not getting rid of this baby, Tony. It's too late now. I have to go for my scan tomorrow.'

I got out of bed and put my robe on and went downstairs. I started making a coffee. Tony's reaction had been confusing. It seemed as though he didn't want to discuss it.

He came down into the kitchen and stood behind me and put his arms around my waist gently. 'I am a married man, Francesca. And we're having a baby, not you. This is part of me.' He laid his hands on my stomach and stroked it. 'That is us, Francesca, you and me together. Do you know when you're going to have our baby?' His voice was warm and soft.

I told him I thought that I'd got pregnant the night he had come back from Paris.

He smiled and nodded, remembering it well, while nuzzling my neck. 'It was different that night, wasn't it, Francesca? I needed you so much. I needed to see you, to hold you. I would have walked across the Channel just to spend an hour with you. Can I come to the scan with you tomorrow? I want to see my baby. Oh and, Francesca, I will have no more talk about trapping me and definitely no more talk about getting rid of my baby. That bundle of joy in there is a little Lambrianu bambino.' He smiled.

Tony took my hand, and we went back to bed. He stroked my body and made love to me. As an afterthought, he asked me if it was okay to carry on with things, considering my condition. I assured him that everything was fine. Nothing had changed.

The next day, as I lay on the hospital trolley, my bladder full and ready to burst, Tony sat at my side, holding my hand. We waited as the nurse looked at the monitor and then her eyebrows furrowed. She ran her scanning equipment over my stomach again, then she took off her gloves and told us she would be back in a moment, as she needed to fetch a doctor.

Fear gripped me. Tony and I looked at each other. We didn't

speak. We just held each other's hands and waited. I felt tears well up in my eyes. Minutes seemed like hours. Eventually, the doctor came into the room and ran the sensor over my stomach and looked at the monitor. He then nodded to the nurse.

'Mr and Mrs Lambrianu, I am pleased to inform you that you are having twins. Look.' He ran the sensor over my stomach again. And there, as though by magic, were two tiny heartbeats.

Tony put his hand to his face and rubbed it. He was grinning from ear to ear and kept asking the doctor if he was sure. The doctor nodded and showed him again. We hugged each other and it was the happiest I had been in my whole life.

In the car on the way home, Tony was on a high. He was all excited and barking orders. Firstly, he demanded I give up work immediately, and rest.

'Tony, love,' I tried reassuring him, 'I work at a doctor's surgery for a few days a week. I couldn't be in safer hands. And I have Elle to help and you by my side. All three of us' – I patted my stomach – 'are just fine, Daddy.'

The grin on his face said it all.

As soon as we arrived home, he flew down the hallway, shouting Elle's name. She was sitting in the kitchen having a coffee with Julie. They had both gathered to hear the outcome of my scan. 'Ladies!' Tony shouted. 'We're having twins.'

Julie and Elle looked at me and then back at Tony.

'Twins?' said Elle. 'That is twice as lovely, Tony. Congratulations.' She was hugging him, and he was all smiles. I thought he was going to burst.

He took out the scan photos and started showing them.

Of course, Julie being Julie had a different slant on things. 'Twins? Well, after this, Tony, you're going straight down the vets. We're having you done, you randy old sod.'

31

SCAT KATZ

All the newspapers were on the alert about the forthcoming twins' due date. There had been all kinds of headlines about the babies and photos of me waddling along the seafront walking Susie. There had been 'Double Trouble for Tony' and 'Tony and Fran and their Bump in the Night'. Every week, there was something. In the end, I had taken Julie's advice and ignored it.

On the last scan, we had been asked if we wanted to know the babies' sexes. Tony was biting at the bit to find out, but I'd declined, telling him we would find out soon enough. We had a month to go.

One night, while Tony was staying at the apartment after a late business meeting, I couldn't sleep, so I got up and made a drink. Going back upstairs, I checked on Bobby and then went into the beautiful nursery that Albert had created for the babies. It was filled with two white cots, mobiles hanging above them. There were white chests of drawers and wardrobes bursting with baby suits and clothes. It had a walk-in cupboard, which was piled high with nappies. Cuddly toys were everywhere, in the rocking chair and on the windowsill. We were ready to go.

My back hurt, and I still didn't feel well. I telephoned Elle, who came straight away. I knew what was happening – I'd been there before – but I couldn't breathe with the pains. I was walking around the kitchen holding my back and then my stomach, panting with every contraction. Elle telephoned Julie.

'It's too early. Maybe it's just a false alarm,' said Julie, trying to comfort me.

I gave out a loud cry and then my waters broke.

'Time to go, Fran,' said Julie. 'Elle, see if you can get your friend Minnie to look after Bobby and come when you can. I'll send the car back for you. Oh yes, you had better ring Tony. No, second thoughts, ring Ralph. Tony will run all the way.' She burst out laughing at her own joke and got me into the waiting car.

Once they had checked me at the hospital, they all kept saying the same thing. 'Babies come when they're ready, Mrs Lambrianu.' And that was that.

It was agony. I needed to push. Julie was holding my hand. Elle had got there and was on the other side of me. We were all pushing and panting together.

'Just one more push, Francesca. You're doing great,' said the nurse.

Then the door of the delivery room flung wide open, with Tony running in just as the first baby was born. The nurses took it away to check it out, while Tony hovered over them watching their every move. Jake and Ralph were behind him.

'Bloody hell, you lot,' said Julie. 'We're not selling tickets, you know.' Even at times like this, Julie never lost her sense of humour. She always had some comment up her sleeve to make you smile.

Within a minute, the pains started again. I pushed and panted while the three men looked on. Another cry and another baby was wrapped in a blanket and taken aside while they checked it out.

'Do they have all their fingers and toes?' asked Tony.

Julie gave him one of her disbelieving stares and then looked up at the ceiling. 'Is that mad Italian for real?' she said. 'Fingers and bloody toes. Have you asked what sex they are, Tony?'

'Well, Daddy,' said the nurse, giving Tony a big grin. She handed Tony a bundle wrapped in a blanket and placed it in his arms. 'Say hello to your daughters.' She smiled at him again, seeing his stunned face.

Tears fell down his face as he looked at a tiny mirror image of himself. There was no mistaking who the father was.

'Look,' said the nurse. 'She even has your cleft chin.'

Tony was rooted to the spot, holding his daughter and staring at the other one, who was being brought over to me.

The twins were more or less identical, except only one had a cleft in her chin.

The nurse was telling us that they were both around six and a half pounds and that everything was okay. But Tony wasn't listening. He moved the blankets away from their faces for a closer look. By now their lungs were wide open, and their cries filled the room, bringing Tony back to reality.

'They are beautiful, Francesca. Take a look at them. We did this.' Tony was hypnotised. He had always been a ladies' man. Somehow, it seemed right that his twins were girls – two more women in his life.

Photos were taken, and Tony seemed to come back to life. Everyone was congratulating us, and the smile on his face couldn't have been wider.

'Well,' said Julie, 'are you still going to call them what you said?' She smirked at me, knowing she had dropped a bombshell.

'Names?' said Tony. 'Oh, God, I have never thought of that. They have to have names, don't they?' He had a worried expression on his face, which made everyone laugh.

'For a great businessman, Tony, you can be really stupid at

times,' Ralph said. 'What are you going to do, call them the twins all their lives?'

'One of my favourite movies,' I began, 'is *Gone with the Wind*. I know it's supposed to be Katie Scarlett O'Hara, but they always call her Scarlett first. So the oldest one by one and a half minutes is going to be called Scarlett and the second one Katie. Scarlett and Katie Lambrianu. What do you think, Tony?'

Tony repeated it to himself and then smiled. 'Yes, I like that. It's different.'

'In fact,' I added, 'Scarlet Toni Elle Lambrianu and Katie Julie Miriam Lambrianu.'

Tony's eyes shot up to look at me when I mentioned his grandmother's name. He nodded approvingly. It was apparent that had touched him deeply.

'You're not calling her Julie,' Julie piped up again, not wanting to be left out. 'God, I hated it, and every girl in my class was called Julie.' But, as much as she disapproved, I could tell that she liked it, and so did Elle.

It felt fitting. The women who had helped me every day deserved some acknowledgement.

Tony was now taking charge again and discussing nannies. 'Why didn't you interview some nannies, Fran? We're going to need one,' he barked.

'Why do I need a nanny, Tony?' I said. 'I have Grandma Elle and Aunty Julie. What more do they need?'

I saw Elle blush. It was the highest honour I could give her. She was the only mother Tony had ever known. Why shouldn't she be the twins' grandma? She had been my rock through all of this.

Eventually it was time for everyone to leave. I was exhausted and fell into a deep sleep.

I woke up in the early hours of the morning and saw Tony in

the room. He was very drunk and had obviously wet the babies' heads.

'Sorry to wake you, Francesca,' he slurred while he held onto the wall to help him stand up. He looked around and saw that there were no cots in my room.

'They are in the nursery, Tony. Everything is fine. They are just letting me have some rest. That's all,' I said, seeing the worried expression on his face. I held out my hand to him, and he came and sat on the edge of the bed.

'Thank you, Francesca, for Scarlett and Katie. *Ti amo.*' With that, he lay his head on the pillow beside me and fell fast asleep, snoring his drunken head off.

When Julie arrived early the next morning with her pink balloons and champagne, she saw Tony fast asleep on the bed.

'I have one of those at home, Fran.' She nodded towards Tony snoring his head off. She was laughing and smiling at the same time. Apparently Ralph had gone home this morning in exactly the same state. There was no need to ask about Jake.

When the nurses brought the girls in, Tony soon woke up. He looked so bleary eyed the nurse brought him in some paracetamol. I fed one baby, and Julie fed the other. Then after a few cups of coffee, Tony had a go. It was his first fatherhood experience, and his suit, creased from where he'd slept in it, was soon covered in baby sick.

When we left the hospital, we were greeted by photographers and journalists desperate to get photos and gossip on the girls. 'Stay away from my daughters,' Tony shouted, angrily pushing them away. 'Get the hell out of here.'

'No, Tony. They've all waited patiently. Let them have their photos, and then we can ask them to leave us in peace for a while.' It seemed good sense to me to get it over and done with.

Tony nodded, although he wasn't happy. We posed for photos

and told them the girls' names, and they seemed happy with that. Tony got into the swing of it. He held them both, one in each arm, and smiled for the cameras. Needless to say, that was the one they were going to use.

The headlines in the magazines and newspapers were variations on 'Tony Lambrianu and the Women in His Life' and 'Scat-Katz for the Lambrianus.'

'ScatKatz?' I asked Julie, who was reading out the magazine column. 'What's that?'

'Don't you know, Fran?' She looked up at me. 'That's what they're calling the girls. Scarlett and Katie, otherwise known as ScatKatz.' She laughed.

It definitely hadn't taken the reporters long to come up with a name for the girls. It made for good headlines, I supposed, and it had a nice ring to it.

It had such a nice ring, in fact, that, after much debate about the newly finished club Ralph, Jake and Tony had built, Ralph suggested calling it ScatKatz. He thought it sounded trendy, and people would know it was part of the Lambrianu empire.

* * *

A couple of months down the road, I was facing another sleepless night when Tony, Ralph and Jake supposedly had a late business meeting to attend and would have to stay over at the apartment.

Both Julie and I knew it was just a poor excuse for the three of them to escape the baby chaos!

'I have an idea, Fran,' said Elle, 'if you want to try it. It's up to you, but it might help.'

Any idea was welcome if it meant I could get some sleep for an hour. I had forgotten what sleep was.

'The cots are enormous, Francesca,' Elle carried on.

I couldn't think what she was talking about. I was so tired I was on autopilot.

'Why don't we take advantage of that? They're twins, Fran. They have been squashed together for months, and now we have parted them. Put them side by side in the cot, and let's see what happens. I think they miss each other.'

It made sense, even to my baby brain. Maybe they were missing hearing each other's heartbeats. We lay them side by side in the cot while their lungs were on full volume, and the strangest thing happened. Once they realised they were together, in her own baby way, Scarlett seemed to reach out for Katie's hand. And then, suddenly, silence reigned, and they went to sleep.

Elle had been right.

As soon as we realised that being together comforted the girls, life was so much simpler. When they were in the baby bouncers during the course of the day, they were happy as long as they were close to each other.

Tony would lie on the sofa with them both asleep on his chest. He enjoyed his own private time with them, and he would get out of bed in the middle of the night just to go and see them. He would sit in the rocking chair watching them sleep. Sometimes I would find him in there fast asleep.

I had sent my mam photos, but it was my brothers who asked when they could come and see their nieces. The last time I'd telephoned Mam she'd told me that George had asked her to marry him and she had said yes.

Obviously, we were expected to go, but it would be a flying visit. We couldn't all stay at my mam's house. There were five of us now, and staying at a hotel would be a nightmare.

Julie came around shortly before the wedding. I could see she had something on her mind.

'Fran, love, don't you find it strange that now you're married and have Tony's children, George has asked your mum to marry him?'

'Not really, Julie. They have been seeing each other for a while. I suppose it makes sense.' I didn't care about George any more. I had more than enough on my plate.

When I spoke to my mam, she mentioned that George had suggested to her that maybe he could run a club in Yorkshire for Tony seeing as he would soon be a member of the family. So that was it, being a part of the Lambrianu family to George meant a meal ticket.

I mentioned it to Tony in passing. He brushed his hair back with his hands. I could see he wasn't happy.

'Fran, I already have businesses in Yorkshire, and they are run by professionals. But if you want me to find him a job, then I will.' He sighed.

I took his hand and kissed it. 'Thank you, Tony. I appreciate the gesture. But what can George do in your line of business?'

'I don't know. But if it makes you happy, I'll find something.' He gave me a kiss on the lips.

'No, my love. Let George make his own way in the world, like you have.'

Tony seemed relieved. I had done the right thing. George liked the idea of fame and fortune, but if he liked it so much, then let him earn it.

I told Julie about it, but she said she'd already guessed. 'You will get used to it, Fran – people wanting to jump on the band-wagon, wanting favours and handouts. You just have to learn to say no.'

She was right of course. I was still naive when it came to money and fame.

'Why don't you tell your mum that it's a good idea, George running a club for Tony, and ask her how much money he's prepared to put in? That way, you're not saying no. You're making a deal. George would have to invest, wouldn't he?' She made sense and I decided that I'd think about her idea.

* * *

Tony and I, along with Bobby and the girls, arrived at the registry office for my mam's wedding. My brothers were happy to see me and meet the girls for the first time. The eldest of my brothers was now fourteen. I told him that, if he ever wanted to come and get away from it all, he could get the first-class train directly from York-shire to London and be picked up at the other end. I gave him an envelope. 'Hide this. This is the money for the train tickets.'

I didn't want them feeling as though I had deserted them. So I made my mind up to sort them out with bank accounts of their own. Then they would never be stuck without money.

George was pleased that Tony went down the local pub where he had organised the reception and introduced Tony as his son-in-law to everyone there. Dearest Antonias gritted his teeth and smiled for the sake of me and my mother and bought drinks for everyone all night.

George had pulled me aside during the reception and asked me what I thought of his business proposition. Remembering Julie's words, I'd asked him how much money he was going to invest into this new venture. I saw his face drop. He hadn't expected that. Did he really think that his wedding present was going to be a fancy club with his name above the door?

Thankfully, with the girls being babies, we had to leave early. As far as I was concerned, enough was enough. Poor Tony was being exploited, and he was putting up with it for my sake. What do they say about love? Actions speak louder than words.

* * *

Back home the next day I told Julie and Elle how proud I was of Tony and what had happened.

Julie hushed me. 'Fran, love, are you still sending your mum some of your wages? It's not my business, but are you?'

I nodded and told her I was. It was for my brothers' sakes and to make life easier for her.

'How does it make things easier for her, Fran? She doesn't pay rent any more. You've given her large sums of money, and you're also sending her a regular income. She doesn't need it now that she has George's wages coming in, does she?'

Julie was right of course. My mam would have another income in the house now, and maybe it was time for me to bow out.

So I set up bank accounts for my brothers, and instead of the money going to my mam, I shared it out and put it in a trust for them. No one could touch it until they were of age or had my signature to approve it.

My mam wasn't happy, but it was time for us all to move on with our new lives.

* * *

The New Year rolled around and Julie and I went to the opening of the new club. It was enormous and had every entertainment you could think of on different floors.

It was a club, casino, restaurant, and jazz bar. Of course, another floor had table dancers. There was something for every-one, including private poker tables in VIP rooms. On the entrance above the door in large fancy pink writing was the sign, SCATKATZ. It was emblazoned in lights and gave the place an air of mystery and expectation.

I saw Tony heading towards me as he shook hands with the VIP guests who had turned up. I realised that I didn't feel worried or insecure any more. Those days had passed. I had grown up.

I turned and gave him a kiss on the lips and led him onto the dance floor. I put my arms around his neck and ran my hands through his thick blond hair.

This was my beautiful husband, the father of my children, and finally I felt secure in his love.

32

THE FINAL HURDLE

Sitting here now with my coffee, it seems strange that all of that uncertainty was eighteen years ago. Looking up at the Lambrianu building, I smiled. How time had flown, and each day was happier than the last. Everyone was grown up now. Bobby was at university studying to become a doctor. Josh designed web pages for famous companies and made a lot of money doing it. Scarlett, Katie and Diana were all at college.

I had gone back to work at the doctor's surgery when I could. If nothing else, it got me away from the telephone, which Scarlett's head teacher constantly rung to tell me she had been fighting again. Tony always smoothed things over when the school threatened to suspend her. He had contributed to school funds and bought the school a whole load of new gym equipment.

Katie was more studious. She liked school, but being quiet and shy, she had been a target for bullying. Not for long though – Scarlett had been there, her fists flying, and it had stopped.

We always seemed to be at loggerheads, and Tony, who was supposed to reprimand Scarlett, always sided with her. She grew more like him every day. They both had long blond hair and the same blue eyes.

Katie always made the peace. She was more like me.

Tony seemed to get more handsome with age. His hair had the odd wisp of silver grey, making him look even more distinguished than ever.

But things hadn't been right between us for a couple of weeks now. I felt like my life had been turned upside down and I needed space to myself. I needed time to think.

I knew Tony had a big business meeting today, and I would catch him at the club. He hadn't answered my calls, and when I had telephoned Jake, he'd told me he would pass on the message. Whether he had or not, Tony hadn't called me back.

Taking a deep breath, I was just about to open the door to the club when it flew open in front of me. Standing there with an embarrassed look on their faces were the two women I had seen earlier through the glass pane of the club door – the ones who'd had their arms around Tony's waist and had been laughing and joking with him, his head thrown back with laughter and Jake joining in.

'Hi, Mum. Bye, Mum,' they both said in unison. These two tall leggy blondes with their wavy hair flowing down their backs were our eighteen-year-old daughters.

'Wait.' I stopped them. 'Aren't you supposed to be in college today?' I knew I was going to get some excuse and I was prepared for it.

'It's a study day, Mum. Anyway, Papa said it was okay, considering it's nearly the holidays.' Scarlett stuck her chin out in exactly the same manner as Tony did when trying to prove a point.

I looked at my daughter. She was holding a handful of money. So they had both been to see their father and swindled him again.

It didn't take much. They only had to smile at him and give him a hug, and he had an open chequebook.

Katie, the peacemaker, kissed me on the cheek. 'Are you okay, Mum? You and Dad, I mean?' She looked worried.

The girls had obviously noticed Tony's absence around the house, and he had probably given them a list of excuses, not wanting to upset them. But they weren't stupid. Even through their busy schedule they had noticed that I hadn't been myself lately.

Nodding, I let them leave. The money was burning a hole in Scarlett's pocket, and the shops were waiting.

I walked in and saw Jake. 'Is Tony in his office?' I asked.

Jake looked shocked to see me. 'I'm not sure where he is. I'll go and check. Wait here.' He was lying his head off.

'I know the way, Jake,' I said, pushing past him.

I heard Jake shout for me to wait. He sounded panic-stricken and was running after me. 'Wait, Fran. Please!' he asked. We were both standing outside the office door.

Slowly, he opened it and spoke to Tony. 'Fran is here, and she wants to see you.'

Tony was changing his shirt before his meeting. He looked at Jake and swept his hands through his hair. 'Tell her I have a meeting. I will call her later,' I heard him say.

'No you won't,' I shouted, walking into his office. I could see the shocked look on his face. 'I am not the hired help, left to wait outside. I need to talk to you, Tony, and I am not going anywhere until I have.'

Tony turned around. His eyes were dark and his face was flushed. He lifted his arms, and with one sweep, he cleared all the contents of his desk onto the floor, sending papers flying.

'I know why you're here, so you can just pick up your fucking bag and leave. Get out,' he shouted at me. His face was red, and those blue eyes of his, which always got darker when he was angry and upset, stared at me.

'Tony, sit down and let me speak. I'm the wrong side of forty, and you're ten years older than me and our lives are about to change. I need to discuss something with you!' Feeling the tears stinging my eyes, I looked up at him pleadingly.

He sat down on his large black leather chair. He looked quite the dominant figure. Pointing his finger into my face, he looked tired and I guessed I was to blame. 'You're not leaving me, Francesca. That is the end of it. What's all this about age? Is he younger than me, this fancy man of yours? Is that it? I have watched you, locked away in that bubble of yours, miles away. I have reached out to you in bed, but you have pretended to be asleep.'

I sat there in silence while everything he had been feeling all came out in one go.

'This man of yours better have a good hiding place, because when I find him, I'm going to kill him. And then I am going to kill you, Francesca!' he shouted.

What do you do when an angry Italian starts ranting and raving at you? As the years had shown me, you sit and wait for him to run out of steam.

His elbows were on the desk now, and his head was in his hands. He looked broken and it was all my fault. 'Go on then. Say it. I dare you, Francesca,' he said.

'Tony, do you remember that hot sunny day in June when the house was empty for once? I was in the garden pruning my roses, and you came home early. Do you remember, Tony?' I enquired.

Now I could see his face softening under all that anger and frustration. He raised his head and looked at me; there was a hint of a smile. 'Of course I do, Francesca.' His voice was husky. 'It was a beautiful afternoon, just us together.' He reached out and took my hand.

It had been one of the hottest Junes recorded in a long time, and I was wearing my shorts and vest top when Tony came home and out in the garden to see me.

Looking up, I'd shielded the sun from my eyes with my hand to see him properly. 'What are you doing home so early?' I had asked.

'It's too hot to work, Francesca. I needed to get away. Where is everyone?' He'd looked handsome. His hair, bleached by the sun, seemed blonder than usual. He was in a white shirt, which was starting to stick to his back where he had sweated slightly from sitting on the leather seats in the car.

'Everyone is out. I have the whole house to myself for once. Do you want a drink?'

I was just about to stand up when he knelt down in front of me. I saw that familiar look in his eye. He leaned forward to kiss me, and before long, we were romping around naked in the garden. Clothing was thrown everywhere.

The blossom from the cherry tree fell on our naked bodies in the sunlight. It was heaven. We made love often, but it was rare to get this kind of freedom to do as we liked without interruption. We had clung to each other and passionately succumbed to each other's needs. Lying on the soft grass with the scent of roses filling the air made it feel erotic and exciting.

My legs were wrapped firmly around him, and I pulled him closer to me, feeling that wonderful throbbing sensation inside of me. Tony was a good lover and took his time, teasing and coaxing my body to reach its peak. And we had. Together. Afterwards, we had laid in the shade under the tree, wrapped in each other's arms, like Adam and Eve – naked in the Garden of Eden.

It was a glorious day to remember and definitely one to put on my top ten memory list.

Tony had gone to the kitchen and come out with a bottle of wine and two glasses. We'd nakedly drunk wine under the tree, locked for once in our own little paradise. We had been out there for hours, free from any kind of responsibilities.

It was shortly after that that I'd started to feel unwell. I presumed I was maybe starting menopause early so I'd decided to go and see a doctor.

Now Tony broke into my thoughts. 'Why don't you want me any more, Francesca? I love you; you know that.' He kissed the palm of my hand. His voice was much softer now, and I could tell even saying what he just had was causing him pain. 'Dear God, Francesca. It's always been you, which is why I'm not prepared to lose you. And I won't. You're not leaving me.'

'I'm pregnant, Tony,' I shouted. 'There's no other man. There never could be, you fool. Who could follow in your footsteps? I am going for a scan in half an hour,' I told him. 'I'm nearly five months pregnant. I'm going to be in my sixties when this baby is twenty. People are going to think that I'm its grandmother. And God knows what the girls are going to say, especially Scarlett.' Now I was breathing heavily. Everything I had been thinking about these last few weeks came pouring out to a dumbstruck Tony.

Our lives had started to become our own again. This baby was going to be a great big upheaval, and I wasn't getting younger. The very idea of carrying and having a child now frightened me. The doctor had already called me an older mum when I had been to see him. I had needed to get used to the bombshell he had dropped on me before telling anyone else. What would Tony say? What would our friends say? I was confused and emotional, which was why I had been so distant and locked in my own thoughts for weeks.

The angry worried lines seemed to leave Tony's face instantly. He rubbed his face with his hands and laid his head back on the chair. Then his face broke into a great big smile. 'Francesca, are we really having a baby? Is that what we planted in the garden in June?' His face was beaming, and he gave me that boyish naughty grin. 'For God's sake, I have been in agony, avoiding you because I didn't want to hear you say that you no longer loved me. And all this time you've been worried because you're going to be a middle-aged parent? Listen to yourself, Francesca. Against the odds, we are being blessed with a baby, and you make it sound like a death sentence. Francesca, we are having a baby!'

Tony came around to my side of the desk, stood me up, and wrapped his arms around me. He held me close to him, like he never wanted to let go. All of his worries were washed away.

Jake had obviously heard us shouting and knocked on the door. When he saw Tony and me in each other's arms, he seemed to breathe a sigh of relief.

'Sorry to interrupt you, Tony, but the guys are coming through the door. The meeting? Do you remember?'

Letting me go, Tony turned and picked up his jacket. He put his head around the door frame and saw all the men he was due to meet that day. He shouted to get their attention.

'Everyone, please, go to the restaurant. Order anything you want. I will be back in a couple of hours.' Taking my hand and pulling me towards him, he announced, 'Francesca is pregnant, and we're going to the hospital right now to see the first picture of our baby.' Tony leaned in to kiss me.

I heard Jake give one of those fake coughs people do when trying to get your attention. Both of us turned to look at him.

'So,' Jake laughed. 'There is life in the old dog yet, eh, Tony? Congratulations, Fran.'

'Jake, my little tadpoles are Olympic gold swimmers. I will be back later.' He was smiling and seemed to have grown a foot taller as he strutted out of the room.

A huge weight had been taken from my shoulders, but there was still the girls and Bobby to tell. I was especially nervous about what Scarlett's reaction might be.

We looked at the monitor in the hospital. There was a little heartbeat and the shape of a baby. Tony seemed a little disappointed that there was only one heartbeat and one baby this time, but he accepted it with grace. It's a wonder he could get his big head through the door.

'Let's not tell everyone until Sunday lunch, Tony, when we're all gathered around the table.' I could see he wasn't happy about waiting, but he was prepared to go along with it.

* * *

At last, Sunday lunch was upon us. When we were all sitting around the table, I gave Tony a nod, indicating he could at last spill the beans!

Tapping his fork against his glass to get everyone's attention, he waited. 'I am very proud to announce that we're going to have another addition to our family. Francesca and I are having a baby.' He took out the ultrasound picture and passed it to Julie.

'Oh my God,' said Julie. 'That's beautiful.' She came around to our side of the table. 'Are you losing your touch, Tony? Only the one baby this time, is it?' She put her arms around both our shoulders and squeezed us tight.

'Well, I think it's disgusting.' Scarlett's voice echoed around the table. 'You're too old to have a baby. What will my friends say when they find out my old mother is pregnant? Yuck.' Scarlett stood up to leave the table.

This was what I had been dreading – too old to have a baby; an embarrassment to my family.

Tony leaned over the table and hit it hard with his fist,

knocking over the water jug. His eyes were full of anger. Over the last few days, I had told him why I was worried.

'You, Scarlett, can shut your mouth. Don't worry, you selfish girl, your inheritance is safe,' Tony shouted. He was shaking with anger.

The room went silent. He had never lost his temper with Scarlett, no matter what she did. Now she watched him, tears falling down her face while he shouted at her. Then he told her to leave the table. He couldn't look at her.

'Wait.' I put my arm around Tony's shoulder to calm him. 'Whatever you may think, I am having your brother or sister. Thank goodness Bobby didn't kick up such a stink when I announced I was having you. Now sit down, dry your eyes, and shut up,' I said.

Katie held my hand. 'That's great, Mum. When is it due?' Yet again, Katie knew exactly what to say.

I told her the due date was around March and gave her a big hug and thanked her.

'Sorry, Papa,' Scarlett said. She looked at him pleadingly, wanting his forgiveness. 'Sorry, Mum. It's great news.'

* * *

As the months came and went, everything was painted and decorated. Albert was overseeing things, and Tony was strutting around like a teenager. Each time he stroked and kissed my swollen stomach, he beamed with happiness.

Scarlet had spoken to her father in private and apologised. She loved Tony and didn't want to lose his love. She had been jealous of the thought of a new arrival that might take her place in Tony's heart and had spoken before her brain had started working. She was definitely Tony's daughter.

Standing in the kitchen, I suddenly felt ill. From nowhere, it felt as if I had been kicked in the stomach. There was a wet patch on the floor, followed by another pain and then another one. The girls were panicking and asking if I was okay.

I couldn't breathe. Another pain shot right through me. It felt like my whole body had electric bolts shooting through it.

Julie took command. She turned to the girls. 'Scarlett, ring your father. Katie, call an ambulance. Bobby, get over here. You're a bloody doctor.'

Poor Bobby took a breath and looked between my legs. 'The head's crowning, Julie. She's giving birth now.' They both looked at each other. 'Mum, listen to me. You're going have to push. Do you trust me?'

I nodded. Julie held my hand, and I waited for the next pain and pushed, giving it everything I had.

I heard the door crash open, and Tony, Jake and Ralph came rushing in with the paramedics hot on their heels. My little Bobby was in full charge of the situation and was talking medical jargon to the paramedics. They all agreed it was too late for any medication and it was all over within an hour.

Panting, I looked up at Tony and waited while Bobby cut the cord.

'Mum, Dad, say hello to your son. And bloody hell, was he in a hurry,' said Bobby.

Bobby handed me over a little naked bundle, who was still screaming his head off. 'Jesus Christ,' shouted Tony, 'we have a son, Fran.' Then Tony realised what he had said and looked down at Bobby. 'You know that you're my son, don't you, Bobby. I love you, always have. Thank you, Bobby.' Tony looked a little embarrassed at having said all that in front of everyone, but he didn't care.

'It's okay, Dad. I know what you mean.'

The paramedics wrapped my newborn baby up and said they

were taking us to the hospital. Tony wanted to know why and what was wrong.

Bobby was on hand to put his mind at rest. 'It's procedure, Dad. They have to check them both out. It's okay.'

Tony was even more proud when the paramedics turned to Bobby. 'Thank you, Dr Lambrianu. You did a great job.'

The baby and I were taken to the hospital. Tony came with us, not wanting to leave our side for a moment. He was hypnotised by this dark-haired version of himself.

Our little miracle baby had my dark wavy hair and my nose, but the rest was all Tony, including the cleft in his chin. His blue eyes seemed to twinkle, beneath his long dark lashes. He was beautiful. Lying in the hospital bed holding my baby, with Tony beside us moving the blanket away from his son's face for a closer look, I smiled. This was a real family moment. It was our moment together before the rest of the family turned up. Tony kissed me and then kissed our little boy.

'Thank you, Fran, for everything. I am the happiest man alive, and that is because I have you.' Just as he was going to kiss me, Julie burst through the doors with the girls, including Diana and Elle.

'Congratulations, you three.' They were holding balloons. Julie had a bottle of champagne and some plastic cups and was passing them around. Ralph and Jake came in, took a drink, and then started taking pictures.

Everyone was looking at my little son, who flashed those blue eyes of his, surrounded by long dark lashes, making all the women's hearts melt.

'You know what, Tony? He's going to be better-looking than you and younger.' Even now she had to tease him. 'Come on then, Fran,' said Julie, 'what are you going to call him?'

I looked at Tony and smiled. There was only one name for this miracle baby. 'Adam,' I said, 'Adam Antonias Lambrianu.' Adam had to be the name, because this little one was made in our very own Garden of Eden. I looked at Tony and could see he knew exactly what was going through my mind.

'Adam Lambrianu,' said Tony, saying it out loud to himself. 'Adam Lambrianu – it has a nice ring to it. Wait a minute. Those are my initials, Fran,' he said, surprised.

'So they are, my love,' I said and kissed him.

Julie was in the background, commenting on how long it had taken mastermind Lambrianu to work out the initials were the same. She raised her glass of champagne to make a toast with the others.

'To Adam Antonias Lambrianu – in fact, to the Lambrianus. The next generation, God help us.' She burst out laughing.

ACKNOWLEDGMENTS

To Avril, Sue, Leanne and Kath, who encouraged me to follow my dreams and write *Francesca*.

To my son, Robert Godden, the wind beneath my wings.

Many thanks to my editor Emily Ruston for all her painstaking guidance and patience. You're simply the best.

And lastly, for all the people who are reading this book and enjoying it as much as I have enjoyed writing it.

MORE FROM GILLIAN GODDEN

We hope you enjoyed reading *Francesca*. If you did, please leave a review.

If you'd like to gift a copy, this book is also available as an ebook, digital audio download and audiobook CD.

Sign up to Gillian Godden's mailing list for news, competitions and updates on future books.

http://bit.ly/GillianGoddenNewsletter

Dangerous Games, another gripping gangland thriller by Gillian Godden is available to order now.

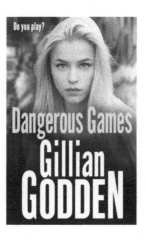

ABOUT THE AUTHOR

Gillian Godden is a Northern-born medical secretary for NHS England. She spent thirty years of her life in the East End of London, hearing stories about the local striptease pubs. Now in Yorkshire, she is an avid reader who lives with her dog, Susie.

Follow Gillian on social media:

 facebook.com/gilliangoddenauthor
twitter.com/GGodden

Boldwood

Boldwood Books is an award-winning fiction publishing company seeking out the best stories from around the world.

Find out more at www.boldwoodbooks.com

Join our reader community for brilliant books, competitions and offers!

Follow us

@BoldwoodBooks

@BookandTonic

Sign up to our weekly deals newsletter

https://bit.ly/BoldwoodBNewsletter